D0499894

# CONSEQUENCES

Timothy Leary's dead.
No, no, no, no, he's outside
Looking in. . . .

Ray Thomas,
*Legend of a Mind*

# ▪ 1 ▪

TROUBLE WAS GONE. Cerise had known it from the moment she entered the strangely neat apartment, the inevitable clutter—disks, books and papers, here a sweater, there a pair of shoes—all missing along with Trouble. She went through the two rooms in the greyed light of the winter afternoon, checked the single closet and the battered trunks that held the rest of their clothes, not looking at the computers until the last, already sure of what she would find. Half the system was gone, Trouble's half, the portable holo-multex drive and the brainbox and the braid of cables and biojacks that carried signals to the implanted processors in their brains. There was no paper note.

A light was flashing on the media console, and she touched the code keys to retrieve the single message. The voice that broke from the speaker was familiar, but not Trouble—Carlie, babbling on about something she couldn't be bothered to hear right now—and she killed the message, not bothering to save it for later. She turned away from the wall of blank screens and cubbies filled with data decks and players, the ugly oyster-grey carpet squeaking underfoot, and looked around the little room as though she was seeing it for the first time. Outside the single window, the sun was setting beyond the buildings on the far side of the little park, throwing a last cold light across the grey stone and concrete. A reflection like a spark flared from the highest side windows of the Lomaro Building half a mile away—three-quarters of a kilometer, she corrected automatically—and faded as she stared. The sun dropped into a bank of dirty cloud, and the light went out as though someone had flicked a switch. On the horizon, beyond the five- and six-story buildings of the local neighborhood, neon flickered to life, running like lightning along the edges of the buildings.

She shivered, and reached overhead into the web of invisible control beams that crisscrossed the apartment, waved her hand twice to bring on the main lights. A yellow light flashed on the display by the door instead, warning her that she hadn't replaced the main battery. She swore under her breath—that had been Trouble's chore—and went to the panel herself, switched lights and heat to full and touched the button that brought the opaque screen down over the window. It was sheer indulgence, this system, costing at least two months' rent to install, but once the security—black security, black-market and blackest-night effective, run off an illegal direct-line power tap—had been in place, it had seemed a shame not to install the convenience systems as well. She remembered Trouble balancing on an uneven chair beside the door, drill-driver in hand, bolting the last of the extra control boxes into place. That had been their indulgence for a job well done, right before the hearings began, three months before David Terrel was actually convicted of armed robbery because of a particularly brutal icebreaker he carried in his toolkit. The last good times, she thought, feeling at the moment only the cold, and turned back to the dismantled machines.

Seeing the system broken, the empty spaces where Trouble's machines had been, made her shiver again, something like fear or rage or sorrow threatening to break through the numbness, but she shoved the feelings down again, and went back into the bedroom for the things she needed to repair the gaps. She had spares of everything that Trouble had taken, machines she had used before she'd met Trouble, and she hauled their cases out from under the bed, brushing dust from the lids. The wind moaned through the rungs of the fire escape that slanted down past the bedroom window; she glanced at it, hearing loose bolts rattle on the landing one story above, and went back into the outer room.

It didn't take long to rebuild the system. Trouble had worked with her usual precision, taking nothing that wasn't hers, leaving the backup disks stacked prominently in front of the dusty keyboard. There was a hollyblock there, too, holographic storage, and Cerise moved it impatiently aside to plug her own holodrive into the multiple sockets. She replaced Trouble's dedicated brainbox with her own—an older model, but still serviceable, still fast enough to let her run the nets without danger—and found a length of cable to reconnect the various components. She looked at the hollyblock, but did not pick it up, turned instead to the rarely used keyboard and began methodically to recreate her machine.

The screen lit and windowed as she worked, giving her a schematic view of the reconstructed system; she touched keys, reestablishing virtual links that had been broken when the physical links were removed, and watched the schematic shift, rotating in the uppermost window to show her the new links outlined in red. A string of text asked for confirmation. She gave it the code it wanted, and watched as the red lines slowly turned to yellow and then to green, blending in with the rest of the design. When she was sure it was complete, she dismissed that image, and sorted through the directories until she found her private mailbox. It took two keys to open it, one a name—she made a mental note to change that—the other a meaningless string of letters, but she found nothing new in the lists of files. That was as she'd expected, and she closed the program, reaching instead for the hollyblock. If Trouble had left her anything, any explanation, it would be there.

She fitted the box carefully into the replacement multex drive, and touched the keys that initiated the test sequence. Everything came back green, and she pressed a second set of keys to access the drive. A dozen files, each indicated by an individual symbol, an icon, bloomed on her screen. She frowned then—she had expected more, some message, some more useful labels, something—but touched the first icon. The file blossomed in front of her, filling the screen with a peculiar half-squashed, half-stretched image that she recognized at once as the two-dimensional representation of a three-dimensional network file—of their network map, she realized suddenly, of the map she and Trouble had painstakingly built over the four years of their partnership. It was one of their more useful tools: there were no commercial maps available—not covering all the nets—and the ones that did exist were deliberately flawed, deliberately distorted to hide the control areas from people who had no business having access. And there were plenty of corporate spaces, privately owned systems that nonetheless also existed in the unreal "space" of the myriad networked computers that was the nets; all of those preferred to be invisible, at least to an outside eye.

On the net itself, of course, things were different. Once you plugged yourself into the system—either via the implanted dollie-box and dollie-slot, the direct-on-line-image processor system, which gave a text-speech-and-symbol interface, or through the full-sense brainworm, with its molecular wires running directly into the brain that let you experience virtuality as though it were real—it was easy enough to find your way around the nets. There were signposts, vivid neon images, and the swirling rivers and lines of light that were the virtual reflection of the data itself, which anyone who'd been on the nets for any length of time could read like a tracker read spoor. But the map was useful for planning a job, when you had to enter the nets from the safest point, so that the security programs, watchdogs and trackers and callback systems, and all the panoply of IC(E)—Intrusion Countermeasures (Electronic)—would either lose your trail in the confusion of conflicting data or never have the chance to track you down. Remotely, Cerise was surprised that Trouble had taken the copy with her, though she supposed it was possible that Trouble had made two copies out of the network files, their own secure space. But then, Trouble had said it was time to give up cracking.

It was very quiet in the apartment, too quiet, just the distant sound of wind and the occasional rattle of the fire escape in the other room. Cerise winced, and reached for the main remote, jabbed at buttons until the media center lit. Trouble had left the main screen tuned to the news channel, and the blare of the announcer's voice filled the room.

"—top story, the Senate today voted to override the presidential veto of the Evans-Tindale Bill, joining the House in handing the president a resounding defeat. Marjorie Albuez in Washington has more on the story."

"Thank you, Jim. By accepting the compromise bill sponsored by Charles Evans and Alexander Tindale, Congress today seems to have ensured that the United States will remain the only industrial nation that is not a signatory to the Amsterdam Network Conventions."

The voice droned on, but Cerise was no longer listening. She swung back to face the linked computers, the remaining files forgotten, and reached for the dollie-cord snugged into its housing at the base of the dedicated brainbox. She tilted her head to fit the cord into the dollie-slot behind her right ear, but did not launch herself directly onto the nets. This was why Trouble had left. She had been talking for months about what would happen if the U.S. rejected the Amsterdam Conventions, about how even the supposedly benign Evans-Tindale Bill would destroy the cracker community, bring them all finally under an alien, ill-conceived, ill-fitting law. For a moment, Cerise almost believed those prophecies of doom. No one had believed that Congress would buy Evans-Tindale, it bore no relation to virtuality. . . .

"—completes what the so-called Nunberg Act—the Industrial Espionage Act, as it is more properly known— attempted to provide two years ago." That was a new voice, but Cerise didn't turn to identify the speaker. "The Evans-Tindale Bill codifies the various provisions of the Nunberg Act, and creates a new entity within the Treasury Department that will have enforcement responsibility on the nets, replacing the patchwork system currently in place. In a nutshell, Evans-Tindale, like the Nunberg Act before it, redefines so-called cyberspace as a particular legal jurisdiction, and establishes a code of law governing these electronic transactions."

Which means, Cerise thought, that we're all screwed. She sat for a long moment, staring at her screen, at the distorted image displayed in its central window. That map no longer mattered, because now there was no reason to keep those secrets, at least not in the legal world of the bright lights: there was a new law out there, and one that could be enforced in the real world. And for the shadows—the illegal world of crackers and grey- and black-market dealers, the world where she had lived ever since she'd run away from her home, her true name, and the secretarial school that had been her second home—it meant the end of an era. It would no longer be possible to dodge the law in one jurisdiction by claiming that you, or your machines, or your target, were located elsewhere; it would no longer be possible to argue that there was no theft where there was no real property. All that had been decided, and by fiat, not the nets' own powerful consensus. And Evans-Tindale also meant that there was no longer any possibility of legalizing the brainworm. The old-style crackers and the legal netwalkers had proclaimed their innocence by blaming everything on the brainworm and its users, and no one in authority seemed to know enough to know that they were lying.

She reached for the safety, cupped it in her left hand, hesitated, and wound the cord twice around her wrist, just in case. If she pressed that button, or its virtual analogue, the system would shut down instantly and automatically, dumping her back in the safety of her own home system, her own body. She took a deep breath, fighting back despair, and used her right hand to touch the sequence that opened a net gateway. The brainworm responded perfectly, its impulses overriding the merely physical input of the apartment, and she flung herself out into the glittering perpetual night that was the net.

*Alice in Wonderland, Alice down the rabbit hole, Alice out in cyberspace, flung along the lines of data, flying across fields of light, the night cities that live only behind her eyes. Power rides her fingers, she moves from datashell to datashell, walking the nets like the ghost of a shadow, her trail vanishing behind her as she goes. She carries power in the dark behind her eyes.*

*And she needs it, tonight, in the chaos that whirls between the islands of the corporate spaces, their boundaries marked by heaps and new whorls of glittering IC(E). The bulletin boards, the great sink of the BBS where all the lines of data eventually meet and merge and pool into a sink of slow transfer, limited nodes, and low-budget users, are in upheaval. The familiar icons and signpost-symbols that guide the unwary are gone completely, erased by their owners or remade in new and somehow threatening form. Icons whirl past her, some representing people she knows, has worked with. She smells fear sharp as sweat, hears the constant rustling murmur of the transactions that surround her as the brainworm translates what is truly only electrons, data transferred from computer to computer, to sensation in her brain. She glimpses a familiar shape, a hint of flowing robes that move against the current of the datastream that enfolds them, and tries to follow. But the crowding icons—balled advertising, jostling users, once a virtual pickpocket, groping for useful programs in other people's toolkits—block her way and she loses the robed icon at the main exchange node, where the data flows down from the outer nets like a waterfall of lights.*

*She turns back toward the center of the maze that is the BBS, following the shape of the underlying structural spiral rather than the illusion of shops and storefronts and tented stalls—unfamiliar shop-icons, old names and symbols blanked or greyed or simply missing—heading for a node where someone will surely know where Trouble has gone. Trouble will have left a message there, if she left anything at all. This is free space, unprotected, and the air stinks of it, the salt sea-smell the brainworm gives to undefended bits of data. At any other time, she would stop to taste, to savor, to see what news is drifting in the wind—and maybe especially tonight she should stop, listen to the whispers and shouts and read the posts that fill the message walls, but Trouble is gone, and that matters more than any law. She can hear voices, snatches of conversations, names repeated, not her own, but familiar nonetheless: the netgods have spoken, the oldsters who built and managed the first nets, and they've thrown their weight behind Evans-Tindale. Cerise sneers at that, and doesn't care that the brainworm broadcasts that emotion. The old netwalkers are out of touch with the new conditions, with the better, faster, and wider-band dollie-slots and especially with the brainworm; of course they'd support this law as a way to keep their own power supreme.*

*In a blank mirror that was once the center of a pair of swinging doors, she sees herself reflected, her icon blond-girl-in-blue-dress-and-pinnie, the child she never should have been, and then the mirror empties, and she puts her hand through it just like Alice and walks, her feet barely touching the illusion of a floor, into a temporary space.*

*Inside the mirror is a cave of ice, not the warm wood saloon she had expected, lined in IC(E) to keep out the intruders; the cowboys and the piano player are all missing, vanished into chill white silence, and a personal icon stands in the center where the bar had been, a woman-shape dressed like a dance-hall girl in snow-white velvet and silver fringe and silver-spangled stockings, the cloth drawn back into a bustle, cut down at the bodice to reveal breasts like hills of snow. Cerise feels the chill of the IC(E) on her skin, tingling down her spine like danger; she smells a tracker program, sharp as burned cloves, can almost taste the candy-sweet data that lies like shards of glass below the illusory floor. Miss Kitty deals in that data, stolen, borrowed, invented, even imagined, and in the commerce of messages passed unread.*

*\*I'm looking for Trouble,\* Cerise says, and waits.*

*She gets no answer, Miss Kitty's icon stands still and silent, and Cerise frowns and takes a step forward. And then she smells it, the scent of rotten meat, the corpse-smell the brainworm uses to signal absolute disaster. Even as she turns to run, the walls fold inward, IC(E) spiking downward. She feels its cold driving at her, lifts a hand to ward off the nearest spine, and its jagged tip scores a deep line along her arm. The brainworm reflects its touch as searing pain and the thin trace of blood ghostly along her icon-arm. There's no reason for this attack, she's no danger to Miss Kitty, never has been, has been in fact a good supplier, but there's no time to form a protest. No time even to reach for an icebreaker, or any of the other programs she carries in her toolkit; this is serious IC(E), deadly serious, and she closes her hand convulsively, triggering the safety. The world dissolves around her, the spikes of the IC(E) fading to static as they touch her skin*

and she leaned back in her chair, untangling her fingers from the cord of the safety. The screen in front of her flashed a bright-red icon, and a text message below it: SESSION ABORT. She glared at that—it was an admission of defeat to trigger to the safety, to run away from danger—and then, belatedly, became aware of the faint scent of hot metal rising from the linked machines. She frowned then, and touched the brainbox. The casing was warm, warmer than it should have been. Her frown deepened, and she set the safety aside, touched keys to call up a diagnostic program. The session-abort icon vanished, replaced by a spinning clock-face; a moment later, it, too, disappeared, and the program presented her with a list of the various components and their conditions. Two of the five fuses had tripped in the brainbox, and one had gone in the biotranslator as well. Cerise shivered, even though she'd expected it, and reached for her box of spares. Miss Kitty's IC(E) had been set to kill—and what the hell the woman thought she was doing, Cerise added silently, transmuting fear to anger, I don't know. The whole nets have gone crazy—they must have, if anybody's actually supporting Evans-Tindale. And if Miss Kitty tried to kill me. Though that probably wasn't personal. She closed her eyes for an instant, remembering the frozen icon and the sudden smell of death. No, probably not personal at all, she decided. If I were abandoning a grey-market space—and I think she must've done just that—that's the way I'd play it. A striking icon to catch people's attention, and then hair-trigger IC(E) to go after whoever tried to follow me. Or, like Miss Kitty did, whoever showed up first.

She rubbed her arm where the IC(E) had touched her—there were no marks on her skin, just the tingling reminder of a near miss in her nerves—and then began methodically to shut down the system. She couldn't replace the fuses with the machines running, and she couldn't go back out onto the nets until the fuses were replaced: no choice, she thought, and swung away from the system. The media wall was still talking at her, the screen now showing a panel of suits discussing the implications of the change. She scowled at them, worked the remote to mute the sound, and only then recognized one of the suited figures as George Aferiat, who had written software for the first dollie-slots and their associated implants, and who had also run a shadow space in the BBS before he'd gotten law. There was nothing more zealous than a convert. She lifted her middle finger to the screen, and turned back to the message board.

It didn't take a lot of work to retrieve Carlie's message from the trash—even cheap machines had the option these days, and her system was far from cheap. She glanced at the linked machines—everything was shut down and saved; all she had to do was wait for the chips to cool and trigger the playback. Carlie Held's voice poured from the little speaker, as perfect as though he himself stood beside her.

"Cerise, Trouble, if either of you's there, pick up, we're in deep shit." There was a pause, and Cerise pictured him standing in the tiny office that served his storefront surgery, the privacy handset swamped in his huge hand. "OK, you're not there. OK. If you haven't heard, Evans-Tindale passed—goddamn Congress overrode the veto—which means the worm stays illegal, and Treasury gets to make the law on the nets. I need to talk to you—we all need to talk. Call me as soon as you can."

Cerise heard the click of the connection breaking, and a red light flashed on the tiny status screen: end of message. She swore under her breath, and reached for her own handset, touched the codes that would connect her with Carlie's surgery. She heard the beeps as the system routed her call—a local, twelve sharp musical tones, seven for location, three for payment, two for privacy—and then waited as the ring pulsed in her ear. She counted six, and knew Carlie wasn't answering—wasn't there—but let it ring a dozen more times, staring at the posturing suits in the media screen, before she finally hung up. Carlie was gone, too.

And that was ridiculous, she told herself. She jabbed buttons again, punching in another number—Arabesque, Rachelle Sirvain in the real world: another local call, just in the next ward, five minutes away by the subway. The phone rang, rang again; she counted ten before she hung up, fighting sudden panic. It was almost as if she was the last one of them left, the last survivor— She shoved that thought away, and punched a third number. This time, the answering machine picked up on the third ring.

"Hi, you've reached five-five—"

Cerise broke the connection—Dewildah was gone, too—and punched a final set of codes. In the media screen, the talking suits had disappeared, to be replaced by a head, a serious-looking woman who wore secretarial goggles. The phone rang, rang again, and then a sharply accented voice said, "Hello?"

Cerise let out breath she hadn't realized she was holding. "Butch. Thank God you're home."

"Cerise? Are you all right?"

She could hear the concern in Butch van Liesvelt's voice, and managed a shaky smile. "Yeah—well, no, Trouble's gone and there's all this with Evans-Tindale—"

"Yeah." There was a little pause, and Cerise could hear in the background the indistinct sounds of someone talking—television, probably, she thought. In the screen, the image changed again, became a pair of lists showing the differences between the Amsterdam Conventions and Evans-Tindale. In one corner of the screen, a much smaller talking head—male this time—babbled away, mouth moving without sound.

"Look," van Liesvelt said abruptly, "I'm heading over to Marco Polo's. Carlie called from there, he said he and Max were there already, and that Arabesque was on her way. I was just going to call you and Trouble, I talked to Dewildah already—"

"Trouble's gone," Cerise said again.

"Gone? What do you mean, gone?"

"I mean she's gone. She packed up her stuff and left, I don't know where she is." Cerise took another deep breath, fought back the baffled anger. "Or why, exactly, but I think I can guess. I'll meet you at Marco Polo's. We can talk there."

"You sure?" van Liesvelt asked, and Cerise felt her eyes fill up with tears. Of all their oddball group—a half-dozen or so crackers who had dared both the brainworm and the risks of real-world contact—it was van Liesvelt, shambling, physically graceless Butch, who'd done the most to take care of all of them.

"Yeah, I'm sure. I'll see you at Marco Polo's."

She cut the connection before van Liesvelt could ask anything more. She set the handset back on its hook, taking ridiculous care with the placement, waiting until the tears were gone again before she turned her mind to business. She worked the remote again, shutting down the media wall, and grabbed her leather coat off the hook by the door before she could change her mind.

The wind had risen since the afternoon, curled in as she opened the door, bringing the smell of the wet streets and driving a handful of tattered leaves around her ankles. Cerise shivered, tucking her chin down into the coat's high collar, then had to reach back to pull the door shut behind her. She jammed her hands into her pockets, wishing she'd remembered gloves, and tore the lining again where she'd cut the pocket for a borrowed gun. This wasn't a particularly bad part of town, no more than most, and better than some, but there had been times when she needed a gun's threat to balance the odds. Or to get them out of whatever Trouble had talked them into. It hadn't happened often—Trouble was generally reasonable, cautious—but every now and then she'd accept a challenge, even one that hadn't been meant, and they would all have to live with the consequences. Like now.

Cerise shook the thought away, the memory of Trouble furious and confident, facing down a pair of local boys with knives. She had downplayed it later, always pointed out that the kids had been maybe thirteen, fourteen years old and obviously trying their first mugging. But Cerise had never forgotten the crazy grin, the sheer, black-hearted determination, and had been, herself, more than a little afraid. She had caught the look again four months ago, when Evans-Tindale passed the first time, and had done her best not to see it. Trouble had said then that she was quitting, that they couldn't go on if the bill passed, and she had obviously meant it.

It was almost dark out now, and all the streetlights were on, swaying gently in the cold wind. Cerise shrugged herself deeper into her heavy coat, stepping more quickly across the moving shadows, heading for the nearest subway station at the corner of Elm and Cass. Not that it was all that far to Marco Polo's, less than a dozen blocks, but it was cold, and dark already, and the secretary gangs, the dollie-girls, tended to lurk on the fringes of New Century Square. As she came out into the brighter light of the intersection, however, she saw the lines waiting beyond the ticket booths, men and women huddled into drab, windproof coats, here and there the brighter cloth of a student uniform, and she muttered a curse under her breath. The system was backed up again—it had never been built to handle the current loads—and she could easily walk to the Square before she even made it down onto the platform. She lengthened her step, heading up Cass into the teeth of the wind.

Once she had passed the intersection, with its bright lights and the low-standing brick station, foot traffic thinned out. This was mostly small shops and offices, all of which closed promptly at five to let their people get out of the city-center before full dark, and the doors and ground-floor windows were barred, steel shutters or heavy grills drawn tight over their vulnerabilities. Security lights showed like blue pinpoints in the corners of a few windows, and there were metal mesh sleeves across the swaying streetlights, casting webbed shadows over the pooled light. A few of the lights were broken anyway, leaving patches of greater dark, and she crossed them warily, wondering if she'd been stupid after all. But she was already past the bus lines at Stadium Road—not that they were running, it wasn't a game night—and it would take longer to walk back to the station than it would to keep going. She could see the lights of the Square in the distance, the haze of gold neon bright at the end of the street, the gold-and-red bars of the Camberwell Beer sign just visible between a pair of buildings: only another four or five blocks to go, and she'd be in the relative safety of the crowded Square. She kept walking, not hurrying, glad of her soft-soled shoes and the dark coat that helped her pass unobserved, and reached the end of Cass without encountering another pedestrian.

New Century Square was as busy as ever, lights glaring from the subway kiosk at the center of the circle, more light, red and gold and green neon, flashing from the signs and display boards that ringed the Square, and from the signs that glowed and flickered over the myriad doorways. The gaudy lights helped to disguise buildings that hadn't been new eighty years ago, when the century turned and the Square had been rechristened in hopes of attracting a new clientele for the new years. Maybe half a dozen suits were standing outside the station, staring up at the news board and its displays—currently a pretty dark-skinned actress showing teeth and tits and a new shampoo. There were more suits inside the ticket booths, men and women alike looking tired and irritable, and Cerise guessed that the system still wasn't running properly. A handful of dollie-girls were hanging out under the awning outside the discount store, watching the suits. The youngest looked twelve or so, the oldest maybe sixteen, and each of them wore a parody of a corporate suit—the skirts too short, slit thigh-high, the jackets too tight and sexy, their faces layered with clown-bright makeup. Their shoes, bright neon-satin pumps, had three- and four-inch heels sheathed in steel, and there would be flip-knives and maybe a gun or two in the sequinned handbags. They belonged to the secretarial so-called college over on Market Street, Cerise knew, kids who had indentured themselves to the school and its placement service to get the implants, dollie-box and dollie-slot, that could eventually win them a decent job with a corporation. They had found out too late, they always found out too late, that they didn't automatically get the training or the bioware that would let them walk the nets, or even use the systems to their full capacity. It was no wonder they took to the streets to get a little of their own back. She had been one of them, eight years ago, before she'd figured out how to get into the BBS and found the grey-market dealers there, and she gave them a wide berth, knowing what they, what she, were capable of doing. She was aware of their stares as she passed, the anger buried under the troweled-on color, and ignored it, knowing better than to meet someone's eyes and trigger a confrontation. Trouble would have laughed—if she was in one of her difficult moods, she would have said something, anything, earned her name yet again. But then, Trouble had somehow never learned to lose. How she'd managed that, Cerise didn't know, even after four years together working the nets, and three years as lovers: she wasn't corporate, and besides, the corporations taught you early to lose to them. But she sure wasn't city-trash, either.

She heard the click of heels behind her, steel on stone, and then a second set of footsteps, the same sharp almost musical clink not quite in synch with the first, and did not turn. The wall of a store rose to her right, solid brick banded with neon: no place to run, except into the street and the traffic, and that would mean losing anyway. The skin between her shoulder blades tingled, an electric touch at the center of her spine. She had played the game before, knew exactly what was happening, and then she heard the voices, rising shrill to be certain she, and all the others, heard.

"—that hair."

"Pull it out, girl."

Cerise turned then, the fury rising in her, caught the dollie-girl by the lapel of her too-tight jacket, swung her sideways into the brick of the wall. The girl staggered, losing her balance on the high heels, and Cerise hauled her up bodily, using both lapels this time, and slammed her back against the bricks, narrowing missing a light tube. She caught a glimpse of the second girl, mouth open in shock, falling back a step or two at the sheer craziness, and looked down at the girl in her hands. She hung dazed, one button torn loose, her eyes unfocused and filled with reflex tears. Cerise shook her, not caring that her head bounced off the bricks, felt her scrabble without result for safer footing.

"You touch me," Cerise said, "and I'll fucking kill you."

She hadn't spoken loudly, sounded calmer than she felt,

but the girl heard, eyes widening so that a tear ran down her painted face, drawing a long line of scarlet from her mascara. Cerise lifted her, barely feeling the effort, and let her go again, saw her slide gracelessly to the bottom of the wall and sit for an instant, long legs sprawling, before the other girl moved to help her up. Cerise turned her back on them, not caring, daring them, even, to follow her. There was nothing, not even a catcall, last defiance, and she felt the sharp sting of regret before the reaction set in.

She was still shaking a little, adrenaline-anger and fear mixed, when she turned down the narrow street that led to Marco Polo's and pushed open the door badged with a neon cactus and pagodas, wincing as the twanging steel-string music hit her like a blow. The downstairs room was filled with a mix of suits and lower-level tech-types and a fair number of secretaries and temps of both sexes on the hustle. Most of them were standing four-deep at the bar, bellowing indistinguishable orders at the sweating bartenders, or crowded in groups of six or seven around the tiny tables. A few, maybe a dozen or so, were already on the little dance floor, arms linked across each others' shoulders, feet moving in approximate coordination. Twin television monitors hung at the ends of the bar, and the news anchor beamed down like a benevolent deity. His words were inaudible through the music and the shouted conversations, but the logo beside his head was the familiar computer-chip-and-gavel that had come to stand for Evans-Tindale. Cerise made a face, seeing that, and began to work her way through the crowd toward the stairs that led to the upper bar.

It was a jovial crowd, this early, everybody loose but not yet drunk enough to think of trouble, and it wasn't difficult to get through the mob, no need to resort to elbows or stepping on toes. She smiled mechanically at suits, and they edged smiling away, letting her worm through the spaces. She fetched up at the foot of the stairs in a sudden pocket of silence as the song ended, and stood there for a moment catching her breath, looking back toward the monitors. The Evans-Tindale logo was still in place, though the image be-

hind it had changed: the screen was filled with protesters, all
waving placards that called for the U.S. to sign the Amsterdam Conventions. The camera focused on one sign, carried
by a black woman who looked young and serious enough to
be a student at a real college; it read, in bright red letters, A:
U.S. AND LIBERIA. Q: WHO HASN'T SIGNED? That wasn't quite
true, Cerise thought—she vaguely remembered that there
were a couple of Asian nations that hadn't yet agreed to the
Conventions—but it was close enough. At her side, a tallish
suit, good-looking, broad bones and a not-too-neat mustache, shook his head.

"I don't get it," he said, to no one in particular. "What's the
problem?"

Cerise looked at him in disbelief, wanting to say something but not knowing where to begin. Evans-Tindale was
going to change everything, was going to destroy the nets as
they were, and offered nothing to replace them— A suited
woman edged up to the man, handed him one of the two
beers she carried, holding them well away from her body.

"Technies," she said. "If they can't have their toys—"

The music started again, with a wail of synthetic brass,
drowning out her words. Cerise shook herself—there was
nothing you could say to some people, nothing that would
make any difference—and started up the stairs.

The upstairs room—it had never had another name,
wasn't even officially reserved for a netwalker clientele,
though the occasional suit or temp who wandered in from
downstairs usually left quickly enough—was much quieter,
and she let the heavy door thump shut again behind her with
a sigh of relief. There was no music here, just the occasional
murmur of voices and the overlapping noise of five or six television monitors, each tuned to a different channel. Most of
the little tables scattered across the dimly lit room were occupied by netwalkers who sat alone or in twos and threes, muttering together or with their eyes fixed on the monitors
mounted from the ceiling. She recognized some of the
faces—Johnny Winchester, for one, scrawny and greying,
who had been on the nets since the invention of the dollie-

slot, and was syscop, the on-line legal authority, for one of
the official public spaces. He'd been to D.C. four times to testify, supporting the Amsterdam Conventions, had argued at
the last that Evans-Tindale was better than nothing. I hope
you're satisfied, Cerise thought, and headed for the bar, giving his table a wide berth.

The bar itself was mechanical, which meant a limited selection of drinks, but Marco didn't have to pay a fifth bartender.
Cerise fed a couple of slips of citiscrip into the machine, and
it whirred to itself for a moment before filling a plastic cup
with wine. In the dim light it looked more like water, and she
sniffed it to be sure before she turned away. There were a few
other faces she knew, not many: netwalkers didn't as a rule
congregate in the real world. It took something like this to
bring them together, and even then most of them weren't
talking to each other, just sitting and listening to the monitors. She recognized a pair of women from the Arts Round
Table, sitting together with a man she didn't know. All three
looked grim, and they had their heads close together; as she
made her way past the table, she saw that they had a portable
machine set up, and were staring avidly at its screen. Neither
of the women were on-line, and the man didn't even seem to
have a dollie-slot; what good they thought they could do, she
didn't know. There was another familiar shape at a table at
the back of the room, a rangy man, bearded and scowling, a
flashing pin in the shape of his red-hand icon fastened to the
lapel of his neat suit-jacket, and Cerise looked hastily away.
Bran-Boru, or whatever his real name was, had a reputation
for being chancy, and she had no desire to attract his attention.

Then at last she saw van Liesvelt, skinny and blonde and
rumpled, even sitting down taller than the others at the corner table. He lifted his hand in greeting, beckoning her over;
Cerise waved back, not trying to hide her relief, and came to
join them. The others were there, too: Carlie Held still in
working whites under his grubby jacket, Arabesque slowly
crumpling the fingers of a VR glove—the old-fashioned vir-
tual-reality interface, not good for anything but games and

blunt-instrument science anymore—into an ungainly fist,
Max Helling with his partner Jannick Aledort at his back,
Aledort listening, not quite part of the group, while Helling
talked. Max was always talking, Cerise thought, and took the
last chair, next to Dewildah Mason, who looked up at her
with a wry smile and a nod of greeting.

"So where's your other half?"

"Trouble's gone," Cerise said, and to her horror heard her
voice crack. She took a sip of the wine to cover it, swallowed
wrong, and choked. Mason reached over to pound her on the
back, brown eyes wide with concern.

"That's what you said," van Liesvelt said.

Giving me time to pull myself together, Cerise thought,
and nodded her thanks, setting the wine down again.

"Yeah." Her voice was still strained, and her throat hurt,
but at least she didn't sound as though she were going to cry.

"Evans-Tindale?" Helling asked. He was a thin, feral-look-
ing man, a little older than the rest of them. He'd been on the
net for years, had more business connections in the shadows,
knew more about buying or selling black-market programs
and data than any of the others. Cerise sometimes thought he
only stayed friends with them because they were all queer,
and the old-style netwalkers still didn't approve of him,
wouldn't approve of him no matter how good he was because of it. She suspected he'd taken the risk of the brainworm for the same reason: the old-style netwalkers wouldn't
respect his work once he'd gotten it, but then, they hadn't
ever respected him. The brainworm did give you an advantage on the nets, let you use the full range of your senses, not
just sight and sound, to interpret the virtual world. The old-
style netwalkers claimed to hold it in contempt, said that it
was a crutch, something for second-raters, but Cerise suspected, had always suspected, that they were just afraid. The
worm entailed risks: implantation and direct-to-brain wiring
was always tricky, could leave you a mental cripple if the operation went wrong, and the oldsters had never quite been
able to face that possibility. The dollie-slots and the associated implants didn't touch the brain, ran along existing

nerves—less of a risk, and more of a challenge to use, or so the oldsters said.

"Trouble wouldn't just run away," Arabesque said. She set the VR glove down on the dented tabletop, curled her own hand over it, matching finger to finger. Her skin was only a little lighter than the black plastic, and both were like shadows in the indirect light.

"She said she would," Held said. He shook his head, laid his huge hands flat on the tabletop. It was hard, seeing them, to believe that he was as good a cybermedic as he actually was; harder still to believe that he was qualified to install and modify brainworms. Or at least he was qualified in the EC, where he'd trained: the worm was still illegal here, and there wasn't any chance of legalizing it now that Evans-Tindale had passed. "She said from the beginning she wasn't going to stick around if Congress overrode the veto." He shook his head, and pushed himself back from the table. "Anybody else want another drink?"

Van Liesvelt shook his head, and Mason said, "Yeah, thanks, Carlie." She held out a glittering strip of foil, and Held took it, turned away toward the bar.

"That wasn't all she was bitching about," Arabesque said, and gave Cerise a hard look. "Last time I talked to her, she said you two'd had a disagreement over a job."

Cerise made a face. This was the part she hadn't wanted to think about, the part she hadn't wanted to remember: she'd been warned, and she'd miscalculated badly. "There's a new corporate space, with new IC(E). I didn't recognize the system, but I thought we could crack it. Trouble doesn't—didn't agree. But it's interesting IC(E)." She could almost see it, taste it, in memory, a massive cylinder of glass, light spiraling slowly up its side, to drift down again in a faint haze, hiding the codes that make up the real security. She had never seen IC(E) that tight before, could hardly wait to try to crack it. . . .

"What was the company?" That was Aledort, leaning forward a little further over the back of his own chair and Helling's shoulder.

"I don't know yet," Cerise answered. "I told you, it's a new space to me."

"Better hold off a while," Helling said. "You don't know what's going to happen under Evans-Tindale."

Van Liesvelt nodded agreement, for once unsmiling. His mustache looked more ragged than ever, as though he'd been chewing on it.

"I can't believe Trouble just left," Mason said.

"Neither can I," Arabesque said, and Cerise glared at her.

"I told you what happened. We'd been talking about the job—"

"You can't call it a job," Helling objected. "If you don't know who made the IC(E) or what's behind it, it's not a job."

Cerise ignored him. "And she said she wasn't going to do it, it was crazy with the second vote coming up. She said if Evans-Tindale passed, if they overrode the veto, she wasn't going to stay on the nets. And when I came home this afternoon, she was gone, and all her equipment with her."

"Jesus," van Liesvelt said.

"I called about three," Held said, reappearing with two glasses. He handed one to Mason, along with a couple of plastic slugs, and reseated himself next to van Liesvelt. "So I guess she was gone then. I'd just got out of surgery, heard from a guy in the waiting room." He shook his head. "Man, I couldn't believe it. They won't sign the Conventions, and then they turn around and pass this shit."

"I was on my way back from campus," Mason said unexpectedly. She had been a student at a real college, still held an extension card from the university. "I was waiting for the commuter train, there must've been twenty of us, and this guy—I hardly know him, his name's Bill something, or maybe Paul. Anyway, he comes up to me and says, 'You're on the nets, right? Did you hear they overrode the veto?' And I looked at him—I still can't believe I did this—and I said, 'You got to be kidding. That can't be right, you must've got it wrong.' And he says, 'No, they've got the monitors on in the pizza place'—there's a pizza place right next to the train station—'and they broke into the soaps to make the announcement.' So I went over there, and sure enough, the monitor's on, and the screen's showing the vote count. And I just stood there. I thought for a minute he'd gotten the story backward, that we'd won, because the numbers were so high for Evans-Tindale, but he hadn't. They'd overridden it, no question. No appeal, no nothing. I damn near didn't bother getting on the train."

"I was on the net," Helling said. "I—" He stopped, glancing over his shoulder at Aledort, who was scowling, and began again. "I'd just drifted back into the BBS, riding the stream, and I thought—I don't know what I thought. It felt like an earthquake, everybody trying to log on or off or to do something, all at once. I mean, the ground shook." He waved his hands in the air, miming the motion. "Literally. I couldn't keep my balance for a minute. And then everybody starting talking, shouting, and I ran for the nearest node and got the hell off the system." He shook his head. "It's still crazy out there. I got back on before I came over here. I thought maybe somebody would be talking sense out there, but it's insane. Half the old spaces are shut down, the BBS is clogged solid with traffic, there's new IC(E) in half the corporate spots I looked at. It's just crazy."

"Miss Kitty shut down the saloon," Cerise said. "And left some very nasty IC(E) behind her." She didn't need to add any more to it: they all knew Miss Kitty, did business with her, and knew Cerise as well.

"Well, she was in a really bad position," Helling said. "Under the new laws, my God, everything she traded in was felony material."

"Wonderful," van Liesvelt said. "I have to admit, Trouble's got a point. It's not exactly going to be safe, staying in the shadows."

"Only if you're not careful," Cerise said.

Arabesque nodded. "Yeah. It changes how we do business, ups the risks and the stakes. My God, you know what we can charge now?"

"Yeah, and end up like Terrel," Mason muttered. "Serving

five-to-ten for a so-called armed robbery—you just better be very careful what you carry in your toolkit now."

There was a little silence, and then van Liesvelt said, "I was over on the Euronets when the news came through. I'd just told a couple of old friends there was no way the override would happen. It took me twenty minutes, realtime, to work my way back to home node. I thought I'd have to hit the safety before I found a way through the traffic."

Cerise whistled under her breath. Twenty minutes in realtime, not the subjective time of the nets, was ridiculously long. Usually one could make one's way from one side of the nets to the other—traveling twice around the world in the process—in that time.

"What in the world," Mason said, "are we going to do now?"

"Do?" Arabesque fixed her with an angry stare. "Pretty much what we've always done, that's what we're going to do. Cracking was always illegal, don't kid yourself, 'Wildah. We'll just have to be more careful—and that's all."

"I don't know," Held said. "I think it's different." He shook his head. "Very different."

Van Liesvelt nodded in morose agreement, and wiped beer out of his mustache. "I was wondering about Europe, heading there, I mean."

"The real business—most of the real targets, real data, data worth money—is still in U.S. jurisdiction," Helling said. "Or can claim it is. And they've explicitly overruled appealing to Amsterdam Conventions. It's in the law."

"Fuck," van Liesvelt muttered, and took another swallow of his beer.

Cerise said, "I'm with Arabesque. We got to stick with it. What else can we do?"

"Go straight?" Helling murmured, with a curl of his lip.

Held laughed without humor, and Arabesque shook her head. Van Liesvelt said, "Not likely."

Cerise allowed herself a sour smile, acknowledging the pun—the one thing they all had in common, besides the brainworm, was being gay—but it faded quickly. Going

straight, moving out of the shadows into the bright lights of
the legal world, the legal nets, would be difficult: they, none
of them, had the corporate connections to become the sort of
consultant that would let them go on paying their bills, and
none of the other jobs that were open to freelancers were particularly challenging, or particularly well-paid. And corporate employment . . . Unconsciously her mouth twisted again
as she tried to imagine herself, any of them, fitting into the
polite, restrained world of the corporations. If any of them
had been suited to the corporate life, he or she would already
be part of it. The perks of a corporate job were too good, despite the risk of layoffs, to be passed up lightly.

The noise from the monitors changed, flared briefly, and
then settled to a single voice. Cerise turned in surprise to see
that the three monitors in her line of sight were now tuned to
the same channel—so were they all, from the way Jerry Singlar's voice coalesced out of the hubbub. Singlar was one of
her least favorite anchors, an ex-cracker gone to the bright
lights with a vengeance, a man who pretended to know and
love the nets even as he proved he didn't understand anything about them. She made a face, but did not look away.
The others were looking at the monitors, too, not just at their
table but all across the room, and the talk faded quickly, leaving only Singlar's voice crackling out of the half-dozen
speakers.

"—commentary. The override of the presidential veto of
Evans-Tindale has brought consternation to the nets, a result
not unexpected among those of us who have walked the nets
for the past decade. Despite attempts at self-policing, the nets
have long been a lawless place, a haven for a criminal minority as well as for the law-abiding majority. This situation has
become impossible to tolerate, as the depredations of the so-
called crackers, descendants of the criminal hackers of the
twentieth century, have become the center of a criminal economy that rivals the Mafia in scope and enterprise."

Arabesque made a rude noise, half laughter, half spitting,
and Mason waved her to silence. Helling muttered some-

thing under his breath that sounded like, "I wish," and Aledort laid a hand on his shoulder.

"This economy, which thrived only by the absence of law,
has spawned a number of subcultures, all dangerous in their
own right. But the most dangerous of these, the one that has
caused the most talk and the one that the Evans-Tindale will
do most to control, is that of the brainworm. These untested
and potentially deadly implants—far more dangerous than
the common dollie-slots, because the brainworm requires
placing hardware in the brain itself—have contributed to the
spread of the cracker culture by giving these hard-line crimi-
nals access to a new technology that is unbeatable by people
equipped with only ordinary, and legal, implants."

"Oh, bullshit," Cerise said.

Held said, in the voice of a man making an old, and losing,
argument, "The brainworm is legal in Europe, and there's no
more cracking from the Euronets. And people don't die from
installation there, either."

"It figures," Arabesque said, with suppressed fury, "it just
figures they'd try to blame the worm."

"It's easier than writing intelligent laws," Helling said.

"They have laws that make sense," van Liesvelt said. "All
they had to do was sign the Amsterdam Conventions. . . ."

"Oh, shut up." That was Johnny Winchester, weaving to
his feet at the center of the room. He stumbled slightly,
nearly overturning his table and tipping his beer so that it
slopped over the edge of the glass to form a slowly spreading
puddle on the tabletop. "Jerry's right, if you people hadn't
brought in the worm, gone cracking with it, none of this
would've happened."

"Bullshit," Cerise said again.

Arabesque said, "Dream on. They've been looking for an
excuse to crack down for a hundred years."

"Yeah, and you people gave it to them." Winchester stared
accusingly at them. Behind him, the spilled beer began to
drip off the edge of his table.

"Fucking wireheads," someone else said, from the darkness behind him.

"Hey, people," Held said, voice dropping into his best street-doc register. "This hurts all of us."

"And there are plenty of people cracking without the worm," van Liesvelt said, not quite quietly enough.

There was an ambiguous murmur from the rest of the room, not agreement, not rejection, an undirected anger that made the back of Cerise's neck prickle with sudden fear. She had heard that note before, on the streets when she was fifteen, running with the gangs, the sound of a group looking for a scapegoat; she had never thought to hear it here, among the people of the net, and never directed at herself. She looked around the room as though for the first time, seeing the majority of pale faces, male faces, sitting for the most part alone or in twos and threes: nothing like her own group, none of the easy realworld friendship. She had never before seen so many of the others together off-line.

She looked back at the others, and saw Aledort leaning back a little, eyes narrowed. He had heard the same thing she had, and Aledort usually went armed.

Helling said, "Nobody's going to wipe out cracking anyway. The multinationals pay too damn well."

He had said the right thing, Cerise realized. There was a little ripple of scornful laughter, and, underneath it, the release of tension like a sigh. She took a deep breath, reached for her wine, and took a long drink without really tasting it. In the background, Singlar droned on, his voice alternately reproving and paternal by turns, but she determinedly ignored it, concentrating on the wine. She set the glass carefully back in its wet circle, wondering what she was going to do. Whatever else Evans-Tindale had done, it had broken the old community of the net, divided the old-style crackers, the ones who relied on the dollie-boxes, from the ones who used the brainworm—and was that the intention? she wondered suddenly. It would be more subtle than she would have expected from people who didn't know the net—and conspiracy theories are usually wrong, she told herself sternly. The only certainty is that the nets have changed irrevocably. And

Trouble is gone, my life changed with that as much as with the new law. The only question is, what to do now.

She took another deep breath, still looking at the glass of wine in its wet circle. Singlar's voice rumbled on behind her, but she didn't turn to look again at the monitors.

"—establish a new enforcement agency—something like the Texas Rangers, if you will, bringing law to the virtual frontier—"

Arabesque was right about one thing, though: it was going to be a lot harder to make a living cracking without ending up in a real jail. She would need new equipment, top-of-the-line machines to replace the old systems she and Trouble had owned, maybe new bioware to bring her brainworm up to speed, and that meant a trip to Seahaven—the real one, she amended, with an inward smile, not the virtual town that went by the same name. The seacoast town was the East Coast's greatest source for black- and grey-market netware, hard and soft alike. But it was correspondingly expensive: she would have to crack that IC(E), the IC(E) Trouble had refused to face with her. Anything with that big a fence around it had to be valuable, and there would be a grace period before Treasury got itself together. She could take what she needed, sell it, and be on the road to Seahaven, the real Seahaven, before anyone knew what had happened. And it would serve Trouble right, prove she'd been wrong to leave—

"Cerise?" Van Liesvelt was leaning forward slightly, both elbows on the tilting tabletop.

"Hey, careful," Held said, and Arabesque pressed down on her side of the table, steadying it.

"You all right, Cerise?" van Liesvelt asked.

Cerise nodded. "Yeah, I'm all right," she said, and thought she meant it. She smiled, calculating the effect. "I'll be going to Seahaven. After I've done some—work."

Helling said, "That was serious IC(E), Trouble said. And you don't know what's behind it."

"If there's that much IC(E)," Cerise said, "it has to be worth something. And I want to do some shopping."

"Your credit's good with me," Held said. He had done her other implants, from the original dollie-slot and box to the brainworm. Cerise nodded her thanks.

"I appreciate it, Carlie, but I don't take charity." She looked around the table. "Anyone interested in coming in on this with me?"

Mason shook her head. "I'm—I think I'm going to lie low for a while," she said, and Cerise was suddenly certain that was not what the other woman had meant to say.

"You're quitting," Arabesque said, the words an accusation, and Mason glared at her.

"I don't know yet, but I'm damn sure it's the smart thing to do."

"Butch?" Cerise said.

Van Liesvelt looked down at his beer. "I think Dewildah's right. I'm going to lie low, see how things shape up before I take on anything else."

Cerise nodded. "Arabesque?"

The other woman hesitated, made a face. "I know the job you mean, and I'm not taking on that IC(E) with what I got right now. You wait a month, let me get my new bioware tuned in, and I'll go in with you."

"I'm not waiting," Cerise said flatly. If I wait, she thought, if I wait, Trouble may come back and try to talk me out of it again—or worse still, maybe she won't come back, and I'll be left truly on my own. She shook the thought away. "Max, you interested?"

"I've plenty of work of my own, thanks," Helling answered.

"Fine."

Held said again, "Cerise, I do give credit—"

"And I don't take charity." Cerise shook her head, shaking away temptation. "Thanks, Carlie, but I can't." I don't care what Trouble says, what any of them say, she thought. I'm not going to let things change.

# TROUBLE

# • 2 •

TROUBLE'S ON THE nets tonight, riding the high data like a cowboy, the plains of light stark around her. The data flows and writhes like grass in the virtual wind, and she glides along the shifts and shadows, a shadow herself against their virtual sun. At the starpoint node, she slides from that high plane into a datastream like a canyon, falls suddenly into shadow, its warning cool along her skin.

IC(E) rises to either side, prohibiting the nodes, great heaps and coils of it like glittering wire, and the old urge returns. She studies it, and knows that she has keys in her toolbox that will unlock them all, fingertips tingling with the memory of their touch smooth as silk. She can almost taste what lies behind that barrier, files and codes turned to candy-color shapes good enough to eat, and remembers the sweet-sour tang, the glorious greed of gorging on the good bits, sorting them in an eye-blink by taste and smell, faster and more sure than anyone else in the business. She lifts her hand, the icon shimmering into existence, familiar routine half-invoked, but makes herself turn away. The IC(E) glitters behind her, lights trembling as though something behind it laughed, and she thinks she hears the whisper of a giggle.

The same sensation touches her like a finger of flame, a taunt literally stinging like electricity, but she has learned long since to ignore that cleverest of lures. She leaves the way she came, sliding oblique along a trail of untouched data, slick beneath her feet like a film of ice, and glances back to see the net healing itself behind her, closing to leave no trace she's ever been there. This night's city flows beneath her, data streams like rivers of cars, and she walks the nets down again, merging with the data until it pools and slows and feeds out into the great delta of the BBS. Here are all the temptations of the world, spread out in the broad meanders and the bottomless swamps, where slow transfer is common and the sheer volume hides a multitude of sins. The air around her thickens as the brainworm reads the data as sensation, and she flings back her *head, smelling spice and oil and a bitter tang like vinegar, carried on a virtual breeze that wraps itself around her illusory body. She pauses—not lost; she is never lost, not here, where the brainworm does its best and a lesser netwalker could drown in the sheer overload of sensation—but savoring the taste and scent of rich and unprotected data, the salt ebb and flow of freedom. And then the reminder sounds, Cinderella chimes at the back of her mind. She finds a quiet current, a soft and transient node, and lets it carry her home.*

The flat dull light of the basement workspace was blinding after the glittering contrast of the nets, and it was cold. She blinked twice, the lines of this night's city still ghosting across her vision, reflections of the net covering the real world, and reached for the cord plugged into the dollie-slot behind her ear. She popped it free, feeling the dull snap as the connection was fully broken, and her screen lit, displaying a record of the evening's ramble as a series of node connections and transfers. Her private accounting program was running alongside, erasing and diffusing those connections, and the notations vanished one by one as the program progressed. Everything was as it should be, and she stretched and went to the high window, peering up at the dark glass. It ran with rain, and the lines of the net across her sight crossed and recrossed the running water. She stared at them for a long moment, held by an illusion of meaning, the deceptive gnosis of the nets, where every shape held a dozen contrary secrets. But off the nets, the images were random, and to demand more was a step toward lunacy. She shook herself, and turned away.

There was no point in turning up the heat, not when she would be going upstairs almost at once. She shivered, touched keys to trigger the program that would erase all traces of this night's wanderings. She should know better— she was legit now, a syscop, even, and syscops didn't need to walk the nets under false pretenses—but the wires woven directly into her cortex made every excursion onto the nets an adventure, and she had never been able to resist that challenge. The only trouble was that the brainworm was absolutely illegal here—had been since Evans-Tindale passed three years ago—and particularly for a syscop, but the net was nothing but colored lights without it. She grinned to herself, watching the screen flash from grey to white, icons flickering past—THREE PASSES COMPLETE, DATA DESTROYED, ATTEMPT RECOVERY: YES/NO?—and touched YES. Despite Treasury propaganda, the wire wasn't addictive—she was living proof of it, had lived two years with her implants disabled, until she couldn't stand the boredom any longer—but it was hard to go back to the sight-only, black-and-neon-glitter world when you'd had it all. The screen changed again, displayed an empty box: the trash program had finished its work. She set her toggles, putting the gateway to sleep, loosed her best watchdog into the household net, then, stretching again, started up the stairs toward her apartment.

It was later than she had realized, well into the new morning. Even Ned Paiso's workshop was dark, and the security lights blazed over the co-op's empty central courtyard, a haze of raindrops filling the cones of light. A smaller security field set blue haze around the well-filled bike rack: it wasn't a killing field, wasn't even attached to a call box, but everyone hoped it would deter the casual thieves. She paused in her tiny kitchen, staring absently out the window, but decided she didn't really want anything. She had eaten her fill already, at dinner, and then on the nets. She turned away, feeling the lack of sleep finally dragging at her bones, and started toward the stairs that led to her bedroom.

The noise came from her tiny porch, a rough, breathless noise like a snarl. She froze, her eyes racing to the alarm system's display beside the kitchen window. Nothing but green lights, but all that meant was that an intruder was good enough to bypass the system. The sound came again, more loudly. More like an animal, she thought—a raccoon, maybe? They came into the compound sometimes, looking for food or shelter in the one still-empty condo. The thought was reassuring, and she moved quietly toward the short flight of stairs that led down into the little living room. She did not turn on the lights—now that her eyes had adjusted to the darkness, she would be able to see whatever was out there quite clearly—but she reached for the poker that hung from the woodstove she never used. She lifted it cautiously, not wanting to make a noise and alarm whatever it was, and edged toward the sliding door. Rikki the metalworker had made them all shutters two years ago, when he couldn't figure out any other way to pay his co-op fees, and for the first time she was grateful for them. Very carefully, she reached for the first vertical slat, and jumped as the sound came yet again. It sounded like a drunk's snoring—if it was a raccoon, she thought, it wasn't long for this world. She twisted the slat, and it gave a little, as it was designed to do, giving her a tiny window onto her back porch.

A man was sleeping there, curled into a ball on a battered chaise that he had dragged into the uncertain shelter of the trellis, a quilted jacket drawn tight around his burly body. Even in the half-light he looked dirty, and more than a little ill. She blinked, unable to believe what she was seeing—I thought he was long gone, gone back to Europe, or dead—then reached for the box that controlled the window. She touched the sequence that sprung the locks and lit a single light above the door, then shoved curtain and door aside and stepped out into the rain. The man's eyes opened slowly, and then he seemed to recognize the lights and rolled painfully into a sitting position.

"What the fuck are you doing here, Butch?" the woman asked, and the man gave her the old familiar goofy grin. He hadn't shaved in long enough that the mustache was beginning to lose definition in a general waste of stubble.

"Hello, Trouble," he said.

"Jesus Christ," Trouble said, and bit off the rest of it. You look terrible, she would have said, and she really didn't want to know. "Come on inside before you freeze to death. How long have you been here?"

Van Liesvelt shambled to his feet, still hugging the jacket tight to him, and she could see where the rain had left darker patches across his shoulders. He looked sideways, still grinning a little, and she gave a sigh of relief: at least he hadn't had to sell his implants.

"Oh, an hour or three," he said. "I didn't want to wake everyone."

He had lost most of the accent, Trouble thought, sounded more like a Kiwi or something, which was probably just as well. White Africans hadn't been popular folks for some decades, and queer white Africans were even worse. She shook the thought away as an irrelevance born of her own fatigue, and stood aside to let him in through the sliding door. "But what are you doing here?" she said again, and a thought struck her. "How the hell did you find me?"

"You told me your name, your realname, one time back in Crystal City. I remembered it, and then I got lucky. You're on the rolls as the local syscop, you know."

"It's not that uncommon a name," Trouble said—the year she was born, every third child had been named India, after the U.N. Festival—and van Liesvelt nodded.

"That's why I waited on the porch. I didn't want to wake you, if it wasn't you."

Trouble nodded, appeased. "I'm not in the business anymore, Butch."

Van Liesvelt nodded back. His jacket was beginning to give off a once-familiar smell, cigarettes and musky aftershave and uncleaned wool in heady combination. "I remember. Whatever happened to Cerise, anyway?" He looked around as though he expected the other woman to materialize out of the shadows, and Trouble grimaced at the memory.

"We haven't been back in touch," she said, and made her tone a warning not to pry.

"Oh." Van Liesvelt would clearly have liked to ask further questions, and Trouble cut in firmly.

"Give me your coat, you're dripping on the carpet. You want a drink?"

"Thanks," van Liesvelt said, shrugging himself out of the wet fabric. He was a big man, the kind of blond who went red in the summer, and he carried a little more weight than he had the last time Trouble had seen him—a modest roll of flab hanging over the waistband of his jeans. That, at least, was reassuring; maybe the rest was just fatigue and bad habits and falling asleep in the rain, she thought, and went back up the stairs into the kitchen. Whatever else he was or had been, he had been a good friend on and, less commonly, off the nets; she owed him at least this much attention. She hung the coat over a chair so that it could drip on the tiling, then flicked the heating switch to maximum and poured two thick tumblers of neat vodka. Unless he'd changed his style, van Liesvelt would rather drink that than the wine that was the only other choice. She came back down into the little living room, carrying the bottle as well as the glasses, and was not surprised when van Liesvelt finished his drink in a single gulp. He held out the glass again and she filled it, saying, "What's it all about, Butch?"

"You're in trouble," van Liesvelt said, and seemed to find it funny. Trouble eyed him without amusement, and was meanly pleased when he did a double take, looking hard at his glass. "What the hell's the flavor?"

"Coriander."

"Jesus."

There was a little silence, and van Liesvelt looked away from her, staring at the faded carpet as though there was a message encoded in its dull patterns. Trouble said, "So why am I in trouble?"

Van Liesvelt sighed, put the glass down with the second drink barely tasted. "If I have much more, I will be drunk." He turned back to face her, grey eyes gone suddenly more serious than she had ever seen them. "You sure you went legit, Trouble? 'Cause I've seen some work on the nets that's real slick, in your style, and goes under your name. Treasury is getting pissy about it."

Trouble shook her head. "I'm clean. I've been clean for, what, just about three years now."

"Somebody who calls themself Trouble has been hacking the industrials," van Liesvelt said. "And they're on the wire."

"Ah." Trouble took a sip of her own vodka, the alcohol stinging her lips. That moved the stranger out of the hordes of crackers who infested the nets and into an elite group, the far smaller number of netwalkers, legitimate and not, who had had a brainworm installed. She and Cerise had been part of that, once. . . . She put that memory aside, looked back at van Liesvelt.

"And, on top of all that," van Liesvelt said, "they're bragging about it."

"I never did that—"

"And that's got everyone's attention," van Liesvelt went on, as though she hadn't spoken. "It's not so much what they go away with—as best I can hear, it wasn't much—as that they made some big-time security look like shit, and the powers-that-be are pushing for Treasury to make an example of someone. Trouble, for preference."

"Fucking idiots," Trouble said, and wasn't sure herself whether she meant the Treasury's network cops or the boasting cracker who'd stolen her name. It had always been stupid to boast about a completed job, was suicidal now; the smart operators did what they were paid for and kept their mouths shut, and that silence brought them more customers in the long run. The trouble was, half the illegal operators still thought Treasury was a bunch of network-nellie fools who got lost every time they left the corporate systems. She had never made that mistake, and she was startled to realize how angry it made her to have her name linked to that particular behavior.

"There's a major sweep on," van Liesvelt continued, "ID checks, body scans, toolkit search, pattern matching—the works and then some. The warning went up on all the boards for anyone ever connected with Trouble to lie low, but I figured, since I'd heard you went legal, you might not get the message. And, of course, I didn't dare risk the mail."

"You figured right," Trouble said. It had been months— maybe as much as a year—since she had last logged on to any of the temporary BBS, the pirate bulletin boards where most of the virtual economy functioned and the illegal and

quasi-legal jobs were traded. She had kept a low profile, not
even lurking, her presence dimmed until she could barely
feel the virtual winds, barely taste the data, relying purely on
the visual images rather than the brainworm's translation.
She frowned, adding up the points where her new identity
intersected with the old. There were more of them than she
liked, and she could feel her frown deepen. "How's the
check being run?"

"On-line, mostly," van Liesvelt answered. "But there are
some off-line checks as well, following up on this new Trouble's contacts."

I wonder if any of them are being made up this way? Trouble thought. She put that aside, something to deal with in the
morning when she could ask a few discreet questions of the
sheriff's computer flunky, and said, "Thanks, Butch. I appreciate the warning."

Van Liesvelt shrugged, reached for his glass again.
"You're family. All us queers have to stick together."

Trouble smiled. "How'd you get up here? You need parking, or transport home tomorrow?"

"I left my bike in the woods," he answered, and waved
vaguely toward the stand of trees that stood invisible beyond
the metal shutters. "I figured nobody would want it bad
enough to chop down a whole tree for it."

Trouble felt the laugh catch in her throat. Van Liesvelt had
come up from the city on his ancient motorbike, almost an
antique already, three hundred miles in the rain, to warn her
that someone was using her name, and that she might catch
some fallout from it. She touched his shoulder gently, and he
looked up in surprise. "Thanks," she said again, softly, and
van Liesvelt shrugged, looked embarrassed and pleased all
at once.

"Like I said, we got to stick together."

There was a chair that folded out into a narrow mattress in
the oversized closet that passed for a second bedroom. Trouble found sheets and a blanket, and pulled the second quilt
and the extra pillow from her own bed to make up a serviceable extra bed. Van Liesvelt protested, but only for form's

sake, and she left him to strip and went on into her own room. She undressed slowly, her mind still busy with van Liesvelt's warning. It had been three years since she'd . . . retired. It had seemed the thing to do at the time: corporate security had been getting better, as were the various law enforcement groups—Treasury, Interpol, ECCI, ko-cops and all the rest—assigned to watch the nets, and then Congress had rejected the Amsterdam Conventions in favor of Evans-Tindale, making convictions possible and even commonplace. Even before Evans-Tindale, things had been going badly. She could still remember the shock, the taste of it, bitter fear, when she'd heard that Terrel was actually going to jail on an armed robbery charge, just as if the icebreaker in his kit had been a gun. . . . Cerise had said that it was stupid to panic, that blind drunk they were better than Terrel was at his best, but Trouble had been certain then that things had changed. Eight months later, Evans-Tindale had passed, and she had been out of the business for good, and on her way to reestablishing her original identity, alone.

She sighed, and crawled into bed, waving her hand through the signal beam to cut the lights. She could hear the rain, louder now, here under the roof, and, as her eyes adjusted to the darkness, her furniture became familiar shadows. The courtyard lights cast a faint pattern on the far wall, even through the curtains. I don't want to leave, she thought, I like it here. The co-op had been a safe harbor, a quiet, easy refuge—dull, but there had been something comforting about the very predictability of the routine. Maintaining the local net, shepherding the co-op's business through the nets: it was easy, and she would regret losing it. She made a face in the dark, annoyed with herself, turned noisily onto her side so that she was looking at the blank wall. If I was really that contented here, I wouldn't've turned the brainworm back on—wouldn't've been out on the net tonight. So where does that leave me?

She had been careful when she retired, had taken seven months to reestablish herself, her new/old identity, before she'd gone back onto the nets, and by that time she'd created jobs to explain the time she'd been invisible. The documentation for those jobs was the weakest link, of course—some of it was outright forgery, like the six months she'd supposedly spent waiting tables in Seahaven, and all of it depended on "employers" being unable to remember their minimum-wage help clearly enough to notice that she'd bought someone else's workcard. Still, an early adulthood spent hopping from one low-pay, no-status job to another wasn't particularly uncommon, especially for artists, and the story that she'd told the co-op when she applied to run their networks for them was not inherently implausible. Kids dropped out of school all the time to try to make it in the arts, and found out too late that their talents didn't lie in that direction at all. When the Treasury cops showed up—if, she amended, without conviction—she would just have to hope that the story held up. It had held up when the local sheriff's office had run the security check that cleared her to receive a syscop's license. *But the sheriff's office doesn't exactly check things out as carefully as Treasury will,* a voice whispered in her mind. She ignored it, and disciplined herself to sleep.

She woke in the chill light of dawn to hear someone tapping on the doorframe. She sat up, blinking, to see van Liesvelt peering in at her.

"I got to be going," he whispered, and Trouble shook herself fully awake.

"Why? You're welcome to stay for breakfast, have some coffee, at least. . . ."

She had spoken in her normal voice—there was no one around to hear—and to her relief van Liesvelt did the same. "No, thanks anyway. I have to be back in the city by noon."

"So you could leave at seven," Trouble began, and van Liesvelt shook his head.

"There's some people I've got to see first. And I want to be out of sight of here before full light, anyway."

That was a kindness, and Trouble was briefly ashamed of her own relief. "If you're sure," she said, and threw back the covers. "I'll let you out."

She padded down the stairs behind him, shivering a little

in the thin T-shirt, unlocked the back door, and then fiddled the security system to let him past the main perimeter sensors. Van Liesvelt walked away across the damp grass toward the stand of trees where he'd left his motorcycle, his disreputable jacket flapping loose around him. He turned back once, lifting his hand in casual farewell, and then disappeared back into the shadows of the trees. Trouble waited until she was certain he'd had time enough to pass the perimeter, counted off five more minutes by the kitchen clock, then reset the security system and went back to bed.

She woke again at nine, feeling somewhat more in control of things, and showered herself completely awake. She dressed, and headed across the compound to the community hall where the news-service machine was kept. It was a cool morning even in the sun, and the maples outside the compound were already showing a few yellow and flame-red leaves among the general green, bright contrast against the vivid blue of the sky. The rain had left the air unexpectedly clear, and she could hear the hum of traffic on the feeder flyway that ran less than two kilometers from the compound.

Inside the residents' entrance, the community hall was as disorderly as ever, the walls papered with notices and children's art, but quiet: most of the other inhabitants were already at work or school. Trouble went down the long corridor and out into the main room, bright with the sunlight that streamed in through the skylights. The glass was set on clear today, and the plain wooden chairs and benches in the public lobby seemed to glow in the warm light. The dining room was closed, of course, but the coffee machine was still active. She punched her codes into the news-service dispenser, and poured herself a cup of coffee while the machine whirred to itself and finally spat half a dozen closely printed sheets. She collected the thin papers, squinting at the print— the machine's ribbon needed changing, and she made a mental note to take care of that later—and nearly ran into Oba Alvarez, one of the co-op's half-dozen potters and a member of the management committee. He smiled at her, rather vaguely, and headed on into the management office.

Trouble shook her head, nearly spilling her coffee, and started back toward her condo. Dory Gustafson, busy draping a photoprint stand with a length of treated cloth, looked up long enough to call a greeting, but did not pause in her work. Trouble waved the papers at her. The co-op still seemed vaguely unreal to her, especially after her days in the city. She knew better than to be nostalgic for the dangers, the hovering fear, the adrenaline edge that the chance of random violence gave to the simplest things, but she still had trouble quite believing in the co-op's basic—niceness. It was easier when they were having trouble with the zoning boards, or the bills, or fighting about a new member's work: she could deal with all of that almost better than she could cope with the good times.

She shook her head again, unlocking the condo's door, and went into the kitchen. She still had the monthly accounting to prepare for the sheriff's office—not a particularly pleasant task at the best of times, and doubly not after van Liesvelt's news. Part of her obligation as the co-op's syscop was to keep a log of local net usage, and to watch out for any attempts either to crack her system or, more likely, to use it as a springboard to other, richer nodes. It was a painstaking job at the best of times, and usually involved hunting down two or three individual members to see if they remembered doing certain jobs. This time, though . . . this time, she would have to check her own records very carefully, and maybe do some judicious editing before she turned them over to the sheriff. She made a face, put the rest of her coffee in the microwave for later, and started down the stairs to her workspace.

The big display board flickered to life at her touch, showing only normal activity, familiar iconage. A CADset was up and running, Natalie Dreyer was on one of her interminable excursions to the university libraries, and someone—Rikki, probably—was running the story-sculpture program that took almost as much space as the graphics programs. Her routine checks were all in place, watchdogs lurking dormant: nothing new there. If anything changed, if anyone tried anything out of the ordinary, her watchdogs would notice and alert her.

She made a face, impatient with herself, and spun her chair to face the board, slipping the cord into place. Instantly the world hazed around her, sparks and shadow overwriting her vision, the ghost of new and unrelated sensations tingling along her nerves. She ignored the feelings, reached for her keyboard, and typed the sequence that changed its mode from standard to the specialized format that allowed her to control the brainworm's settings. She hit a second sequence, and then her private code, the password that gave her access to the internal account. An instant later a light flared, and a new window popped into existence, displaying the brainworm's virtual controls. She sighed—it was much more fun working fully wired, but the brainworm inevitably leaked some feedback into the system; a good syscop could tell whether or not another netwalker was on the wire—and moved the virtual levers to damp down the input. The tingling faded, and the lights that floated between her and the screen dimmed slightly, until she was looking at a display that was almost what any other netwalker would see. She made another face, and touched a final icon to set the changes. Then, dismissing the brainworm's controls, she turned her attention to the monthly accounts.

She pored over the accounts for three hours without finding anything out of the ordinary. Her own monitors had been doing their job, erasing any signs of her occasional fully wired forays onto the main nets, and there was no sign that this new Trouble, whoever it was, had been using her nodes as a staging area. She shrugged to herself, and touched the keys that would drop her notes into a working file for later revision into the sort of report the local sheriff appreciated, then leaned back in her chair, stretching to work out the kinks. The iconage of the co-op at work danced in front of her eyes, and was echoed a moment later on the main display: Dreyer still in the libraries, two CADsets working now, Mineka Konstenten running a blocking program. Her eyes lingered on Konstenten's icon, flickering from pale blue to a blue dark as midnight as her demand on the system changed. Konstenten was still an enigma, had come over one night to see the computers, stayed until morning, and had neither returned nor allowed the subject to be raised again. Trouble's smile shifted with the memory, became rueful. She still didn't know how she herself felt about the whole thing. Konstenten was a good friend, a clever designer, and an attractive woman; a vest she had made, Japanese patchwork of black-and-white fabrics, hung on Trouble's wall as a work of art when it wasn't being worn. But she was not precisely what Trouble wanted in a lover—or at least not now, not here—and, all in all, it was probably smarter to live celibate just a little while longer. . . . Which was where that train of thought always ended these days. Trouble stretched again, making herself concentrate on the pull of muscles across her shoulders, then laced her fingers together and pulled until the tendons tightened all the way into her wrists. If the brainworm had been fully operational, the movement would have sent feedback into the net, a flicker of sensation translated as light and sound, tangible even to the unwired masses. . . . She turned her attention back to the screen.

"Indy?"

Trouble looked up, startled, touched keys to open the intercom. "Yeah?"

"There's a couple of suits who want to see you," Gustafson went on. "Oba's got them in the main hall."

Trouble swallowed hard, the copper taste of panic filling her throat, and kept her voice steady only with an effort. "What sort of suits?" She made her hands move on the keyboard, saving her work and putting her system to sleep, leaving only the watchdogs loose on the household net.

"Something to do with computers, I think," Gustafson said. "They said they wanted to talk to the syscop."

Trouble let her breath out slowly, reached for the remote that would signal her if there were any anomalies in the system, and tucked it into the pocket of her jeans. If they just wanted to talk to the syscop, it might be all right, be just another routine check. And if it was what van Liesvelt had warned her about, people looking for Trouble, her present documentation should get through the first checks. She pushed herself away from the board, and went up the basement stairs.

Gustafson was waiting outside the main door, one hand still on the intercom controls, the sunlight pointing up the corn-silk texture of her hair and the bright barbaric splendor of her working smock.

"So what do you think?" Trouble asked, and was rewarded by a quick grin.

"Not corporate, I don't think," Gustafson said. "The suits aren't good enough."

"Thanks," Trouble said, and started for the community hall. Like anyone who lived this far outside the mainstream, Gustafson had learned to read the nuances of the corporate dress codes as well as or better than the corporate souls themselves: if she said cheap suit, she meant it, and cheap suits meant cops.

The hall was still very bright, though someone had adjusted the skylights so that the glass was bright amber, filling the hall with heavy color. It helped to hide the worn upholstery on the lobby furniture—the space had been furnished from the discards of the co-op's households—and the merely serviceable rugs. The two men waiting there had their backs to the light, throwing their faces into shadow, but Trouble could tell they were cops just from the way they held themselves.

"India." Alvarez emerged from a side room, the management committee's current offices, a sheaf of green-stripe paper in one hand. "These people wanted to talk to you."

Trouble nodded and stepped forward into the sunlight. "I'm India Carless," she said, and waited.

"Thanks for seeing us, Ms. Carless," one of the strangers said. He was the taller of the two, Trouble realized, as they both came to their feet in polite acknowledgment. They were definitely cops, by the movement as well as the suits, cheap copy-Armanis, and she held herself very still.

"Unless you need me, India," Alvarez said, "I've got to get

back to work." He let his voice trail off, making it almost a question, and Trouble shook her head.

"I can take care of it, thanks," she said, and Alvarez turned away. Trouble looked back at the strangers. "Is there a problem?"

"I don't think so," the smaller man said.

His partner cut in smoothly. "We just have a few routine questions. We've been talking to most of the syscops who monitor systems that use the BVI-four gateway into the national net."

Trouble let herself relax a little. Anyone who called it the national net didn't know the system—or else, she thought, they're trying to lull me into being careless. If they're looking for Trouble, they'll be playing it very canny. "If I can help, sure. Can I get you some coffee?"

There was a quick exchange of looks, and then the taller man said, "No, thanks. We've got a lot of driving to do." He slipped his hand into his jacket pocket, came up with a thin folder. "I'm Bennet Levy, that's John Starling. We're from the Treasury."

Trouble accepted the folder with what she hoped was convincing uncertainty, studied the ID card and hologram badge as though she'd never seen one before, and handed it back to Levy. She didn't recognize either of their names, but then, she hadn't expected to: even if she had heard of them, and she had been off the shadow nets long enough to make that unlikely, she would only have heard their work names, not the names that were actually on their badges. "Why don't we go in the other room?" she said, and gestured toward the door that led to the smaller of the two conference rooms. "It's not as sunny."

"Thanks," Starling said, and the two of them followed her into the little room. Trouble motioned for them to take a chair, and let the door fall closed behind them.

"Have a seat, please," she said. "You sure you don't want coffee or something?"

"No, thanks," Levy said again. He and Starling pulled chairs away from the table and sat down, apparently very much at their ease. Trouble did the same, hoping she seemed equally calm. The chairs and table were less battered than the furniture in the lobby: this room was used for negotiations with outsiders, and the fittings were correspondingly better.

"So how can I help you?" Trouble said again, and the two agents exchanged quick glances.

"We've had some reports of cracking and intrusions that have been traced back to BVI-four," Starling said. That would make him the technical expert, Trouble thought, and kept her face expressionless. "But we lose the perpetrator there, at BVI-four—we haven't been able to trace him on any of the major outgoing lines—so we're checking all the local nets that use that gateway, in case he's staging through one of them." He paused. "You're the only syscop for this system, Ms. Carless?"

In spite of his best efforts, Trouble heard a whisper of incredulity in his voice, and bit her tongue to keep from responding to it. A lot of people still assumed that a woman couldn't run a bulletin board on her own, much less act as solo syscop; if they wanted to make that mistake, this was not the time to enlighten them. "That's right," she said aloud, and waited.

"Do you mind telling me about the setup here?"

"Not at all." Trouble paused and took a deep breath, willing herself to switch to enthusiast's mode. "This is an artist's co-op here, we're registered with the NEA and the state foundations. Because of that, we need versatile machines, a lot of raw power that can be turned to different uses at different times. We have a local net within the compound, mostly home machines and famicon, to facilitate load-sharing, and a couple of linked minis for graphics—one of our people is a fractalist, and we also rent time to some other graphics people who can't afford their own machine suite. We have four printers here, too, all top of the line, and a babybox to run them. All of that is on the local net, so that we can pool jobs when we have to, or buy time from other co-ops. Seara— she's the fractalist—she takes some odd commissions sometimes, things that need a lot of power."

"Such as?" Starling asked.

Trouble shrugged. "Last year, somebody wanted fractal wallpaper, and we had a printer that could run it. The design took everything on our net, plus a hundred hours of bought-time just for the formulae, and then it tied up the printer and the babybox for a month."

"Fractal wallpaper," Levy said.

"I didn't care much for it myself," Trouble said, and there was a little silence, almost companionable, as the three of them contemplated the possibilities.

"What about your net connections?" Starling asked, shaking himself back to business.

"We have two basic nodes, one general, one high-speed data," Trouble answered, "both transfering through BVI-four. I monitor both on a random schedule, and keep a watchdog running at all times."

That was the standard procedure, and Starling nodded. "So graphics is the primary business of your net?"

"Yes and no," Trouble said. "It's the reason we have this much power, and the high-speed connection, but most of the time people don't need much more than their home machines. We tend to use the BVI-four gate primarily for information and trading, and once every couple of months we run a big job through it. And, as I mentioned, we do sell time when we have it." She paused, gauging the agents' response, and ventured a question of her own. "I'm assuming you're looking for someone sneaking packet data through the high-speed node?"

"Among other things," Starling said.

"What about access to the big nets?" Levy asked.

Trouble looked at him. "Do you mean who has it, or how we work it?"

"Who has it?"

"We have a household account on Tele-net, through BVI-four, which I manage through some homebrew accounting routines. All the adults have access. It's a standard password setup. I try to get them to change the codes regularly, and never use anything from a dictionary, the usual routine, but you know how that goes." Trouble shrugged. "We get odd charges—stuff I can't identify, and nobody admits to—maybe once or twice a year."

"What about kids?" Starling again. "Are there any, and do they have access?"

Trust Treasury to ask first about the kids, Trouble thought. She said, "Yes, and yes. We gave everyone full access to the local net, but I gave the kids special passwords that access a different set of programs—games, mostly, some arts and science tools. If they try to use the gateways when they've logged on with those passwords, I've set the system to flag me. If they've got a reason, schoolwork or something, or their folks' permission—and if they're not going into one of the really expensive datastores—I'll generally let it go through."

"What about kids using their parents' passwords?" Starling asked. "Do you get much of that?"

"I don't think so," Trouble said. "Certainly I haven't spotted any anomalous activity patterns on any of the accounts. We've only got half a dozen kids in the compound, and they don't seem to be into computers much."

"Lucky," Levy said.

Starling said, "Have there been any changes in usage patterns? Or any signs of intrusion, charges you can't account for, say, over the last five months?"

Trouble frowned, hiding the annoyance at being addressed as a total novice, and did her best to simulate genuine confusion. "No, nothing recently. And I keep good records—they're filed with the sheriff every other month." That much was required by law; she doubted she needed to tell Starling, at least, that the files were thoroughly edited before they went to county records. Starling grinned as though he'd read the thought, the first human expression she'd seen from him.

"Do you spend a lot of time on the net?" Levy asked abruptly.

Trouble looked at him warily. "Depends on how you define 'a lot of time.' I handle all the co-op's on-line business, time sharing or selling, anything like that. I'm the one who deals with the net when people need it. Why?"

Levy ignored the question. "Has anyone locally been talking about any kind of unusual charges, intrusions, unexpected problems in their local systems?"

"No," Trouble said, with more confidence, recognizing where the question was headed. "We share time with a lot of local nets—we're all small-scale around here, a couple of mom-and-pop datastores, town libraries, things like that. If anybody was having troubles, they wouldn't tell the rest of us, for fear it would cut into their income."

"Would you tell us?" Levy asked.

Trouble smiled. "I'd tell you," she said, and emphasized "you." Go ahead, pursue that line, she thought. It would only lead them into the tangle of the BBS, and they could spend the next ten years there, chasing their tails, without finding anything useful.

"I wonder if you've heard of someone coming back into the shadows," Starling said softly. "Netwalking, cracking—you know the sort of gossip on the BBS. Especially in the syscops' forums. The talk-name is Trouble."

Trouble froze for a heartbeat, made herself move again with an effort that was almost painful. "I've heard the name before," she said, dry-mouthed. It would be suspicious to say anything else; she had been a name to conjure with, once upon a time. "But not recently—not for a couple of years, at least. I thought somebody told me Trouble died."

"The reports were greatly exaggerated," Starling said.

Levy said, "So you haven't heard anything about Trouble?"

Trouble shook her head. "Like I said, I haven't heard that name in a couple of years."

The two agents exchanged a quick, unreadable glance, and Starling said, "Can you show us the setup? The physical plant, I mean."

"Sure," Trouble said, and pushed herself up out of her chair, hiding her unease. "It's across the way—everything's in my basement so that I can keep an eye on things full-time." She palmed open the door, and led the way out into the lobby, Starling and Levy following at a polite distance.

She took them through her condo and down into the basement work area, where the minis sat behind a heavy dust-wall, and the smaller machines—the network controller and its backup, and the souped-up home machine that she used for her own access—sat side-by-side on their low table. Levy glanced around as she pointed out the various features, but she could see Starling's eyes tracing every cable and connection as she explained the system.

"And you're on-line yourself, of course," he said, when she had finished.

"Yes."

He stepped up to her control board, ran a long-fingered hand along the edge of the casing—a netwalker's hand, Trouble thought, superstitiously, and felt a surge of fear. He tugged the datacord out of its housing, and his attention sharpened abruptly. "You must spend a lot of time on the nets," he said, and pulled the cord out to its full length, displaying the double head.

Trouble froze again, damning herself for her carelessness. A double jack, high-speed data line and regular dollie-jack combined, was the tool of the serious netwalkers; it was also the only way you could process enough information to satisfy the brainworm. Most users—even most syscops—made do with the ordinary jack, and lived with the time lags. If she had stood up and shouted, the message couldn't have been plainer. "I do spend a lot of time out there," she said, deliberately misunderstanding. "Like I said, we do a lot of graphics, both in-house with the fractals and as a time vendor. I spend a lot of time monitoring those jobs, and you have to be able to shut down fast if something goes wrong."

"Oh?" That was Levy, sounding almost interested.

"Yeah. When you're running the big color printer and there's a glitch in the program, well, the faster you can close it off, the less ink and paper you waste. And Seara uses a lot of unconventional materials, all of them expensive." She gave Starling a guileless glance, and did not think he was impressed.

"You must do test runs to prevent that kind of thing," Starling said.

"Oh, sure," Trouble answered, and let a genuine grievance color her voice. "But you don't know artists. They keep fiddling with a program even after it's supposed to be set, and when you run what's supposed to be the final job, you find out they've added a line or two of code—" She let her voice go high and thin, imitating Seara. "—just a half-tone difference in one color mask, that's hardly a change at all—and that will be the thing that screws up the entire run."

"Uh-huh." Starling was still looking at the double-headed cord, his eyes moving from its housing to the host machine to the main display. Trouble kept her expression open and innocently helpful, hoping that he believed her—but that was almost too much to expect, with the shadow-walker's cord staring him in the face.

"When did you send your last report to the sheriff?" Levy asked.

"The beginning of August," Trouble answered. She could feel the fear swelling in her belly, took a slow, deep breath to keep it down, and tucked her hands into her pockets again.

"So the next one's due any day now," Starling said.

Trouble nodded. "I was working on it when you called me."

Starling looked at Levy. "I think we might as well wait until that one's in, Ben."

"Whatever." Levy looked back at Trouble. "Will you send us a copy as well?" He held out a card, and Trouble took it mechanically.

"Sure. Is there anything I should be looking for?"

Starling shook his head. "Just the usual. You will let us know if you hear anything—anything at all—about Trouble?"

"Absolutely," Trouble said.

"Or anything else," Levy said. "Any talk of intrusions,

funny accounts, anything at all. Our numbers are on the card."

Trouble looked at it, the codes barely registering, looked back at Levy. "I'll let you know," she said again, and doubted they believed her.

She walked them back upstairs and let them out her front door, watched them walk away across the lawn. They hesitated for a moment at the entrance to the community hall, but then Starling said something, and they turned away, heading toward the compound gate and the carpark beyond. They walked in step as if by habit, and Trouble shivered despite the sunlight. They were bound to be suspicious—they had to be suspicious, after she had been careless enough to leave the double jack out in plain sight. It was just a question now of what she would have to do. She closed the door gently, throwing the locks out of old habit, and started slowly back down the steps to the basement.

She seated herself in front of the keyboard again, but did not reach for the datacord. They would expect her to do that, to go on-line to find out anything she could about them—the netwalkers would know, as they knew all the important enforcement agents; it was just a matter of asking the right people—and if they were any good at all, they would be monitoring her system from their car. If they were as good as she suspected Starling might be, her system would already be crawling with their watchdogs, lurking programs to track her progress across the nets. . . . She shook herself then, clamping down hard on the panic that had seized her. She had checked the system this morning when she went on-line—though maybe not as well as she should have, after what Butch said—and there had been nothing out of place, nothing she didn't recognize. She just hadn't expected Treasury to show up so quickly.

She made a face and reached for the datacord, slipped it into the slot behind her ear. The main thing now was to control the damage, find out what, if anything, they had running in her system; failing that, she would need to find out why they had connected her with the stranger calling itself Trouble. And that would take some fancy shadow-walking. In the old days, it would have been simple to deal with the problem: she would simply have packed up her machines and gone to a new city, found an apartment and started over again. It had always taken months for the law to track her, and the one time she'd been unlucky and they'd found her right off, it had still taken them so long to figure out who had jurisdiction that she had been able to get out of town before the warrants could be issued. But that was a very long time ago, before she'd met van Liesvelt—before you met Cerise, a voice whispered—and things hadn't been that easy in years. Not since Evans-Tindale—and all of that, she admitted silently, was less the problem than the fact that she herself was out of practice. It had been three years since she'd walked the shadows, at least in any serious way.

She leaned back in her chair, staring at the screen that mirrored the image that hovered in front of her eyes, not really seeing the lines of minuscule type and flickering icons. The first thing she needed to do was find out why Treasury had come here looking for this new cracker. Once she knew that, knew whether she was actively suspected or if she'd just been unlucky, then she would know what more she had to do. She hesitated, wondering if it was worth the risk, then entered the sequence that recalled the brainworm's control panel. She adjusted virtual levels until she was running at half strength, the setting that would give her the extra control she needed but minimize the inevitable feedback from the brainworm itself.

*Virtuality steadies around her, becomes faintly tangible, a hint of roses and lavender filling the air. Everything seems to be in order in the local net, but she whistles anyway, summoning the nearest watchdog, and it comes lolloping over. She stoops to pet it, feels the spikes of its code sharp under her hand, touches ears and nose and finds them cold as ice. It, at least, is in perfect health, and she says, seek, boy, and lets it run, following its track in the pools of phosphorus it leaves behind. It comes cantering back in half an interminable* second, lolling tongue trailing drops of fire, flops at her feet: nothing amiss, nothing to hunt and catch. Stay, she says, and strides out toward the gateway, heading for the main nets and the information she needs.

# ■ 3 ■

*C*ERISE WATCHES FROM *the edge of the board, surveys her domain. The programs stretch before her, dark squares laced with the hot red-gold of the internal datastream, live unreal wires pulsing with the ebb and flow of information. The light squares swarm with golden haze, warm light like butter melting, folding over the pastel flicker of the workers in their core. Overhead arches the blue of IC(E), hard-edged, geometric, walling in the chessboard that has become her world.*

*And it's a good world: her thoughts flash like darts along the angled tracks, flicker along the lava cracks of the datastreams. She pauses at the edge of the golden shell, and a program like a snake's tongue tastes the bytes that whistle through her. A hundred lights bloom and fade before her: all is as it should be, her pawns—the company's pawns, if she'd admit it—controlled, contained, and protected by her lattice of hard IC(E). The data itself slips unconstrained through the internal nets, the brainworm turning it sharp and sweet as candy, like a taste of honey in the wind.*

*A light flares, hot pink, winks instantly to the blue of IC(E), but she's seen it and is moving, launching herself along the familiar paths. She draws armor about her as she goes, blue-grey IC(E) as sharp as steel, slips within the datashell in the blink of a code. The bright shards of data slid past unchanged, stinging rain against her skin. Nothing missing, nothing spoiled—but she queries the system and finds nothing there, too. No one has been there, the system says, and that is wrong. She sets the intruder alert wailing, sends the message racing along the datastream, confining all but the highest-level users to their own spheres. The lights dim around her as the internal codewalls thicken. Beyond it, the alarm flares like lightning, crackling along the lattice of the external IC(E); behind*

*her, the junior syscops and their watchdogs come on-line, bright
shapes coursing the system, leaving her to deal with the hole in the
heart of their most secure system.*

Inside the cracked shell she finds the flaw, and behind it teases
out the tangled bits that were her favorite monitor, and something
else. She lays the pieces out module by module and line by line,
bright against a slab of black she conjures out of nothing, and sepa-
rates her own program from the stranger. She recognizes the hand
at once, and swears softly, checks the routines again. It's a familiar
program, anyway, though there's no guarantee that the one who
wrote it was the one who launched it against the company—but she
feels the knowledge cold against her, the fragments of data pricking
her fingers like shards of glass.

Overhead, a syscop calls from where the system IC(E) was
dented. It's a bruise along the edge of one bright bar of the codewall,
but it's all the trail she'll ever find. She leaves the scraps of program
to the nearest watchdog, and lets herself out the way the stranger
came in—the stranger who may not be a stranger, not at all. She
puts that thought aside, and launches herself out into the greater
net.

Power lies before her, planes and fields and streams of light, the
familiar night-city that lies always in her core. She smiles her pleasure even as she shapes a tool to filter the information, searching for
a method that was once as familiar to her as her own best tools, a
hand on the keyboards as clever as her own. The program darts
away, a shape vaguely like a bird, spiraling out across the glittering
fields, finds a trace and stoops to it, transmitting codes. Numbers
flash in front of her eyes—MATCH INEXACT, PROBABILITY OF MATCH
70.09%, FOLLOW YES/NO—but she barely sees them. The brainworm translates the same input into a touch, a scent and a feeling,
like and yet not the same as the hand she thought she'd followed.
Frowning now, she signals FOLLOW and lets the program run, drifting armored along the lines of light, through datastreams like rivers
of white fire. She passes a familiar node, and then another, bathed in
sudden flares as systems challenge and then accept her presence.
She knows even before the stream slows and swells and tangles in
and around itself that she will lose this trail in the spreading

*swamp of the BBS, the market delta where all the data in the world
eventually collects, puddles, and, muddied, goes free.*

*The trail ends, her program vanishes with a spark like an excla-
mation point. She slows herself, surveying the vast and marshy
space, where lines and lights merge and cross and twine like para-
sites around each other's roots. There are few shadows here, at least
to the sight, but the steady glow, the slow pulse and steady buzz of
unprotected data, hides more than it reveals. She gives herself a moment longer, savoring the salt tang of the free data, then finds a
familiar line and follows it, moving through the crowding symbols
and the overloaded petty-nodes with the ease of long familiarity. A
major node flashes green and welcoming at last, terminus and gateway for a thousand low-budget users. She touches it, whispers code,
and lets it snatch her home.*

Coigne called the meeting for breakfast the next morning,
leaving her six hours to prepare. She didn't really need the
time, had done all that could be done in the first few minutes
after the codewall had been breached, but she complained
about it anyway, knowing Coigne would respect her more
for objecting to his plans. She spent another hour or so re-
viewing the data her hard-working staff had culled from the
records—there were no surprises there, nothing she hadn't
already figured out in the seconds it had taken her to analyze
the wreckage of the program and to trace the stranger's
trail—and went to bed.

She was up before the alarm, showered and dressed to the
familiar murmur of the in-house news service spilling from
the muted screen. There was no word of the intrusion, even
on the high-level channels that she was cleared for, and she
didn't quite know if she was glad of it, or worried. She listened with half an ear to the latest profit projections broken
down by division—an exercise in controlled intimidation
that she usually followed religiously, because the number-
two and last-place divisions would be ripe for on-line mischief—and wondered what she was going to say to Coigne.
As little as possible, she thought, as always, and reached into
her closet for the rest of her suit. Most of her look was already

in place, her nails painted the hard dull-surfaced fuchsia that looked like the icing on a cookie, a flat, cheap color that worried the suits who saw her because they didn't know how she'd dare. She had painted her lips and cheeks and eyes the same hard color, shocking against the careful pallor of her skin, and the black of the chosen suit only intensified the effect. It was subtly wrong for her job, like the rest of her look—like all of her, wrong sex, wrong class, wrong attitude most of all: the skirt a little too short, the jacket too mannish, with none of the affectations or compromises of corporate femininity. The heels of her shoes were painted the same stark fuchsia as her nails.

She looked hard at herself in the mirror, straightening the narrow skirt a final time. It would do—she would do; the look would remind them none too subtly that she could dress the way she did, could walk into their boardroom on her terms because they needed her. She could afford to dress this way—she was the only one who could afford to dress this way—because she was who and what she was. She was the only one, of all of them, who had to.

She put that thought aside—not something she could afford to acknowledge, not with Coigne waiting—and turned to the banked consoles to collect the pocketbook system with its downloaded data. Everything she needed was there, from the sanitized version of her report—Coigne would get the real one—to the software that would let her display and manipulate those figures for the board, to the home-brew stripped-down interfaces that let her achieve limited access to the nets even from the low-powered pocketbook. It wasn't enough to feed the brainworm, gave her only a standard view, but it was enough to work with. She touched an icon to check the directory one final time, then hit the sleeper key and folded the screen away. She took extra care to double-lock the flat's door behind her when she left.

A car was waiting in the driveway, just outside the courtyard gates. Coigne's car, she realized in the split second before the nearest window slid down to reveal the hard-boned face.

"Good morning, Cerise. I thought you might need a ride."

"You still don't trust me, Coigne." She smiled to hide the cold knot in the pit of her stomach. It had not been in her mind to run, but the fact that Coigne had thought she might made her wonder if she should have done so. "I'm disappointed."

"So am I." Coigne's face disappeared, and the door snapped open.

Cerise slid into the car's dim interior, into the faint smell of leather and the sunlight cut by the smoky bulletproof windows. Coigne was outlined against the far window, a thin, fair man with white-blond hair cut close to the stark planes of his skull. His wide mouth twisted into a brief, humorless smile, and he leaned forward to touch a button on the control panel mounted just below the divider that separated the passengers from the driver's pod. The door closed itself, and the car slid smoothly into gear, picking up speed as it passed through the courtyard gate and out onto the expressway feeder. It was all corporate land here, manicured to expensive perfection in front of the identical blocks of flats and houses bought from the same prefab supplier, allowed to go to an approximation of wilderness in the ditch that separated the access road from the feeder and the overarching flyway.

"So what happened?" Coigne asked.

Cerise reached into her carryall, handed him the disk she had prepared. "That's my report."

Coigne took it, slid it into the datadrive set into the armrest beside him. He slipped a pair of glasses from his breast pocket and plugged the fine cable into the drive before fitting the temple pieces over his ears. The dark backing on the display lenses made him look blind. "But what happened?" he said again.

"Pretty much what you see," Cerise said, and then, because she knew he expected more, "Someone—a pretty skilled someone—pried a gap in main IC(E) and penetrated the Corvo division subgroup. Response time was excellent, and as far as I can tell nothing was damaged or stolen."

"Copies?"

"Impossible to tell." She gave the bad news without flinching, refusing to apologize or justify.

"Find out."

"The only way I can do that," Cerise said, "is to wait and see if anything shows up on the market. I've already got feelers out, but it's too soon to tell."

"I see." Coigne unplugged the dataline, then lifted the glasses off and slipped them back into their pocket. "I've heard a name in all of this."

"Have you?" Cerise made herself relax against the heavy padding, felt the draft from the comfort systems cool on her legs. The car topped the rise onto the flyway, slipped sideways through a gap in the traffic, and settled into the passing lane. Cars flashed past to her right, overtaken in the slow lane, their shapes blurred by the smoky glass. The regular compound-to-compound commuter shuttle rumbled past, trundling along its track in the center of the flyway. For an instant, the low sun caught and flamed in its mirrored windows, and then it was gone.

"The word is," Coigne said, "that Trouble's back on-line."

Cerise sat very still, knowing better than to speak the lie that had sprung instantly to her tongue. Trouble's dead—but Trouble wasn't dead, and it would be too easy to find out that truth, and then it would be too late to convince Coigne that she could still be trusted.

"I don't suppose you know anything about it," Coigne said.

Cerise shook her head, managed a faint, one-shouldered shrug. "It would be the first sign I'd seen of Trouble since I came to work for you." She paused, and tried the lie. "At one point, I heard she was dead."

Coigne ignored it. "You and Trouble used to work together. I would've thought you'd recognize the style."

"Anyone can copy style," Cerise said, and laced her tone with faint contempt. "Hell, I see my own programs on the nets, copies of my own work trying to break my IC(E). Style isn't an ID, Coigne."

"Not legally, but I would have thought it would be enough

for you. Especially since it was enough to set other people talking." Coigne looked sideways at her, met her eyes for the first time. "I'm sure I can rely on you, Cerise."

He didn't need to articulate the rest of the threat: he—Multiplane officially, but mostly, directly, him—knew perfectly well what she had done before he hired her, and had the evidence to boot, evidence that was a guilty verdict suspended for only so long as she worked for him. She lifted an eyebrow at him, achieved a quick smile. "That was a long time ago, Coigne."

"Three years."

"On the nets, that's eternity. Besides, our cracker wasn't Trouble."

Coigne looked at her for a moment longer, then turned back to the window. "Don't fuck this up, Cerise."

Cerise ignored him, and he seemed content to let it go. She turned her head slightly, looked out the smoky window without really seeing the thickening stream of cars that converged on Multiplane's central compound. It hadn't been Trouble yesterday, she was sure of it, just someone who'd learned a lot, stolen a lot, from Trouble. But Trouble had been her partner back in the glory days before Evans-Tindale, and that tainted her judgment, in Coigne's eyes. He wouldn't believe her until she found the intruder, this cracker who was using Trouble's programs, and proved that it was someone else. And *God help me if my Trouble's still on-line somewhere, still in the business; I'll never convince Coigne it wasn't her.* She rejected that thought even as it formed, her lips curving with the start of a smile. Trouble had walked away from the business three years ago. She wasn't about to reappear now.

The car slowed and tilted, following the flyway as it curved down in a graceful double-spiral that joined the semicircular road that curved in and out of the central compound. There were other cars ahead of them, more of the heavy-bodied black limos that signified junior executive status and were abandoned for more practical vehicles once the rider made it into the boardroom. Coigne frowned quickly, and glanced at his chrono. A shuttle pulled past them into the main building's terminal—the elevated tracks ran directly into the fourth-floor lobby—and Cerise found herself wishing she had been on it. She was entitled to a car and driver, but rarely took the privilege; she enjoyed the crowds on the shuttle, and the illusion of anonymity, coupled with the certainty of an audience, let her hone her attitude for each day's work.

The car slowed still further, braked to a crawl as it took its place in line behind an identical vehicle. Coigne leaned sideways—trying to read the license number, Cerise knew, see who it was ahead of him—then settled back in his place, his mouth twisting in a faint, dissatisfied frown. They slid at last into the docking point, and a security guard, soberly suited, but with the mirrored glasses that hid a heads-up display, and at least one minigun concealed in his perfect tailoring, keyed open the door. Two more guards, so closely matched in age, size, and coloring that they could almost have been siblings, waited in the shadows of the door, ready for trouble. Not that there had been that many invasions of transportation engineering firms; that had been reserved for more controversial businesses, biotech and the direct-on-line computer firms, but Cerise was never entirely sorry for their presence. The first guard nodded a greeting, murmured, "Ms. Cerise," in a voice so soft and deferential that she could ignore it if she chose, and turned his attention instantly to Coigne.

"Excuse me, Mr. Coigne, but there's a direct-flash for you."

"Damn." Coigne scowled at the guard, whose expression didn't change.

"I'm sorry, sir, but it's noted urgent."

Coigne grimaced. "Put it through to one of the cabinets, will you? Cerise—" He stopped abruptly. "I'll see you upstairs, then."

"Of course," Cerise said, and slung her bag more securely onto her shoulder. One of the other guards held the door open for her, and she went into the building, her heels loud on the polished stone floor. She heard the door of one of the communications cabinets that lined the first lobby close behind her, sealing Coigne into its gleaming interior, but did not look back. She rode the moving stair up to the main lobby, where a quartet of well-dressed secretaries staffed a long counter that was as much barrier as service center. Overhead, another shuttle train hummed almost silently along its guidepath, bright against the brown-toned glass that formed the building's outer shell, and disappeared through the arch that led to the fourth-floor lobby. The massive pillars that supported the rails cast long shadows across the warm-toned floor. Cerise stepped up to the counter and passed her ID disk through the nearest scanner. One of the secretaries, a dark girl who looked barely old enough to have a network license, looked up as the numbers flashed across her screen.

"Good morning, Ms. Cerise. Your meeting's in conference dining three."

"Thanks—" For the life of her, Cerise could not remember the younger woman's name, and compromised with a smile. "When is it scheduled for?"

"You have fifteen minutes," the younger woman answered, and her own smile in return was faintly conspiratorial.

Cerise nodded, stepping around the barrier, and made her way into the elevator lobby. There were two banks of elevators, one on each side of the shuttle's guidepath, polished bronze columns that ran the height of the five-story outer lobby and then continued up the outside of the building itself. The express was running to the executive dining levels at the top of the building, where her meeting would be held, but she ignored it, waiting impatiently for a local car instead. It came at last, and she wedged herself in with a dozen or so others, tucking her carrycase carefully under her arm. With luck, she would be able to check in with her own people without being too late for her meeting.

Network Security took up most of the twenty-first floor, a suite of offices around the perimeter and then a maze of cubicles surrounding the protected core where the mainframes and their backups lived. Cerise stepped out of the car into the tiny metal-walled lobby, and waited while yet another security guard passed her ID through his scanner. Only after the machine had cleared her did he smile and mumble something that might have been a greeting. Cerise nodded—try as she might to accept them as a necessity, the precautions never failed to annoy her—and passed through the heavy door into her domain.

Most of the day staff was already at work, crammed with their machines into their shoebox cubicles. A few were still off-line, drinking a last cup of coffee or going over a hard-print report from the previous night, but most of them were already limp in their chairs, cords plugged into dollie-slots, out on the nets. Everything was as it should be, and Cerise made her way around the perimeter of the maze to her own suite of rooms. The outer door was open, and a dark woman looked up from her keyboard in surprise.

"Cerise. I thought you had a meeting."

"I do." Cerise came to stand behind her chief assistant, and stared unabashedly over her shoulder at the screen. "What's this?"

"Autopsy of that program you found yesterday," Jensey Baeyen answered. "It's homebrew, or at best heavily modified commercial. I got a sixty percent probability on the maker, though."

"What's the name?" Cerise asked, already knowing the answer.

"Someone called Trouble. Been inactive for a few years, just came back onto the nets in a big way, is what it looks like," Baeyen answered.

"Who made the match—which data bank, I mean?"

"Treasury."

That figured. Cerise nodded. "Make me a copy of the autopsy and put it on disk for me, would you? What about copies? Any sign of them on the grey markets?"

"Not yet," Baeyen said. She touched keys, and slipped a datablock into one of her subsidiary drives. "I put Sirico on

it; he should have a report for you within the hour. Someone's been bragging, though."

"Shit."

Baeyen grimaced. "I know. It's just the usual stuff, 'look
how smart I am,' with nothing real to back it up—"

"—but the board isn't going to like it," Cerise said. She
sighed, made a face at the screen. "Make me a quick copy of
what you've picked up so I can look it over before my meeting. So Treasury thinks it's Trouble?"

"That's what the match says," Baeyen said. "But Trouble
was never one to boast, or so I hear, so the boaster and the
cracker may not be the same hand, which would explain why
nothing's showed up on the markets yet. But it looks like
she's back—Trouble, I mean. It was a she, wasn't it?"

"Yes," Cerise said, in her most colorless voice. Oh, yes, she
added silently, Trouble's a woman, all right, a tough and
sexy, smart-ass broad who walked out on me—but she didn't
boast, and she didn't take stupid chances. She accepted the
datablock, glanced up to check the time. "I've got to get moving, but tell Sirico I want to talk to him as soon as I get back."

"All right," Baeyen said, and turned her attention back to
her displays.

Cerise went back out of the office, past the rows of cubicles
staffed by limp bodies, and the security checkpoint, rode the
elevator to the executive dining area. The conference rooms
were on the lower of the two floors, a maze of linked rooms
with movable walls to accommodate groups of various sizes.
Dining room three was smaller than she had remembered
from the last meeting, just a single oval table with half a
dozen chairs and place settings, but the view from the enormous window was just as she remembered it. The room
faced northeast, and the towers of the city gleamed in the distance, bright as steel against the vivid blue of the sky. It
looked best in the morning, before the daily haze settled in;
the channels of the salt marsh that lay between Multiplane's
compound and the main connector flyway were full, reflecting the sky like a tarnished mirror.

The others were there ahead of her, Lenassi of Marketing,

Mr. Koichiro from the Executive Committee, Guineven from
R-and-D and Brendan Rabin from the Corvo subgroup, looking distinctly uneasy at being in such high company, Coigne
himself for Main Security—most of the important people on
the Internal Affairs Committee, plus a representative of the
group involved in the intrusion. Cerise nodded a general
greeting, and took her place at the table. A young woman in a
neat black uniform drifted over to take her order.

"You're late," Coigne said.

Cerise looked at him dispassionately, said to the waitress,
"Just coffee, please, and a display stand for my system." The
woman nodded and backed away, and only then did Cerise
turn her attention to the people at the table. "I know. I
stopped in downstairs to see how the autopsy was going."

"Autopsy?" Lenassi asked sharply.

"My people spent last night dissecting what was left of the
intruding program," Cerise said. "They've achieved a recon-
struction, but I'll want to look it over myself before I can say
if we've got anything useful."

The display stand arrived then, trundling into place under
its own power, and Cerise turned to fit her pocketbook into
the cradle. Her coffee arrived a moment later, a full pot and a
delicate cup-and-saucer displayed for a moment on a silver
tray, before the waitress whisked everything into place in
front of her. At the same moment, a rather handsome abstract painting slid aside to reveal the larger of the room's
two projection screens.

"Are we all set, gentlemen?" Koichiro asked, and nodded
to the waitress before anyone could respond. "That will be
all, thank you, Consuela."

"Yes, sir," the waitress said in a colorless voice, and
slipped away, closing the door behind her.

Koichiro looked at Coigne. "So. Derrick, you wanted this
meeting." As always, he sounded a little conscious of the first
name, as though he were still getting used to the alien custom. He was older than most of the Board, older than most of
the executive committee, and Cerise had never been able to

determine if his posting to Internal Affairs was a sign of his rank or a graceful step toward retirement.

"That's right, sir," Coigne said, and gathered the table's attention with a look that was as eloquent as shuffling papers. "As you know, we had an intrusion yesterday, into the Corvo subgroup's research net. As far as we can tell, no actual damage was done, but it remains possible that copies were made of crucial data. I felt that Internal Affairs should meet as soon as possible to discuss both the immediate consequences and any long-term effects. And, of course, any possible solutions to a continuing problem. Cerise, would you give us a rundown of yesterday's event, and your department's response to it?"

"Of course." Cerise reached across the display stand to touch the start-up key, cupped her hand around the remote, almost hiding the controls. Letters and symbols flashed onto the wall screen, shaping a schematic outline of Multiplane's internal network. Bright blue lines formed a boundary around the image, showing the IC(E) that walled in the systems. "I've made disk copies for each of you as well, but this is the summary. The intrusion lasted about five seconds, realtime, before the syscops spotted it, and was directed into Corvo's secondary storage volume—that's the space linked to Bren's principal workspace." On the screen, the affected nodes glowed briefly red. "Five seconds is not a lot of time to make copies, but I have people checking for any signs that the intruder is trying to market stolen goods. The program used was a cracker's tool, probably homebrew, or maybe a commercial product that has been extensively rewritten. We are autopsying what's left of it, but we haven't gotten a solid match to any known crackers."

She was taking a risk there, and knew it, but sixty percent wasn't a solid match by any stretch of the imagination. She glanced from face to face, gauging their reactions. Both Rabin and Rand Guineven looked relieved—as well they might; most of their projects were too complex to be significantly affected by such a short intrusion. Lanessi still looked worried, which was no surprise. Public relations was part of Marketing's concern, and he would have heard that someone was bragging already. Coigne wore his usual faint, faintly patronizing smile, but she couldn't read Koichiri's expression at all.

"I was on the net when the intrusion occurred," Cerise went on, "and tracked the incoming path to a dead-end node in the BBS. I've begun other lines of inquiry, but I don't expect to hear much from those sources until later today."

She touched the remote again, dimming the big screen. It had not been the most useful presentation she had ever made, but the Board seemed to expect to see visuals no matter what the topic. There was a little silence, and then Lanessi cleared his throat.

"I understand that there has already been publicity about this on the nets."

The shadow of a frown flickered across Coigne's face, but he said nothing. Cerise said, "That's right."

"Most unfortunate," Koichiri murmured.

Cerise glanced warily at him, saw no expression at all on his broad face. "But unavoidable," she said. "A short intrusion like this is likely to have been made for advertising—to prove that someone can do the job, not actually to copy anything. Of course whoever did it is going to boast."

"And by boasting, tell every other cracker out there that we're vulnerable," Lanessi said. He shook his head. "It'll get back to clients and shareholders at this rate."

"Not necessarily," Cerise said. "Right now, the intruder doesn't have anything real to boast about—and everyone on the net, at least, will know that. They'll ignore it until the intruder comes up with something useful. And that we can prevent, now that we're warned."

"We've taken the usual precautions," Coigne cut in smoothly, "doubling the sweep frequency, running more watchdogs, putting more syscops into the system. And we're devoting a particular effort to tracking down the intruder, making sure she's stopped for good."

"She," Lanessi said. "Then you have an ID?"

"A possible ID," Cerise said, overriding whatever Coigne

would have said. "A rumored ID. We have a name, nothing more."

"And a sixty percent match in the autopsy," Coigne said, soft and deadly. "To a name that matches a known cracker. I consider it a little better than possible, Cerise."

Cerise smiled at him blandly, wondering which of her people had leaked the autopsy report. "I'd prefer to say possible until I've confirmed it. There are some important discrepancies involved, as well as the sixty percent match. It's better to be conservative in this, I think."

"Who is this person?" Koichiri leaned forward in his chair, resting his elbows on the table. Age spots showed on the backs of his steepled hands.

Coigne looked at Cerise, visibly passing the question to her. Cerise chose her words with care. "Rumor says it's someone calling themselves Trouble—Trouble was a big name on the nets three or four years ago, but dropped out of sight, hasn't been heard of since. There was some talk that she was dead. This person, this new Trouble, may be the old one returned, or just someone using her name and programs: as I said, this doesn't match the old Trouble's style in some significant ways."

Coigne lifted an eyebrow at that, a fleeting gesture, but said nothing. Koichiri said, "You'll pursue this." It was not a question.

"Of course, sir," Cerise said, and allowed herself a faint note of injury.

Guineven said slowly, "I'm more concerned that this episode might lead to further attempts on the system. What can we do to prevent it?"

"We've already set up extra security," Coigne said, "and we'll maintain it for as long as necessary. And catching the intruder should discourage any further attempts."

"How will that extra security affect the net?" Guineven asked, and Rabin nodded.

"Yeah, we're already high-loading—" He stopped abruptly, as though he hadn't meant to speak.

"It's going to run a little slower," Coigne said. "It can't be helped."

"Mr. Rabin," Koichiri said. "What would the intruder have been looking for?"

Rabin gave a suppressed shrug, as though he wanted to be more expressive and didn't quite dare. "We have the MADCo station shuttles on the boards, and the estimates would be worth something to anyone else making a bid on the project. Or there's the Genii design."

Guineven shook his head. "I don't think so. That's so close to production that it wouldn't benefit anyone anymore."

"Derrick," Koichiri said. "I think you should also look into who would benefit from such a theft. You might be able to find your intruder that way."

Coigne hesitated, as though he wanted to refuse, and Cerise bit back the desire to grin. Looking into potential rivals' activities would keep him busy, away from her investigation, and give her a chance to handle things her way. Lanessi said, "I can give you what we know about competitors' bids, Derrick. If that would help."

"Thanks," Coigne said, and sounded sour. There was no refusing either the offer or the order. "I'd appreciate it."

Koichiri nodded once, decisively. "Thank you, gentlemen. I think you are well on your way to controlling a potentially troublesome situation."

It was unmistakably a dismissal. Cerise sighed, worked her remote to close down the pocketbook, then reached to work the machine clear of the display stand. The others were gathering their belongings, too, collecting papers and mini-boards. Koichiri pushed his chair back and started for the door. Lanessi and Guineven followed more slowly, but Rabin hung back, paused to lean over Cerise's shoulder.

"I wonder if I could talk to you at some point about what the intruder got into?" he asked, softly.

Cerise nodded, but before she could say anything, Coigne said, "Cerise. I'd like to talk to you now, if you can spare a minute or two."

Cerise sighed again—she had been expecting that command ever since Koichiri had brought up rival firms—and looked at Rabin. "I'll try to get in touch with you this afternoon, Bren, if you'll be free."

"I'll be available until three," Rabin answered, with a wary glance in Coigne's direction, and eased away.

"I'll talk to you before then," Cerise said, and looked at Coigne. "All right, what is it?"

"My office," Coigne said, softly, though the room had emptied around them. Cerise nodded, and slipped the pocketbook back into its case.

"Fine."

She followed Coigne down the three-level staircase—supposed to be reserved for fire access, but everyone used it—and then around the curve of the building to his office. The two rooms faced directly east, over the ocean, and the windows were darkened against the morning light. Coigne seated himself behind his massive desk, ran his hand across an edge-mounted control bar to light the displays beneath the polished surface. Cerise settled into the chair opposite him, crossing her legs to display stockings and the bright-heeled shoes to their best advantage.

"What do you mean, this doesn't match Trouble's pattern?" Coigne asked.

Cerise blinked. "This person—even if it's calling itself Trouble, it's not behaving the way Trouble used to. Boasting, for one thing: that's something Trouble never did." The memory caught her unaware: Trouble pacing the length of their two-room apartment, swearing in rhythm with her drumbeat walk, all because a friend had boasted once too often, and now he was dead, another body rotted in the harbor water. "She said it was stupid, it used to infuriate her when other people did it." Especially friends.

"Maybe," Coigne said. "Or maybe, since she's been off the nets so long, she feels she needs the advertising."

That was plausible—if you didn't know Trouble. Cerise said, "All right, but even granting that, the program autopsy isn't conclusive, either. It's like Trouble's hand, but there are some tricks she never used."

"Again, she's been off the nets a while," Coigne said. "Why shouldn't she have learned some new tricks?"

"Where?" Cerise asked. "And besides, these aren't new tricks. It's old stuff, stuff she did differently—routines she always sneered at." And it feels different, she wanted to say, it doesn't taste or smell or feel like Trouble's work. But that was arguing from the brainworm's evidence, and she still didn't know for sure that Coigne knew she had one installed. She was almost certain that he did—he would almost have to know—but until she was sure, she didn't want to betray herself unnecessarily.

"Could she be covering her trail?" Coigne asked.

"Possible, but unlikely," Cerise retorted. "Why is it so important for it to be Trouble?"

There was a little silence, and then Coigne looked away, conceding. "It's not so much that I want it to be Trouble," he said, "as I want to be sure you'd tell me if it was Trouble."

"I do my job."

"If it is Trouble," Coigne began, and let the words hang. Cerise watched him, unblinking. She had never wasted time justifying herself to him, refused to begin now.

"At any rate," Coigne went on, "I expect you to deal with the intruder. Which brings me to my next point." He smiled, not pleasantly. "I want this person stepped on, and stepped on hard. In other words, Cerise, this isn't something that I want to take to court. Find me the intruder, and give me the location. I'll take care of the rest."

Cerise sat very still, not daring to move for fear of betraying her anger or the sudden fear. It had been years since the corporations had felt safe acting as their own law, since well before Evans-Tindale—since the Amsterdam Conventions, in fact—years since it had been necessary. For Coigne to be trying those tactics now—it could only mean that there was something not quite right about Corvo's project, something that wouldn't stand the scrutiny of a proper trial. And if she was wrong, if Trouble was involved . . . If any shadow folk were involved, they still had more claim on her loyalty than Coigne did. And at the very least, they deserved a trial, not

Coigne's goons jumping them from some back alley. She said, her voice carefully expressionless, "You're taking a lot on yourself, Coigne."

Coigne looked back at her, pale eyes, grey as ice with a darker ring at the edge of the iris, utterly unreadable. "I have my—priorities."

Or your instructions, Cerise thought. "All right," she said, "I'll keep you informed." She rose to leave, and Coigne's voice stopped her in her tracks.

"I want more than that. I want this intruder, Cerise. I've never been more serious."

Cerise looked back over her shoulder, wondering just what Coigne had been up to to produce what was, for him, a kind of panic. "I won't forget," she said, and slipped through the door before Coigne could call her back. It had been a petty effort—and useless, too; if Coigne wanted to continue the conversation, all he would have to do was ask for her— but it helped to take away the fear.

She made her way back down through the familiar tangle of corridors and elevators to Network Security, waited again while the guards processed her ID and waved her through into the inner rooms. A trio of operators was off-line, clustered around a bluebox junction that looked homemade, and Cerise suppressed the temptation to stop and join the analysis. Instead, she went on into her own office, where Baeyen was still working at the lesser terminal.

"Sirico's got his report," Baeyen said, without looking up from her screen, and Cerise nodded, glancing quickly over the other woman's shoulder. Nothing new there, just the usual security schema, and she pushed open the door to her private office.

The mail light was flashing, but she ignored it, touched buttons instead to signal the best of the three secretaries attached to the department. An instant later, her screen windows, and Landy Massek's sharp face looked out at her.

"Yes, Ms. Cerise?"

"I need you to set up a meeting for me with Brendan Rabin

at Corvo, sometime this afternoon for preference. Will you do that, and get back to me as soon as possible?"

"No problem," Massek said cheerfully, and his window vanished.

Cerise sighed, and turned her attention to her mail. As she'd expected, the largest file was Sirico's report, and she flipped through it quickly. He had been as thorough as ever, and had come up with nothing—which means, she thought, whoever it is, this new Trouble's had trouble selling whatever s/he got. And since that's not likely, unless Rabin has something really unexpected to tell me, like they're not working on anything at the moment, it should mean that s/he didn't get anything at all. She touched keys, flipping quickly through the remaining files, then switched to a different program and tied herself into Sirico's last reported position. There was a brief hesitation, and then another window opened on her screen, displaying Sirico's icon, a samurai-armored head and shoulders that looked vaguely robotic.

"Cerise?"

"Who were you expecting?" Cerise began, and cut herself off. "You did a nice job on the report, Pol."

"Thanks." The icon's expression could not change—Sirico didn't have a brainworm, was too obedient a networker for that—but the voice sounded faintly smug. "I don't think they got anything, boss. Somebody'd be buying, if they had."

"I think you're right," Cerise said. "Tell me, what else have you heard about this Trouble?"

There was the faintest of hesitations before he answered, just enough to convince her that there was something more. "Just talk. Nothing real."

"Such as?"

There was a longer silence, and then Sirico blurted, "Word is, you used to work with somebody called Trouble."

"That's right." Cerise had been expecting the question for almost twenty hours now; she found herself remotely surprised that none of the others had brought it up before. Except, of course, Coigne. "We were partners. You knew I came out of the shadows, Pol. Everyone does."

"So, what do you want us to do about this one? Go slow?"

Cerise blinked at the screen, startled and a little touched by the offer. "No. I want to stop any more problems before they get started—and besides, I don't think it's the Trouble I used to know."

"There are people saying that," Sirico said. "And there are a lot of people who are pretty pissed at this one. He/she's been teasing the big names, and stirred up a lot of security in the process."

Definitely not my Trouble, Cerise thought. "Any word on how to contact this Trouble?"

"What else?" Sirico asked, and the icon would have grinned it if could. "Seahaven."

"Ah." Cerise leaned back in her chair. She had expected nothing less, of course, would have been disappointed if she had gotten any other answer. Seahaven was the last and greatest of the virtual villages, the last survivor of a dozen similar spaces that had existed before Evans-Tindale. It was a virtual space run by and for its unknown architect, the Mayor, an unreal place policed, positioned, and created entirely at his whim. If you entered its influence, you agreed to abide by its rules, to subordinate whatever filters you used to interpret the net to its own system. It was a spectacular effect, and a dangerous one; there were always people who tried to beat the local system, force it to bend to their whim, and while they always failed, the fallout could be disastrous. It had always been a cracker's haven; now it was one of the last remaining spaces where the shadow walkers could conduct their business. It was also one of the net's greatest temptations, and home of its greatest dangers: Trouble had said once that if it were on any map, it would have to be labeled, quite literally, HERE BE DRAGONS.

"Do you have any idea where I'd look for Seahaven these days?"

Sirico's icon shifted color, went yellow for a brief instant, the equivalent of a shrug. "New Hampshire?"

"Very funny." Cerise frowned at the screen. Seahaven was also a town on the New Hampshire coast, maybe ninety-five kilometers to the north. It had once been a summer resort and a fishing town, but as the beaches became dangerous, racked with high UV sunlight, eaten away by pollution and the shifting tide-line, other businesses had dwindled, until the entire population was dependent on the secure hotel built just outside the town on pilings driven into the salt marsh. The hotel was highly rated among the multinationals who needed absolute security for their negotiations—there had never been a successful raid, virtual or real, on the facility, and only a handful of attempts—and the lack of other work in the area kept its prices lower than most. Seahaven, the off-line Seahaven, existed now only to service the hotel, and the hotel and the town government worked hand in glove to keep it that way. Cerise had lived there for an interminable eight months after Evans-Tindale—the old beach-front Parcade was one of the best sources along the East Coast for black- and grey-market ware, and she had been desperate for new hardware—and had hated it. The ghost of a town, worse still, the ghost of a virtual town, hopeless and dying, with nothing to do but serve the hotel and throw rocks and bottles at straying strangers: live free or die, Cerise thought, only they can't seem to do either. She shook away the flash of memory, salt air and the smell of oil smoke drifting along the beachfront, said aloud, "The Seahaven that matters, Pol. Any ideas?"

"I don't know. The last I heard, if you wanted to go to Seahaven, take a walk through the Bazaar. But that was a week ago."

Cerise sighed. "Right, thanks. Keep an eye out for any sale from this intrusion, will you?"

"How long do you want me to watch?" Sirico asked.

"Give it another thirty-two hours," Cerise answered. "If we haven't seen anything by then, we're not going to."

"OK."

"Thanks, Pol," Cerise said, and cut the connection. She stared at the screen for a moment, then touched keys to sound the net. The system flashed an instant list of everyone's position on-line. The simplest thing would be to post a general message, but traveling to net-Seahaven was still something a little questionable, a long step toward the shadows; for her people's sake, it would be better to ask them individually. She studied the list, then blanked the screen. None of the duty operators were likely to admit knowing the road, even if they did know it, which wasn't terribly likely; better to hit the net herself, head for the BBS and the Bazaar that lay at its heart, and find her own way from there. And, she admitted, with a wry smile at her own frailties, it would be more fun to do it herself.

Before she could tie in, a chime sounded, and Massek's face appeared in the corner of her screen. "I've set up an appointment with Mr. Rabin, Ms. Cerise. Is two-thirty all right with you?"

Cerise made a face. "Can you make it any later, Landy?"

"Sorry. Mr. Rabin's got a meeting at three as it is, and he expects to be there the rest of the day."

"All right," Cerise said, and knew she sounded irritable. "Two-thirty it is."

"Thanks. I'll tell Mr. Rabin." Massek vanished.

That changed the parameters somewhat. Cerise pushed herself up from her desk and went to the door of the office. "Jensey. I'm going out on the net for the next few hours. I'll be back by two—it's to do with the incident yesterday, if anyone asks." She meant Coigne, and Baeyen knew it.

"I'll tell him," the dark woman answered. "Do you want me to sound a recall for you?"

"I'll set one," Cerise answered, and turned away. She returned to her seat, adjusting the chair controls to a more comfortable setting, one that wouldn't leave her crippled after a few hours. She checked the toolkits and the standbys already displayed on the screen, and touched keys to have the system warn her when it was time to go home. Then she took a deep breath, and launched herself out onto the net.

*She is flying now, bursting like a rocket through the company IC(E), exploding onto the net like a firework. Overhead, a light gleams like a moon, full and brilliant: an open conference, and she hesitates, tempted, but makes herself turn away. The lines of the nets expand before her, roads and rivers of data like glowing highways; she chooses one, not quite at random, and lets it carry her down toward the BBS.*

*The rivers move more slowly here, where talk is free and the lines are overburdened. She disciplines herself to that meandering pace, drifts silently from node to node. The Bazaar is the great center of the BBS, the link of traders' nodes where anything and everything is bought and sold. Lights flare around her as she drifts closer, bursts of compressed iconage like the cries of a street hawker, and the air smells of burnt cinnamon. She bats the most persistent symbols idly away, feeling them break like bubbles against her hand: familiar advertising, most of them, some of them not, new names and faces, new services, strangers on the net. She drifts past, not bothering to make any reply, her own icon dimmed and ghostly in the midst of all that brilliance, seeking the sellers that lay behind the walls of light, behind the barriers of the obvious. She tests the virtual winds, tasting the data, but finds none of the familiar markers that hint at the road to Seahaven. At the Polar Flare, where there is always news of the shadows, she catches the ball of light that is flung at her, unwraps the spinning advertisement without bothering to read the icons: there is nothing at its center, and she frowns, and tosses the glittering shards like confetti back onto the net. There are other nodes; she crosses them, finds at last a familiar symbol, and touches it. The shape within becomes a presence, a scent and then a swirl of light, a hand-icon inviting her inside. She reaches into her own toolkit, finds the right shape to answer it. Their icons merge, weaving together into a sphere that will provide at least the illusion of privacy, and the familiar presence speaks.*

*Haven't seen you in a while, Cerise. Are you buying or selling?*

*He knows perfectly well she's gone legit, gotten a real job, a legal job, and Cerise smiles, letting the brainworm display the expression for all to see.*

*Neither, Max. As you should know. I'm trying to get to Seahaven.*

*As she expects, that stops him, and there is a little pause, the* light flickering around her like a silent fire. She hangs in its warmth like a salamander, happy in her element, and hears a faint intake of breath.

*The road's closed today, or so I hear. Come back tomorrow.*

*Trouble?*

She makes the question ambiguous, and hears Max Helling laugh.

*I thought you left her.*

He knows better than that, he was there, and Cerise keeps her tone cold and level. *If it's her—and she left me.*

*If—?* There is another little silence, and then Helling laughs again. *So that's the way you're playing it. I heard this Trouble got into Multiplane.*

*That's the way it is. Or so I hear.* Her echo of his words is malicious, and she hears it strike home.

*I've retired, too, Cerise. Don't push me.*

That is news, and Cerise lifts an eyebrow, knowing the brainworm will relay the gesture, asking without speech whatever happened to Aledort. She says nothing direct, however, waits, lapped in the golden light. She waits, and it is Helling who speaks again.

*Like I said, the road's down today. Try tomorrow—through Eleven's Moon.*

He flips away, shattering the sphere that encloses them into a thousand shards like flying knives. Cerise ducks in spite of herself, in spite of knowing she should have expected it, and Helling is gone. But he's told her what she wanted, what she needs to know; there's nothing more she wants from him, not for now. She smiles, delighting in the glittering air, the crush and bother of the advertising, the slow and complex rhythm of the data tides that lie beneath the BBS, and turns along a curve of blue-green light, taking the long way home.

*T*ROUBLE PLAYS JIGSAW *well, even by the standards of the nets. The crystals dance through the playing sphere, flickering from blue to green to yellow, racing up and down the spectrum in an unpredictable pattern, and she reaches for the red ones, catches them just as they blush from orange into red, and slings them into their place in the growing structure. The twisted sculpture, a fantastic, spiraling tower like a mad single-branched candelabra, shivers under a sudden shower of pieces, her own and her last opponent's, flickering like a flame between blue and red. Around the inner surface of the sphere, the eliminated players cluster in ones and threes, bright icons at the corners of her vision, redetermining the playing area. She smiles, fierce behind the mask of her playing piece, the brainworm turned up full, so that she feels every unreal motion, and launches a crystal—already red, too late in its cycle to use—toward an icon who's drifted too close, a silver shape like a Scottie dog. She turns away before she sees it hit or parried, to catch another drift of crystals. A few are shading toward red; she catches three in quick succession, tosses them, slowly, not with all her strength, so that as they approach the twisted tower they are just turning red. Her opponent, a wedge of iridescent silver like a fighter plane, knocks the first away with a well-placed crystal of her own, but the second and the third sink home, and the tower shades imperceptibly closer to the true red that would mean Trouble's victory. Trouble smiles behind the masking icon, and launches herself up and over the wavering structure—it sways even wider, but she has timed it perfectly—and finds a rich field of crystals on the far side, all ripening toward the red she needs. The iridescent fighter swoops sideways, swinging wide around the structure, gathering crystals of her own, but Trouble is ahead of her. She slings the last five crystals into place, banking them off the nearest part of the sphere to snap into the lattice at the bottom of the tower, the hardest of all shots to execute but the most certain, done right. The tower flares scarlet, flashes victory; victory flares around* *her own icon, bathing her in sheer delight, direct pleasure, and she gasps inside the encircling field of color. The other icons, the glittering fighter, the Scottie dog, a stylized Ferrari, and all the rest, drop slowly to the common plane of the net, and the playing sphere fades around them.*

*\*Nice game,\* the fighter says, gruffly, and Trouble smiles again.
\*Thanks.\**

*\*I didn't catch your name,\* the Ferrari says.*

*Trouble pauses, savoring the moment she had known would come—she had planned for it, came out to play in order to provoke it, and now she intends to enjoy it. \*Trouble,\* she says at last. \*The original,\* and before they can react, before they can do more than absorb the words, she's launched herself for the nearest node, leaving only the shell of the icon behind her. The cutouts flare as she drops through the node, and she vanishes from the net in a shower of smoke and flame that obscures her trail beyond recovery.*

Trouble lay back in her chair, jolted by the drop from virtuality, let herself sit for a moment, until her heartbeat slowed to normal. She had spent the last three days tracking the person who called themself Trouble through the net, and had gotten nowhere, found nothing except a file full of crackers' gossip. And Treasury was still too interested in her system to make it possible for her to chase down the rumors. She checked the main screen automatically, saw Starling's watchdog still patiently chasing its tail, and touched the keys that released the crude muzzle. The program unfolded itself, sent a burst of codes across her screen, found nothing, and went dormant again, momentarily satisfied. Trouble eyed it uncertainly—she couldn't be sure that it hadn't spotted her interference, working with a three-year-old muzzle—but there was nothing she could do about it if it had. The worst it could do was testify that she had a brainworm—bad, but not an unbeatable charge. At least it could not, by itself, prove that she was Trouble.

And she had made a good start. Trouble smiled slowly, savoring the memory of the Jigsaw game. It had been fun to play again, to play at her own top capacity; it had been even more fun to name herself, and watch the panic set in. Once

she was known to be back, she herself, the original, the only
Trouble, someone would tell her who this pretender really
was. And then she could deal with it, either by shopping the
pretender to the cops—she had no obligations there, after
the stranger had stolen her name, her style—or by revealing
the pretense on the wider nets. The latter was probably the
more satisfying option, though selling out the pretender was
safer, and she allowed herself a grin, contemplating the possibilities.

Her fingers were cramping inside the tight shell of the
metal-bound glove. She winced, working her hand against
servos gone suddenly stiff and unresponsive, and sat up
enough to unplug the glove. The pain eased, and she
stretched cautiously, opening and closing her hand, until she
was certain the cramps would not return. Then she snapped
open the catches, and eased the glove away from her fingers.
Trouble's return—the return of the real Trouble, she
amended silently—would be the talk of the nets within half
an hour. All she had to do was back it up.

Fortunately, that wouldn't be hard. But before she could
go much further, she needed a new toolkit, and probably a
new implant to manage data transfer to the brainworm. After
three years, the old chip was outclassed, and while she could
make or steal much of the software and bioware that she
needed, it would be quicker and more efficient—and safer,
too, in the long run—to buy what she needed from one of the
shadow dealers who infested the coast. She had the money
for it, a little more than five thousand in a mix of citiscrip,
bearer cards, and an ugly grey-green wad of oldmoney; and
besides, she told herself, buying a new kit would be one
more way of announcing her return.

A chime sounded from the intercom, and she jumped
before she realized what it was.

"India?" A female voice too distorted to recognize paused
briefly, static singing through the speaker. "India, are you
down there?"

Trouble touched the answer button, her heart still racing
painfully. "I'm here. What is it?"

"Are you on line? I—we'd like to talk to you."

"If I was on line," Trouble said, "I wouldn't be answering you." She stopped, took a deep breath, backing away from the bravado of the nets. "Sorry. Who's we?"

"Me, Oba, Mike, and Terri Lofting."

At least half of the Management Committee, plus whoever was doing the talking. Trouble took a deep breath, feeling the sudden chill run along her spine. "I'll be right up."

She took the time anyway to shut things down properly, so that no one could complain of her work as syscop, and went upstairs. The delegation was waiting at the main door, the evening sky behind them glowing red and orange between the layers of clouds, like embers in a banked fire. She studied them for an instant as she opened the door—it was the entire Management Committee, plus Judy Merric, who had once been a paralegal and did most of the legal talking for the co-op—and beckoned them into the brightly lit kitchen.

"What's up?" she asked.

"You tell us," Teresa Lofting said. She was the oldest member of the committee, grey-haired and soft-bodied, but there was a will of iron beneath the grandmotherly exterior. She had built the co-op almost out of nothing, and was fiercely protective of its rights.

"Let's sit down," Alvarez said hastily. "If you don't mind, India."

"No," Trouble said, without sincerity, and waved them on into the living room. She thought for a moment of offering coffee and tea, but, looking at the grim faces, suspected that it would only put off the inevitable. "What's this all about?" she said again, and sat down on the chair beside the unused stove.

The others took their places reluctantly, exchanging glances, and at last Alvarez said, "The Treasury agents, the ones who were here the other day. What do they want with you?"

"They were asking about a cracker who may have been going through my—our—nodes," Trouble said, and wondered why she bothered. "I told them I hadn't seen anything, and gave them a copy of the sheriff's report—my report to the sheriff. That's all."

"And had you?" Lofting asked. Trouble frowned, and the older woman amplified, her voice still sweetly reasonable. "Had you seen anything?"

"No," Trouble said, and didn't bother hiding her annoyance.

"Hey, people," Merric said softly, and Mike Ishida said, "Yeah, let's begin at the beginning. India doesn't know what's been going on today."

Trouble looked warily at them, already not sure she wanted to know, and Alvarez said, "All right, Mike, you tell her."

Ishida gave a wry smile, careful to include all of them—but Lofting, at least, wasn't buying, Trouble thought, and Alvarez didn't look too happy, either. And if Merric's here— she might only have been a paralegal, but she had a good sense of the legal process. If she was worried, then Treasury might well be close to an arrest.

"We've been getting a lot of attention from the authorities all of a sudden," Ishida said. "I got a phone call from a Mr. Levy, who says he's with the Treasury, asking about you, India—asking how you came to work for us, what we know about you—asking me in my capacity as a committee speaker. Oba and Terri got the same kind of inquiries, and when I asked around, a lot of people had been getting informal questions. So what's going on?"

Trouble spread her hands. "I don't entirely know. What they told me was, they tracked a cracker using my nodes, my net. I checked into it, of course, and didn't find any signs of anyone, but what I hear on the net is, there's a cracker come back from the dead, somebody nobody's heard of in years, who's causing a lot of trouble. What the connection is with me, I don't know." And everything except the last sentence was absolutely true.

The other four exchanged glances, Lofting still with that gentle, implacable moue of distaste that was more alarming than any overt threat. Merric leaned forward slightly. "India—"

"Very well," Lofting said, riding over whatever the ex-paralegal would have said. "I can accept that you don't quite know what's happening, I can even believe that you didn't know that this—cracker—was back in business, but I find it hard to believe that you didn't know this person. If that's what you tell us, however—" She paused, clearly waiting for a denial. Trouble made her expression as guileless as possible, and, after a moment, Lofting continued. "—then we have to accept it. But I—we of the Management Committee—cannot support you if you've been involved in illegal activities. I want that clearly understood."

"We knew perfectly well when India came to us that hiring any syscop out of the shadows might present problems," Ishida began. "And we agreed then—"

"Do you understand?" Lofting said, as if the younger man hadn't spoken.

Oh, yes, Trouble thought, I understand, and bit her tongue to keep from speaking it aloud. You're washing your hands of me, regardless of what I've done—or, more precisely, because you believe I've done whatever it is they're accusing me of.... Which of course I did do, once upon a time and sort of, because I was—I am—Trouble. It would be funny, if it wasn't so serious—hell, it is funny. She sat still for a moment longer, considered and discarded three different answers. It was quiet in the condo; she could hear, in the far distance, the dulled, steady rush of traffic on the flyway. She said at last, "You don't leave me many options. As it happens, I haven't been running shadow jobs here—" She used the cracker's phrase deliberately, and saw Merric wince. "—but that doesn't seem to matter, to you or to Treasury. Like Mike said, you knew—I told you—what I'd done before I came here, back when it wasn't illegal, and you said then it didn't matter. However, I don't intend to involve you, the co-op, in my troubles."

Ishida flinched at that, and Alvarez looked up, as though he would protest. Even Lofting had the grace to look faintly uncomfortable, but she rallied quickly. "The co-op can't afford your troubles—can't afford cracker troubles," she said. "The law—Evans-Tindale is very clear about what makes an accessory. You know that."

She had been looking at Trouble, but it was Alvarez who nodded. "I'm sorry, India," he said.

"So," Trouble began, and Lofting cut in.

"I want you to understand that we, the co-op as a whole, will do whatever we can to cooperate with the Treasury's investigation."

"Make sure you fill out the reward form correctly," Trouble said. "But remember to clear out your personal systems first." She had meant that as a threat—she had dealt with plenty of grey-market programmers for the co-op, trying to get good programs at prices the artists could afford—and she was pleased when Alvarez looked away.

Lofting ignored her, looked around the room, visibly gathering her delegation. "That's all we came to say. I appreciate your time, India."

"Not at all," Trouble said, and bit down hard on a profane response. It wouldn't work—wouldn't impress Lofting, wouldn't anger her, would merely be what she'd expected, and Trouble wouldn't give her that satisfaction. She walked them to the door, moving with care, and was surprised when Merric hung back at the doorway, glancing over her shoulder as the others moved away into the growing dark.

"If you need it," she began, scowling, and then her tone changed abruptly. "If they come down on you, India, remember, you don't have to talk to them. Even if they arrest you, you don't have to talk to them without a lawyer, and we have a contract with my old firm." She reached into her pocket, the movement screened from the others by her body, and came out with a thin piece of pasteboard. "The callcode's there, and our account number. You'll still have access."

Trouble took the card wordlessly, and knew from Merric's shiver that her fingers as they brushed against her hand were as cold as ice. "Thanks," she said, and was remotely pleased that her voice remained steady.

"I hope to hell you don't have to use it," Merric said, and turned away.

Trouble shut the door quite gently behind her, and went upstairs to her bedroom. There was no point in putting it off, and no point in staying here any longer; with Lofting firmly ranged against her, the rest of the co-op would soon fall into line. Which meant she needed the toolkit right away, and the new implant as soon as possible, and the machines downstairs would no longer be safe. . . . She put those thoughts aside, recognizing incipient panic, and began methodically to pack.

It didn't take her long. She had accumulated more things than she'd realized, clothes and books and disks and the plain-but-decent furniture, but most of it would have to stay behind. She collected what she could carry, what would help her in the weeks ahead—Trouble's clothes, the best of her pieces, costume from the old days and the few new things that matched that image—and then went downstairs to break up the system. Some of the hardware would have to stay—she couldn't risk having the node simply vanish, tempting as it was to deprive the co-op of its connection to the outside world—but she stripped the more portable machines away, reaching awkwardly around the shelves to unhook dusty cables. She had done this before, and shied away from the memory, suppressing the thought that Cerise would say it served her right. She sneezed, startled, and went back upstairs for a rag, cursing herself for her carelessness. She'd never stayed in any one place long enough for that to be a problem. Finally, however, she had everything broken down; she folded the last cable neatly into its housing, took a last look at the net monitor obligingly blinking on the main screen—everything was green, most of the house machines shut down for the night, a single blue-toned icon that was Mineka Konstenten, working late on one of her designs— and turned away. It had never been particularly hard to leave, before. Even leaving Cerise had been easier.

She paused in the living room, set the system carrybag on the floor beside the lighter backpack that held her clothes. It was a strange thought, not something she'd really considered before. It wasn't so much that it was hard to leave the co-op—though, given the choice, she would have stayed, and that was startling—as that it had been, well, easy to leave Cerise. Not that I wasn't right to do it, she thought, but still. . . . She could remember packing that day, loading the machines and the clothes haphazard into the only bag she had, wrapping the delicate brainbox at the center of a cocoon of jackets and shirts, packing the storage blocks in underwear, hurrying because she couldn't stand the thought of arguing anymore, because Evans-Tindale had become law and she'd known Cerise wouldn't see reason, because if she hurried she didn't have to think too much about what Cerise would say, coming home to the empty flat. No, easy wasn't the right word, but she hadn't felt this same regret, a nostalgia, almost, for the time she'd spent. It had been fear then, certainly, and anger. She was angry now, too, but she hadn't expected the co-op to support her. She had expected Cerise to come with her, in the end.

She checked the kitchen controls a final time, making sure the household systems had spooled down to standby, set the environmental system at fifteen degrees, then left the remote conspicuously in the center of the table. She pocketed the old-fashioned keys, and let herself out the sliding door, locking it carefully again behind her. She hesitated then, weighing the keys in her hand, then turned not toward the gate but into the compound, walking back along the row of houses, skirting the pools of light that spread from the porches. At Konstenten's house she hesitated, but made herself step up onto the porch, and tapped gently on the reflecting glass. For a moment she thought the other hadn't heard her, that she'd been too immersed in her work to hear, but then the mirror-image rippled, the line of trees, her own brighter shape wavering, and the door slid open a few inches.

"What is it, India?" Konstenten asked, and slid the door open the rest of the way. She was a tall woman, chestnut hair held back by an embroidered scarf; threads clung to her T-shirt and the legs of her jeans. Behind her, light gleamed on her quilting frame, spotlighted in the center of the room. "Or should I ask?"

"I'm leaving," Trouble said. She held out her keys, and Konstenten took them mechanically, stood holding them still with her hand up, as though she wasn't sure what she wanted to do with them. "I may be back—I hope I'll be back, but I wanted to ask if you'd keep an eye on my stuff."

There was a little silence, and then Konstenten said, "You're leaving me responsible for your place. And whatever's in it. All with Treasury breathing down your neck, and the talk everywhere that you're going to be busted any day now. Fuck you, Indy."

"There's nothing in there that could get you into trouble," Trouble said. "They think I'm a cracker, you're not involved in that."

"Fuck you," Konstenten said again, and threw the keys at Trouble's feet. They landed with a splash of metal against concrete. "Why do you even bother telling me you're going?"

Because I didn't tell Cerise, Trouble thought. But that was not an answer that Konstenten would understand. She said, "Because I thought I owed you."

"Because you needed my help," Konstenten answered. The keys lay gleaming at Trouble's feet.

"Fine," Trouble said. She shifted the bags on her shoulder, took a step backward, letting the keys lie where they'd fallen. "Yeah, I could've used some help, but it's OK. Leave it, let the committee, whoever, deal with it. But I wanted to let you know."

She turned away, started walking fast into the shadows, heading toward the edge of the standing trees and the path that led to the main gate. Behind her, she heard a scrape of metal against concrete, but did not look back to see if Konstenten had picked up the keys.

She caught the night shuttle into Irish Point, the train chugging down the center of the flyway that gleamed like an oil slick in the headlights and the silver glare of the rising moon. To the south, the city lights filled the horizon, the distant buildings little more than shadows behind the broken geometry of their lights, further distorted by the scratched windows. She watched them, trying not to think too much, until the flyway split away to either side, ramps spiraling down to the ground roads, and the shuttle itself dipped toward the terminus. She had made sure that Jesse's still existed, was still in the same ratty storefront where he had always kept shop; that was all she could do, and she put her worries and the anger aside for later.

She took a trolley from the terminus into the town center, got off at the familiar end-of-Main stop. Main Street was less crowded here, toward the edge of Irish Point's shopping district, fewer cars in sight. Less than two miles away, the street ended at the concrete of the sea wall, and Trouble could see the lights of the Coast Guard tower rising above the distant buildings. She made her way past the closed storefronts, their windows protected by metal grills or heavier solid shutters. Here and there, someone had tried to pry one of the barriers away, leaving a corner curled up, and everywhere red and green pinlights glowed in corners, signalling wide-awake security systems.

There weren't many people on the street, either—a young woman hurrying past, who vanished through the locked door that led to an upstairs apartment; a couple of middle-aged men who walked slow and unsteady, arguing about something in an unfamiliar creole; a twenty-something man in jeans and a too-tight T-shirt, hands in his pockets, scowling—and Trouble felt vaguely that she ought to be afraid. She was too angry for fear, however, beyond the always present need to keep an eye on the shadows, too angry still even to admit her anger, except as a white-cold intensity that she honed like a weapon, focusing her thoughts on the meeting. She would not think of Konstenten, of the co-op, not yet. She turned off Main Street at last, striding through the orange glow of a streetlight, and saw the familiar sign ahead of her.

Jesse's was a small place, a clapboard storefront with a dirty display window filled with faded posters and a few old-fashioned pocketbooks and travel decks. The door was open, however, just a screen separating the main room from the street, and she could hear the music two doors away. It was old music, familiar rhythms, and she found herself falling into step as she came up to the door.

The main room was just the same as it had always been, bare wood floors badly in need of polishing, shelves filling the side walls and the wall behind the bare metal counter with its row of open outlets. Just inside the door, an overfilled notice board advertised everything from used chips and bioware to a secondhand tricycle. A quartet, all young, all nondescript in jeans and military surplus, none of them familiar to her, sat at the center table, a notebook's internal works spread out among them like a card game or the entrails of some sacrificial animal. They all looked up at the sound of the door, and she felt their eyes on her as she walked past them to the counter. None of them would be of significance—if they were at all important, they would be in one of the back rooms—and she ignored them, fixing her eyes on the woman behind the counter. She would be one of Jesse's innumerable girls, one of the harem who cooked and cleaned and did the tech work and kept the store running while Jesse played on the nets, and Trouble approached her with the same wary respect she used to all of Jesse's women. The woman, tall, stringy, very black, her hair fastened in a club of braids at the base of her neck, looked back at her with a weary, deliberately unnerving stare.

"What you need, honey?"

"I've got some shopping to do," Trouble answered. "And I want to talk to Jesse."

"We got stock out here," the woman answered, with a vague wave of her hand at the crowded shelves, "but Jesse's on-line. You'll have to make do with me."

Behind her, Trouble could hear a soft sound from the group at the table, a rustle that might have been a stifled laugh. She ignored it, still looking at the stringy woman. "I need custom work. And I still want to talk to Jesse."

There was a little silence, and the woman said, "Will Jesse want to talk to you?"

"Tell him Trouble's here."

The woman's head came up, her mobile face drawing down into an angry scowl. "I don't take kindly to pretenders, sweetheart, and we don't deal with hot merchandise—"

"The real Trouble," Trouble interjected. "The original. You can tell Jesse that I'm back, and I'm pissed. Nobody takes my name in vain."

The woman stared at her, her anger replaced by speculation, and Trouble heard one of the quartet whistle softly. She could see their reflection in one of the shiny metal boxes that held sterile components, a distorted image, but clear enough to see them all four staring, the notebook forgotten on the tabletop. She waited, willing to let the woman take her own time in deciding how to handle this apparition from Jesse's past, and the curtain that covered the door into the back rooms was swept back abruptly.

"Problems?" a familiar voice asked, and the woman turned toward her with ill-concealed relief.

"This woman wants to talk to Jesse—"

"Trouble?" Annie Elhibri sounded less than enthusiastic in her recognition, and Trouble allowed herself a slight, unpleasant smile.

"Good to see you again, Annie."

"Jesus."

"Not yet," Trouble murmured, and Elhibri rolled her eyes.

"What the hell are you doing here? We heard you'd left the shadows."

"Someone's taking my name in vain," Trouble said again. "I'm—not best pleased."

"Right," Elhibri said. "I guess you better talk to Jesse."

She held the curtain aside, and Trouble ducked under the faded fabric. The inner rooms had changed even less than the outer, the walls still painted with bold sweeps of color and stylized suns-and-moons from the last psychedelic revival. In one side room, a couple of crackers sprawled on mattresses laid out beside a strip of datanodes, cords snaking across the floorboards from their dollie-slots to disappear into the nodes. In the next room, a man and a woman leaned close over a viewlens, the woman pointing out features in its circle. Trouble looked, but couldn't see what lay in the lens's magnifying field. The surgery was empty, not usual in the old days, not on a Thursday night when most people had just gotten paid on their real jobs, and she glanced sharply at Elhibri.

"Where's Carlie?"

Elhibri looked back at her, thin eyebrows rising. "Dead. Didn't you hear? He died last winter."

"AIDS?"

"Yeah."

"Shit." Trouble closed her mouth over anything else she would have said, any apology for not having known. Carlie Held had installed her first dollie-slots and BOSRAM, had implanted her brainworm and rigged most of the later upgrades and improvements to the mixed system. It was hard to believe he could be dead—and someone might have told me, out of all the old gang. But she had walked away, not they.

"We got a new girl doing installations," Elhibri went on, "name of Karakhan. Carlie trained her—it was his idea to have her take over."

Trouble nodded, swallowing her grief and the regret that she hadn't known sooner, and Elhibri stopped in front of the final door.

"Wait here," she said, and pushed through the beaded curtain before Trouble could say anything. There was a murmur of voices, and Elhibri reappeared, holding the curtain aside. "Jesse says come on in."

"Thanks," Trouble said, and stepped under the draped beads.

Nothing much had changed here, either, except for Jesse himself. He still sat behind the massive desklike shape of a salvaged miniframe, extra processing towers sprouting from its corners like buttresses, but his hair was grey, and the lines of his face had deepened. The eyes, however, were the same, brown and deceptively warm, and so was his expression, smiling and closed all at once.

"So the prodigal returns," he said, with the same heavy joviality that he had always used when he wanted to buy time. It was a familiar pose, and Trouble took a savage pleasure in the old routines.

"Not exactly," she said. "I just need to pick up a few items for my toolkit. You're still the best, Jesse, or so they say."

Jesse lifted an eyebrow. "Still, Trouble?"

"It's been a while."

"So it has," Jesse agreed. "What is it precisely that you're looking for?"

"Just a couple of routines," Trouble answered. "I need a set of icepicks and some tracers. And I want to buy a muzzle for a watchdog."

"You do realize," Jesse said, "that all of this is illegal now?"

Trouble smiled. "And I want an upgrade for my worm."

Jesse sighed. "All right, I can get you the icepicks, no problem, deliver as soon as you pay and I download. Tracers, hell, take your pick, I've got a pretty good selection. Now, for the muzzle—what kind of a watchdog is it, anyway?"

"Treasury," Trouble answered, and was pleased when Jesse winced.

"You don't ask for much, do you? Come back into my life, without even so much as a hello, darling, and tell me you want sixteen varieties of naughtyware, including a new chip for the worm. What the hell are you up to—or, no, don't tell me. Icepicks, tracers, muzzles, implants—Christ, you don't want much from me."

Trouble waited until the spate of talk had run out, smiled again. "Hello, darling. It's good to see you again."

There was a little silence, and then, reluctantly, Jesse smiled back at her. It was a real smile, acknowledging her attitude and skill, and it transformed the blank roundness of his face. "I didn't think it could be you making all that trouble. Just not your style."

"It's not," Trouble said. "Which, of course, is why I've come shopping."

Jesse nodded, touched controls hidden somewhere behind

the bulk of the miniframe. "I think I can fit you up, except maybe for the implant. Karakhan's good, but she's not up to the worms yet. I'd have to get somebody in."

"Who's the best, now that Carlie's dead?" Trouble asked.

"Woman in the city," Jesse answered. "Her name's Huu, H-U-U—Dr. Huu, get it?"

"Got it," Trouble said, and wished she hadn't.

"She's part of Butch van Liesvelt's crowd, if you still talk to any of them," Jesse went on. "I could get you an introduction, but you'd be better off going through the family."

"Yeah, you're still a straight boy," Trouble said. "I'll talk to Butch. What about the rest of the stuff?"

"I can get it for you," Jesse answered. "At a price, of course."

"Jesse," Trouble said, and let her voice go deep and teasing.

"I mean it, Trouble. This stuff doesn't come cheap anymore, and you want some pretty specialized routines."

"I don't have time to waste," Trouble said. "I'll give you three thousand for the lot."

"Three thousand?" Jesse's voice scaled up with mock-disbelief. "Three thousand for icepicks, tracers—my best tracers, which is what I know you'll want—and a muzzle?"

"That's right." Trouble waited, hooked her thumbs into the pockets of her jeans, knowing that all she really needed to do was wait.

"I'm sorry," Jesse said, and shook his head for emphasis. "I'm sorry, I can't do it. I've got a business to maintain, expenses, employees to pay—we've got a pension plan and health care now, in case you didn't know."

"Both of which are mandated by the government," Trouble said. "Three thousand, Jesse. I told you, I don't have time to waste."

There was a little silence, Jesse shaking his head, and then, still shaking his head, he spread his hands in surrender. "All right, three thousand. But you'll have to take straight-off-the-net routines. I can't afford to do any custom work at that price."

"I can make my own modifications," Trouble said demurely.

"All right," Jesse said. "Let me start pulling things."

"Thanks," Trouble said, and Jesse waved vaguely toward a chair that stood in the corner of the room. It was as much of an invitation as she was going to get, and Trouble dragged it over to the miniframe. Jesse leaned close over his multi-screen, hands busy on keyboard and shadowscreen, her presence already all but forgotten. He would be checking his inventory, Trouble knew, the legal and illegal storage spaces he had scattered in the house and across the nets, along the virtual chain that made up his network presence. If she closed her eyes, she could almost see the flare of lights as Jesse leapfrogged from node to node, muddying his trail.

It took nearly an hour for him to locate the programs he wanted. He surfaced long enough to announce that fact, but it took another twenty minutes to extricate himself from the nets without leaving traces. Trouble waited patiently enough—someone less skilled could easily have taken three times as long, without producing what she needed—but when the data drives began to whir she pushed herself to her feet and went to watch them spin down.

"I hope you like what I found you, after all that," Jesse said, rather sourly, and Trouble looked over her shoulder to see him unplugging himself from the last system block.

"I'll let you know when I see them."

Jesse rolled his eyes heavenward. "There's gratitude for you."

"Can I run off your system?" Trouble asked. The green light came on, signaling copy-complete, and she triggered the release.

"Oh, go ahead. Why not?" Jesse waved toward a trio of nodes, and Trouble slipped her board from her bag and set it on the ledge, opening it just enough to give her access to her machines. She carried several versions of analysand in working memory, and ran the new programs through the most comprehensive of the group, barely watching the lines of code as they flickered past on the screen. An image formed behind her eyes, drifting hazily in unreal space, coupled with a cascade of sensation as the brainworm kicked in, translating the numbers into her personal codes. She flipped from the icepicks, elegant, lean programs, cold and hard as steel, to the baroque complexity of the tracers, and smiled in spite of herself, feeling a familiar touch, a routine of her own buried in the secondary structure. The program lolled in front of her, willing and eager and clearly skilled; fleetingly, she felt the sensation of glossy fur, and nodded to herself, accepting that the program was in good shape.

"Good bones," she said aloud, and Jesse grunted.

"Good genes," he answered. "You remember Max Helling? That's about a third-generation variant of his old Toby."

Trouble nodded. She remembered Helling, all right, from the old days, a bony, hawk-faced man who specialized in tracers and virus killing, though Aledort—a cracker, as well as an eco-teur—had kept him away from the circle as much as possible. "Whatever happened to him, anyway?"

"Went legit," Jesse answered. "Or so I heard. I haven't seen his work much, outside the marketplace."

And that was a pretty good indication that he was indeed legitimate: only the crackers could afford to give away their programs for nothing. "Who wrote the variant?" Trouble asked, and Jesse shrugged again.

"Signs itself TG—which stands for Toujours Gai, or so I hear. The work's reliable. TG doesn't do much, and what there is tends to build on other people's templates, rework flawed stuff, but what's out there is choice. Word is, if you need something redesigned, TG's the one to do it."

"Nice to know," Trouble said, and touched keys to begin shutting down the system. "This is good stuff, Jess, thanks."

"Always a pleasure doing business," Jesse answered, without conviction. "Three thousand, you said? Plus five hundred for my commission."

"Three thousand," Trouble answered. "Nice try."

"Three thousand."

Trouble nodded, reached into her bag, came up with the folder of mixed cash. She found what she wanted and handed it to Jesse. He counted it, stacking it gravely into three piles, multicolor citiscrip foils, the dull silver of the bearer cards, the final, smaller grey-green wad of oldmoney. "All there," he said at last, and swept the piles together, stuffed it all somewhere out of sight. "Anything else I can do for you?" His tone suggested that he hoped there wasn't.

"Two things," Trouble answered, and grinned at the suddenly wary expression on the man's face. "Nothing complicated—not even anything illegal."

"Right," Jesse said, without conviction, and sank back into his chair.

"First, I saw out there somebody had a trike for sale. Is it still available?"

Jesse nodded warily. "Yeah."

"Do you know anything about it?"

"No more than anybody," Jesse said, and Trouble sighed theatrically. She was, she realized, enjoying herself.

"It's your fucking store, Jesse, you know every piece of string that goes through here, never mind the chips and the hardware. Don't give me that."

"It's pretty much as advertised," Jesse said, stung. "Good condition, probably needs a tune-up, kid's selling because he's out of college and can't afford the freight to get it home to wherever it is he comes from, São Paulo or someplace like that, and he doesn't want to drive it."

Trouble nodded slowly. The machine—an OstEuro Starrider, the notice had said—wasn't particularly fancy, wouldn't win races or carry extra armament, would probably get you killed if you tried outrunning police vans and flyers, but it was a good steady platform for the long haul, would carry a decent cargo. "I'm interested in it, Jesse. Will you broker for me?"

"At fifteen percent, sure," Jesse answered.

"Used to be ten."

"Inflation," Jesse said.

Trouble considered, running the numbers in her head, but she already knew she could afford it, even with Jesse's commission. "All right. But I won't go above the asking price, no matter what he throws in."

Jesse started to leer, then thought better of it. Trouble said it for him, "No, not even his own hot body. Not my type."

"Agreed. I'll need a deposit—earnest money."

"I'll give you three hundred now," Trouble said, "and another two hundred over the commission if you can make the deal before I leave."

Jesse nodded, and typed something into his desktop. A chime sounded faintly. Trouble reached into her pocket, pulled out a second folder of bearer cards. She found one that rated two hundred and fifty, then paged through a half-empty book of foils until she came up with the remaining fifty, and passed them together across the desktop.

"I'm trying to contact him now," Jesse said, and made the money vanish into a pocket without looking up from his screens. "You said there was more?"

"Second thing," Trouble said. "I need to go to Seahaven, Jesse. Can I walk out through your nodes?"

There was a little silence, Jesse busying himself with the desktop. "Seahaven's changed some," he said at last.

When he didn't say anything more, Trouble lifted an eyebrow at him. "What do you mean?"

"It's changed." Jesse grimaced, looked annoyed with himself for having betrayed anything like uncertainty. "The Mayor—he's gotten a little more autocratic these days, and the interface is a lot slicker, a lot more IC(E) in it, nasty IC(E). There was an incident last year that caused a lot of talk. The Mayor turned in somebody who was working out of Seahaven—he said the guy was cracking without good sense, screwing around where he couldn't possibly make a profit, but a lot of people thought it was personal."

"I heard some of that," Trouble said. There had been a rumor last year that someone, not a cracker, had been shopped to the cops for screwing around with someone else's pillow-friend. If that was from Seahaven—well, it had to have been a nasty quarrel, and wide-ranging, for its echoes to have reached her in the bright lights.

"So a lot of people are off Seahaven these days," Jesse went on, "or at least they're watching their step."

Trouble shrugged, only partly out of bravado. Whatever truth was behind the rumors, Seahaven was still the only place left that you could do certain kinds of business, the only place that had successfully defended itself against the various agencies whose job it had become to police the nets. "I need to get a message out," she said, and Jesse sighed.

"Then you want to go to Seahaven," he agreed. "Try through Eleven's Moon. You're welcome to use a node, any room you want. But—be careful, Trouble."

"Thanks," Trouble said. "Is there someplace I can be private? Not just for me," she added, seeing Jesse's mouth curl into a grin, "but to keep you people out of it."

Jesse sobered instantly. "Yeah." He touched more controls, and Trouble heard a chime sound in some distant part of the building. "You can have the little room upstairs."

That brought back memories, all right—she had worked there before, done some of her best work in that little, blue-walled space, both when she was starting out and then later, when she and Cerise had needed to do a job on the fly—but she said nothing.

"Ah," Jesse said, and looked down at his screens. "I found the kid."

"Offer him two-thirds," Trouble said.

"Don't you trust me?" Jesse asked, rhetorically, and his fingers danced over the keyboard. There was a little pause, and then he smiled. "Done deal. That's another fifteen hundred, Trouble."

"Rounded up?" Trouble asked, but reached for her money.

"Rounded down. I'm wounded."

Trouble slid a short stack of bearer cards across the table, added a booklet of citiscrip. "Where is the trike?"

"Out back," Jesse answered. "You can have it whenever you want it—" He broke off as the curtain slid back and Elhibri appeared in the doorway.

"Annie. Trouble's going to be working upstairs."

Elhibri nodded, and Trouble followed the other woman out of the room and up the narrow back stairway to the blue-painted room. It was empty except for the node, its box mounted in the center of the floor like an inside-out drain, and a patched foam-core armchair.

"You want coffee?" Elhibri said, grudgingly, and Trouble nodded.

"Yeah, I'd appreciate it."

"I'll bring you a pot," Elhibri answered, and disappeared, closing the door behind her. Left to herself, Trouble began setting up her system, main box, data drives, the specialized add-ons that interpreted the net, then plugged the cord into her dollie-slot, careful to keep the power low for now. She loaded the new programs, ran the installation routines, and sat back to run a quick diagnostic scan. Elhibri reappeared halfway through, a small, two-cup thermos and a mug on a tray, and Trouble thanked her abstractedly, barely aware of her presence or her departure. The scan showed green, a multibranched tree of indicators; more than that, she could feel the system in tune, a gentle harmony, and she shut down the scan.

The gateway icon returned to the center of the screen, a multibranched, ever-changing shape that seemed always on the verge of falling into a regular polygon but could never quite be defined. Trouble evoked the control program, touched the virtual levers, bringing the brainworm fully on-line, and heard the seashell rush, the traffic rumble of the net. The realworld hazed and faded, overwritten by the images transmitted directly to her brain.

*She rides the fast datastream toward the BBS and the delta, slides away from it as the data slows around her, using her own separate momentum to carry her a little further into the swirling light, the bright icons of the advertisers and the punters and the users blending into a single shifting layer like the flow of a visible wind. She passes familiar stations, nodes and virtual spaces that are shops and meeting grounds and informal brokers of one thing or another, but no one seems to notice. No one sends her more than the usual glittering chaff, and she smiles at her conceit that made her expect* more. It is probably just as well, this virtual anonymity, or discretion, but she doesn't have to like it. She finds a mail drop, a red-and-blue glittering box, and, after only the slightest hesitation, steps within. Inside is the illusion of a post office, and the illusion of privacy; she invokes a routine that makes the latter real, and quickly shapes her message. BUTCH—I NEED YOUR HELP TO CONTACT DR. HUU, AND A PLACE TO STAY. MEET ME AT MICKEY'S WILD GOOSE AT—she glances sideways, checking realtime, and makes the calculation—5 A.M. TOMORROW. THANKS. She adds the mailcode and dispatches it, through a tried-and-true cutout node. Smoke flares briefly, a stink and a flash of heat across her face, and she knows the system has erased the local copy. She smiles, and dismisses the program that gave her the moment's protection from prying eyes.

She moves on through the shifting pattern of the virtual streets, spirals eddying within a greater spiral, following their shape rather than the outward image, and finds herself at last in front of a symbol she recognizes, an icon man-tall, X and I barring a shape like a full moon. She lifts her hand, knocks, and, a fraction late, feels wood beneath her knuckle. A heartbeat later, the icon fades a little, becomes pliable to the touch. She drifts through it, and feels the local interface seize her, drawing shadowy shapes around her. The walls of a store tower to either side, dark shelves crammed with dark and unimaginable objects that slink away from view when you try to see them clearly; a shapeless figure, a demon carved of light so white that she can't see any detail, sits behind a high counter, waiting.

*You rang?* it says, deep voice stolen from an actor famous for horror films, and Trouble smiles to herself. She gestures, overriding the local system, and calls into being her old icon, harlequin dancing, the one everyone remembers.

*I'm on the road for Seahaven,* she says, and ignores the faint intake of breath that betrays the human hand behind the demon.

There is a little pause. She feels the faint pulse of a probe, pressure, a tickle, against her skin, and then the stronger surge of her own kit repelling its interest, so that she appears to the other as an icon without a source, without the faint silver cord that ties most icons to their point of origin and makes the skies above the BBS a cat's-cradle of glittering lines. The demon shape nods and gestures, creating a doorway out of nothing.

*Enter,* it says, in its most sepulchral voice, and Trouble touches hand to forehead in mock salute. The door opens at her approach, and she steps through into Seahaven.

It is Venice, today, or perhaps Amsterdam—Trouble has been to neither—all tall, narrow houses lining a canal that reflects trees made of light. She smiles, acknowledging its genuine beauty, and walks on into the image, ignoring the door that closes and vanishes behind her. Light glitters from the black water at her left hand; more lights glow in the windows of the houses to her right. Overhead, grey on black, clouds flow too fast across a starless night. She doesn't recognize these buildings, but some things never change in Seahaven, and she starts walking, following the slow curve of the canal, until, just where she'd expected it, she finds a bridge. She crosses that, still walking alone, her footsteps ringing on the stone, striking sparks, no sign of other visitors, turns left, and emerges abruptly into a crowded plaza. At its far end looms a terraced pyramid like an Aztec temple, winged lions and eagles poised in combat on each corner: always the same symbol, always the same place, here at the heart of Seahaven: the Mayor's palace. She strides through the crowd as though they don't exist—and most of them are pale, compared to her, unwired—ignoring the occasional surprised murmur, just her name, *Trouble*, like distant thunder, and walks up the steps until she stands under the arch of the Mayor's palace.

*Mr. Mayor.* She is playing to the crowd as well as to the presence that made the city, and enjoys it, enjoys their leashed interest, the pretense of indifference that deceives no one. There is a pause, and she wonders if the Mayor is going to make her wait, punish her for her presumption, and she resolves to rip a hole in the wall before she lets him do that to her. But then the arch lights, slowly, and a ghostly shape takes shape within it, wraith-thin, wraith-pale even without the black drapery, crowned in black and the pale blue-silver of stars.

*So,* the voice says, too soft to be heard beyond the portico, and an instant later she feels the air congeal as the Mayor seals the space behind them, surrounding them with a cool sphere of opal light. *It is you. I heard you were dead.*

Hoped, maybe, Trouble thinks—they were not enemies, but were

*never friends; she was wary of Seahaven, respectful but not adula-
tory, and the Mayor has always preferred something close to wor-
ship. She says, *It's me.*

*And what does Trouble want here?* the Mayor asks. *I'm not at
all sure we want trouble.* He isn't wired, or his icon would have
smiled; still, his tone points up the double meaning, childish though
it may be.

*I have business,* Trouble says, *and as a courtesy, I thought I'd
give you notice.*

*Fair warning?* the Mayor murmurs.

*If you like. Someone's been using my name, causing me prob-
lems—Treasury's down on me, from the old days, and I'm not
happy. Maybe this new Trouble thinks I'm dead, thinks the name's
free for use, maybe it's just stupid, I don't know. But I want my
name back. No one uses my name for the kind of shit this new Trouble's been pulling.* She stops, pulling back from the anger, continues more calmly. *This is fair warning, and I want to make sure
this punk sees it. I'm back, I'm the only Trouble there is, and I don't
take kindly to imposters.*

There is another silence, the Mayor's icon looking down at her
with the same faint, unchanging, superior smile she remembers
with annoyance, and then he says, *Why come here?*

He wants his tribute, and she gives it, grudging: *Because Seahaven's still the center of the business—always has been, probably
always will be. Because I know everyone who's anyone will come
through here, in time. This—new Trouble—will get my message if
I leave it here."

The icon bends its head in regal thanks, complex display for
someone not on the wire. Showoff, Trouble thinks, says nothing.
The Mayor says, *I'll post it myself, red-line warning, if you'd
like.*

Trouble lifts her head, surprised—it's not like the Mayor to offer
anything, much less something actively useful, and least of all to
her—and the icon gestures stiffly with its working hand.

*The new Trouble, as you call it, has been attracting too much
attention. I've had to shut down for a couple of days myself—I'm
only just up again. It's time it was warned to behave.*

*I'd appreciate it,* Trouble says.

*Then give me a name-sign.*

Trouble reaches into her toolkit for the seal she hasn't used in three years, wakes the program and waits while it churns a tiny image out onto the net. It is her icon, the dancing harlequin; imbedded in the image are more fragments of code that by their presence identify it as hers alone and by their absence betray any attempt to tamper. She hangs it in the air in front of her. The Mayor waves his hand, and it shrinks; he makes a gesture like putting it into his pocket, and the shimmering image vanishes.

*I'll post that message,* he says, and Trouble answers, *Thank you.*

The opal sphere dissolves. She steps back through the last wisps of it—they cling to her for an instant, cold and damp as fog, then curl away—and sees the others watching, openly now, as she walks back across the square. She doesn't recognize many of the icons— it's been three years since she's walked the shadows, and three years is long enough for most of her peers to have vanished, the hands behind the icons retired, imprisoned, or dead—but they know hers, and they make way for her, no one quite daring to question. She walks back out of the crowd, out of the plaza, feeling the old joy singing in her, the old delight at her mastery, and turns left across another illusory canal. A few of the icons follow, slipping discreetly after her; she grins to herself, readying a program of her own—just let them try to follow me home—and gestures, looking for the nearest outbound node. It has always been easier to leave Seahaven than to enter it: a door appears almost at once, and she opens it, steps back out into the hubbub of the BBS. Two icons follow, with an attempt at stealth. She laughs and makes no attempt to conceal it, sets her program free, and in the same instant cuts her connection, letting the prepared retrieval snatch her home.

# • 5 •

T ROUBLE STRAIGHTENED SLOWLY, shrugging her shoulders against the inevitable stiffness. One foot had gone to sleep, despite her precautions; she made a face, working her ankle until the pins-and-needles faded to a distant buzz. Then she unplugged herself from the system and began breaking down the machines. The euphoria was fading rapidly, curdling to melancholy, an inevitable reaction. The coffee in the thermos was still warm, and she drank it in gulps, more for the liquid and the caffeine than for the taste. It was late, but she still had time and to spare to make her rendezvous with van Liesvelt. If he gets the message, a voice whispered in her brain, but she pushed the thought aside. You could rely on Butch—she could rely on Butch; that had been demonstrated a dozen times in the past, and the fact that he'd come up to the co-op to warn her only proved that nothing important had changed. But of course it had: all the important things had changed. She wasn't with Cerise anymore, wasn't even legal anymore, despite her best efforts, and Carlie was dead and David was in jail and the survivors, the old gang, all van Liesvelt's and her friends, Cerise and Helling and Aledort and Arabesque and Dewildah, scattered God knows where— She shook the memories away, angry with herself now for indulging her mood, the down side of her net triumph. Better to stay angry, she thought, and slung the bag of components up onto her shoulder, leaving the thermos and the cup for someone else to deal with.

As promised, Jesse had the trike ready for her in the back lot, complete with temporary registration and jane-doe ID chip, and a secondhand helmet that carried a heads-up display and a datacord. She loaded her bag into the cargo box slung between the rear wheels and pulled on the helmet, plugging herself in to the machine's limited control system. Lights flashed green, and she felt the faint buzz of pleasure that confirmed the diagnostic's report. For a moment she hesitated, wondering if she should try to make the drive tonight, but she was still tense and angry from her conversation with the committee—and besides, she told herself, you made a deal with Butch. Might as well use the adrenaline. She kicked the trike to life, and swung it out of the crowded lot before she could change her mind. It was a heavy machine, stiff in the steering, but reasonably powerful, and she knew she had the hang of it by the time she'd worked her way through the tangled streets to the entrance to the main flyway. Lights flashed in the helmet display, warning her that the flyways were under grid control and urging her to tie herself in as well. She hesitated for an instant—jane-does, temporary registration, were just that, temporary, and could set off alarms; on the other hand, the surest way to get stopped by a traffic patrol was to stay off the grid—and touched the yes/no pad under her thumb. The machine steadied under her as she picked up speed, and the lines of the grid gleamed in her helmet screen. She leaned forward, letting the noise and the wind carry away the worst of her anger.

She reached the outskirts of the city a little after three, as the class-two bars were closing and the after-hours clubs were opening for business, rode the flyway in over the darkened suburbs, spiraling down the ramp at the Park exit as the gridlines vanished from her helmet. McElwee Park was as apparently deserted as always, but she gave it a careful berth anyway, knowing that the shadows hid a small army of dealers. The Park District was less busy than usual, only a few smaller trucks stopped outside an occasional shop, tired-looking crews slinging boxes down through the sidewalk hatches in the orange glare of the loading lights, but she drove cautiously anyway, paralleling the arch of the flyway. Most of the old landmarks were still there, though there was just the raw scar of a foundation where the Teleos Theater had been, and at last she turned onto the side street that ran into the shadow of the flyway. The club was there, just where it had always been, tucked into the shadow of one of the massive supporting pillars; she wondered, not for the first time, how Mickey had managed to bribe or beat the gangs away from his door. The business lamp was lit, casting a sickly yellow light onto the pavement. The street to either side was crowded with vehicles, inexpensive runabouts and cycles sharing space with bigger, meaner machines that glittered with security: Mickey's Wild Goose was, unmistakably, still in business.

Trouble found a parking place between the streetlamps and set the unfamiliar security fields, then slung her bags over her shoulder and started toward the door. She was more tired than she had realized; the anger had worn off somewhere on the long drive, and the exhilaration of the drive itself was fading. She could feel a dull stiffness in her shoulders and down her back from the trike's steering, and knew she would be sore in the morning. She sighed, laying her hand over the tiny call-plate, and waited, feeling the night chill creep over her, until the panel that covered the bulletproof peephole slid open.

"Private club." The voice came from a speaker below the peephole. The panel started to slide closed again, but Trouble caught it, exerting all her strength to keep it open.

"I'm a member."

"Yeah?" The voice was frankly incredulous. "Let's see some ID."

Trouble bit back a curse and reached into her pocket, came up with a silver disk engraved with her dancing harlequin. She had thought, before, that it had been stupid to keep it. She smiled, bitterly amused by her own assumptions, and held it in front of the peephole. There was a little silence, and then the voice spoke.

"Well, fuck me like a dog. I guess you better come in."

The door opened, and a wave of smoke and sound came with it, so that she blinked and nearly stumbled on the high threshold. The main room was unexpectedly crowded, two dozen men, maybe more, gathered around the little tables, and all of the data towers along the walls were occupied: a very busy night, she thought, or else Mickey was running a promotion. Van Liesvelt was not among them. She made her way toward the massive bar at the center of the room, very aware that she was the only woman present, and the only person not wearing the cracker's elaborate regalia, chains and leather or silk and suit. She could see herself in the dull gold mirror behind the bar: a tall woman, broad shoulders made even wider by the army surplus trenchcoat she wore over jeans and jacket, her silhouette made even more bulky by the bags slung over her shoulder. Her face looked pale in the uncertain light, pale and grim. She had forgotten, until just now, how much she had always disliked Mickey's Wild Goose.

The senior bartender ignored her as she leaned against the bar, but the junior, a stocky woman with a worn, rawboned face, came sliding down to meet her. Trouble controlled her annoyance at the slight, but heard her voice rough and irritable anyway. "Get me a cup of coffee, please. And I'll want to use a phone."

The woman nodded, but made no move to reach for the coffee urn. "There's a five-dollar minimum now," she said, and glanced up, meeting Trouble's eyes in brief, woman-to-woman apology. "Excluding services."

Trouble looked at her for a long moment, but knew it would do no good to confront her. She could hear the silence behind her, the conversations not quite picked up where they had been left, the whispered speculation. "Is the kitchen still open?" She didn't dare drink, not as tired as she was, but food could only help, might keep her awake until van Liesvelt arrived.

"Yeah," the bartender said, and touched a hidden pressure point. A menu lit beneath the bar's surface, displaying a dozen different items.

"Fine." Trouble scanned it quickly: junk food, the kind of thing the shadows seemed to thrive on. "Give me a double burger with everything, fries, and the coffee. And I'll still want to use the phone."

The bartender nodded, her fingers moving on a hidden touchpad, and Trouble heard a snort of laughter at her shoulder. She turned, not fast, and saw a forty-something man in a decent business suit standing beside her. He had braced himself against the bar, and she could smell the gin on him.

"You're not watching your weight, I guess."

Trouble lifted an eyebrow at him, and his face changed, as though he'd realized that she might be someone, after all. "Not that you need to, of course."

"And not that it's any of your business," Trouble said,

quite gently, and laid her ID disk on the counter for the bartender, icon-drawing upwards. The man's eyes flicked from it to her and back again, widening slightly in recognition.

"No. Sorry." He looked down the bar. "Hey, Millie, what do I have to do to get served?"

"Sorry," the bartender said, wearily. "That's another gin-and-tonic, and a scotch, up?"

"Right."

Trouble lifted an eyebrow, but said nothing. The bartender worked her machines, produced two more short glasses, and set them down in front of the stranger. He took them with the care of a man who's already had too many, and turned away without leaving a tip. The bartender's mouth tightened, but she looked away. "You wanted coffee?"

Trouble nodded. "Please."

"Cream and sugar?"

"Black."

The bartender nodded, and headed back down the bar toward the coffee machine. Trouble leaned against the heavy display top, watched the menu flashing under her elbows. This was what she hated most about the on-line world, the shadows as much as the bright lights of the legal nets: too many men assumed that the nets were exclusively their province, and were startled and angry to find out that it wasn't. They were the same people who feared the brain-worm, feared the intensity of its sensations, data translated not as image and words alone, but as the full range of feeling, the entire response of the body, and, rather than ever admit fear, they walked with raised hackles, looking for a fight. It had gotten worse since Evans-Tindale: the new laws had broken the fragile alliances that had held the nets together, rewarding one set of netwalkers over the rest. Behind her, she could hear the conversations slowly starting up again; she could also hear the edge to them, ready to tumble into mockery or hostility. She loosened the belt of her coat, let it hang loose over her jacket and the open-necked shirt, and reached for the mug that the bartender slid toward her.

"You said you wanted a phone?" the bartender asked.

"Yeah," Trouble said, and took a cautious sip of the coffee. "Can you run it here?"

"Sure." The bartender reached under the counter, came up with a familiar black-and-silver comset, set it in front of the other woman. Trouble took it, smiling her thanks, and reached around the side for the datacord. This was precaution more than necessity, and she was not surprised to feel a faint pressure, the trace of another presence haunting her line. She blinked once, saw familiar icons overlaid on her vision, let herself fall into the fast time of the net—

—and sees lines running silver across her eyes, weaving through the bar, sees a stranger on the line, an unknown icon, generic in shape—there to listen? to spy? simply to harass? She carries nothing more than utilities in her bioware, runs the rest from hardware—and cuts that thought as useless. The phone system is there, and the local machine that drives it, and that's weapon enough, in her hands. She reaches for the phone buttons, fingers impossibly slow, touches four keys to override the local system—syscop's privilege—and then she's in the heart of the system. She finds a dormant tracer, long unused, and launches it. It strikes gold at once, and as the numbers come up in front of her eyes, she repeats them, ties herself to the stranger's phone and sets her fingers on two buttons at once, letting the shrill noise echo painfully through her ears, into the nerves where the brainworm can amplify it to the point where even the unwired can hear, and feel—

—and blinked away the silver lines, the blinding icons, to see one of the men at the corner table, a young man, spike-haired in a leather jacket draped with chains, jerk the cord out of his head, wincing at the feedback.

"Wired, by God," someone said, not quite softly enough.

Trouble smiled, very slightly, and nodded toward the spike-haired man. She could feel herself falling into the old stance, all lazy confidence, one thumb hooked into the pocket of her jeans, the open coat swinging from her shoulders like a cape, and disciplined herself to show no further sign of the delight that bubbled up in her. It had been a long time since she'd had to play that game.

She turned back to the bar, certain now that no one else

would try to bother her, and keyed in van Liesvelt's codes. There was a little pause, the signal pulsing in her head, and then the machine clicked on.

"Hi, this is Butch. I'm not home right now—"

She cut it off, knowing—hoping, anyway—that van Liesvelt was on his way, and pulled the cord free of the dollie-slot, letting the hidden spring tug it back into its housing. She was suddenly very tired, but didn't dare relax, not yet, not in front of this crowd. She took another swallow of the hot coffee, and the bartender slid a plate onto the counter in front of her. Trouble nodded, and looked around for the chit to thumbprint.

The bartender waved a hand, the gesture screened from the rest of the bar. "No charge," she said softly.

"Thanks," Trouble said, startled, but the other woman was already looking away.

"You done with the phone?"

"Yeah, thanks," Trouble said, and the bartender carried it away. Trouble shrugged to herself, and turned her attention to the food.

She realized that she was hungry as soon as she took the first bite of the hamburger. The meat was rare, the way she'd always liked it, and seasoned with coarse black pepper; the tomato tasted of summer. She finished it quickly, along with the first cup of coffee. The bartender, silent, still not meeting her eyes, refilled the mug, and Trouble started on the fries. The club seemed to be getting used to her presence: the conversations resumed, and once or twice she heard ordinary laughter, though the men who came to the bar for drinks gave her a wide berth. She ignored them, and they ignored her; still, she knew a few of them were staring when they thought she wasn't looking, not entirely hostile, now, but curious and, maybe, just a little bit afraid. The unregenerate shadow-walker in her rejoiced at the thought.

She was finishing the last french fry when the door opened again, and she looked up to see van Liesvelt standing silhouetted against the dawn light. She lifted a hand in greeting, and pulled herself up from against the bar. Van Liesvelt came to meet her, holding out his arms in greeting. It was done for effect, she knew, to annoy the watching netwalkers, who held back from physical display off the nets, fastidious to the point of prudishness. She returned the embrace with interest, was enveloped in his familiar smell.

"So you're back in the game. You look," van Liesvelt said, "like a gunslinger."

Trouble laughed softly, not entirely displeased by the image. "I'm back," she agreed, loudly enough for the entire bar to hear, and reached for the bag she had left at her feet. "I appreciate the favor."

"No problem at all," van Liesvelt said, and held the door.

Trouble walked past him into the morning light, the rising sun throwing shadows the length of a city block. The air smelled of oil and dew. Somewhere in the distance, she could hear the rumble of an early train; closer at hand, a truck engine whirred and finally caught, settled into a steady rhythm.

"Sorry about the short notice," she said, "but I'm in a bit of a bind."

"It's all right," van Liesvelt said. "I'm sorry I'm late." He looked around, blinking a little in the strong light. "What are you driving?"

"I bought a trike."

"Bring it," van Liesvelt said. "I bought a place with parking last year."

"That's new." Trouble started toward the tricycle, reaching into her pocket for the security remote, and van Liesvelt grinned.

"The fines were getting expensive." He stopped beside a rust-mottled runabout, tugged the door open. "You can follow me. There's not enough traffic this time of day to complicate things."

Trouble nodded, and deactivated the trike's security field. She slung her bag back into the carrier, thumbed on the engine, and then sat, motor idling, while van Liesvelt coaxed the runabout into reluctant motion. She followed him along the uncrowded main street, back past the park, and then along the edge of the district until they came to the black-glass walls of the Interbank complex, and finally turned down a side street she didn't recognize. At its far end, they turned again, into a cul-de-sac that was still entirely in shadow. Van Liesvelt pulled his runabout to a stop outside a tired-looking wooden door, popped the driver's door, and climbed out. Trouble pulled the trike in behind him, lifted off her helmet.

"What's this?"

"My place." Van Liesvelt snapped open an ancient padlock, and hauled at the door. "Give me a hand, will you?"

Trouble came to join him, put her own weight against the door. It resisted for a moment longer, then slid open, the unoiled hinges shrieking. She winced, and said, "You could fix that, you know. You could even get a motor, and a remote hookup."

"You can jimmy electronics a lot easier than you can fiddle this," van Liesvelt said, and stepped back into the runabout.

That was true enough, Trouble thought, and went back to the trike, waiting for him to roll the runabout into the darkness. The machine vanished, and its engine cut out; a moment later, a light came on inside. Trouble sighed, and pushed the trike into the garage, edging as close to the walls as she could. There was just enough room. "So, what have you been up to, that you need that kind of security?"

"Stuff," van Liesvelt answered, and grinned. He was standing at another door, this one opening onto a stairway.

"Sorry," Trouble said, and lifted her bags out of the trike's carrier.

"I'll tell you when you've had some sleep," van Liesvelt said, and led the way up the stairs.

She was never fully sure, afterwards, just how she got into the apartment, woke at sunset to the soft sound of voices in the outer room. As she had expected, her shoulders were tight from the trike's steering, and she stretched cautiously, working the muscles until they loosened. She sat up carefully, tilted her head to listen, until she was sure she didn't recognize the voice of whoever it was with van Liesvelt—a woman's voice, certainly, but that was all. She swung herself out of the narrow bed, scanning the room—landlord-white walls, the bed, her bags set on top of the only table, bare soft-tile underfoot, typical cheap city flat—and padded naked across the floor to collect her clothes. She wondered briefly if van Liesvelt had undressed her, or if she'd managed it herself, then shook the thought away and began pulling on clothing.

Dressed in jeans and loose pullover, she pulled the door open, found herself looking out into a hallway drenched in red light. The setting sun was framed in the window at the end of the hall, sinking into the jagged skyline; the voices were louder, van Liesvelt and the woman, and she started down the hall toward them, her bare feet silent on the tiles. She paused just outside the only open door, and heard van Liesvelt laugh, low and genuinely amused. That sounded safe enough, and she stepped into the doorway. Van Liesvelt was standing in the center of the crowded, brightly lit room, a small glass in one hand, a frosted bottle in the other, and a fat woman sat on the couch in front of him, looking up. The television flared soundlessly behind her, displaying a weather report. She saw the movement behind van Liesvelt, and leaned sideways, frowning. Trouble lifted both hands, displayed them empty, and van Liesvelt turned to face her.

"Good morning to you, Trouble."

"Good morning. Or whatever." Trouble came on into the room, aware of the fat woman's eyes on her, and was careful to keep her hands very much in sight. There was something about the stranger's stance, the controlled stillness of her heavy body, that made Trouble feel the need for caution.

"You want a drink?" van Liesvelt went on, and Trouble nodded. "Vodka all right?"

"I expect it'll have to be," Trouble answered, and van Liesvelt's grin widened.

"It's what I've got."

"It's fine." Trouble looked sideways, saw the stranger still watching her, looked back at van Liesvelt. "It'd be nice if you'd make introductions, Butch."

"Oh, yes." Van Liesvelt filled another of the small glasses and handed it across. Trouble took it, feeling the cold of the vodka even through the heavy glass. "This is a good friend of mine from the nets, the lady you were looking for—she's since your time, Trouble, but she's very, very good. Michellina Huu."

The fat woman nodded, gravely.

Van Liesvelt went on, "And this is Trouble—not the one you're thinking of."

Huu smiled at that, almond eyes narrowing. "I'm glad. No one needs that hassle."

"That's what she's here about," van Liesvelt said. "Am I right, Trouble?"

Trouble seated herself on the edge of the chair nearest the door, said, "That's right. I don't take kindly to someone usurping my name."

Huu said, "Who does?" She was very well dressed, Trouble saw, a heavy silk suit that almost had to be bespoke, and a few pieces of what looked like carved jade. Her sleek black hair was cut in an angled cap that flattered her broad face, and Trouble felt distinctly plain by comparison.

"I told her you'd be wanting to do some business," van Liesvelt said, and Trouble nodded.

"Yeah, thanks. I've been working in the bright lights for a few years," she said, talking through him now to Huu. "It's about time I had an upgrade."

"Well," Huu said. She looked from Trouble to van Liesvelt and back again, and her impassivity broke into a sudden good-natured grin. "You're a closemouthed bastard, Butch. You might give me a little more warning. Exactly what are you looking for, Trouble?"

"I told you to bring your kit," van Liesvelt said. "And a full set of spares."

"That might have been for you," Huu said. "God knows, you're always blowing something."

Trouble said, "I need a new processor, for a worm. I've been hearing about the Prior high-speed set, but I'm open to suggestions."

"It's a good set," van Liesvelt said.

"Expensive," Huu said.

"How expensive?" Trouble looked from one to the other, and van Liesvelt shrugged.

"It runs about thirty-five hundred, installed," Huu said.

"I heard you were family," Trouble said.

"That is the family price," Huu answered.

Trouble lifted an eyebrow.

"That includes the board, and the plate, plus the linkage," Huu said. "And everything's new, straight-out-of-the-factory steriles, so you don't have to worry about who had them last. And the BOSRAM update, of course. Plus installation. And I don't take plastic."

Trouble sighed, calculating. She could afford it, but it wouldn't leave her much for other expenses. "I've got thirteen-fifty in citiscrip and twelve hundred in bearer cards. Another four-fifty in U.S. dollars."

Huu looked at van Liesvelt, who nodded slowly. "I'll cover the rest."

"That's not necessary, Butch," Trouble began, and van Liesvelt waved away her protest.

"Yes, it is."

Huu said, "Pay me three thousand up front, you can owe me the rest."

Trouble nodded. "When can we do this?"

Huu spread her hands. "Butch told me to bring my kit. Now, if you'd like."

"Worm and all?" Trouble asked sharply. The linkages were complex; even though the original installation had done the hardest work, running the molecular wires directly into the brain, fitting the new processor to the input channels needed painstaking care.

"I was trained in Europe," Huu said, and grinned. "Amsterdam."

Van Liesvelt nodded.

Trouble nodded back, reassured. Amsterdam was the great center for legal training. "You've got a Prior with you?"

"Everyone wants them," Huu answered. "Of course I carry them."

"All right." Trouble looked at van Liesvelt, recognizing her own reluctance and impatient with it, but unable quite to control it. "Can I get something to eat?"

"Not until I'm finished," Huu interrupted.

"I'll put something in the nuke," van Liesvelt said. "You want to use the bathroom, Doc?"

Huu nodded, but stayed in her place. Cash in advance, Trouble thought, and pushed herself up out of her chair. "I'll get the money."

The hall was dark now, lights gleaming in the buildings beyond the window. She made her way back into the little bedroom, switched on the blinding overhead light, and rummaged in her bags until she'd collected the money. It was probably the best thing for her, doing the installation more or less spur of the moment, and she knew she should be grateful to van Liesvelt for setting it up like this. She hated the installation process, which he knew, hated it more each time she had to go through it, and it was better not to have to spend a night or two sweating over it. It wasn't so much the risk of a screw-up. That was there, all right, less likely than an accident on the flyway but worse to contemplate, brain miswired, or damaged, leaving her a drooling idiot. It was a risk she'd learned to live with, faced every time she confronted serious IC(E) or even, on some level, every time she stepped out onto the net itself. Power surges happened, rare but real, overriding the inbuilt safeties of the implanted systems, and there was nothing you could do about it, except stay off the net altogether. No, it was the installation itself she hated, and tuning her reflexes to the new system, body given over to pure sensation, inflicted without passion, without feeling, by a stranger's hands. Maybe that was why the serious netwalkers, the original inhabitants of the nets, hated the brainworm: not so much because it gave a different value, a new meaning, to the skills of the body, but because it meant taking that risk, over and above the risk of the worm itself. Maybe that was why it was almost always the underclasses, the women, the people of color, the gay people, the ones who were already stigmatized as being vulnerable, available, trapped by the body, who took the risk of the wire. And you are trying to put this off, she told herself firmly. Get on with it.

She went back into the main room, laid the money on the low table in front of Huu. The citiscrip foils glittered in the light, bright against the bearer cards and the crumpled wad of oldmoney. Huu counted it quickly, and slipped the pile into her jacket pocket.

"All right," she said, and stood, reaching for the bulky case that stood at the end of the couch. "Shall we get started?"

"Fine," Trouble said, and didn't know if she was glad that Huu was a woman. It had been easier with Carlie, they'd been old friends, and there was no possibility—well, no likelihood—of sex between them.

"It's down the hall," van Liesvelt said. "Last door on the right. I should have anything you need, Doc."

"Thanks," Huu said, and motioned to Trouble. "After you."

The bathroom was bigger than Trouble had expected, with room enough between the shower and the sink and toilet for a solid-looking table. Huu set her bag on its white-painted surface, popped the latches, and began lifting out equipment. "Have a seat," she said, and plugged in a portable sterilizer, then turned to shrug out of her jacket, hanging it neatly on the back of the door. The clean-field lit with a whine as the sterilizer warmed up, and a bright cone of purple-tinged light formed in the center of the table. Huu set a handful of instruments under it, and drew on rubber gloves, white and dead-looking against her dark skin. "And then let me have a look at what you've got in there now. What's your status?"

"Negative." Trouble lowered the toilet lid, sat down warily.

"Tilt your head."

Trouble did as she was told, looking down and to her left to expose the dollie-slot. Rubber fingers ruffled the short hair, probed gently, and then Huu took her hand away, smoothing the other woman's hair as absently as she'd disarranged it.

"That's a nice chip you've got in there now. Do you want to keep it, or trade it in? I'll credit you for the balance of what you owe, for a trade."

There was no point in keeping the extra chip: it wouldn't run in tandem with the Prior system. "Make it seven-fifty, and you've got a deal."

"Six."

"Seven?"

Huu hesitated, then nodded. "Seven." She turned back to the table, and Trouble heard the whine of an electric razor. "Tilt your head again."

Trouble looked down again, and a moment later the razor's tip tingled against her neck, hair dropping away from around the dollie-slot and down the back of her neck. Huu brushed away the last stray pieces and picked up an injector the size of her thumb.

"This is going to sting," she said, and put the tip against Trouble's skin.

Trouble hissed at the touch—it was more than a sting, it was a definite jab, a deep stab of pain right through to the bone—but didn't pull away. The pain was followed by an immense cold, and then a numbness, spreading out from the dollie-slot. It crept up her scalp, tingling at the top of her head, wrapped around her neck, and took in her whole right ear.

"Jesus," she said, and couldn't feel her jaw moving in the right-hand socket. "That was quick."

"That's how it's supposed to be," Huu said. She set an instrument tray—also hazed with purplish light—on the back of the toilet, and turned Trouble's head into position. "Keep still."

Trouble froze, and felt the distant pressure of Huu's arm, her left forearm, against the back of her scalp. Something tickled near the dollie-slot, and, it seemed a long time later, she felt something damp on her back just below the knob of her spine. Metal clashed once behind her head, then again in the instrument tray. She slanted her eyes sideways without moving her head—she couldn't have moved her head if she'd wanted to; Huu's weight held her steady as a rock—and saw something like a piece of raw meat, tossed beside the bloodied scalpel. A moment later, Huu's hand came into sight, laid the thick wafer of the old chip into the tray, and Trouble realized that she had been looking at a piece of her own scalp. There was another brief moment of pressure, and Huu grunted softly.

"All in. Now I have to attach it. You know the drill, it's going to hurt, but it'll be over in a second."

Trouble winced—she did indeed know the drill, had done this twice before without it getting any easier—and braced her hands against her knees, digging her nails into the denim as though the extra pain would help.

"Now," Huu said, and Trouble felt a fat snap like a giant static charge at the back of her head. She jerked in spite of herself, and the pain ebbed to a dull, distant ache. It throbbed slightly, in tune to her heartbeat.

"In and on," Huu said. She took her hand away, and Trouble lifted her head cautiously. The anesthetic was starting to fade; her neck hurt, but not too badly, yet. Huu held out a towel that smelled strongly of antiseptic. Trouble took it, dabbed gently at her head and neck, and brought it away spotted with blood.

"Calibration next," Huu said, her voice perfectly neutral, and slipped the head of a datacord into the sterilizer's field. Trouble looked back over her shoulder, and saw the instrument bag gaping open to reveal the square black shape of an output box, all its telltales lit and the display screen glowing pale grey. "Ready?"

Not really, Trouble thought, but nodded. "Let's get it over with."

"Right. Look away, please," Huu said.

Trouble took a deep breath, and swung around so that she was sitting with her back to Huu. She leaned forward, bracing her forearms against her thighs, and felt Huu's fingers cold on her neck.

"I'm beginning now," Huu said, and Trouble took another deep breath—

*and sprawls out into darkness, like but not the net, blind and deaf and dumb and insensate. The worm in her brain lies dead, and she is nowhere, nothing—and then light sparks, brilliant red and gold explosions across her eyes, surrounding her. The feeling comes next, hot wind and then more, sheer heat, slamming against her body with the hot smell of gunpowder, fireworks, and sound follows, a great inchoate roar that fills her ears to bursting and then reverberates, soundless, in her bones. She would cry out, turn away, but the explosions are already fading to a drab landscape, light grey plane under dark grey sky.*

*\*Stand up,\* a voice says, and she does as she's told, the flat grey ground spongy under her feet. She hears a snatch of song as she moves, harsh and incongruous—\*got nipples on my titties big as the end of my thumb, got something 'tween my legs make a dead man come\*—but the memory-music fades as Huu tunes the system tighter. \*Walk.\**

*And Trouble walks, steps out across the endless and unchanging plane. A wind touches her, gentle at first, caressing her naked body, then harder, stinging slaps against back and thigh and breast. She tastes sand, smells heat and rubber. She keeps walking, and walks out of the wind, the plane tilting underfoot so that she is now going uphill. She lengthens her stride, enjoying the challenge, and the ground gets steeper, so that she's breathing hard and finally leans forward into the slope, pulling herself up with hands as well. Her fingers sink for an instant into the grey mass, a sensation like dust or fog between them, and she feels the shock of panic, as though she will fall through a barrier that is solid to her feet and legs. Then the slope steadies, first to soft mud and then to the same smooth rubber that she feels under her feet, and she keeps climbing, until at last she tops the hill and stands upright again.*

*The plane steadies around her, takes on color and three dimensions. Grass grows underfoot, cool and tickling, and she laughs in spite of herself, feels warmth on one side of her body, and turns to blink up into blue sky and the blinding disk of the sun. She looks down again, and sees a table in the distance, an ordinary picnic table, the kind you see in children's books. There is a box on it, black, one side open into empty darkness. The pleasure fades, seeing it, and she is tempted, as always, to turn and walk away, ignore that last step, but she knows better. She takes another deep breath, walks toward the table, the sun warm along her right side, the grass cool and dew-damp underfoot, smelling of spring and acrid growth.*

*This is the last step, the thing that all the rest leads to, the final tuning of body and brain wire. She looks down at the box—there is always the option to stop now, the cybermeds always give you that choice, but it's a choice to live half-aware, half-blind, clumsy and grotesque on the net. She's been on the wire too long to live like that, and she reaches for the box before she can think too long. She slips her hand into the opening, and the world vanishes in a sheer rush of sensation, pure feeling filling every nerve in her body. She throws back her head, and the feeling turns to pain, pins-and-needles swelling to racking cramp to pure fire, an agony swirling through her until she's nothing but pain. And then it peaks and vanishes, leaving her gasping for an instant before the pleasure starts, rising from the tickle of desire to soaked arousal to racking, orgasmic delight.*

She leaned forward further, pressing her elbows into her thighs, not yet ready to look up and meet Huu's eyes. The blood-spotted towel lay between her feet, where she'd dropped it, and she fixed her eyes on it as though it was something important. Her crotch was hot and wet, body lagging behind her brain, and she smelled of sex. She could hear the sucking sound of Huu peeling off the rubber gloves, and wanted for a painful instant to feel the other woman's hands between her legs, gloved fingers pressing into her clit— She took a deep breath, shook that thought away.

"You're likely to be sore tomorrow," Huu went on, heedless, or, more likely, Trouble thought, diplomatically blind and deaf, "and you should run at quarter power for a couple of days, let yourself get used to the new interface before you try to go at it full on—but you know the drill, you shouldn't have to worry about it. The calibration's good—"

Trouble snorted and stretched to pick up the towel. It ought to have been good, the way she was feeling.

"—perfect to four decimal places, so you shouldn't feel too much difference from your old system, except the speed. Pickup should be a little more precise, too, so you might want to spend some time playing with your precision tools before you actually use them. Swab the incision with alcohol a couple times a day for the next month—I'll give you a dummy plug, if you don't have one."

"Thanks," Trouble said, and accepted the flesh-colored plug, larger and broader-headed than the usual jacks, that Huu held out to her.

"It's a good system," Huu went on, and dumped the contents of the instrument tray into van Liesvelt's sink. "I think you'll like the way it'll run now."

"Thanks," Trouble said again, and pushed herself to her feet. Her jeans were damp between her legs, flesh swollen and unsatisfied. Over Huu's shoulder, she could see the water in the basin tinted faintly pink, the piece of scalp sticking to the side just below the waterline. "I think I want a drink."

She had several. Van Liesvelt had defrosted several entrees, his usual prodigal generosity, and she had some of each as well, as though the food and the alcohol would help ground her. Huu ate with them, devouring noodles and broth with confident pleasure, and she and van Liesvelt spent most of the time debating the relative merits of Stinger and Monaco bioware. Trouble let the familiar talk wash over her, letting herself adjust to the aftershocks, the occasional frisson of unrelated sensation as the swollen scalp around the new implant triggered a reaction. It would take a day or two to settle down fully, and she would use that time to rest, recuperate, stay off the nets and see what could be done in the real world to locate this new Trouble. Once the incision was mostly healed, she would go back on the nets, and start looking in earnest.

She slept better than she'd expected—Huu had left her with pills and strict instructions—but woke with the kind of dull headache that left a person fit for nothing but the lowest grade of television. She had at least half expected it, treated it with more of the pills and a day spent sprawled on van Liesvelt's couch, staring at shopping channels without really seeing either the products or the perky, high-breasted women pitching them. Van Liesvelt ignored her, busy with his machines, gone first into local space composing some small utility, and then out in the net itself, but she was too sore, too tired and aching, even to feel envious. They had dinner delivered, from the Indian restaurant on the edge of the District, and Trouble relaxed into the familiar taste of curries and thick, greasy breads.

By the second day she felt better, so much so that she borrowed van Liesvelt's setup and took her first steps back onto the net. She tuned the brainworm as low as she could, barely a ghost of the usual sensations, but even so, her skin crawled and tingled, itchy with extraneous sensations bleeding in from the healing incision, and she logged off almost at once, swearing to herself.

"Want a cup of tea?" That was van Liesvelt, standing in the doorway of the little room. It was barely more than a closet, windowless and stuffy, warmed by the banked hardware, and Trouble felt suddenly trapped, claustrophobic.

"Yeah, thanks," she said, and, mercifully, van Liesvelt moved his bulk out of the doorway.

"I was thinking," he said. "If this new Trouble is in the business—not just farting around, I mean—then there aren't that many people left who'd have anything to do with it."

"That's true," Trouble said, and followed him down the long hall to the kitchen.

The kitchen itself was unexpectedly bright, overhead lights and electric kettle plugged into the main work island, bright-orange cords stranded through the room's central volume. Outside the double window, the sky was brassy-white, a few more substantial clouds floating above the general haze. They overlooked the alley and the attached garages, low sheds jutting out into the rutted street. The doors were strongly reinforced against thieves, and most were brightly painted, garish against the dull stone. The kettle whistled, and van Liesvelt poured the tea, set the mugs solemnly on the long table.

"So," Trouble said. "Who'd you have in mind?"

Van Liesvelt shrugged. "The usual suspects. Dieter, the Snowman—"

"I heard he was out of the game," Trouble interjected. "In fact, I heard he turned state's evidence about a year back."

"You should know better than to believe everything the syscops tell you," van Liesvelt said, grinning. "He got caught, all right, but beat the rap. They put the story out on him out of spite."

Trouble nodded. "What about Devil-boy?"

"Gone legit."

"That does narrow it down."

Van Liesvelt nodded, fished the teabag out of his mug. "Yeah. It's pretty much Dieter, and the Snowman, and Jimmy Star and Fate."

Trouble pulled out her own teabag and took a wary sip of the spicy, bright red liquid. "I don't know about Dieter, I heard he mostly deals viruses."

"Oh, no," van Liesvelt said, his voice suddenly accentless, mimicking Dieter's thin tones, "not viruses. Never viruses. Just code fragments."

"My ass," Trouble said.

"Not to my taste," van Liesvelt said automatically, and Trouble lifted her middle finger at him. "So, Fate or the Snowman, or maybe Jimmy Star. I think you're right about Dieter. Do you want me to see what I can find out?"

Trouble made a face, but had to admit the logic of the suggestion. She wasn't ready yet for that kind of netwalking, and she didn't have time to wait until she was better, not with Treasury on her heels. "Yeah. Anything at all would be useful."

"Do you want to listen in?"

Trouble hesitated, tempted, but shook her head. Even just lurking, using the brainworm on its lowest setting to follow van Liesvelt's activity, would be as bad as walking the net on her own. "Let me know if you find anything," she said, and van Liesvelt nodded.

"I'll do that." He picked up his mug, and wandered away again, only apparently aimless. Trouble watched him go, bit back her irrational jealousy. She hated the attunement period, hated not being able to walk the nets as freely as she normally could. You survived three years off the wire, she told herself firmly. You can put up with this. She picked up her mug, and went back into the living room to investigate van Liesvelt's collection of tapes.

He had a lot of anime, typical of a netwalker, and one in particular that was familiar, an old favorite of Cerise's: americanime, surreal, queer, and violent. She put it in the player, settled herself on the couch to watch, wondering if she would like it as well without Cerise's commentary. It was old-style, the drawing mannered, elongated, improbable figures against sweeping, computer-managed backgrounds, but the conventions were easy enough to relearn, and she watched, caught up in spite of herself by the stylized plot and people. The latter were real enough, netwalkers she had known and admired years before drawn larger than life, made heroes, and she remembered, suddenly, Cerise talking about the filmmaker. She—it had been a woman, Trouble remembered—had been a netwalker back in the glory days, when the nets had just opened out, before she'd retreated to anime. The brainworm had been very new then, the risks outrageous; safer to draw and dream, Cerise had said.

"Got it," van Liesvelt said from the doorway, and Trouble looked up sharply, automatically muting the player. "It's Fate."

Trouble touched a second button, shutting down the entire system, and stood up. "Is it, now?"

Van Liesvelt nodded. "And he's taking some heat for it— gone to ground, they say, but I know where his bolt-hole is."

"What kind of heat?" Trouble asked.

"Treasury's been interested in him, subpoenaed all the files on that board he runs. Plus local cops set watchdogs on

the system—I heard from Kid Fear that Fate's spent most of
the last few days taking potshots at them."

"Kid Fear?" Trouble lifted an eyebrow at the name, and
van Liesvelt shrugged one shoulder.

"I know. It's either fifteen or pretending to be."

"Is it reliable?"

"So far." Van Liesvelt shrugged again. "You think we
should have a few words with Fate?"

Trouble smiled slowly. "I think so. In person." Fate—his
real name was Kenney, Lafayette Kenney, or something like
that—was notorious for hating to work off-line, so much so
that it was rumored that he had once turned down a million
in citiscrip because it would have involved too many face-to-
face meetings with the client. The story was probably an ex-
aggeration, but it summed up Fate's attitude pretty well.
"You sure you know where he is?"

"Trust me," van Liesvelt said, not even bothering to sound
offended, and Trouble waved away her words.

"Sorry." If van Liesvelt, who made it his business to know
the off-line world as well as the nets, said he knew, he knew.
"When's a good time?"

Van Liesvelt looked at the carpet, checking the time.
"Now's as good as any. He'll be there."

"Good enough," Trouble said. "Shall we take the trike?"

Van Liesvelt shook his head. "My runabout. I don't want
you driving off the grid."

Trouble grinned—she had a reputation from the old days,
not always deserved, as a reckless driver—but went back
into the spare room for her jacket. When she emerged, van
Liesvelt was checking the battery of a stunstick. She gave
him a questioning look—most netwalkers, even from the
shadows, didn't risk running afoul of the strict weapons
laws—and he shrugged.

"I don't think we're heading into trouble, but Fate's got
some heavy friends. I'd rather be careful."

Trouble nodded, accepting the necessity, and followed van
Liesvelt down the stairs into the darkness of the garage.

Traffic was heavy, as always, but van Liesvelt was patient,

easing the runabout through the tangle of cargo haulers and passenger vehicles at a steady pace, until at last they emerged from the District and he could turn onto one of the major cross-town arteries. Here the traffic was just as heavy, but the lines of runabouts and bikes moved more quickly, and they made better time toward the neighborhood where van Liesvelt said Fate had his bolthole. It wasn't a bad area, mostly row houses and the occasional corner storefront complex—groceries, liquor, drugs-and-sundries, a couple of cheap-electronics shacks—and Trouble relaxed against the battered seat cushions. Van Liesvelt found a parking place along the street, beneath a streetlamp, and Trouble climbed out while he fiddled with his security system. The air was cool, the few stunted trees in their iron cages in front of the houses already turning yellow. Trouble fed a couple of foils into the meter, and turned to van Liesvelt.

"So, where is it?"

"About two houses down," he answered, and tilted his head toward a house at the middle of the block, where an adolescent—at this distance, it was hard to tell the gender through the hunched body and the spiked hair—sat on the low steps, staring at nothing.

"That's his security?" Trouble murmured.

"Probably," van Liesvelt said. "Kids are cheap."

Trouble nodded, and followed him toward the house. The boy—at least, she was almost certain it was a boy—looked up as they started up the stairs, but said nothing. The main door was unlocked, but gave only onto a grim-looking lobby, all grey tile and a cluttered letterboard beside the barred door. It looked impressive enough at first glance, but Trouble couldn't repress a grin. The first thing she'd learned when she'd moved to the city was how to jimmy those boards. . . .

"You want to do the honors, or shall I?" van Liesvelt asked.

"Oh, go ahead," Trouble answered, and van Liesvelt produced a credit-card-sized databoard from one pocket. Its reverse was scarred with the lines where new chips had been inserted into the minimal systems. He flourished it once, and inserted it into the keyreader. There was a brief pause, and Trouble, leaning past his shoulder, could just see lights flickering in the tiny display square as the machine searched for a matching code. To her surprise, the lights stayed orange for a long moment, and then a voice crackled from the speaker above the lock.

"Christ, van Liesvelt, is that you?"

*Fate,* van Liesvelt mouthed, and Trouble nodded. Fate had always been good.

"That's right," van Liesvelt said aloud, quite cheerfully, and there was a sigh from the speaker.

"Then I suppose you'd better come up before you break something." The mechanism clicked loudly, and Trouble pushed the door open.

"Only your codes, Fate," van Liesvelt said, and they went up the stairs.

Fate lived on the third floor, at the back, where the fire escape led directly into a side street. Trouble saw the ladder plunging past the landing window, and was reminded of the last apartment she had shared with Cerise. They had wanted the near-impossible, a decent kitchen, quiet bedroom, at least two entrances or a good way out, and as few cockroaches as possible. . . . She shook the memory away as van Liesvelt knocked on a rust-painted door, bracing herself for the meeting with Fate.

The door opened at once, but it was a stranger, blond and stocky in a cheap suit, who looked out at them. He grunted when he saw van Liesvelt, but scowled at Trouble. "What do you want?"

Van Liesvelt said, "Hey—"

Trouble smiled, said, in a voice soft enough to brook no argument, "We're here to talk to Fate."

The blond's scowl deepened, and a second voice said, "Leave it, Phil. Let them in."

Grudgingly, the blond stepped back, opening the door into a surprisingly pleasant apartment. The walls were painted dull cream to match the carpet, and there were a few pieces of good art scattered here and there. Fate was standing in the middle of the room, hands jammed into the pockets of his jeans, long hair caught back in an untidy ponytail. The scar on his face, running from cheek to chin, looked more prominent than before.

"Do you want me to stay?" Phil asked, and Fate shook his head, grimacing impatiently.

"No, I know them."

"Do I search them?" Phil went on, and leered in Trouble's direction. "I'd enjoy searching the double-dollie."

"Go ahead," Trouble said, with the smile she'd cultivated for just that insult, "and I'll be in your records by morning. How's your credit, straight boy?"

Phil flushed, and Fate said, "Don't mess with the net, Phil." His voice was flat, without emotion. "I told you, this was my business. I'll deal with it. You can go."

"Mr. Sinovsky's going to hear about it," Phil said, but turned toward the door.

"Fine," Fate said, and waited. There was a little pause, and then Phil shouldered past, deliberately jostling van Liesvelt. The door slammed behind him.

"Didn't know you were working for the mob these days, Fate," van Liesvelt said.

Fate looked at Trouble. "I didn't know you were back on line."

Trouble nodded. "I hear you've been dealing—fencing for someone using my name. I'm not happy, Fate."

"Your happiness," Fate began, the southern accent suddenly strong again, "—ain't my responsibility."

"I'm making it your business," Trouble said, and took a step closer to Fate. "Treasury made it mine."

Fate stepped backward, maintaining the distance between them. "Treasury's been down on me, too. That's what goddamn Phil was here about."

"Oh," van Liesvelt murmured, "Sinovsky's not going to be pleased about that."

Fate darted an angry glance at him, but said nothing.

Trouble said, "I'm looking for this new Trouble, Fate. I want him, her, or it very badly, because I lost a damn good job because of it, and it's going to pay. Now, you're its fence, you can tell me where it works out of."

Fate shook his head again. "I can't do that, Trouble. I'm running a business now—"

"I don't give a shit about your business," Trouble said. "I'm prepared to bring it down, and you know I can."

There was a little silence, Fate still unmoving, keeping three meters between them, and van Liesvelt said thoughtfully, "Sinovsky can't be pleased by all this attention, not when he's trying to keep a low profile after those shootings."

Fate glanced at him again, grey eyes wary. Trouble said, "He really won't be happy if I have to take action."

Fate looked back at her, took a deep breath. "Trouble—newTrouble—works out of Seahaven."

"Where else?" van Liesvelt murmured

"That doesn't tell me very much," Trouble said. "Hardly worth my time."

"The other Seahaven," Fate said. "His realworld address is somewhere in Seahaven."

Trouble nodded slowly. That made sense: the off-line Seahaven, or at least the beachfront Parcade, was the best source on this coast for grey-market electronics. Where better to live, if you dealt in stolen codes—and besides, from everything she had heard, the new Trouble would probably appreciate the obvious irony of having the same address on- and off-line. "Right, then," she said. "I think I'll pay him a visit. Thanks, Fate."

"Don't mention it," Fate muttered, and van Liesvelt grinned.

"Wouldn't dream of it."

Trouble smiled too, and turned toward the door, opening it for van Liesvelt. She was about to follow him into the hall when Fate called her name.

"NewTrouble's on the wire. I thought you should know."

Trouble turned back to face him, nodding slightly. "Thanks," she said, and then, because that wasn't enough, "I appreciate the warning."

It was more than just a warning, and they both knew it; it

was a declaration that Fate had chosen sides. If newTrouble was half as good as he seemed—and Trouble had no real doubt about it, from the rumors she'd heard and the work she'd seen—then any direct competition between the two of them would be decided by millisecond advantages. Knowing that he, newTrouble, was on the wire might give her just that faction of an edge, the difference that would mean beating him face to face.

Fate made an odd, unfinished gesture, barely more than half a shrug, hands still deep in his pockets, and Trouble remembered that he had never been on the wire. Gossip said he'd gone as far as Carlie's once, actually left his flat and walked cross-town to the storefront clinic where Carlie had been working in those days, and turned around and left before Carlie could even ask what he wanted.

"He's crazy," Fate said, and managed a malicious smile. "Better get Cerise to watch your back—if she's still around."

"Fuck you," Trouble said, and slammed the door behind her. Van Liesvelt gave her a wary look, and she shook her head, suddenly tired of the whole thing. "No, let it be. I got what I wanted."

"All right," van Liesvelt said, visibly doubtful, but Trouble ignored him, starting down the stairs toward the lobby. She had what she came for, newTrouble's address, realworld and on-line, and that was enough. She'd check Seahaven again— virtual Seahaven, the one that mattered—and then . . . She smiled, slowly, without humor. Then she would head back north along the coast highway, to the other Seahaven, and see what this usurper had to say for himself.

# SEAHAVEN

# ▪ 6 ▪

TODAY SEAHAVEN IS a city in flight, and Cerise walks through uncrowded streets while the stars whirl overhead and under her feet, easily seen through the transparent sidewalks. The Mayor's palace looms ahead, always Aztec no matter when the setting, but she ignores it, wanders instead onto the mall where the merchants, legal and not, collect in rows, and a wall displays a thousand messages. Her current icon is known—a comic-book woman, all tits and hips and Barbie-doll waist, but done in one dimension only, exactly like a comic book, so that the shape is paper thin, absolutely flat from certain angles—and so is her current affiliation: the crackers give her a wide berth, and she pretends not to see or recognize the familiar icons. She is interested in Trouble, not trouble, and there's no point in antagonizing the people who might most be able to help her.

She is early at her rendezvous; she walks the length of the wall, scanning the displays. Art swirls through and over the messages, screening content in glorious colors—the Mayor pays in time for artists without other access to decorate his wall—and she enjoys that more than the words, until she reaches the midpoint. And there, in neon-red, hot Chinese red, the artists giving it a wide berth, is a familiar symbol: Trouble's harlequin, brilliant against the dark seeming-stone of the wall itself. Cerise reaches for it, feeling the familiar flicker of codes against her fingers—Trouble's work, no mistake, no forgery, the real thing, not the pale imitation of the new Trouble's work—and the message spills into the air around her.

I'M THE ONLY TROUBLE THERE IS. I DON'T TAKE KINDLY TO IM-POSTERS—FAIR WARNING, LAST AND ONLY WARNING.

Cerise puts the message back where she found it, watches the red symbol reappear around it and flatten itself back against the wall, glowing like fire against the darkness. So my Trouble's back now, she thinks. I knew it wasn't her who did the boasting. For an instant she considers copying the message for Coigne, using it to *force him to admit that her Trouble wasn't the intruder, but common sense intervenes. He will say that this is more clever planning, more evasive advertising, and, from anyone else but Trouble, he could be right.*

She turns away, the stars wheeling overhead, streaks of light in a cloudless dark, wheeling underfoot as well, as though she and the city lay on a plain that bisected a sphere spinning through space. The buildings look sharper-edged, as though seen against fireworks, but she ignores the effect, scans the plaza for Helling's icon. She sees it at last, almost doesn't recognize it—he's changed the symbol, gone from the old blue biplane to a blue thunderstorm, almost invisible, an inky shadow against the greater darkness.

*So you've seen it,* Helling says without preamble, drifting closer, and a tiny fork of lightning briefly touches the dancing figure.

*How could I miss it?* Cerise asks, and hears herself hard and bitter.

*No one else has, either,* Helling agreed. *It's been up for a hundred-twelve hours.*

Cerise whistles softly, amazed that the Mayor would allow anything to occupy space for so long, and Helling goes on, *Treasury's seen a copy, too—and it's been downloaded out of town, of course.*

*Of course.* Cerise looks up at the spinning sky, dizzying herself. This is Trouble's style, this warning: one warning, and God help you if you don't listen, because she won't give another one, or any quarter afterwards. . . . She remembers Trouble, long ago, earning the name she'd taken, tracking a man who hadn't paid her through the nets, and, once she'd found out exactly what he was doing and where in the realworld he was doing it, passing details and location to the police, once a day every day for three weeks—always through complex cutouts; she'd been just as deep in the shadows as her victim—until they'd caught up with the dealer. Trouble had sat smiling at the evening news, and never had to do it again. Cerise shakes her head, shakes the memory away, and looks back at Helling. *I hear you're consulting these days.*

*That's right,* Helling says, and she hears him suddenly wary.

*I also hear you've got a friend at Interpol.*

*Yeah.*

*Anywhere accessible? In reality, I mean.* It occurs to her that she no longer knows where Helling is based—she had heard he was in London, but that was a year ago.

*To you, yeah,* Helling says, sourly. *I'll tell him to have his people call your people.*

*Thanks,* Cerise says.

*One thing, though,* Helling says, and Cerise looks back at him. *Vess wants Trouble, too.*

*I thought Interpol only dealt with multimillions or germ warfare,* Cerise says, already dreading the answer.

*The new name's been linked to a couple of nasty viruses.*

*Bullshit.* The word triggers a lurking watchdog, which materializes as a small and yapping terrier, sparks flying where its claws strike the transparent paving. Cerise glares as it circles her ankles—the Mayor's delicacy never fails to irritate her—waits until it dissolves before she goes on. *Also not Trouble's style. Even less so than boasting.*

*Vess never knew Trouble,* Helling says. *He's a Eurocop, they move in different circles. You sure you want to talk to him, Cerise?* His face shows briefly in the thunderstorm, smiling.

No, Cerise thinks, but says, *I'm sure. Tell him, will you?*

*I'll tell him,* Helling says again. The icon brightens slightly, lifts away from her, lightning flickering through it to outline the clouds.

She watches it go, fading to nothing against the moving sky, makes no move to call him back. There's nothing more to say, not to him, and she walks back down through the plaza under the spinning stars.

Helling was as good as his word, as Cerise had expected. Interpol's local office contacted her secretary, and they juggled schedules until they found a mutually acceptable time for lunch. She took a car and driver—not her usual habit, but she wanted time to think—and as the car slowed in the clotted traffic on the main approach to the downtown business district, she began to wonder if she was doing the right thing. That uncertainty was unlike her, and she frowned, annoyed with herself, and pushed the thought away. What she needed from Interpol was simple, an accounting of the false

Trouble's activities—it would be useful to have something to show the board, to prove that Multiplane was not the only corporation targeted by this particular cracker, plus it would be nice to have more evidence to analyze, to prove to Coigne that it wasn't her Trouble—and maybe, just maybe, she could trade her own information, her knowledge of the old Trouble and her certainty that this was someone else, for Interpol's files. After all, she thought, I was Trouble's partner, and anyone who's been anything in security, even a Eurocop, has to know that. It's the least I can do, for old times' sake. And if I have to, I have other coin to trade. The pun pleased her; she smiled, and saw the driver cast a fleeting glance into his mirror.

The car turned off the flyway, rode the ramp down into the crowded streets. Cerise leaned back in her seat as the hordes of pedestrians flowed around the car like water around the rocks in a streambed, not wanting to pay attention to them, men and women in cheap-corporate suits, the middling sort who kept the companies running and the money flowing. Trouble would have teased her for her contempt, called it arrogance—and she would've been right, had been right about it, but I was right, too, when I said I'd earned it. Cerise frowned slightly, the old apartment coming back to her in a rush of memory, the plain two-rooms-and-a-bath, with a kitchen unit mounted into the wall above the freezer, and Trouble lounging on the foam-core folding couch that was their only piece of furniture. It had been two months before they'd gotten a job that let them pay for anything else, and right after it they'd seen a play on the culture channel that took place entirely in a bed. For weeks, just the thought of it had been enough to send both of them into giggles. Bad enough to be crackers, Trouble had said, that was enough of a stereotype, but artsy crackers. . . .

And this was not the attitude she needed to take to this meeting. Her frown deepened to a scowl, and she took her thoughts firmly in hand. Helling's friend from Interpol was going to want value for any information he let slip; she would have to be at her best, if she was going to win this game. The car slowed again, eased to a stop directly in front of the black glass-fronted building that housed the restaurant they had chosen. The driver locked the engine, and came around to open the door; Cerise climbed out easily, just touching the automatically extended hand.

"I'll be back for you at three, Ms. Cerise?" the driver asked, and she nodded.

"That'll be fine," she said, and went up the shallow marble stairs into the lobby.

The light was darker here, dimmed by the smoky glass, but she knew her way without having to consult the direction boards placed discreetly inside the entrance. She climbed the double staircase and nodded to the man in evening clothes who waited just outside the door.

"Cerise," she said. "I'm meeting a man named Mabry."

The security man nodded back, fingering the silver square of the annunciator clipped to his lapel, and Cerise stepped past him into the suddenly warm light of the restaurant. It wasn't crowded, and a pair of waiters came hurrying to meet her.

"May I help you?" the first—a dark, curvy little woman in a black skirt a little too short to flatter her short legs—asked, in a voice that held the hint of a musical accent. Cerise smiled in spite of herself, in spite of business.

"My name's Cerise," she said again. "I'm here to meet Mr. Mabry."

"Of course. If you'll come this way," the woman answered, and hurried off, glancing back only once to be sure Cerise was still behind her. Cerise followed more slowly, enjoying both the woman's bustling handsomeness and the quiet elegance of the dining room, found herself, as she had expected, at the door of one of the semiprivate rooms. A table for two had been set up there, hidden from any other diners by a standing screen and some towering, broad-leafed plants, and the dark woman gestured toward the table.

"Your party, ma'am."

"Thanks," Cerise said, hoping vaguely that she would be the one to wait on them, and turned her attention to the man at the table. He rose to his feet at her approach, holding out his hand in greeting.

"Ms. Cerise?" It was only half a question, but Cerise nodded anyway, and the man went on, his vowels touched with a flat, European accent. "I'm Vesselin Mabry."

"Pleased to meet you," Cerise said, and allowed herself to be handed to her seat. It was a tactic Eurocops often employed against Yanks, that overdone, unfamiliar politesse, but she had faced it before, rather enjoyed the brittle game of it. He was not quite what she had expected, looked more like an overage rocker than a netwalker: a big man, broad through the shoulders and thick-bodied, with a mane of untidy, greying curls and a fleshy, broad-boned face. Only the jacket betrayed him for a cop, even though he wore it over jeans and a charcoal-grey T-shirt: it was not top-of-the-line, a less expensive copy of a good designer. She smiled to herself, reassured, and leaned forward in her chair.

"Max said you might have some information for me about a cracker I've been hunting."

Mabry didn't even blink, just smiled slowly, the lines at the corners of his eyes tightening with what looked like good humor. "Funny, that's what Max said to me."

Their waiter—not the dark woman, Cerise saw with some disappointment—arrived then, stopping the conversation. He offered menu boards, pointed out the order mechanism, and vanished again, but the interruption had been enough to defuse any advantage she might have achieved.

"I heard on the net that Multiplane had had an encounter with Trouble," Mabry said. "Frankly, I was disappointed that you didn't notify us at once."

"Question of jurisdiction," Cerise said, promptly and plausibly, using the easy lie. "Interpol's network authority comes from the Amsterdam Conventions, and you know we never signed."

Mabry sighed heavily, put his menu aside. "You and I both know that's bullshit. Any law enforcement agency can be notified now, and the word passed to a more appropriate entity if necessary."

"Also bullshit," Cerise said. "We have a responsibility to be certain that our response to an intrusion is overseen by the agency most directly concerned. Which may or may not be your agency—all of which is made moot, of course, by the fact that the company is U.S.-based."

"Multiplane is multinational," Mabry murmured. "You have subsidiaries in Switzerland, Eire, and Germany, just to name Europe. That certainly falls within my brief. And multinationals have traditionally obeyed the Conventions."

Cerise nodded, willing to surrender her position—she had better and stronger ones in reserve—and said, "Which is part of why I'm here, Mr. Mabry."

"Vess. Please."

Like calling a cobra "Cuddles," Cerise thought. It's cute, but it doesn't make me any less careful. "And I'm Cerise."

"No other name?"

"I never needed one." Cerise smiled at him, looked down at her menu, then touched the order strip to select her lunch.

"Except Alice," Mabry said, and matched her smile.

"That was a long time ago," Cerise answered. She had expected him to know that—anyone who was halfway competent on the nets would have found out her old workname, never mind that Helling could have told him—and she refused to be disconcerted by it.

"Yes, it quite dates me," Mabry answered, and Cerise caught herself warming to him. That was dangerous; still, Helling liked him, and Max had never been a fool.

"But we are interested in the same person," Mabry went on. "I would be very glad indeed to see any data you can give me regarding your intrusion."

"You didn't say, we're both interested in Trouble," Cerise said.

"That's the second thing I'd be interested in hearing from you," Mabry said. "The word on the nets is that Trouble is back—the old Trouble, your former partner, I believe—and that this intruder, this cracker who writes viruses, is someone else entirely. Of course, a week ago, everyone was saying the opposite."

"I think it's two different people," Cerise said.

"Why?"

Cerise leaned back in her chair as the waiter appeared with their salads, grateful for the interruption. When the man had left, she went on, "Because none of this is Trouble's style. Not the cracking—our work was surgical, we did exactly what was needed, nothing more, nothing less—and not the boasting afterward. I hadn't heard about viruses until I talked to Max—you must be keeping that very much under wraps, Mr. Mabry—but that's even more not our style, not Trouble's style. Germ warfare is too double-edged. We never messed with it."

"What, never?" Mabry murmured, with a lift of his bushy eyebrows. "I thought it was a rite of passage."

"Don't play devil's advocate with me," Cerise said. "You're old enough to remember the old days. There were standards, even before the law moved in. Responsible people didn't do viruses." She shook her head, the anger cooling rapidly, continued more quietly. "I know, we were breaking the law, off-line law, but we did keep to our own rules."

"I wouldn't have thought you a romantic," Mabry said.

"You were there, too," Cerise answered. "You tell me."

There was a little silence, and then Mabry looked away. "Yes, I know," he said, softly. "I get tired of hearing about it sometimes, that's all."

He was never one of us, Cerise realized suddenly, had never worked the shadows. She eyed him with new wariness and a new respect, not quite sure which she felt—more like what she would feel for some new and exotic species—and Mabry smiled with what looked like self-mockery.

"Still," he said. "Cops should stick together—shouldn't we?"

Cerise smiled, acknowledging the point: whatever he hadn't been, whatever she had been before, right now they were on the same side.

"Max said this wasn't like Trouble," Mabry went on, "or not like the Trouble he knew, and now you're saying the same thing. I find that very interesting."

Cerise hesitated, then, deliberately, touched one finger to her dollie-slot. "This new Trouble doesn't feel the same."

"A brainworm?" Mabry's thick eyebrows rose, and then he grinned. "A European job, I presume."

"Of course," Cerise said, blandly.

"Yet the Treasury savants make a match of it."

"Sixty percent accuracy," Cerise said. "All that means is that they've never seen the newbie before, and that it's using some of Trouble's old programs—which would make sense, if it's stealing Trouble's name. All of which you know."

Mabry grinned again. "Tell me about Trouble."

Cerise looked at him in genuine surprise. "What's Max told you?"

"Very little," Mabry said, and there was a touch of bitterness in his voice. Cerise lifted an eyebrow, and Mabry took a deep breath. "Max and I have been—together—for about a year now, but we don't, he doesn't talk much about his old friends."

"I didn't know you were family," Cerise said.

Mabry touched his own dollie-slot. "Depends on the family," he said, and this time the bitterness was clear.

Cerise nodded once, careful not to show too much comprehension. Helling was on the wire, of course—they had all been, van Liesvelt, herself and Trouble, Max and his then-partner Jannick Aledort, Carlie Held, Arabesque, Dewildah Mason, and David Terrel. They had lived within a subway ride of each other for three years, and had seen each other off the nets perhaps even more than on—and that was part of what the wire had brought them, the desire to know each other in reality as well. And it would be hard for Mabry, a man who stayed within the law, who adapted to the rules of the net—one of the most ironclad of which was, never try to contact the human being behind the net persona—to know that his lover had not only managed an illegal career with an illegal implant, but had broken that rule as well. "Whatever happened to Aledort?" she asked, with apparent inconsequence, and Mabry grimaced.

"He was shot to death," he said, after a heartbeat's pause.

"Two years ago. No one was ever charged, but it was probably Planetaries."

Cerise nodded, feeling suddenly cold despite the restaurant's expensive environmental system. That was two down, out of the old gang, Terrel in jail—still—and Aledort dead, and maybe more gone, if she'd been able to keep in touch. It was no surprise that Aledort had gotten himself killed—ecotage was a dangerous profession, and the Planetary League was a particularly bad group to cross; and besides, Aledort had a nasty streak that almost invited murder—but it was still a little unnerving to contemplate.

"And yes," Mabry went on, with another little smile, "I'm a bad winner."

So we know where we stand, Cerise thought. She said, "We all thought Max could do better than Aledort." She carefully did not say that she thought he had done so, and Mabry's smile broadened for an instant.

"To return to business," he said. "Tell me about Trouble."

Cerise paused, took a deep breath, and was pleased that when she spoke, her voice stayed steady, remote. "We lived together, worked together, for just about four years. She's a brilliant cracker—also on the wire, we all were—with a good sense of place and timing, a nice hand with tools. She used to write most of her own, or modify them. I'm probably a little quicker—she's bigger than I am, and that shows even on the net—but she's probably a little more accurate in the long run. She liked to run really clean programs, the architecture mattered to her, she'd polish things just for the satisfaction of it. That's what's missing with this newTrouble, that sense of precision. Trouble liked to keep things clean." Including leaving me—at least it was clean for her. Cerise put the thought aside along with the flash of memory, Trouble's body pressed against her own, the feel of Trouble's muscled back beneath her fingers as she pulled the other woman closer into a twining embrace, and said, "What's Interpol's interest in all of this?"

There was a little pause, but then Mabry said, "As you know, this new Trouble has been causing a lot of commotion.

Treasury is looking for her—or him—here, ECCI and Interpol are mounting their own investigations as well. Since Trouble, either one, has always worked out of the U.S. nets, I've been sent over to keep an eye on the Treasury investigation, just in case they turn up something we can use. There have been a series of intrusions, scattershot attacks, into the industrial nets in Europe, but we—Interpol is most worried about the viruses."

"Reasonable enough," Cerise said. In spite of herself, she felt another touch of fear worm its way along her spine. You couldn't steal much in a five-second intrusion, but there was plenty of time to leave an infectious program. In fact, she thought, if I were trying to virus a system, that's probably how I'd do it. Break in, leave my virus, and then deliberately trigger the alarms in the hope that the syscops would be too busy trying to trace the intruder to spot any stray bits of code. She bit back the desire to call her people immediately with the warning—they had run scans as soon as the intruder had been spotted; she had returned from her futile chase to find the printouts waiting—and said instead, "The same style?"

"All the ones that have been reported," Mabry said, "follow a similar pattern. A quick intrusion, sometimes a virus inserted, more often not, once a definite theft and subsequent sale, but always boasting afterwards."

"That sounds like what we had," Cerise agreed. "I have a transcript of the event with me, if you'd like to take a look at it."

"I'd like to keep it." Mabry held out his hand, and Cerise slid the disk across the table.

"Please do," she said. "We haven't had any signs of infection, but I'll double-check when I get back to the office."

"I can give you a sample of the payload," Mabry said. "Which hasn't been particularly destructive. And also what we've salvaged of the main code." He produced another disk from his pocket, and held it out. Cerise took it, nodding her thanks.

"If you find anything," Mabry went on, "would you save

it for us? Most of it's been set to self-destruct, but still, any fragments are potential evidence."

"Of course," Cerise said, and slipped the disk into her carrier.

"There's one more thing," Mabry said, "and I'd rather you didn't answer than lie to me. Do you keep in touch with Trouble?"

It was not the question Cerise had been expecting. She hesitated, choosing her words carefully, thought vaguely that he'd paid her back for asking about Aledort. "No. We didn't exactly—part friends. Right before Evans-Tindale passed, we had, well, a disagreement about it, about what we should do. Trouble wanted to bail out then and there, go legit, and I wanted to go on. I had a job in train that I wanted to do, you see." She could almost see the remembered IC(E), almost taste the sharp codes, a new system then, one she'd never broken before, a gaudy, glittering challenge, utterly irresistible to any netwalker of spirit. "We were still arguing about it, about the job, when Evans-Tindale passed. She left. I haven't seen her since, bar her name on the nets." The worst of it was, Trouble had been right.

Mabry nodded slowly, as though he'd guessed her thought. "Treasury will be wanting to talk to you nonetheless."

"I might've known." The words came out more bitter than she'd intended, and Mabry smiled slightly.

"They want Trouble—either one—very badly. If you know of a way to get in touch with her—" He broke off, shaking his head.

I certainly wouldn't tell you, Cerise thought, and said, "I'll bear that in mind." Or was he hinting I should warn her? she wondered a split second later. It was possible; he was Helling's lover. Max had obviously spoken well of them, from the old days, or at least the little he'd said had been good. And there was an old rivalry between Treasury and the Eurocops.

"They'll probably be getting in touch with you soon," Mabry went on. The waiter appeared with their food, a plate balanced in each hand, served them with economically graceful gestures. Mabry waited until he had gone to continue. "John Starling is handling the on-line investigation."

Cerise froze for a fleeting instant, the delicate flavor of the chicken gone to ashes in her mouth. She knew Starling, all right, at least by reputation, and didn't much like him—another netwalker who'd never known the shadows and had a chip on his shoulder because of it. He used a soaring bird as an icon, a deceptively simple sweeping line, bright as light on metal. "I'm sure I'll be hearing from him, then."

Mabry nodded, she thought in sympathy. "I'm inclined to agree with you and Max, this isn't the Trouble you knew. But now that Trouble's back on-line—well, I suppose they have to take action."

"If I were looking for Trouble," Cerise said, "I'd look in Seahaven."

Mabry smiled then, with genuine amusement, the lines tightening around his eyes. "So easy for some of us to get there."

"Ah, well," Cerise answered, and matched his smile. Mabry would not be welcome in Seahaven, any more than she would be welcomed in the near-mythical bat caves reserved for the real cops. "Are you based in the States these days?"

"London, actually." Mabry accepted the change of subject with equanimity. "This is a temporary assignment." They talked through the rest of the meal about minor things—Mabry's time in London, her own life at Multiplane, never how he and Helling had met—and came back to the new Trouble's techniques over dessert.

"Frankly," Mabry said, "I think this Trouble, the new one, is very young. The technical aspects—the routines I've dissected have managed to be brilliant and sloppy all at the same time. Not mature work."

"And very much not Trouble's style," Cerise said.

"Not if she liked—likes—precision work," Mabry agreed.

"And it's asking for trouble, being that sloppy," Cerise said, and grimaced at the inadvertent pun. A drop of raspberry sauce escaped from the wedge of chocolate terrine, landed on the pristine edge of her plate. She dabbed it up abstractedly, the fuchsia of her nails clashing with the deeper red, licked her finger without really thinking about it.

Mabry smiled wryly—he was having coffee, black, decaf— and said, "Yeah. I think this newTrouble is going to trip itself up one of these days."

"What about tracers? Any luck?"

"Now there this Trouble seems to have learned quite a lot from someone." Mabry leaned forward, planted both elbows on the cloth. The table tilted slightly under his weight. "I'm good at tracking, and we've had some other experts in—Max among them."

"I remember Toby," Cerise said. It had been the best tracer she'd ever used, was still a part of her frontline toolkit.

"Yes. But we still haven't been able to get any kind of a fix."

Cerise finished the last bite of the terrine, and leaned forward herself. "It may be because this guy's using some of Trouble's old routines, modified. Trouble knew Max's work, used to enjoy playing hide-and-seek with him, and most of the current tracers use some of the Toby routines. That's part of the problem with all of this. This guy's using Trouble's tools, so it is her work, her hand, that shows up on autopsy. But it isn't her."

"I wondered why so many of the shadow-folk were staying so quiet," Mabry said. "Usually, when someone boasts like this, stirs up this much heat, you get a lot of talk. The shadows either close ranks, wall us out, or there are half a hundred people wanting to shop him."

"Trouble was well respected," Cerise said. It wasn't precisely true, but it was as close as she felt like coming to the full explanation. Trouble's skills had been universally respected, but the wire had made the old netwalkers keep their distance, and there had always been the whisper that Trouble was only as good as her chips. It was more that Trouble had been the most visible of the group on the wire, and one of the best crackers around; like it or not, she'd been a symbol to both sides. "Now that she's back, you may hear more."

"So you believe in this message I've been seeing everywhere."

It wasn't really a question, but Cerise answered anyway. "*That's* Trouble's style."

There wasn't much to say after that, and Mabry signaled for the check. They argued politely over it, and, after some insistence Mabry let her pay. Cerise was still smiling when she emerged into the cloudy afternoon to find her car waiting as she'd asked. She told the driver to take the long way back to Multiplane's compound, along the ring road that surrounded the city, and leaned back against the seat, trying to sort out her thoughts. She would almost certainly have to talk to Starling—or *maybe I could send Sirico, or maybe Jensey?* she wondered. *The real question is, am I going to try to warn Trouble first? Can I afford to take that chance?* She sighed, turned her head sideways, not really seeing the other vehicles—dozens of dark, heavy-bodied cars that matched the one in which she rode—crowding the travel lanes. *Trouble more than half deserves this, the way she ran out on me— but she gave me fair warning, the one warning she always gives, she told me she wasn't going to crack that system. . . . And I don't like John Starling's reputation.*

That wasn't entirely fair, and she knew it—he was a dedicated cop and a skilled netwalker—but she refused to look further. *I don't like him, and I don't think Mabry likes him either. And besides, I owe Trouble at least this much. The trick now is to find her—or, of course, someone who knows how to find her. I wonder if Butch kept in touch?* It was quite possible, and she felt a faint pang at the thought. But then, she told herself, *I didn't exactly make an effort to keep in touch with him, or with any of them, after I went legit.* She had not been proud of herself for taking the job with Multiplane—it had not been entirely her choice, and it was not something she had been going to boast about to her old friends, not something that she had wanted to discuss at all, if she could help it. And the easiest way to avoid questions had been to avoid the people altogether, at least until she was well-known as Multiplane's chief syscop, and by then so

many of the shadow-folk and the worm-carriers had fled into
security that she was relatively invisible. She could put the
word out discreetly—one of the others, Helling, maybe, or
Dewildah, or even van Liesvelt, if she could find him, might
be willing to help—or she could take her own advice to
Mabry and look in Seahaven. That was probably her best bet,
and she shifted against the cushions, wishing now that she'd
told the driver to take the flyway. She curbed her impatience
sharply, made herself sit quiet as the car churned its way
through the heavy traffic. Seahaven was always a temptation
and a challenge: she could only welcome the excuse.

The car let her off at Multiplane's main entrance, where the
same deferential security was waiting. The first pair murmured greetings as one held first the car door and then the
door into the lower lobby, but the second pair, one seated behind the high desk that half blocked the entranceway, the
other standing hidden behind a pillar and a potted palm,
looked up at her approach, and the taller man stepped out
from behind his pillar.

"Excuse me, Ms. Cerise, but I've got a message for you."

Cerise stopped, frowning in spite of herself—she hadn't
expected Treasury to catch up with her so quickly—and security went on, "Mr. Coigne would like to talk to you as soon
as you get in. He said, if you'd drop by his office on your way
up."

That was not a request. Cerise frowned more deeply, wondering exactly what Coigne wanted, and shook speculation
away as pointless. "All right, thank you. You can let him
know I'm on my way."

"Thanks, Ms. Cerise," the woman behind the desk said.

Cerise nodded and went on past, to ride the moving stairs
up to the main lobby. She had to wait for an elevator—not
unusual, so late in the day—and stood for a long moment
staring at the elevated track that carried the compound-to-
compound shuttle. The frame embedded in the massive
grey-glass wall was designed around the track and its enclo-
sure, the brass struts radiating like a sunburst from around
the triangular entrance. Even on a cloudy day, the metal

seemed to gleam with a light of its own; in better weather it was spectacular, and Cerise allowed herself a quick moment of regret, wishing it were sunny. It was easier, at the moment, to think about architecture. The elevator came then, and she stepped inside past the hurrying squad of brightly dressed secretaries, keeping her mind blank as she rode up to the twentieth floor.

Coigne was expecting her, of course—security had, inevitably, notified him of her arrival—and the secretary, a quick-moving, painfully serious woman, waved her on into the inner suite. The door to Coigne's office stood open, and she paused there, tapped once on the black-enameled metal of the frame. Coigne looked up with well-simulated surprise, beckoned for her to come in.

"I heard from the Treasury today," he said, without preamble.

Cerise seated herself in the guest's chair, arranging her skirt to show a comfortable amount of thigh. She had dressed carefully for the meeting with Mabry, in the black and hard fuchsia that was her trademark, and knew she looked good. She had realized long ago that it annoyed Coigne to find her attractive, and she enjoyed the delicate game of provocation. "I'm not surprised," she said. "I assume they're interested in Trouble?"

Coigne frowned. "If you were expecting them, Cerise, you might have warned your staff."

"I thought," Cerise said, "that they were capable of handling routine matters."

"The Treasury doesn't seem to think it's routine," Coigne said. "Neither does your staff, for that matter."

Cerise hid her irritation, an annoyance mixed almost equally with apprehension, and said, "I don't see the problem."

"No problem," Coigne answered, and laid gentle stress on the word "problem." "However, they do want to talk to you."

"So I'd heard." Cerise leaned back in the padded chair, crossed her legs and let one foot swing, the shoe hanging momentarily from her toe before she pulled it back. "I gave a precis of our information on the intrusion to the Interpol agent handling the case—given that we're multinational, I thought it'd be good to have someone from there looking into the matter—but I'd be happy to provide the same information to Treasury."

"They know that you used to work with Trouble."

"It's no secret."

Coigne eyed her thoughtfully, thin face expressionless, the grey eyes paler than the clouds seen through the windows behind him. He was framed against the ocean and the sky, the water gone cold and grey-green in the dulled light; his fair hair looked washed out, ugly against the strong greys. On the horizon, a rust-red shape was briefly visible: a ship, a tanker maybe, standing out to sea.

"Listen to me, Cerise," Coigne said at last. Cerise did not move, did not change her politely attentive smile, but every muscle in her body tightened. She recognized that tone all too well: Coigne meant every word, and would back them up, precisely and exactly, with all his considerable skill and resources. "I want this Trouble—I've told you that before, and I mean it. I don't intend for us to put up with this kind of shit from two-bit crackers. I don't really care if this is the woman you used to live with, but if it is, I expect you to put her away. You work for me now—for Multiplane—and don't forget it."

"All right," Cerise said. She sat up abruptly, enjoying her anger. "You've said your piece, now listen to me. I will put a stop to this new Trouble—who is not my ex-lover; my ex-lover is back and thoroughly pissed off on her own account—and I don't need your threats to make me do my job. I have a system to protect: that matters to me. But I am not going to be able to do it while you or Treasury are breathing down my neck, and I'm not going to find him or her or it on the nets. You want me to catch this new Trouble, fine. But I'm going to need more freedom of action than you're used to putting up with. And if you won't give it to me, I don't want to hear any complaints about me not doing my job."

Coigne blinked twice, looked down at his desktop, looked back at her, his face still without readable emotion. "What do you need?"

Cerise paused, startled by his capitulation—which means that he wants this new Trouble, much more than I realized— said, slowly, trying to hide the fact that her own plans were still unformed, "First, I'll need to make Jensey—Baeyen— acting chief for the duration."

Coigne nodded.

"Then—" Cerise took a breath, pulling her thoughts together. "I'll need to devote myself to this job exclusively. I have net access, I'll want extra time without questions, and I'll want a company car—no driver, just the car. Also leave, with pay, no questions where or why, and a company draft, at least ten thousand."

"You should have that in your budget," Coigne said.

"I'll need your signature on the forms."

Coigne nodded. "You'll be going after her—or him—yourself, then?"

"Yes," Cerise said, and realized that she was shaking. She folded her hands, laced her fingers together—she had not expected Coigne to agree, still had not realized how important this was to him—and smiled deliberately. "It's my job, isn't it?"

"Yes," Coigne said, "it is."

Cerise pushed herself up out of the chair before the silence could grow into a threat. "Then I'll pass this information to Treasury, and put things in train."

Coigne nodded again. "Send me the papers. I'll approve your requests."

"Thanks," Cerise said, and turned toward the door. Coigne's voice stopped her in the doorway.

"Don't fuck this up."

"I don't intend to," Cerise said, and let the door close gently behind her.

She made her way back to network security like a woman in a dream, barely aware of the delicate pastel murals that decorated the public spaces or the carpets chosen to be soothing. She showed her ID to security, a stocky woman sitting hunched behind the bulletproof glass of her cubicle, and went on into the main room. It was very quiet, the only sound the gentle hum of half a dozen individual stations mingled with the softer hiss of the environmental system. Her staff, Sirico, Macea, Czaja, and the rest, sat or sprawled bonelessly in their cubicles, supported by the heavy chairs, out on the nets. She ignored them, stepped into her own office to find Baeyen sprawled vacant-eyed at her station in the outer office. Her mouth hung slightly open, and a thin line of spittle trailed down her chin. Cerise walked past her, knowing better than to try to reach her from the realworld, went into her own office, and keyed commands into the waiting machine. A few seconds later, Baeyen's icon flashed onto the screen.

"Boss?"

"Sorry to interrupt you," Cerise said, "but we've got a project to set up."

"Let me close this down," Baeyen answered promptly, "and I'll be on my way."

"Thanks," Cerise said. The icon vanished, and she turned her attention to the schematic of the corporate net that bloomed automatically in her screen. Everything seemed to be in order, and live security was tight; she touched another key sequence, and confirmed that her extra watchdogs were in place. So far, so good: all that remained was to warn her people to check again for viruses. She flipped away the schematic, typed a code command, and added identifying icons from machine memory; an instant later, the screen split, showed Czaja's flying-crane icon in one half, Alec Zemtzov's dumptruck, bright as a child's toy, in the other.

"Boss?" Czaja said.

"Sorry to drag you away," Cerise said again, "but I picked up some—worrisome—news at lunch today, from Interpol. Seems that the Eurocops have been finding viruses in a few of the intrusions, and they gave me a sample disk. We need to scan for it right away."

"We ran a solid scan as soon as it happened," Czaja said.

He was in charge of the section of the net that included Corvo's research volume. "We didn't turn up anything—"

Zemtzov's icon flickered, signaling an interrupt. "Nothing that matched existing patterns, anyway." His on-line voice was far crisper than his real voice, and Cerise was, as always, briefly amused by the contrast. She smothered her smile as he continued, oblivious to the differences. "What does Interpol say about payloads?"

That was always the real question, the virus's intent, and Cerise nodded her approval. She had picked Zemtzov to be the system's virus researcher, and was pleased to see her decision borne out. "Nothing too bad, or so Mabry said, but there's still been some damage."

"Collateral or primary?"

"I don't know for sure—don't know if they know." Cerise slid Mabry's disk into one of the transfer drives. "I have the dissections Interpol did."

"Ah." Zemtzov's icon shifted color again—he was an expressive communicator—and she could hear the satisfaction in his voice. "Then if there was anything—and I think Shaja's right, the intruder didn't leave us any presents—we should be able to track it."

"Good," Cerise said. "I'm copying you Interpol's files. I want you to take another run through the system, especially Corvo's volume, Shaja, and sweep specifically for anything that's in the file."

"You got it, boss," Zemtzov said.

Czaja said, more slowly, "I'm going to get complaints. The system's already running slow."

"They'll have to live with it," Cerise said. She looked up to see Baeyen standing in the doorway, still rubbing at the damp line on her chin. "Blame it on me if you have to. I'll handle any complaints."

"I'll try to keep them calm," Czaja said. "But they won't be happy."

"They'll survive," Cerise said. "We need to do that sweep."

"All right," Czaja said.

Cerise sighed—he was good at his job, but painfully negative, always ready to find the bad things about any suggestion—and said, "Let me know when you're finished." She cut the connection as soon as they'd begun their acknowledgments, looked up at Baeyen. "Sorry, Jensey. Have a seat."

"No problem," the dark woman said equably, and settled herself in the chair opposite Cerise. "What's up?"

Cerise smiled. "Enough. I've got Shaja and Alec running another sweep of the Corvo volume. Interpol says that the intrusions they've been dealing with have involved viruses."

Baeyen made a face, spread her hands wide. "That's going to slow down everything."

"So I've been told," Cerise said. "I also hear Treasury was wanting to talk to me."

Baeyen's eyes slid sideways. Embarrassment? Cerise wondered. Or guilt? "That's right," the dark woman said. "I didn't know what you wanted to tell them, so I told them they should come back." She hesitated. "I didn't mean to make trouble with Coigne."

"You didn't," Cerise said. It wasn't true, but the other woman's concern had made her feel vaguely protective. "When they come back, give them—no, we'll make a couple of disks for them, analysis and a transcript of the event. Get Sirico to pull that together for me, will you, and copy it to me when he's done."

Baeyen nodded, and slipped a notepad machine out of her pocket, began chording notes into its memory.

"If I'm here," Cerise went on, "I'll talk to them, and if I'm not, see if you can get them to set up an appointment, all the usual stuff."

"Right," Baeyen said. "Like I can tell Treasury what to do."

"I know," Cerise said. "Do your best. This isn't the main thing, though."

Baeyen looked up warily at that, and Cerise leaned forward, steepling her hands on the desktop. "I'm going after Trouble—the new Trouble—myself," she said. "Which means I'll be leaving you in charge of the systems, Jensey."

Baeyen's eyes widened, a look of shock replaced almost at once by one of calculation. Then that, too, was gone, and she looked back down at the notepad's tiny screen. "What do you need me to do?"

"As I said, you'll be handling the systems once I leave," Cerise said. "I don't know exactly when it'll happen—it all depends on how long it takes me to track down newTrouble—but I want to get everything in place now." She watched Baeyen as she spoke, saw the other woman's struggle to keep the excitement from her face as she chorded information into the notepad: Baeyen was no less ambitious than anyone at Multiplane, and she could see the possibilities. Not that it mattered, Cerise thought. She was still better than Baeyen. "Aside from getting you briefed, I need to arrange for a car, not with a driver, to be available for me on an hour's notice—less if transport can manage it—and to get the paperwork written up so I can draw on the emergency funds."

Baeyen nodded, head still down, watching words scroll past on her screen. "All right. I'll put the paperwork in train—I can do it myself, or I can give it over to one of the secretaries, if you don't mind word getting out."

"That's why I asked you to do it," Cerise said.

"I'll take care of it, then," Baeyen said, without annoyance. "Ditto for the car. I'll also get on that disk for Treasury."

"Sirico can do that," Cerise said, and Baeyen nodded.

"After that—whenever you want to start showing me things, I'm ready."

"Get the paperwork going," Cerise answered, "then come talk to me." She was startled by her own reluctance, took herself firmly in hand. "I'll start putting together notes for you tonight."

Baeyen nodded, chorded a final bit of data to her notepad, and rose gracefully to her feet. "I'll talk to you before you go home, anyway," she said, and let herself out, closing the office door behind her.

Cerise sighed, and looked down at the desktop with its scattered icons. She should really start on the package for Baeyen, and she knew it, but she reached instead for the input cord. It wouldn't hurt anything to go out on the nets for an hour or two, might even help her give Baeyen an up-to-the-second picture. . . . She grinned at the thought, well aware of what she was doing, but plugged herself in, pushing a stray piece of hair back out of the way. She did need to see how people were responding to Trouble's challenge—and besides, she thought, I just might be able to pass Mabry's warning to Trouble. That was an odd thought, that she might encounter the other woman on the nets after all these years, an uncomfortable thought—she had always somehow assumed that Trouble had quit for good, left the nets entirely—but she put the idea aside. She owed Trouble this much: that was all that mattered.

*She wanders through the fields of light, past familiar signs, moving toward Seahaven, but not in pursuit of it. Her work is, mostly, done: two hours on the nets already, longer in virtual time, long enough for anyone, and ample for her. There is only Trouble to consider, but she floats, drifting from node to node, not quite willing to take the next step, to turn down toward the BBS and the hidden roads that lead to Seahaven. IC(E) arches to either side, coils and spills of it concealing a link of nodes that leads to unidentified corporate space, glittering like razor wire in sunlight. She studies it idly, mapping its weak points and its strengths, and wonders if she should find the maker of one particularly clever piece of code, beg, borrow, or steal it for her own nets. She files the thought, and the location, for later, and turns away, letting a rush of traffic carry her down into the BBS.*

*She touches down on the virtual plane that carries the Bazaar traffic, lets her icon interface completely with the system around her. Balls of advertising burst overhead and at her feet, spraying bright images, gilded promises, so that she walks at the center of her own hailstorm of light. Very little is of interest, but she smiles anyway, enjoying the brilliance, the sensation like soap bubbles against her skin, and does not dismiss them out of hand. Other icons glide past her, some like her haloed with the confetti of the advertising, many not—real crackers, they say, don't tolerate this misuse of the net's potentials, and many others copy the affectation, true or not. She ignores them all, follows the currents that spiral in toward the* center of the bazaar. At Eleven's Moon, further in today than the last time she found it, closer to the hubbub of the central board where real business is transacted and transformed, she lifts a hand to the demon, who scowls but says nothing. The door opens for her, and she steps out into Seahaven.

It is quiet today, a muted space, trees with jewels for leaves lining black-glass avenues, while the illusion of water rushes through an arrow-straight canal, reflecting equally illusory stars as strands of golden light. She looks down, and finds her icon remade, the cartoon woman rounded out to become something close to human. She frowns—Seahaven is in a realistic mode today—and gestures, dismissing the icon. A warning sounds, a shape like a gryphon forming in the dark air to inform her that she can't go naked/invisible here, but she ignores it, chooses another shape from her bag of tricks. This one is closer to her true image, in a style that will match the Mayor's whim, an alabaster woman, austerely thin, draped in black and touched with the color that is her name. The gryphon vanishes, accepting the change.

She continues along Seahaven's streets, following the pattern that remains constant no matter how the trappings change, finds herself at last in the market square. She moves through a gathering made unfamiliar by the Mayor's choice of convention, human shapes rather than icons, male mostly, out of anime, a few caricatured women and robots, once a Masai prince striding with a spear, and makes her way to the heart of the space. There the wall glows neon-bright, prodigal images splashed along its surface, overlapping, overwriting each other. Here and there a message glows among the designs, and she walks along its length, following the threads. Trouble's message is gone at last, but Cerise keeps walking, looking for some other trace of her old partner. There is nothing, not even among the tangles of artists' imagery, and she stands for a long moment, considering the wall. There is someone watching her among the moving people, a shape she almost certainly will not find familiar even if she looks. The brainworm translates the code to a prickling between her shoulder blades, itchy, uncomfortable, but she takes her time anyway, framing her own message, before she turns around. It is a woman, a girl-shape, really, thin and angular, big eyes in a sharp and pointy face above black leather.

*The girl-shape smiles, pure mischief, impure invitation; Cerise blinks, intrigued in spite of herself, but returns to business.*

*She knows what she needs to say, and phrases it without apology—*Treasury/Starling *(the joined icon, not the words)* are looking for you, take precautions—*but hesitates for an instant over the identifier, and settles at last for the smiling cat that will, for better or worse, evoke the old days. She wraps the words in a gaudy package that is much stronger than it looks, and seals it again, this time with Trouble's harlequin, using the codes that they once shared, and hangs it on the wall before she can change her mind. She hears a murmur of surprise and curiosity behind her, but she does not look back.*

*And then the girl-shape is there in front of her, still smiling: on the wire. Cerise blinks again, assessing the image, bad-girl chic, black leather and silver chains and the unmistakable curves, and dispatches a quick query-program of her own. It is rebuffed, as she'd expected, but the flavor of the other woman's work comes with it, smoke and mirrors and the hint of steel beneath it.*

*Hey.*

*The voice is as much a pose as the rest of the icon, deep and smoky, but it's well chosen. Cerise admits a silent interest, but suppresses all hint of it, because, after all, this may be a different kind of challenge.*

*Hey yourself.*

*The girl-shape shifts, takes up a stronger stance, hands on hips, and Cerise grimaces inwardly, bracing herself for the inevitable. She is known, and a syscop; there are plenty of crackers who have dared her before now.*

*You're playing with fire,* *the girl-shape says, gestures to the harlequin dancing against the wall.* *Sure you're up to it?*

*Cerise laughs, lets the amusement ripple out onto the net.* *Are you?*

*Try me,* *the girl-shape answers, but she, too, is smiling, the mask of the icon-face creasing in a simulation of delight. Definitely on the wire, and Cerise nods, recognizing the skill.*

*Sorry, sunshine,* *she says aloud.* *I don't have the time.*

*You could make time,* *the girl-shape answers, and flings up a hand, throwing out a shape like a mirrored sphere to surround* them, blocking the sights and sounds of the plaza. Cerise reacts instantly, freezing the sphere literally half-formed—just to prove she can do it, she's curious now herself about this stranger—then relaxes and lets the image flow like mercury around them.

*And why should I?* she asks, but makes no move to open the sphere, letting the lazy voice and the hint of contempt hold the other at a distance.

*I'm cute,* the girl-shape answers, and the words are meant to sting. *That's supposed to be enough for you.*

I've seen better, Cerise thinks, and says nothing, lets the silence carry the message for her.

*You a friend of that Trouble?* the girl-shape asks, voice gone sharp with anger, and shapes the piping harlequin in the palm of one hand to make herself absolutely clear.

Cerise nods.

*NewTrouble's not going to be happy,* the girl-shape says, and Cerise's attention sharpens.

*And whose friend are you, little girl?*

*Ah.* The girl-shape's tone changes again, goes faintly smug, the icon preening itself against the silver mirror. *Myself and mine. Maybe yours—if you're interested.*

It's not the challenge Cerise expected, and her eyebrows rise. It's been a while since anyone approached her—being a syscop plays hell with one's wetware. *So just who are you?*

Something scratches at the outside of the sphere, a tarnished shadow against the silver. One of the Mayor's watchdogs, Cerise guesses, groaning silently, come to stop just this kind of conversation. The girl-shape glances up at it, gestures rudely, looks back at Cerise.

*Silk,* she says, *they call me Silk.* She reaches into her toolkit, icon-hand vanishing for an instant, to reappear clutching something that looks like an anarchist's bomb wrapped in green-red-and-gold Christmas plaid. She tosses it gently toward Cerise, and it tumbles heavy to the illusory ground, rolls almost under her feet before it explodes in a cascade of blinding light. The silver sphere vanishes with it, exploding into a shower of gleaming shards. Cerise flinches back as they sting against her, blind for an instant before her filters override the image, and then the girl-shape is gone.

*A watchdog—this one a shape like a hound, black and tan—whines around her feet, seeking a scent. Fragments of red and green litter the ground, bits of codes no longer holding meaning, and out of the corner of her eye she sees a scavenger trundling toward them. She frowns slightly, scans the broken bits again—whatever Silk is, whatever else Silk is, she seems to act with reason, and there must have been some purpose behind the Christmas-colored bomb—and this time sees the mailcode, lying harmless among the clutter. She collects it hastily, stashes it in a holding box, is standing innocent and aloof, the box well sealed, when the scavengers arrive. She steps over them, walks away, out of the plaza, thinking of Silk.*

## • 7 •

TROUBLE DROVE TOO fast, as usual, the speed warning flickering yellow at the base of the helmet display. Ahead, the flyway gleamed like a dirty mirror in the cloudy light, reflecting the grey of the sky. At this hour, dozens of tow-carriers rumbled in the central lanes, mostly heading south toward the markets; the private traffic was sparse, a couple of corporate limos and a handful of light trucks and runabouts, spread out for kilometers along the ribbon of the road. More letters flashed in the helmet display, warning that this was the last exit before the border tolls, and she eased the trike sideways into the slower lane. The exit ramp curved down into the scrubland behind the salt marshes, and the grid lights flashed at her, warning her that local roads were not under computer control. She matched the speed limit here—local cops were less forgiving than the grid—and turned onto the narrow road that led east, toward True's Island and the sea.

The land was relatively crowded here, cluttered with low-built, sagging houses and cinder-block garages. This was car-farm country, a place to buy and sell spare parts and junkers. The road was busier, too, battered runabouts with unmatched panels and the ubiquitous pickups, each with its bed full of miscellaneous machinery. Trouble drove decorously, not wanting to attract undue attention: the border people were an insular group, didn't welcome outsiders and particularly not the ones who took the back roads to Seahaven.

She crossed the border just south of Southbrook, skirting the town itself and its asphalt plains of discount shopping. On the horizon, she could see the neon sign, bright even in daylight, blinking the message that had been the town's salvation, NO SALES TAXES!!! East of town, all the little roads wove together into a rotary, complete with a cop-shop in the center, mixed public and private station, the state insignia side-by-side with the logo of the hotel, The Willows at Seahaven. Only a single road led east, out into the marshes, and Trouble took it, careful to keep the trike just under the speed limit posted on the board at the entrance to the road. A forest-green fast-tank was waiting in the lay-by beside the station, warning lights muted, and she watched it warily in her mirrors until it had faded from sight.

No one else had taken the Seahaven road. The asphalt ran straight and true toward the sea, the marsh spreading golden to either side. It was low tide, and the air smelled of salt and mud even under the helmet. She glanced sideways, and saw a few seabirds wading in the shallow channels, heedless of chemical sands, long legs bleached white by the tainted waters; another bird circled idly overhead, whiter than the clouds. As she drew closer to the coast, the ground seemed to drop away to either side, the road carried on heavy concrete pilings over bare mud and the filled channels that were the creeks. At high tide, it was all water, and only the brookers knew the safe passages, where the creeks and brooks were deep enough to take a boat and cargo without touching the poisoned land. They would fish here, too, in defiance of the law and common sense, scratching a living from the polluted waters that might well be worse than the town jobs they feared so badly.

Ahead, the land lifted slightly, sand and seawall rising to block her view of the ocean. She slowed in spite of herself, in spite of the brookers who could be lurking, as the road went from pilings to the solid sand and stone of Shepherd Hill. It wasn't much of a hill, or even much of an island, just scrub grass and a few straggling pines, bent nearly double by the winter winds, but it was enough to carry the Coast Road. Ahead, the seawall loomed, a massive heap of stone and gravel, with the faded warning sign below it: ROAD ENDS HERE, and then a double-headed arrow. To the right, the road was drifted with sand and rock, barely traveled: only the Plantation lay to the south, deserted since the Hundred-Year Winter, except for public sex and suicides. It had once been a tourist mecca, a stretch of semiwild beachfront, protected from overdevelopment by state and federal governments. There had been a web of narrow roads on the landward side, leading to a pavilion and ranger station just below the main beach, but south of that the beach and scrubland had been left for hikers. In the old days, Trouble had been told, it had been a picnic spot, a twenty-minute walk from the last parking circle to a sweep of beach that looked across the inlet to the Joppa Flats. Now, though. . . . Now it was dead land, or dying—the ecologists weren't completely sure of that, but they had diagnosed the chemical-sands syndrome, and that was an eventual death sentence, both for the beaches and, very nearly, for towns like Seahaven that clung to the water. The sands had absorbed the chemicals that had spilled offshore during the unbelievable series of winter storms that had struck the coast twenty years ago; there had been other spills since, in storms and in fair weather, none quite as bad as in the Hundred-Year Winter, and the sands had bonded to the chemicals, changing the nature of the beaches and of the sea floor. The vegetation, or some of it, had adapted, the algae first, great mats of it washing up on the beaches to carry still more chemicals ashore. Some of the hardier species had developed ways of eating the more noxious chemicals, and a few seaweeds had developed a symbiotic relationship with them, carrying the algae in their nodelike floats or under the broad leaves, until the entire coast was poisoned. Only a few species seemed to hold their own; the rest, fish and birds and the occasional shoreline mammal, were dwindling toward extinction. Trouble turned north, toward Seahaven.

It wasn't a long drive, not half an hour even at the low speed the badly mended potholes and the drifting sand forced upon her, and she could see the arc of the Ferris wheel on the horizon, bright even in the daylight. The road lifted as she reached the higher ground of the Sands, the ground falling away steeply into the mud and grass of the Blood Creek Slough. A boat, high-bowed, with a squarely upright pilothouse in its center, moved slowly along the creek itself, a single figure just visible in the stern. In the far distance, at the inland edge of the Slough, the autumn trees were red and gold against the dull sky.

The land widened, a few houses, low-built, sturdy looking, cinder block and grey shingle, appearing now, and the piled-rock seawall gave way to concrete and sloped sand. This was brooker country, not quite Seahaven, and Trouble touched the throttle, increasing her speed as she passed a fenced-in schoolyard. And then she was past the Sands, the land narrowing briefly to a causeway, the first houses of Seahaven appearing ahead. In contrast to the Sands, they were brightly painted, and crammed in higgledy-piggledy on the rising ground. To her left the Ferris wheel loomed, centerpiece of the Parcade, and a paved road, much mended but clear of sand, turned off toward it. She allowed herself a long look at the low-slung arcades lining the road, and the mock-castle, pink and green and bright as an Easter egg, at the end of it, but kept to the main road. If newTrouble was in Seahaven, he would almost certainly be found in the Parcade, but there would be time to search for him later, when she had reestablished herself in town.

There were more people here, more than she'd seen in any one place since she'd crossed the border, kids in ragged denim and army surplus or cheap-dyed tunics, a few older adults in uniforms from The Willows, heading home to sleep or out to the Parcade to play or deal, other adults in an attempt at cracker's leather and chains clustered in the shop doorways or along the streetside. Most of them would be faking it—real crackers would probably be asleep by now, after a hard night's work, or just waking up—and Trouble's lip curled behind the concealing helmet.

She turned onto the beachfront road, skirting the crowds at the town center, drove between the seawall and the tattered boardwalk, where the shops clustered together, selling souvenirs of a beach no one wanted anymore to see, and cheap, oily food. Beyond the seawall, the ruin of the Pavilion Bandstand loomed, jutting on a broken pier a hundred meters out into the water. Only the junkies and a few whores went there now, sheltered in its leaning shell, and even the craziest netwalkers gave it a wide berth: the net held no weapons that could frighten a people without credit or history.

There was a public lot at the end of the boardwalk, half-filled with runabouts and the occasional home-built truck. Trouble found a space without difficulty, and climbed off the trike, stretching in the suddenly humid air. She needed a place to stay, someplace cheap and, more important, discreet, and she would find that only on this side of the Harbormouth Bridge. Once she crossed the drawbridge into Seahaven proper, people would begin asking awkward questions; better to stay this side of the bridge, safely anonymous and clear of the hotel's direct influence. She knew half a dozen places that met that description, or she had known them; whether they still existed, in the continual flux that was this unnamed section of town, was another matter. Still, there was only one way to find out, and she hoisted her bag onto her shoulder and started walking, the humid warmth closing in around her.

The first hostel was long gone, displaced by an Asian restaurant with purple walls and plastic plates of food in the windows, but the second was still in business. It was tall for Seahaven, almost four stories, sides shingled and painted a faded blue. Trouble stepped cautiously onto the sagging porch, trimmed with pink-and-yellow-painted carving, and pushed open the screen door that led to the little lobby. As usual, no one was in sight, but a camera watched from the corner above the manager's counter. She stared up at it, deliberately acknowledging its presence, and settled herself to wait.

It was only a few minutes before the door that closed the stairwell off from the rest of the lobby swung open, but it felt much longer. Trouble made herself turn slowly, found herself facing a woman she didn't recognize, a woman nearly as tall as herself, with grey eyes and grey-streaked dark hair. Her skin was faintly mottled, sun-scarred, and she'd made no attempt to hide it with makeup or creams.

"Help you?" she asked, in a tone that suggested she didn't care if she could.

"Yeah," Trouble answered. "I'm looking for a room."

The woman just stared at her, lined face without expression, and Trouble went on, keeping her impatience under control with an effort, "Does Mollie Blake still live here? She'll vouch for me."

Something in the woman's expression changed, a shadow of recognition flickering across her face. "I know Mollie. What's your name?"

"India Carless. But everyone calls me Trouble."

"I remember you." The woman stood still for an instant longer, then turned away from the counter. "Wait. I'll see if we have anything."

It was a risk, giving her proper name, Trouble knew, but it was the only name Mollie Blake knew her by. She waited again, leaning now against the counter where the camera was focused, and listened for the sound of footsteps on the steps up to the porch. If the stranger called the cops—though which cops would be interested, here in Seahaven, was always an open question—there was another way out, through the flimsy door and down the long hall to the barren backyard. . . . And then she did hear footsteps, not on the porch behind her but on the inside stairs, and the stranger reappeared in the doorway. A second woman stood behind her, and, seeing her, Trouble gave a sigh of relief.

"Hello, Mollie."

"Hello, Trouble." Blake stepped out from behind the other woman, but did not come closer or offer an embrace. "I thought you were out in the bright lights these days."

"I was." Trouble eyed Blake warily, uncertain how to read the reception. Blake was no cracker, had never been on the nets—didn't even have a dollie-slot, the essential tool for anyone who worked with any network. She was, however, one of the best sources of hardware throughout the Parcade, possibly along the coast. "You might say my past caught up with me. I'm looking for a place to stay, until I find someone."

Blake nodded, slowly. She was a stocky, straight-bodied woman, a little taller than average, her skin tanned almost to the color of her rust-brown hair. At the moment she was absolutely ordinary in jeans and a crumpled, man-style shirt, but Trouble, who had seen her dressed to kill, ready to mingle with the crowds at The Willows, was not deceived. "I've heard something about that," Blake said.

"You're still with Nova, then?" Trouble asked, and Blake shrugged.

"Off and on." She looked at the other woman, still standing silent at her shoulder. "Trouble's OK. She doesn't cause problems—or if she does, she cleans it up herself."

That was letting her know where she stood with a vengeance. Trouble suppressed a moment's annoyance—Blake should talk—and said, "Thanks."

The grey-haired woman stepped around Blake, ducked under the barrier so that she stood behind the counter, and reached for the keyboard of the registration system, pulling it out from under a pile of news sheets. "Carless, you said the name was?"

Blake said, "That's Joan Valentine, by the way."

"Pleased to meet you," Trouble murmured.

Valentine nodded, her expression noncommittal, and poised her hands over the keyboard. "Name?"

"India Carless," Trouble said, and wondered an instant later if she should have chosen another. Treasury knew that name—worse still, it was her real one—but then, she told herself, she didn't have good ID for anything else. That was the one thing she hadn't gotten for herself in the city, new ID to replace the jane-doe registration or her own legitimate papers. She shook the worry away, leaned forward to watch Valentine key the information into the machine.

"They send a disk up to the cop-shop twice a week," Blake said suddenly, and Trouble glanced over her shoulder to see the other woman smiling slightly.

Valentine said, "Local regulations." She looked at her screen, head cocked to one side as she studied the menu. "The only thing they pay attention to is the ID numbers, though."

"Right," Trouble said, and reached into her pocket for the jane-doe disk. She handed it to Valentine, who ran it through the scanner and handed it back across the counter.

"Somebody's going to come asking questions about that," Valentine said.

"When?"

Valentine shrugged.

Blake said, "Come on, Val. You sent the last update, when, yesterday?"

Valentine darted her an uncertain look, but said, "Yeah."

"So you've got, what, it's Thursday—so, you've got until Monday at the earliest," Blake said. "Or Tuesday, if Val forgets to send the disk on time."

"And how likely is that?" Trouble asked, and Blake laughed.

Valentine made a face. "It—can be arranged. Talk to me."

"Let me know the going rate," Trouble said. "In the meantime, though, I'd like to get a room."

"I've got a two-room suite, your own bath and input nodes, on the third floor," Valentine said. "If that's all right with you."

"That's fine," Trouble said, and meant it. She pulled the last cash-card from her belt, set it on the counter. It would certainly be enough to cover a few days in Seahaven—at least until Tuesday, and after that, she could use credit. Valentine accepted it, fed it into the machine, and nodded as the verification codes appeared.

"I'll take you up, then," she said.

"Key?" Trouble asked, in some surprise, and Blake shook her head.

"We got palm-locks last year, Trouble. Even Seahaven changes."

"Right," Trouble said, and followed Valentine through the battered door and up the narrow stairs.

It was warm in the upstairs hall, and the air smelled indefinably of Seahaven, salt and constant damp blending with the scent of oil or burned rubber from the beaches. Valentine led her down the long, dimly lit hallway, and stopped at the last door, fingering the heavy box of the palm-lock mounted above the latch. The door swung open, and Valentine held it, nodding for the other woman to go in.

Trouble stepped into sudden cool and the hum of an environmental unit set on high, reached automatically for the room controls to switch on the lights. The room was bigger than she'd expected, with a desk and table and a couple of comfortable chairs next to a floor-mounted junction box in one room, and a big bed and a video cabinet in the other. She'd gotten turned around somehow, coming up the stairs, so she was surprised when she opened the heavy curtains to see that she overlooked the front of the building and the street outside. She could just see the edge of the neon sign running below the window, and understood why the curtains were made of such heavy fabric. The bathroom was small, but most of the fixtures looked relatively new. She set her bag down, and Valentine said from the doorway, "All right?"

"It'll do, thanks," Trouble said.

"Then we'll set the lock."

It was an exercise in futility—the first thing she would do, after she checked the net, would be to buy an override lock of her own, probably from Blake's shop—but Trouble nodded, and came forward to lay her palm against the sensor plate. Valentine fiddled with the lock controls, and then with her master control, and pronounced the lock ready. Trouble tested it obediently, and the door snapped open to her touch.

"All set, then," Valentine said, and turned away without waiting for an answer.

Trouble shut the door behind her, turned to survey the suite more closely. Nothing seemed out of the ordinary, scarred wood floor, a single throw rug, cheap white-wood furniture, a few posters tacked onto the walls in lieu of prints, but she went methodically through it anyway, searching for bugs and taps and peepholes. She found nothing, either in the walls or under the casing of the junction box, and dragged the less battered of the two chairs close to it, within reach of her machine cords. She pulled the other chair in front of the door, wedged it with the desk, and went back to the junction box to begin setting up her system. The node was standard; she plugged in cables and power cords, and leaned back in her chair to begin a last quick check for lurkers.

She let the diagnostics run, paying less attention to the play of lights and numbers on the little screen than to the flicker of feeling across her skin, hot as a summer wind, and the fleeting taste of the system on her tongue. Everything felt clean, no alien programs hidden in the architecture, no odd loops of code that led nowhere, and she adjusted the brainworm to its highest setting. It was the first time she had run it at full capacity since she'd had the new chip installed, and she sat for a moment, letting herself get used to the sensations. The net felt brighter, as though she were looking at it through freshly washed windows, all her senses sharpened as though she'd shed a skin. She grinned to herself, enjoying the heady feeling, and touched the button that released her onto the net.

*She rides the nets like a roller-coaster, swept along the data-stream, hitching a ride on the lightning transfer just because she can. She laughs aloud, not caring for an instant that the brainworm transmits the ghost of that emotion back onto the net, but then she sobers, remembering what she's come for, and drops back down to the plane of the datastream. Roads of light, highways of data, stretch in every direction, dazzling red and gold and the pure white light of diamonds. She pauses a moment, enjoying the display, the sheer pleasure she had missed for three interminable days—better, actually, than what she had had, a sharper image, faster response— and then she shapes her course, chooses a road that glows like lava, red as molten steel, sinks into it, and lets it carry her away.*

She rides it toward the BBS, buffeted by the taste and smell of the data that enfolds her, her skin prickling with its touch, tingling with security and encryption. The noise of it is jarring, like high-pitched thunder, but she rides with it until it carries her through the final node, the last one before the bazaar. She drops from it then, finds herself abruptly in a space that has been reformed since the last time she took this route. A wall of light flows like water ahead of her, curving in a graceful semicircle; she hears a sound like a thousand voices mimicking water, the flow of conversation in a million languages, and the air is suddenly cool, faintly damp against her skin. She takes a step forward, curious but not alarmed—there is no IC(E) visible, and no warning; the space's creator doesn't seem to mind trespassers, indeed, seems actively to invite them—and an icon/face blooms in the lightfall, the colors running down now over the planes and angles of the face, bright along the scar that bisects one cheek.

*Fate?* she says aloud—it has to be him, even though the icon is new; a startling, unexpected effort for a man not on the wire, an illusion built to lure in the worm-carriers, or one particular worm—and she tastes agreement before she hears the answer.

*Hello, Trouble. I want to talk to you.*

Trouble nods, wary, goes no closer: while she feels no IC(E), Fate has no reason, just now, to be fond of her, and there are other programs besides IC(E) in every cracker's toolkit. *I'm listening,* she says, when the other says nothing.

*Where are you going?*

Trouble hesitates, a heartbeat of time that will seem longer. Fate is certainly no friend, never was—but then, how hard will it be to guess where she is ultimately headed? *Seahaven.*

*I thought so,* Fate says, and the colors shift briefly, flush with satisfaction, and fade again to the rainbow of the lightfall. *There are people there who want to talk to you.*

*Oh?* In spite of herself, Trouble feels a touch of fear—Treasury/Starling, maybe, though how he would get into Seahaven without the Mayor's connivance, or any of her old enemies, or even new-Trouble itself. She curbs the feeling sharply, makes herself wait.

*Oh, yes,* Fate says, and this time she hears the malice in his voice. *You've stirred up a lot of trouble. People want to know your intentions.*

That's different—that she can handle, and she sighs softly. *Thanks for the warning, Fate,* she says, and the icon retreats, fading into the lightfall.

*I'll be watching.*

Fate's voice drifts back to her as if from a great distance, and then the lightfall and the cool air and the rest of the space dissolve around her, fading to grey like a scene from an old movie. Trouble lifts an eyebrow—an enormous effort, just to pass that message—but turns her attention to the business at hand. Overhead, the web of data conduits glitters black-on-silver; she reaches up, touches one, and lets it carry her down into the BBS.

She finds the door to Seahaven without difficulty—she is expected, she thinks, and takes a moment to reorder her toolkit, so that her best defenses, a shield and a dispersion program, are ready to hand. Then she steps through the gateway, and out into Seahaven.

Today it's all black glass, a predatory nightmare of a city, looming buildings that turn the streets into canyons lit only by the graffiti that glows neon-orange against the slick black walls. This is not her favorite incarnation; it means the Mayor is in a bad mood, unwilling to police the virtual violence, or, perhaps and worse, ready to indulge in it himself. She tunes the toolkit higher, evokes the standby call and feels the ghost of a shield bind itself like a weight to her left arm. The linked dispersion program trembles against her right palm, ready for use—it will handle most active attacks, destroy the program that the shield deflects—and she walks carefully out into the glass-walled city.

The streets are empty, or nearly so; she catches the glimpse of an icon whisking out of sight around a corner once, but that is all. Her footsteps echo, ringing on the apparent stone beneath her feet, but no one challenges her, and she reaches the market square without seeing anyone more at all. The market is all but empty, too, most of *the shopfront/icons shuttered, splashed at the Mayor's whim with heavy grills and bright graffiti. Only the wall remains unchanged, and there are icons clustered at its far end, waiting. Two turn at her approach, and she hears her footsteps suddenly ring louder, sparks flying where her heels touch the black ground: the Mayor, making sure no one misses her entrance. Bastard, she thinks, and grins, and keeps on walking, watching the icons shift themselves, spreading out to meet her.*

*She imagines music, West Side Story, Sharks against Jets, and shifts her stride to match the nervous beat, the finger snap of sparks against her skin. Behind the icons, on the wall, she sees her icon dancing against a gaudy familiar packaging, its gloss a little dulled from handling. Someone has been trying to read her mail, but she knows from the pattern of the wrapping and the way the scuff marks lie that the seals—Cerise's seals—have held.*

*The icons are clearer now, some with the tang of the wire about them, their feedback tinting the net around them, others—the majority, but not by much—plaintext. She knows them all, and that is briefly disappointing: it would have been good to meet newTrouble at last, the stranger who's taken her name. She stops when she is about five virtual meters from the nearest of them, waits, hands loose at her sides, the programs trembling against her fingers. One icon takes a single step forward, declaring itself the spokesman: an angular, armored shape like a Japanese toybot.*

*\*Trouble,\* it says, and Trouble smiles, lets her amusement leak out onto the net.*

*\*Dargon.\* She knows what lies behind the massive image, a pudgy, bearded man who lives in his parents' basement; she tracked him once, after he'd crossed her, and found his secret. She lets that knowledge strengthen her, then pushes it aside. Whatever he is in the realworld, they are on the nets now, and she cannot afford contempt—whatever he is in the realworld, on the nets he is a king. She turns her head, surveys the line, names them one by one.*

*\*Nova—\* Blake's partner, a shape perversely made of shadow rather than light, sexless against the dark city walls. \*—Starfire—\* Another shadow-shape, this one filled with stars, as though the icon were a window into the heart of a galaxy. \*—Arabesque, or should I say, hello, Rachelle—\* And here her voice sharpens in spite of her-*

*self*, because Rachelle Sirvain is an old friend, a good friend, from the years before. The robed icon shifts, and Trouble tastes uncertainty, a hint of guilt spiking the air, before Arabesque has herself under control again. *Postmaster, Katana, Jimmy-D, Rogue, Alexi—* The last all plaintext, two-dimensional shapes against the black-and-neon city, without depth and expression, but not, she reminds herself, without tools or the skill to use them.

*Someone,* she says, *someone's been messing with my mail.*

There is a little pause, and in the silence someone, Arabesque, she thinks, laughs soft and low. The Postmaster icon shifts slightly, and she knows he was brought in to do the work, and failed.

Dargon says, *We have reason to be concerned.*

Trouble laughs, lets the sharp sound carry the scent of her anger onto the net. The ones on the wire will feel it clearly; the others will receive a footnote and, perhaps, the faint uncomfortable echo of her feelings. *So do I have a reason to be concerned—and the right. Where were you when this punk cracker took my name?*

That is her best point, the most legitimate argument, and she feels it strike home. Out of the corner of her eye, she sees other icons gathering by ones and twos, staying well back, out of range, but watching. This is a major event, even for Seahaven, and she wonders, briefly, where the Mayor is.

Dargon says, *Rumor had it you were dead.*

*Rumor,* Trouble says, and lets them sweat, lets them wonder which rumor she will mention, which of the nasty stories that circulate about them all. *Rumor had it wrong,* she says at last, and smiles inside, tasting their relief. *I'm still here, and it's my name.*

*You're stirring up a lot of trouble,* Dargon says. *Causing problems for everyone who works the shadows. It can't go on, Trouble.*

*I didn't start it,* Trouble says. *It was forced on me—but I intend to finish it.* She lifts her voice a little, talking now not only to the line of icons but to the lurkers to either side and any others watching invisible—to the Mayor himself, if need be. *This new-Trouble, this person who stole my name, it's compromised me. Not to mention it's gotten everyone else into difficulties, but that's your business, yours to deal with unless you want to make it mine. I *want my name back, and I want this punk off the net. Is that clear enough for you, Dargon?*

*It's clear,* Dargon says, and the color of his armor shifts slightly, takes on the red tinge of anger mixed with the blue of amusement. A grim smile? Trouble translates, and waits.

*Treasury doesn't care which one of you it gets,* he says at last.

Trouble smiles. *But you care, or you should. You don't stop this one now, you don't know what it'll do next—could steal your names, your work and style, could just keep cracking the way it's been doing, and upsetting the cops. But sooner or later you'll have to do something. I intend to do it now.*

There is another silence, this one longer, and she takes the chance to look sideways at the lurkers. Fate is there, plaintext cartoon-icon of his scarred face, and next to him a shape that can only be Max Helling, bright among the rest. The old gang returning, she thinks, and can't decide if she feels better for it. She thinks she sees van Liesvelt too, among the cluttering crowd.

Dargon says at last, *If this newTrouble agreed to stop using your name, would you call a truce?*

Yes, Trouble thinks, if it also agreed to stop using my programs, copying my style, made it clear it was someone else. But this is the net, and the rules are different; she can't concede a position yet, not without losing status. She says, *Has this person agreed to it?*

Dargon hesitates, and the colors fade a little from his icon. *No.*

And that, Trouble thinks, will never do. She can't afford to concede first, not when she's always been on the outside, not quite of the community that polices the net, set apart by the brainworm, gender, and her choice of lovers. She shakes her head, enjoying the sense of the movement—a false sense, really, existing only in her brain, along the brainworm's wires—says, *If it agrees, talk to me then.*

Dargon gives a little sigh—he had obviously expected no other response, would probably never even have asked if she hadn't been a woman, a dyke, and on the wire.

Trouble goes on, not waiting for his answer, *Like I said, sooner or later this person's going to have to be stopped.*

*Stopped or shopped?* a voice—Nova's, she thinks—queries

sharp and amused, and Trouble nods her appreciation of the quibble.

*Treasury will certainly buy,* she says. *And I'm prepared to sell, if I have to. But I want my name back, and an end to this stupidity.*

She has declared herself, fully and completely, and she stops, waiting for their answers. The Postmaster is first to move, drifting back out of the line of icons, away from the wall, away from her, his message clear. He will not help, but he won't stand against her, either. Arabesque steps forward, colors rippling along the sweep of her silken robe, the cloth flying as though she stood perpetually in a strong wind, steps past Dargon and comes to join her. Trouble smiles, and feels an unfamiliar sensation shiver through her— gratitude, certainly, and something more. Starfire backs away, joining Postmaster, and Rogue joins them; a heartbeat later, Alexi goes with them. From the lurkers, van Liesvelt steps forward, a big shambling bear-shape that carries his familiar grin. Blue Max, Max Helling, unmistakable even in the blue thunderstorm that has replaced his biplane, follows more slowly, and van Liesvelt turns to him in surprise. Katana and Jimmy-D turn away, brush past Postmaster, and are gone, lost among the lurkers. Fate steps forward without comment or change of affect, takes his place with Trouble's friends. That she had not expected, a public affirmation of his private choice, and she is careful not to shame him with surprise. Dargon and Nova stand alone between her and the wall, and Nova laughs.

*Later, maybe, Trouble. But I won't stand in your way.* The icon flips away, vanishes in a shower of smoke, and Dargon turns slowly, faintly green, the color of a nodded head.

*All right. For now,* he says, and steps aside.

Trouble hides her smile, mutes the triumph that sings through her, looks at the icons gathered around her. It is so like the old days that she could cry or dance, and she doesn't know what to say, says instead of greeting, *I have to get my mail.*

Arabesque laughs, a muted sound, and van Liesvelt says, *So do it. We'll wait.*

Trouble nods, strides away across the charcoal paving, takes the message down from the wall. Cerise's once-familiar codes seethe against her hands; she matches them from memory, the responses buried in her toolkit, and the message falls open in her hands, a fleeting burst of words that burns itself into memory. TREASURY/ STARLING ARE LOOKING FOR YOU, TAKE PRECAUTIONS. That is unexpected, a warning from Cerise, after everything that's been between them, and she walks back to the others as slowly as she dares, wondering what to do.

*So,* van Liesvelt says. *You got your mail.*

*Was it worth it?* Fate says, and despite the inflexible icon, Trouble hears the irony in his tone.

It triggers her decision, and she nods, speaks before she can change her mind. *Yeah,* she says, *it was worth it—and does anyone know where Cerise is these days, or what she's doing?*

Arabesque draws in a breath, says, in the sharp London voice that goes so strangely in Trouble's mind with the black skin, *What a welcome. Thank you, sunshine.*

*Sorry,* Trouble says, and after a moment the other woman laughs, this time at herself.

*I've missed you, Trouble.*

*And I've missed you.* Trouble waits a moment, gauging her chance to ask again, and Helling clears his throat.

*Cerise is with a company called Multiplane. Chief of on-line security, I think. And she's looking for Trouble—the new one, I mean.*

*I see.* Trouble didn't mean to speak aloud, is vaguely startled when the words drop onto the net, shakes herself with a frown. *I need to get a message to her, privately. Any ideas?*

Arabesque's mouth twists, but she says nothing. Helling says, slowly, *I have a—friend who's in touch with her, but it wouldn't necessarily be private.*

*I know a route,* Fate says. *Do you want the numbers or do you want me to do it for you?*

There is a challenge, intended or not, in his words, and Trouble stiffens. *Give me the numbers.*

The icon does not change, but a moment later a silver wafer appears in the air between them. Trouble takes it, tucks it into memory without looking at it, feels the numbers vibrate in her mind. Arabesque says, *I thought you left her. That's what she said.*

*I did.* Trouble doesn't look at her, doesn't want to explain, and Arabesque laughs again, this time with genuine amusement.

*Trouble, you're too much.* She steps back, her draperies gathering around her as though her private windstorm had changed direction, lifts her hand to find a gateway out of Seahaven. *I'll keep in touch,* she says, and is gone.

Trouble stares after her, regretting the unasked questions—what are you doing these days, are you well, are you happy—then shakes herself, and turns back to business. She has to find Cerise—she owes Cerise the word she herself had gotten, that newTrouble's in real-Seahaven.

Helling says, *It's slick IC(E) at Multiplane, slick and very hard. And not all of it's Cerise's.*

*The route I gave you takes you in obliquely,* Fate says.

Trouble nods her thanks, feeling the numbers, address and directionals, trembling in memory.

*Good luck,* Helling says, and starts to drift away.

*Thanks,* Trouble says, softly, for more than just good luck, and she sees Helling's face appear momentarily in the shadow of the thunderstorm, to show his smile.

*It's good to have you back.*

Trouble grins in spite of herself—it's good to be back—and looks at the others. *And thank you, too.*

*I don't much like viruses,* Fate says. The icon does not change: it never changes, he's not one to indicate feelings, says it all in the choice of his words. Trouble looks warily at him, wondering what lies behind it, morals, the cracker prejudice she shares, some deeper hatred, and the icon fades before her eyes. That leaves van Liesvelt, and she looks back at him, the heavy bear-shape bulky against the neon scrawl behind him.

*I had some news,* he says. *From the doc. She says Treasury's been asking questions.*

*What kind of questions?* Trouble asks, and feels the fear stab through her. How could Treasury have known to go to Huu—how could they have known she needed a new chip? Jesse? It wasn't like him to sell that kind of information.

Van Liesvelt shrugs. *She said it was a general have-you-seen-her notice, just asking if anyone's done any work on a woman *matching your description. It was going under your real name, though.*

*Fuck,* Trouble says, and only with difficulty refrains from kicking the watchdog that appears instantly to snap at her ankles. The co-op, then, and possibly Jesse—he would sell her, if it meant staying clear himself.

*The doc didn't say anything, of course,* van Liesvelt went on, *and she thinks it should dead-end there.*

Trouble nods, her mind racing. When she gets off the net, she'll have to bribe Valentine, see if she'll substitute another name for the one she gave at registration, or maybe hack the hotel system and make the fix herself. That, in Seahaven, won't be easy, and she puts the thought sternly aside for later. She will have enough to do, to leave Cerise the message she needs. *Thanks for the warning,* she says aloud, and van Liesvelt grins.

*Just be careful,* he says, and turns away.

Trouble takes the long way out of Seahaven, through the most complex of the gateways, checks the address Fate has given her, and lets the first node she comes to carry her away from the BBS. She follows the coded numbers through the tangle of the midlevel roads, letting herself fade to obscurity against the brilliant packets of data, until she is all but invisible, little more than a shadow of a ghost. She pauses at the center of a great hub, waits, a dozen breaths, a hundred heartbeats, while the datastreams flow over and past her, until she is sure she is not followed. Only then does she take the final step, the last turn that will lead her to her ultimate destination.

IC(E) arcs to either side, walling off the corporate precincts, sparks dripping like water from the overarching spines. Trouble recognizes the space, a shared system where suppliers and parent corporations meet and exchange data, knows how the protocol works and how to get inside. Fate has done well by her, bringing her here; the only difficulty now is to trace Multiplane's lines. She checks herself, confirming that her presence has been muted, outbound data squelched, turns slowly, watching the datastream slide past her, merging with the IC(E), until she understands the pattern of it, and feels it in her bones. She chooses a packet then, invokes a mirror program from her toolkit, watches it spin an identical image

*around herself, so that she sinks into the datastream, indistinguish-*
*able from the data around her. She lets herself drift toward the*
*IC(E), lets the steady flow draw her into the coils of unreal wire,*
*sharp and cold as steel and hard as bone. She can feel the chill from*
*them as she slides through the spiraling wire, sees it through a pale*
*gold haze of the stolen pattern; her own hands are all but invisible,*
*the gleam of IC(E) bright beneath her skin.*

*And then she's through the first barrier, emerges into a space like*
*a pool, where a structure like a stack of gears stirs the datastream,*
*curving it first into a gentle whirlpool and then sorts it on its way.*
*She slows herself subtly, not daring to fall too far out of the parame-*
*ters, just a backward eddy in the general current, and searches the*
*packets for an address label. They are coded, an unfamiliar system,*
*and she calls Fate's codes from memory. She had hoped not to have*
*to rely on them—she trusts him, but only so far, only so far as she*
*would trust any fellow cracker, except perhaps van Liesvelt and Ar-*
*abesque . . . and Cerise. But the numbers are there, and she evokes*
*them, creates a label for herself that matches the patterns that she*
*sees, and lets herself slide back into the line of data.*

*The current sweeps her closer, stirred by the first level of gears*
*into the general pool, and then, quite suddenly, she's swept up and*
*away, snapped from the stream and flung off into a new and alien*
*conduit. Her stomach lurches as the brainworm relays the motion*
*faithfully—one of the few disadvantages of the wire—and then she*
*steadies, orienting herself against the new perspective. The space is*
*marked off in grids, black on silver, a dozen or more imposed one on*
*top of the other: a mailroom configuration, a limited interface with*
*Multiplane's primary systems. She studies the pattern for a mo-*
*ment, letting the data fall past her to be captured by the various*
*grids, then lets herself fall with them, shrinking as the data shrinks*
*until she matches its shape precisely. The address Fate supplied*
*floats before her; she feels the system probe it, a pulse like a pres-*
*sure, a finger poked hard into her ribs, and then she's shunted into*
*the maze of the grids. She rides the current, tossed abruptly from*
*side to side as the system shunts her from one plane to another, and*
*then, quite suddenly, she's where she wants to be.*

*She hangs suspended, abruptly still, in a space that seems infi-*
*nite, but feels constrained, hemmed in by the walls of the pigeonhole*

*into which she has been dropped. This is the virtual address, the place where the mail waits, and she studies it, reaching with infinite care to feel the other message packages waiting with her. They are all for Cerise; she feels further, finds the password lock that seals the system and recognizes Cerise's hand in the intricate check mechanism. Definitely the right place, she thinks, and sinks back into the still center of the address to compose her message. It is simple, a single word—from her, to Cerise, there's no need for more. Even after everything, it's still that simple, and she shapes the word in its delicate casing: SEAHAVEN.*

*She sets it free, easing it out of the shell that conceals her presence, budding it like an amoeba. At last it pops free, shining like a soap bubble for an instant as the system registers a new arrival, and Trouble smiles to herself. She has done what she can; it should be enough to bring Cerise to Seahaven, the real one— Cerise has already been to the virtual town, she knows what is, and isn't, there. All that remains is to leave as undetected as she's entered. She pauses for an instant longer, considering her options, then grins and shapes another address. The mail routine sweeps by again, and she watches it pass, gauging speed and direction; another dozen heartbeats, and it sweeps past again like a lighthouse beam. This time she reaches for it, places the false address in its path and lets it scoop up the packet, dragging her in its wake. When she's sure it has her bait securely, she reels herself in, recomposes herself behind the mask of the false package. The program flings her back into the grids, and the grid flips her out into the sorting area. She would laugh if she dared, breathless, enjoying the rollercoaster ride. And then she's back out in the IC(E) and she abandons the mail packet, lets the system carry its empty shell on through the walls of IC(E). Someone will be annoyed, receiving a transmission so badly garbled, but she spares less than a thought for them, turns her attention to the IC(E) instead. It is less formidable from this direction, was designed to keep people out, not to hold them in, but she knows better than to be too confident. She eases her way through the coils like diamond and wire, moving crabwise, oblique, across the grain of the net, until at last she emerges from the thicket, hangs once again in the open net.*

*She smiles, allowing herself at least that much of triumph, but does not let her cloaking programs fade. Instead, she takes the nearest datastream, and, still smiling, lets it carry her toward home.*

I T WAS A five-hour drive to Seahaven, under grid control, four hours on manual. Cerise, driving alone, kept the runabout off the grid. She flashed past the corporate vehicles in the grid lanes to her right, barely aware of the figures outlined against the bright-gold windows. Crossing the Merrimack, it was foggy—it was never not foggy at night up here, drifts rippling past in the cones of light from the headlamps—and Cerise cut her speed, the engine easing down from the shrill whine that had annoyed her for the past four hours. Multiplane's loaner fleet was generally underpowered, whether for economic reasons or security she didn't know, but a few days driving at what she considered to be a reasonable speed would generally send the borrowed machines back for a tune-up. She smiled to herself, thinking of the mechanics' faces when she returned this one, and settled herself more comfortably against the padded seat.

A light clicked in the heads-up display at the base of the windscreen, and in the same moment a sign flashed past on the side of the road: one mile to the border toll station. She read the information almost without thinking, feet automatically shifting on the pedals, her hands easing the wheel. Another limo slid past, this time on her left, overtaking her on manual. She caught a brief glimpse of the bright interior, two men in suits seated facing each other across a display console, and then it passed completely, and she saw only the flickering taillights. The driver's compartment had been blacked out, without even the glimmer of red that usually outlined the section. Going to Seahaven? she wondered, and the toll station loomed ahead.

At this hour, almost midnight, most of the gates were on automatic. The grid was signaling to her, more letters and arrows streaking past in the windscreen, and she hit the thumb button to signal that she would obey. The grid computers shunted her toward a middle lane, as she had expected—they would be considering that she was on manual and, driving fast in a small car, would respond more quickly than the heavier limos—and she smiled once to herself at the accuracy of her prediction. A single light flickered in the tollkeeper's booth; the row of gates stretched empty across the road, display lights proclaiming that they were on automatic. Cerise worked the window controls, reached for the passcard as she slid into the gate. The reader was set high, positioned for a limo running on the grid, and she had to stretch to slide the card through the manual sensor. There was a brief pause while the computers considered the verifications and the money was deducted from Multiplane's traffic account, and then the orange-and-white barrier folded back. She touched the accelerator gently, and the runabout slid out into the warm orange light of the toll station. There was a beeping sound behind her, and she glanced up at the mirror screen. The grid had brought one of the limos into the gate badly, and the gate sensors couldn't read the low-powered pass button. She could see the tollkeeper, a stocky man in jeans and a T-shirt, dashing across the pavement toward the beeping car.

Another good reason to stay off the grid, she thought, and returned her attention to the road. The lights from the toll station formed a band of orange across the roadway, the fog drifting through it in seemingly solid clouds. Beyond the lights, the night seemed very black. She timed her acceleration so that she slid into the darkness at the point where the road narrowed again to five lanes, touched the controls to close the window. The fog smelled of peppermint and tobacco, and she wondered what had drifted in from the open sea this time. She was three minutes away from Seahaven.

She reached the Seahaven cutoff in five minutes, slowed by the appearance of a phalanx of state militia in their dull green fast-tanks, coursing along the outer lanes. She pulled over, into the slowest of the manual lanes, watching the warning lights stream along her display band: rear- and side-scan radar, automatic identity query and response, machine check. She kept her speed cautious even after they had passed. At the Seahaven exit, more lights flashed, demanding that she link with the local grid. This was Seahaven: she obeyed, lifting one hand from the wheel to punch in the link codes. An instant later she felt the controls shifting against her touch, and she made herself relax. The runabout swung south, turning along the access road that ran almost parallel to the main north-south flyway. Seahaven—or, more precisely, The Willows at Seahaven, the secure hotel that was the town's economy—preferred to control all vehicular traffic within its borders, and made access to the town as complicated as possible. The commuter trains did not stop there, nor did the buses. They were particularly careful about anything coming in over the causeway; the town grid was both competent and aggressive in its attempts to gain control. She touched a final code, temporarily disabling her controls, and leaned back against the padding, suddenly aware of her own tiredness. It had been a long day, longer than she'd realized: meetings all morning trying to get her department into order and to make sure Baeyen would be able to handle the transferred authority, and then going onto the net to find the message waiting, the unfamiliar packet that she had known, even before she touched it, felt the codes, had to be from her Trouble. It had just been one word, just "Seahaven," but that had been enough: Trouble was back in the game, and willing to share what she'd found. It had taken her three hours to convince Coigne of that, though, and she grinned, savoring the victory. Best of all, though, Trouble was back.

At least for now. Cerise felt her smile turn wry, the old pain stabbing her again. Trouble had left once before, left her in the lurch; there was no guarantee it wouldn't happen again. And even that was getting ahead of things: there was no reason to think that she would see Trouble again even on the nets, no reason to think that Trouble would want to do

more than this, this one message. Cerise stared at the lights of
the heads-up display without really seeing them, thinking
about Trouble. She could almost see her, was tired enough
that it took very little to conjure her, tall and broad-shouldered and smiling, tiger stripes vivid in her thick hair. And
that was not what she wanted to think about. She shook the
image away, frowning now, shook away too the recognition
that she still wanted Trouble, after everything, and fixed her
eyes on the darkened screen.

The roadway lifted, rising up on pilings to cross the bands
of salt marsh that lay between the main highway and Seahaven itself. The dome of the local nuke glowed on the horizon to the south, whitening the fog. Security had to be tight
there, with Seahaven on its doorstep, though whether it was
to protect The Willows' exclusive clientele or to keep out the
lowlifes who lived in the town and along the Parcade, she
had never been entirely sure. Closer in, she could see the Ferris wheel at the end of the Parcade glowing through the fog
like a monster icon. She would check there tomorrow, she
decided, see if she could get word of either Trouble in the
shops and cubicles that lined the street.

The roadway curved, swinging to cross the Mill Race at its
narrowest point, and she looked sideways and back, looking
for The Willows. She could barely find it—the road had been
laid to make it hard to see, from any approach angle—just
the white roofs floating, floodlit, above a screen of trees that
was all but invisible in the dark. She had even been there
once, when Multiplane had been negotiating to buy out a
competitor, had stayed in the cool and perfect rooms,
screened from electronic snooping, live spies, and the threat
of raiders real or virtual, and had hated every minute of it.
The staff had been perfect, discreet, all but invisible in the
conference center at the heart of the compound, attentive and
cheerful in the perimeter buildings; the food had been exquisite, the evening entertainment, tapes and sports, of
course, nothing live, well chosen. But she had remembered
the people she had known, the summer she had lived in Seahaven, the ones who worked at The Willows and the ones

who wanted to, the ones who would indenture themselves to the hotel and the ones who didn't dare, and had found it hard to meet the service people's eyes. The Willows had saved Seahaven, there was no question about it: when the beaches died, there had been no other jobs, no other employers, and the hotel had taken up the slack, employed the fishermen and their children, the small businessmen who suddenly had no clientele. The town had always lived partly off the tourists; it had not been difficult to find people who knew the service trades. But The Willows had also made sure it would have no competition—security reasons, they said, but it allowed no other corporations to settle in the town limits. The Parcade they tolerated only because it brought extra and expensive business, both the bright-light corporations whose people liked the game of a walk on the wild side and the greyer ones who had some dealings with the shadows.

Cerise shook the thought away. She shouldn't have to deal with The Willows, or its security, not this trip, and if she did, Multiplane had clout enough to handle it. Ahead now she could see the lights of Harborside, on the higher ground across the Eel Ditch. Her own hotel was there, a subsidiary of The Willows, of course, built to accommodate spouses and families who couldn't be allowed in the more secure buildings of The Willows itself. Harborside was the nicer part of town, where the better-paid service trades had their houses, and the better shops and entertainment centers were; beyond the Blind Creek it became plain Seahaven again, the acceptable face of poverty, hardworking, stubborn, some of it subsidized to astonish the visitor. But the harbor still held its share of fishing boats, though you had to sail a long way, the fishermen said, push the boats' limits, before you dared eat what you caught, and there were only a few jobs there that had no connection to The Willows.

Lights flashed across her display, and Cerise glanced at the string of query codes. The inboard systems responded automatically—destination, reservation codes, a request that the hotel be informed of her arrival—and the message bar flashed green in acknowledgment. The runabout slowed, the sound of its tires changing as it hit the older pavement of the town roads, and the grid shunted it neatly into the middle lane of Willows Road. Cerise smiled to herself—the locals still called it Ashworth Avenue, a last stubborn gesture of the independence they had already sold—and saw the lights flashing from the drawbridge that spanned the Harbormouth. Beyond it lay the unnamed neighborhoods that lay between the main town and the Parcade, still Seahaven but cut off from the town and The Willows and the jobs by the one-lane bridge: her eventual destination was the Parcade, which she had once known better than she had known the town where she was born. She closed her eyes, shutting out the fog-damp street and the forlorn neon, remembering her Seahaven. There were tiny gardens there, wedged in between the candy-colored houses, with raised boxes of storebought dirt to fight the sand and the encroaching chemicals from the beach. There were triple- and quadruple-deckers, porches jutting off at odd angles, and families crowded into low bungalows never meant to stand the winter, and tidy capes where someone still cared enough to paint and clean and sweep the sand from the concrete before the doorways. She had had a flat on the top floor of what had been a tall vacation house, two rooms and a bath, but with a balcony from which she could see the ocean. It had been hot, even with fans running and all the windows open, and she had slept on the roof with the rest of the housemates more than once, but at least it had been warm through the interminable grey winter.

The runabout slowed and tilted, turning, and Cerise opened her eyes to see the low buildings of Eastman House looming out of the fog. She glanced once to her right, to see the guardhouse at the end of the smaller causeway that led to The Willows, and then looked back toward the doorway, mustering a smile for the uniformed man who appeared to greet her. She touched the interior lock, and he opened the runabout's door for her, smiling with apparently genuine welcome.

"Ms. Cerise. Can I take your luggage?"

Cerise nodded, touched the controls a final time to open the storage compartment, and levered herself out of the driver's seat while the doorman collected her single bag. She pulled the hardware case from its place behind the seat, waving the doorman away when he offered to take it from her, and followed him into the lobby. It was dimly lit, warm amber light, and music drifted gently from the bar beyond a screen of broad-leafed plants—someone singing the blues, Cerise recognized, the sort of music Trouble had liked, in her more mellow moods. She turned to the woman who waited behind the all-but-hidden counter.

"Ms. Cerise?" the woman said, making it a question even though the town grid had signaled Cerise's arrival, and Cerise nodded. "If you'll just look over our form, make sure everything is as requested . . ."

Cerise took the flashprinted form, scanned it quickly—single room, full media suite and net ties, unlimited signing privileges, courtesy of Multiplane's account—and scrawled her name where indicated. The woman took it back, smiling her thanks. She had perfect teeth, like all The Willows' employees, very white against the deep red lipstick.

"Thank you, ma'am." She reached beneath the counter to retrieve a glittering disk of iridescent plastic and a sensor board. Recognizing the system, Cerise laid her hand against the board, and waited while the woman recorded palm and fingerprint and the heat pattern and recorded them on the disk itself. It was a double-check system, the prints recorded both in the disk that served as a key, so that only the registered guest could use it, and in the lock itself. It wasn't impossible to defeat, Cerise knew—she'd done it herself—but it did take more time and equipment and a knack for social engineering that not every cracker possessed.

"You're all set," the woman said, and Cerise slipped the proffered disk into her pocket. "George will take you up, bring anything you need to get settled."

"Thanks," Cerise said, and let the doorman lead her through the lobby to the double elevator. They rode up in silence, and Cerise followed him down the short hall to her room. It was on the end of one of the three wings, she realized as the doorman unlocked the door and held it for her, then followed her inside. In daylight, she would have a clear view of the slough and The Willows itself. She tipped the doorman automatically, declined his offer of a drink from the bar or a late dinner, and let the door close behind him.

There was a kitchen console, coffee machine and hot-water dispenser above a little cabinet of supplies, set into the wall of the main room, and she started a pot of coffee before she turned her attention to the net console. It was pretty much the same setup that she had remembered from her first visit to The Willows, and, at least at first glance, she was certain she carried the right programs to deflect any lurkers in the system. She hesitated a moment, wondering if she should wait until she'd had some sleep, wait until morning before venturing onto the net, then reached for her hardware carrier. She would stick to the local net, take a quick look around tonight, when the local crackers would be out in force, and tomorrow she would look in earnest for Trouble. She put together her system, then poured herself a cup of coffee before coming back to settle herself in front of the console. As she had expected, the management did not provide chairs that would be comfortable for netwalking. She wriggled against the too-tilted chair back, then brought the pillows from the bed to prop herself more comfortably into position. She slipped the jack into the dollie-slot, and dropped easily onto the local net.

*She tunes the brainworm low, enough to feel but inconspicuous to others, and begins to wander, following the spiral curves of the local net. It's a plain system, heavily controlled—she sees watchdogs everywhere, some sleeping and benign, others ranging purposefully, one or two guarding specific gateways, and she marks those last for later investigation. Not that there's anything she wants from behind those IC(E)-walled doors, but the challenge intrigues her.*

*The local trade-net lies ahead, a chain of BBS, a spiral within the spiral, an eddy curling in opposition to the main system that becomes a series of spherical spaces like beads on a string or the cham-*

bers of a nautilus. She considers it for an instant, then lets herself drift down to that plane: it is here, if anywhere, that she will find either Trouble. Her feet touch solid ground, or its illusion, and she walks along a road whimsically marked with yellow bricks.

The BBS surround her, the first sphere filled with gaudy advertising, the icons fizzing against her skin, dancing around her like a cloud of insects. She ignores it—this is a trade space; she recognizes most of the product, and knows this is not worth her while—and the images fade as she leaves that chamber. The next space is brighter still, badged with neon shapes stolen from the Parcade, and she doesn't bother to hide her sneer. This is for the tourists, the ones who want the illusion of the shadows without the danger, a place that plays at being the grey market. She looks close, and sees the watchdogs and the trackers, the silent IC(E) woven into the very fabric of the images, all to protect the people the market is designed to cheat. They have the feel of The Willows, of the security she has already tasted from a distance, and she quickens her pace, knowing this is not a place to linger.

Beyond it lie cocktail spaces, crowded with icons not all of whom represent netwalkers—the local system believes in the illusion above all—and she slows, scanning the space for likely trapdoors. There are fewer watchdogs here, and most of those are focused on the obvious flashpoints, where the BBS intersects most directly with the abstract plane. She walks past, searching for familiar symbols, and finds an icon that she recognizes, tainted by a well-known hand, a touch like a whisper of perfume against the air. She smiles, approaches, and the icon rotates toward her as though there were a live hand behind it. She can feel that fake, however, the chill unreality radiating from it, and doesn't bother to answer the preprogrammed greeting.

*Libera,* she says, the old password, and the icon fades slightly, disclosing the trapdoor. She glances behind her once, unfolding her scan, and sees/feels nothing untoward, no particular attention from the watchdogs. She gestures then, furling her programs, and steps through the nebulous doorway.

She emerges into a new space, green-walled, floor of jagged emerald grass imprisoned beneath an invisible surface, so that she walks above the apparent surface of the ground. It is a lot of effort for a

shadow board, and she looks sharply sideways, letting the scans unfurl around her, but there is nothing untoward, no tang of unexpected security. The watchdogs are bred from the shadows, and she
recognizes at least the pedigree if not the hand that made them—
and in any case, they are turned toward the walls, watching for
intruders, not for the people who use the space. It is less crowded
here—no need for the illusion of a crowd, to bolster the ego—and
she can feel the faint current, gentle feedback, a hint of emotion,
that signifies another brainworm, or maybe more than one. Definitely the right place, she thinks, and lets herself stroll toward the
source of that sensation, walking, almost floating, over the top of
the gleaming grass.

At the center of the space, by the message pole that runs from
floor to arched ceiling, she sees a familiar icon—Mario, his name is,
and he once tried to crack her IC(E), though he was good enough to
get away once she'd jumped him. This is neutral ground, however,
and she gives him a careful distance, feeling his surprise and
quickly controlled anger feed back into the net. He's on the wire,
too, unusually, and she doesn't want trouble from him.

And then she feels it, the familiar warmth, a whisper of sensation
that's like a well-known voice. She quickens her step in spite of herself, in spite of knowing better, and sees, around the pole, the shape
of a harlequin, dancing, pipes in hand.

*Trouble,* she says aloud, and the word comes out exultant, and
she doesn't quite know why.

The harlequin turns, lifts hand to half-mask, and she sees the
mouth below it smile. *Cerise.*

Cerise stops three virtual meters from her former partner, suddenly not sure what to say or do, and Trouble lifts her hand. Evok-
ing a program, Cerise thinks, tensing—she can feel the routine as
yet undefined, its potential trembling in the virtual air around the
other woman's fingers—and Trouble says, *Shall we talk?*

It is the tone, the same tease, half-amused, half-seductive, in
which she would have said, Shall we dance?, and Cerise smiles in
return, deliberately slow and mocking. *Why not?* she says, and
calls her own program, throwing a silver sphere around them, to
keep out the lurkers. Trouble has seen the gesture and in the same
moment launches her own program, so that the two spheres, silver,

silver gilt, meet and mesh so that they stand under a mottled sky that streams with color. Trouble lifts her hand to her face, and her own face appears through the mask—a gesture of respect, Cerise acknowledges, but a cheap one. She can feel the other's presence, the feedback from the brainworm, knows Trouble feels the same, and that if either one of them relaxes that same feedback can spiral, each feeding on the other, until it carries them both away.

*I thought you'd come,* Trouble says, *but I didn't expect you so soon.*

*I'm not particularly happy with the current situation,* Cerise says, and hears herself less sharp than she'd intended.

*No more am I,* Trouble said, and laughs aloud. *For what it's worth, it wasn't me.*

*I didn't think it was,* Cerise answers. *Not your—style.*

*Thanks for that.*

There is a little silence between them, and in that silence Cerise hears the thread of a sound, the ghost of a siren: her passive watchers, warning her that security is interested in the private sphere. Trouble hears it, too, or some warning of her own, looks over her shoulder.

*We can't talk here,* she says, and Cerise nods.

*I'm at Eastman House,* she says. *Join me for breakfast.* She lifts her hand to break the sphere, feels Trouble's agreement even as she dissolves the program's construct in a cloud of buzzing smoke and fragments, and takes a quick five steps sideways so that by the time the smoke clears and the watchdogs arrive, sniffing avidly, she is well away and Trouble is nowhere to be seen. There is nothing else she can do—she has already done more, much more, than she'd expected—and she walks back along the spiral, lost in thought, retracing her steps out of the spiral path until she can ride the data home again.

Trouble sat unmoving in the darkened room, the sea-damp air chill on her bare arms. Beyond the half-opened window, the fog rolled past in slow billows, bringing a smell like peppermint and gasoline with it from the beach. She sniffed it automatically—the peppermint smell was like the one her bioware used to label a particular class of data—but did not move to close the window. The lights, linked for economic reasons to a motion-sensor, had turned themselves out while she was out on the net; they would not go on again until she touched the switch. There was enough light from the window, from the neon on the street below, to show the shapes of the furniture, and the flickering telltales on her hardware cast faint orange light across the table where she'd set up her system. She stared at it, noting successful shutdown with one corner of her brain, thinking about Cerise. She had expected Cerise to come to Seahaven herself—that was Cerise's style, to step briskly in when angels would think twice before acting—but she had not expected quite so rapid a response, if only because she had not expected Multiplane to be able to act so fast. The fact that they had meant that Cerise had been expecting—something, and had set up her departure in advance. *And will I go to breakfast?* Trouble thought, and smiled, seeing the icon again in imagination, Cerise's cartoon-woman walking toward her under the green-glass dome of the BBS. It had been a strange thing to see her again, to feel her presence, silk and steel and taut-strung wire; stranger still to feel her own response, heart turning like a wheel, rolling over into the familiar habit of trust, despite everything—and that was foolish, stupid beyond permission, as Cerise herself would say. Old habits die hard, but die they must: *I'll go to breakfast,* she decided, *but not without setting up some fallbacks of my own first.*

She turned back to the system, wincing a little at unanticipated stiffness in her shoulders and back. She had slipped sideways at some point, come back from the net to find herself slumped painfully against the side of the chair. The dollie-cord slithered across her shoulder, and the healing flesh around the new socket was starting to hurt again, a dull throb of pain at the back of her head. She would make the fallbacks in the morning, she decided, when she was fresh and rested, and freed herself from the system. She undressed in the dark, not bothering with the room lights—her eyes had adjusted now to the dimness, and it seemed pointless to put on a light for the few minutes she would be awake and active—used the toilet, and crawled between the clammy sheets. She fell asleep watching the blink of the system tell-tales mirroring the neon.

She woke to brilliant sunlight, slanting in under the imperfectly lowered shades, lay blinking for a moment before she pushed herself upright. She was still stiff from the previous night's work, and the back of her head felt bruised, puffy and sore to an exploring touch. She grimaced, and swung herself out of bed, hoping that a shower would help. Washed and brushed and dressed, she felt a little better, but the muscles of her neck still twinged with each unwary move. She rolled her head from side to side as she moved toward the media center, touched keys to call up time-and-temperature. It was later than she had realized, well past nine, and she swore under her breath. Cerise wasn't a morning person, and when she said breakfast, she meant ten o'clock and no earlier, but that barely left Trouble enough time to reach Eastman House. I knew I should've taken care of fallbacks last night, she thought, and shook the anger away. It was too late, that was all; she'd have to chance it. But I must stop being stupid about Cerise. She shut down the sleeping system, unplugged the central brain, and shoved it into her bag along with what was left of her money and the disks she had collected—her emergency kit, the absolute minimum that would let her walk the nets—then let herself out of the room, sealing the room lock and the extra override behind her.

It was about a half-hour's walk into Seahaven proper, across the drawbridge that spanned the Harbormouth. Trouble walked easily through the nearly-empty streets, seeing only a few people gathered outside the waffle shop behind the beach arcade. It was low tide, and the air smelled of salt mud, and oil, and, faintly, still, of peppermint. It was cool, the breeze off the water cutting through her vest and jersey, but the sunlight was warm. Crossing the drawbridge, it struck diamond highlights from the water left in the central channel, and lay in sheets across the exposed flats, where the mud was still wet from the receding water. A boat was moving along the dredged channel, heading for the fish docks, and a trio of gulls wheeled behind it, following the scent of food. They were very bright against the autumn trees that lined the horizon. At the top of the bridge, the concrete changed to metal mesh, and Trouble walked warily, careful of the slick surface. From that point, she could see down into Seahaven and beyond, past the seawall that enclosed the town and even out onto the beach itself. The sand lay in ugly patches, green and grey and oily brown, sand changing to sludge at the tideline. Even at this distance, she could see the heaped seaweed smoldering as the air hit it, releasing the chemicals it had collected from the sea. The remains of the Pavilion Bandstand were very bright against the blues of sea and sky, and someone had scrawled the beginning of a word, *K* and *O*, in scarlet across the broken shell. She wondered vaguely what it had been going to say, and started down the bridge into town.

It was more crowded here, runabouts moving along the narrow streets, and a bus passed her halfway up the avenue, carrying the night shift home from The Willows. She kept walking, moderating her pace so that she didn't seem too conspicuous, turned at last onto the little road that led toward Eastman House and to The Willows beyond. The sidewalk here was well repaired, like the roadway itself, and the grass to either side was expensively maintained, the irrigation and fertilizer heads showing like brass nails at regular intervals. There would be one-way filters buried beneath it to keep the beach chemicals from leaching into the new-laid soil, Trouble knew, and security devices laced into the neat hedges that bordered the property. For an instant she wished that she could have approached it on the wire, so that she could see the networked security blazing out of ground and trees, but that was beyond even experimental capacity now.

She did not hesitate at the entrance to Eastman House, but marched between the carved pillars as though she owned the place—as though she'd been invited, which she had. The doorman eyed her warily, taking in the casual, uncorporate clothes, but held the door open, and even offered a smile. Trouble grinned back, unable to keep from enjoying his uncertainty, and crossed the lobby, her bootheels echoing when they hit the strips of marble between the islands of carpet, to fetch up at the reception desk.

The young woman behind the desk frowned slightly, then muted that expression almost instantly, but her hand still hovered over a security button. "May I—?"

"I'm here to see Cerise," Trouble said, and smiled again. "I'm expected."

"Of course," the young woman said. She took her hand away from the button to punch codes into a keyboard, managed an uncertain smile of her own in return. "Who may I say is here?"

"I'm expected," Trouble said again. That was a risk, but less of one, she suspected, than giving her real name. Besides, when the corporations dealt with the shadows, they dealt on the corporation's turf. Let them think that, let them think that Cerise is buying grey-market goods, Trouble thought, and we're home free.

"Of course," the young woman said. She was too well trained to show any hint of annoyance in tone or expression, but Trouble could hear it in the click of fingernails on keys. "Ah, yes," the clerk went on, after a moment. "Don'll show you up."

"Thanks," Trouble said, and turned to face the doorman as he approached. The clerk handed a slip of paper across the counter, and the doorman took it, glanced quickly at it, and turned to Trouble.

"If you'll follow me, ma'am?" He started toward the elevators without waiting for an answer.

Trouble followed, felt the hairs at the back of her neck prickling. This was the tricky part, the dangerous part: if anyone was looking for her, if The Willows had somehow spotted her, recognized her from Treasury have-you-seens, this was the time when they could take her. She kept her shoulders loose with an effort as the elevator doors closed behind them, wishing, not for the first time, that she still had a gun. Or a knife, she thought, or anything.

The elevator doors opened at last, and she kept close be-

hind the doorman, keeping him between her and any lurking
security. They stepped out together into a beige-walled hallway, gently sky-lit, beige shadows on beige carpeting; the
only color was the scarlet of the flowers in a niche at the very
end of the hall. It was very quiet, too, only the faint hiss of the
environmental system, and Trouble felt herself relax slightly.
No one was waiting here; that left only Cerise to worry
about, and despite everything, she couldn't quite be wary of
her. She shrugged that recognition away, annoyed with herself, and the doorman stopped in front of one of the beige
doors. He touched the intercom button, said, in the deferential voice The Willows taught its employees, "Ms. Cerise,
your guest is here."

"Thanks." The voice even through the distorting intercom
was unchanged, the same clear soprano. "It's open."

The doorman pressed the handle, and held the door, and
Trouble walked past him into the suite. The light was
stronger here, and she blinked once, startled, as the door
closed again behind her. Cerise was waiting more or less as
she'd expected, sitting with her back to the west-facing window in one of the hotel's big armchairs, legs crossed, fingers
steepled to proclaim she didn't have a weapon, and didn't
need one. Trouble had never been fully sure whether the
pose was bravado or misdirection, if there really was a palm-
gun somewhere close to hand: Cerise had never owned a gun
when they were together—there had been no real need, all
the aggression had taken place on the nets, virtual violence,
where a woman could easily be as hard and tough as any
man—but she had demonstrably known how to use one.
Cerise did not move, and Trouble took a step sideways, out
of line with the window, so that she could see Cerise's face
against the sky and the slough beyond the glass. Cerise
smiled then, full lips quirking up into something like genuine amusement. She had gone back to dark hair, Trouble saw,
jet-black hair that emphasized the alabaster pallor of her
skin, and was stark contrast with the deep pink of her lips
and nails. The black suit was expensive, top of the line, like
the pink-heeled shoes. It jarred with the makeup, the hard

cheap color flat as the icing on a cookie, but, as always, Cerise carried it off.

"It's good to see you again," Trouble said, and Cerise laughed.

"You're late."

"I didn't want to wake you," Trouble said, and then the amusement vanished from her voice. "And I didn't want to draw too much attention. Someone's been taking my name in vain."

Cerise nodded. "So I'd noticed. So lots of people have noticed." There was a little silence between them then, and Cerise looked up at the other woman. Trouble had changed more than she'd expected, more than she herself had—she was heavier now, though not fat, the sexy child's curves maturing into something fuller, rounder, a shape that promised adult pleasures. She'd let her hair go back to its natural brown, cut short to keep the heavy curls subdued, but she still wore her clothes, jeans, man-style shirt, boots, a Japanese-patchwork vest, all mock-simplicity, with the old understated edge of menace.

"I'm not best pleased," Trouble said, quite mildly.

"Coigne—my immediate superior—wants to shut you down."

"Was it him who set Treasury on me?"

"I don't know," Cerise said. "That may have just been natural causes—this new Trouble's pushing the envelope pretty hard. It was bound to attract attention."

"What concerns me," Trouble said, "is how that attention got turned on me."

"You—we—were pretty well known," Cerise answered. "No one's forgotten Trouble." They had forgotten Alice, though, she thought, with a too-familiar touch of bitterness—or, no, not forgotten, but Alice-B-Good had gone to the corporations, joined the enemy, and her name had disappeared from conversation. She uncoiled herself from the chair, and crossed to the breakfast table set up beside the media center. "Coffee?"

"Thanks," Trouble said, and took the cup held out to her.

"What I'd really like to know is where this punk got the idea my name was up for grabs."

Cerise nodded slowly, poured herself a cup and set the pot aside, all without taking her eyes off the other woman. "You've been less than visible for quite a while. I don't know where you were, and I looked." In spite of herself, the old anger sounded in her voice; she controlled it instantly, and went on with only the slightest of hesitations, "There was a rumor that you were dead. He—she—may have thought the name was free."

"I'd love to know how that story got started," Trouble said, and settled herself on the nearest chair.

Cerise went back to her armchair, set her cup down and tucked her legs back under her. She could feel the narrow skirt straining, riding up on her thighs, and didn't care, was even mildly pleased with the effect. "I wasn't very happy with you," she said, and Trouble gave a wry smile.

"I guess not."

"Did I have cause?"

Trouble looked down into her cup, wrapped both hands around the fragile china as though she needed the warmth, staring into the black liquid. She said, without looking up, "I fucked up, leaving like that. But I was right—I had to go."

Cerise felt her own mouth twist, stared at the top of Trouble's head as though she was trying to memorize the way the hair grew from the other woman's scalp, the short almost-curls springing from a straggling part, tumbling heavily across her skull and over the tips of her ears. "We might've cracked that IC(E) together," she said, in spite of herself, and Trouble looked up sharply.

"Or we might've both gotten caught." It was the old argument, the one that had driven them apart, or as near as made no difference, and she took hold of herself, said, carefully, "I screwed up, I admit it, but that was three years ago. We can't change it."

"No," Cerise said, still with the twisted almost-smile, and then she made herself relax. "I suppose we can fight that out later. What matters now is to find this imposter of yours."

"Not mine," Trouble said instinctively, and was glad to see Cerise smile. "So what have you got on it?"

"Let's trade," Cerise said, and this time it was Trouble who grinned. "You first."

Trouble's grin widened, as though she might refuse, but she said, "I don't know a whole lot, actually. The first thing I heard of it was Treasury showing up on my doorstep—literally, I was working as a syscop for an artists' co-op—"

"You're kidding," Cerise said, and Trouble shrugged.

"It seemed the thing to do at the time. I stayed off the net for eight months after I—left—and then I stayed in the bright lights, got myself syscop's papers and got a real job."

"A syscop," Cerise said, and shook her head. "Well, set a thief to catch a thief."

Trouble said, "But, like I said, I've been keeping a low profile. The first thing I knew about it was John Starling and his partner, what's his name, Levy, I think, showing up to interview me about somebody using my local net as a springboard into the big BBS. I'm pretty sure that was just an excuse to check me out—my records were clean, and I'd've known if someone was screwing around on my boards."

"What happened to the co-op?" Cerise asked.

Trouble poured herself another cup of coffee, buying time. "I left—at their request. They said they couldn't afford my problems." She held up the pot, eyebrows rising in question, and Cerise shook her head. "So Butch van Liesvelt had showed up on my back porch the night before Treasury came down, to warn me they were interested, and when I had to run, I looked him up. I got an updated implant, and then we did some snooping around. Fate—remember Fate?—has had some dealings with newTrouble, and he told me he was based in Seahaven. This one, that is. He was not real happy with newTrouble. I guess he'd spent a couple of days mopping up Treasury watchdogs and snoops after the last time newTrouble was in his system." Trouble took a deep breath. "He did tell me one other thing, though. NewTrouble's on the wire."

"Is he, now," Cerise said softly. "That's very interesting."

"So what do you have?"

"Interpol doesn't know he's on the wire," Cerise said, as if the other hadn't spoken. "They're worrying about viruses at this point." She shook herself, frowning as she tried to organize her thoughts, said, "Hand me an English muffin, will you?"

"You're eating before noon?" Trouble asked, but found one of the still-warm muffins in the bread basket. It oozed butter—Eastman House didn't skimp on cholesterol, it seemed—and she found a plate to set it on before handing it across. Cerise took it with a nod of thanks.

"Help yourself, there's plenty."

"No, thanks," Trouble said, but picked a strawberry from among the garnishes. It was out of season, but tasted better than she'd expected, and she ate another. "So what's this about viruses, and Interpol?"

"I gather that newTrouble's been playing games in Europe," Cerise said, indistinctly, through a mouthful of bread. "But let me start at the beginning. We—Multiplane, that is—had an intrusion. I was on line and tracked it, but lost the intruder in the BBS."

"Naturally," Trouble muttered, and Cerise nodded.

"My programs, and the later autopsy of the icepick that was used, suggested it was your work—I think it was a sixty-five or seventy percent probability, something like that—but it didn't really feel like your hand." She smiled thinly, remembering Coigne's response. "My boss, Coigne, disagreed, said it was you, so I started looking for myself. I didn't talk to Treasury personally, my people did that, but I ran into Max Helling on the net and he put me in contact with someone from Interpol. And he—Mabry, his name is—gave me what they'd picked up, mostly code fragments and the occasional virus. Apparently newTrouble's been doing some cracking in the European nets, and was leaving a few viruses behind him. None of them were really damaging payloads, but the corporations have been—concerned."

"Not unreasonably," Trouble said.

"And Max and Mabry seem to be a couple," Cerise said.

"For what it's worth." She leaned forward, holding out her plate. "Would you hand me another muffin? I have a disk for you, if you want to look at it."

Trouble did as she'd asked. "Yeah, I'd like to get a look at this person's work."

"My setup's there," Cerise said, and pointed to the modules laid out on the shelf at the front of the media center. "The disk is loaded and cued, hit any key to run it."

Trouble picked up a slice of melon, crossed to the media center. "Can I keep this?" she asked, and touched a key to start the display.

"It's yours if you want it," Cerise answered, with another of her thin smiles. She watched as Trouble stared down into the screen, still gnawing delicately on the slice of melon, brows drawing down into the faint, familiar thoughtful frown. And it was strange to think of that expression as familiar even now, and not entirely pleasant, like another, unexpected, betrayal, and Cerise looked away, poured herself another cup of coffee that she didn't want.

"That's interesting," Trouble said, in the controlled voice that had always boded ill for someone. "This person's using most of my old routines."

"Yes," Cerise agreed, with enough mild amusement that Trouble turned to look at her. "Well, what'd you expect, Treasury pulled the match out of thin air? Of course it's using your routines."

Trouble grunted an acknowledgment, her eyes already back on the screen and the scrolling text. "A fair number of modifications, though—and he wasn't working from first-generation copies. Looks like he got them second- or third-hand, with modifications already in place—I think there're two hands in this, at least, or else he's really careless."

"Mabry said, and I agree, from what I saw in the autopsy, that it's immature work. This person—you said he?—doesn't like to do tidy work, only does it when he has to."

Trouble nodded thoughtfully. "Yeah, it's a he, or so Fate said." She ran her hand across the control ball, recalling a section of text, stared at it for a moment longer before going on. "You know, I could be offended that anyone thought this was me."

"And you used to complain I was arrogant," Cerise said.

"Well, you are." Trouble grinned, and Cerise smiled back in spite of herself.

"But I've earned it." She uncurled herself from the chair, stretched legs and arms, and realized with a certain pleasure that Trouble was watching her, enjoying the play of muscles under the thin black tights. And that was playing with fire, she knew, but she had never been able to keep away from matches. . . . "So, what are your intentions?"

Trouble's eyebrows rose in mute question, pointing the double meaning, and Cerise waved it away.

"Regarding newTrouble."

Trouble looked at her for an instant too long, an imperceptible hesitation before she answered, "The word I have is, he lives here, somewhere in town. I've already stopped by Mollie Blake's—you remember Mollie—but I thought I might take a walk along the Parcade, see if anyone wants to tell me where he's at."

Cerise smiled again, picturing Trouble's styles of questioning. "Mind if I tag along? I want this guy, too, you know."

"Dressed like that?"

"I can change."

"Don't tell me you got suited up just for me."

Cerise pushed herself up out of the chair, heard the note of challenge in her voice as she answered, "I thought you should know where I stand these days." She went into the bedroom without looking back, shedding her jacket as she went.

Trouble said behind her, "Head of on-line security for Multiplane. I'd heard. Sort of a glorified syscop—set a thief to catch a thief?"

It was only what she herself had said, her own jibe thrown back at her, but Cerise flinched anyway, and didn't answer. She left the door open, worked the tight skirt down her hips, exaggerating the movements with deliberate anger, walked in tights and heels and thin chemise to the suitcase that stood open on the dresser top. She found jeans and a T-shirt, and looked up again, to see that Trouble had disappeared from the doorway. She could see the other woman's reflection in the grey surface of the media center's monitor, however, and knew Trouble could see her, too. She stood still for a moment, then made herself move away, out of the line of sight.

Trouble looked away from the big monitor, not sure whether she was glad or sorry, not sure exactly what had happened, either, except that she was glad the challenge had been withdrawn. She glanced again at Cerise's machines, touched a key to recall the file, made herself concentrate on the Interpol report. Whoever had written it, this Mabry, presumably, Helling's new lover, had known his business: the analysis was cogent, each step laid out so that anyone reading the file could follow the reasoning behind its conclusions. What was missing, and Mabry had known it, was a sense of why newTrouble had picked these particular targets, chosen to steal these particular bits of data and release his viruses in these particular volumes of the net. Trouble frowned, trying to remember everything Fate had told her. It wasn't much, and most of it was unspoken, but she could assume that it was his dealings with newTrouble that had caused him enough problems to put him firmly on her side. And that was odd, too: any serious cracker would know better than to antagonize a data fence, especially someone like Fate, who worked for the mob. Of course, if newTrouble did all his business on the net, he might not know about that connection. But even so, she thought, you don't mess with a good fence. And Fate is a good one, no question about it.

"You done with that?" Cerise asked, and Trouble turned, to see the other woman standing in the bedroom doorway. She had changed into something like her old style, black jeans, nearly black T-shirt, black jacket, and walking boots, and the vivid makeup was a shocking contrast.

"Yeah," Trouble answered, and stood aside to let Cerise close down the system. "It's got to be a kid, newTrouble does. It doesn't make sense any other way."

Cerise looked up curiously, her hands slowing on the keys. "Why? I think I agree, but why?"

"You first," Trouble said, automatically, and Cerise laughed.

"Give it up."

Trouble grinned. "Because this isn't profitable—none of this that your Interpol buddy found, and none of what I've heard about here, and most certainly not hassling Fate."

Cerise nodded, folding the screen back over the keyboard. "That's more or less what Mabry said, and certainly the intrusion we had was pretty pointless—more to prove he could do it, as far as I can tell, than to get anything to sell. He was in the wrong place—that particular volume belonged to a subgroup that didn't have anything at a crucial stage."

"Besides," Trouble said, "it feels like a kid's work."

Cerise nodded again, slipped a folder into her jacket pocket. "And where best to find a kid but on the Parcade?"

They walked back across the Harbormouth bridge. The tide was coming in now, rising over the flats, and a few gulls were waiting at the edge of the mud, heads cocked to watch something under the shimmering surface. Cerise shook her head, seeing them, said, "I don't know how they survive, given what the fish have been eating. And swimming in."

Trouble shrugged. "Scavengers evolve, too, I guess." But there had been more gulls around when she was younger, she thought, or maybe that was just a trick of memory. She frowned slightly, annoyed at the irrelevance of her thought, and fixed her eyes on the continuation of the avenue ahead. The streets were more crowded now, night workers just starting their day, and the arc of the Ferris wheel showed neon above the rooftops.

The Parcade lay perpendicular to the beach, had once connected almost directly with the beach itself, but the stairs that breached the seawall had been barricaded, riprap piled behind the new concrete walls, and only the occasional plume of sand now passed that barrier. Cerise looked away from the barricades, brighter concrete against the weathered grey, said, "Where to first, do you think?"

Trouble shrugged again, surveying the low-slung build-ings. They lay in two long rows, facing each other across the much-mended street; the ones closest to the beach were sand-scarred, the pastel paint scratched and blistered, but the more distant ones were in fairly good repair, only the sun to fade the gaudy colors. The Ferris wheel and its battered con-trol shack lay at the end of the northern arcade, but even its brilliance was dwarfed by the pink-and-green palace that stood across the end of the road. The mostly green trim was picked out in yellow and white, and purple banners streamed from all six turrets. They would have to end up there, whether they wanted to or not, and Trouble grimaced, thinking of the warren of dealers behind those walls. Not just grey-market there, but black, software, and even hardware dragged out of the deepest shadows, plus drugs and arms and just about anything else that one could want, and the man who presided over it all with genial contempt was a deeply connected player. Or at least he had been: he might be dead by now, she thought, and said, "Mollie's first, and then work our way down the arcades."

"Leave the palace for last?" Cerise asked, but there was no malice in her smile.

"It'll give them a chance to take a good look at us," Trou-ble said, and Cerise nodded.

"Yeah. Tinati was always a little trigger-happy for my taste."

"So he's still running things?" Trouble asked, and stepped up onto the boardwalk than ran the length of the arcade. It was cooler under the sheltering roof, and she drew her vest closed again. Across the street, in the other arcade, a skinny kid in jeans and a sweatshirt came out of one of the store-fronts, began sweeping sand off the boardwalk into the street.

Cerise nodded. "I had some—dealings—with him about a year ago."

Trouble glanced at her. "I thought reputable corporations didn't make deals with the shadows."

"It was a buy-back," Cerise said, indifferently. "Anyway, who told you Multiplane was respectable?"

Trouble laughed. "There's Mollie's."

Mollie Blake had a single storefront toward the beach end of the north arcade, a narrow, dimly lit public room presided over by a thin girl with teased hair piled high over a frame. The shelves to either side of the central desk were piled with a random array of hardware, toys, and useless gadgets mixed with genuinely practical items. Trouble found her eyes drawn to a simple-looking data-dome, wondering if its interior works really matched the manufacturer's name on the touchplate. The override lock she had bought had been top-of-the-line, and Blake's price had been better than fair.

"Can I help you?" the girl said, not moving from behind her desk, and Trouble brought herself back to the business at hand.

"I want to talk to Mollie," she said. "Would you tell her Trouble's here?"

The girl's eyes moved to Cerise, and Cerise said, "We're together. My name's Cerise."

This time the girl's eyebrows rose in open amazement, and she touched something under the edge of the desk. "Ms. Blake? You have visitors." There was a little silence, and Trouble looked again, found the thin wire of an earpiece running down the girl's neck. "Trouble and Cerise."

There was another silence, this one longer, and Cerise glanced sideways, unable to repress a quick grin. It was all too like the old days, and she had forgotten, almost, how much fun those days had been. . . .

"Ms. Blake says go on back," the girl said, and her surprise was audible in her voice. She reached under the edge of the desk again, and an unobtrusive door popped open on the back wall.

"Thanks," Trouble said, and stepped around the desk. She pulled the door open—it was heavier than she had expected, backed with armor sheathing, and the locks were extra-heavy-duty—and stepped through into a narrow stairwell.

Cerise followed cautiously, wrinkling her nose a little at the dust that had drifted behind the threshold.

"Come on up," Blake said from the top of the stairs, and Trouble did as she was told.

They emerged into a bright and pleasant room tucked under the eaves. Twin skylights were open, the armored shutters propped up to let in light and air, and there was furniture, foam-core chairs and a pair of low tables, drawn up around a central test table. Another woman, heavyset, big-breasted and wide-hipped, sat in one of the chairs, one ankle resting on her thigh.

"You know Nova," Blake said, and the heavy woman nodded in greeting.

Trouble nodded back, did her best to hide her surprise, and could see the same startled realization flicker across Cerise's face. She had never met Nova off the nets, neither of them had; she had thought Nova was a man, like most of the crackers who affected that style. Nova smiled crookedly, as though she recognized and did not entirely enjoy that response.

"So," Blake went on, and waved them to the nearest chairs. "What do you want from me now, Trouble?" She looked at Cerise. "Or is this Multiplane's business?"

"Both," Cerise said, gently, and sat down in a patch of sunlight.

Trouble said, "I'm looking for information, Mollie."

Blake made a face, and Nova said, "And Treasury's looking for Trouble." Her tone was absolutely familiar, sharp and ironic, and Trouble knew without a shadow of a doubt that this was the person she had sparred with on the net.

"I'll tell you what we're after," she went on, as though Nova hadn't spoken, and fixed her eyes on Blake, who stood with one hip leaning against the edge of the test table. "Then you can think about it and give me an answer. I'd rather you said you didn't know or wouldn't tell me than lie to me—and I'll find out any lies."

"Oh, I know exactly what this is about," Nova said, and Blake said, "Wait." She looked at Trouble. "Go on."

Trouble said, "Word is that this newTrouble, the person who's stolen my name on the net and who's causing a lot of trouble for all the shadows, lives in Seahaven. If he buys hardware, and he must, no one goes without hardware, he'll have come to you. I want his name, and an address."

"He might not have come to me," Blake said, tonelessly. "Not everyone has your high opinion of my sources."

"Bullshit," Cerise said sweetly.

Trouble elaborated, "He's not stupid, newTrouble. He will have come here—the work he's doing, he'd have to have done."

"Assuming he's in this Seahaven," Blake said. "What's this to you, Cerise? Where does Multiplane fit in?"

"My bosses want Trouble almost as much as Treasury does, and they aren't much more particular about which one they get," Cerise answered, with a thin smile. "I, however, want to see the right Trouble blamed for this shit."

"Personal interest?" Nova murmured, with a lifted eyebrow.

"Get the wrong Trouble, and it's not going to stop," Cerise said. "And surely both sides of the law agree it has to stop."

"Touché," Nova said.

"Well?" Trouble asked, still looking at Blake.

Blake looked down at the test table, running her fingers over the concealed controls. "Give me a few days," she said.

Nova said, "I hate to say it, Moll, but she's right. Trouble, I mean. This punk's got to go."

Blake glared at her partner, got herself under control instantly. "I need to check things out," she said to Trouble. "You understand."

"Fair enough," Trouble answered, and pushed herself back up out of the heavy chair. "Let me know."

"What are you going to do when you find him?" Nova asked.

Trouble looked back over her shoulder, met Cerise's eyes for an instant, saw her eyebrows lift slightly, and then her gaze slid past to Nova, still sitting with her leg cocked up, ankle on her knee. A carved bead hung from a braided leather anklet, catching the light from the window. "Shop him," Trouble said, simply, and Nova nodded.

She went on down the stairs, Cerise following silently, and the door opened again into the shop. The young woman was still sitting behind the counter, but this time a pair of young men in patched denim jackets stood together over a recording deck, muttering to each other about its merits. They looked up as the door opened, startled and unwillingly impressed, and Trouble walked out past them, Cerise falling into step at her side.

"Where to now?" she asked, when they had stepped out onto the boardwalk.

Trouble shrugged, looked down the arcade toward the palace. "We'll stop in a couple more places," she said, "and then we'll hit the palace."

Cerise nodded, a faint, not entirely happy smile playing on her lips, and turned toward the next storefront.

Most of the storeowners remembered them, though not all fondly. Trouble repeated her message four times more, twice to men she had once known well, once to a thin woman who'd done them a favor, back in the old days, and was visibly unsure if she regretted it, once more to a man who had known Cerise, and sweated for it. She looked at Cerise as they left the store, and Cerise smiled.

"So what was that all about?" Trouble asked.

Cerise's smile widened, became almost impish. "He owed me money, and he doesn't know if I remember."

Trouble grinned. "You going to call it in?"

"I haven't decided." Cerise stiffened abruptly, not a movement but a sudden focusing of attention. Trouble shifted, looking with her toward the palace, and saw a man in black leather walking toward them, a red skull vivid on his shoulder.

"I see Tinati's deigned to notice us," she said aloud.

Cerise jammed her hands into the pockets of her jacket, one fist distending the pocket as though she held something there. "That's Aimoto. He's sort of chief thug."

"Great." Trouble kept walking, controlling her steps with

an effort, turning her approach into a saunter that was as provocative as open aggression. As the stranger approached, she could see that he was Asian, or at least part Asian: a big man, broad-shouldered, big-bellied under the heavy jacket, with golden skin and a flat nose and eyes that looked very small.

"He is not," Cerise said mildly, "even half as stupid as he looks."

The big man was within earshot now, and Trouble wondered if he'd heard. If he had, he gave no immediate sign of it, nodding placidly to Cerise. "It's good to see you again, Ms. Cerise. Mr. Tinati was wondering, are you here on Multiplane's business, or is it—personal?"

"A little of both," Cerise answered, still with her hands in her jacket pockets.

Aimoto nodded again, looked at Trouble. "Trouble, I believe?"

Trouble nodded.

"Mr. Tinati would like to talk to you—to both of you."

"Fine," Cerise said, and Trouble nodded again.

"We were wanting to talk to him."

She wasn't sure, but thought a smile flickered across Aimoto's broad face. He said nothing, however, but turned back toward the palace, gesturing for them to go with him. Trouble kept step at his shoulder, not wanting to fall ahead or behind, and wished again that she had some weapon, any weapon. Tinati, and his bosses, were people that even the net did not cross; she preferred to deal with them only at a distance.

They passed through the shadow of the Ferris wheel and climbed the four steps that led up to the palace's main door, plywood painted to mimic pink marble ringing hollow under their boots. Inside, the palace was relatively dark, despite the strip-lights along the halls, the walls painted pink or green or covered with bright, surreal murals. Most of the little doors that led off the hall were closed, each one badged with cryptic symbols or a name printed in letters so small that one would have to be practically touching the door to read them. Cerise glanced curiously from side to side, obviously recognizing at least some of the symbols. Trouble, who had been out of the shadows long enough to lose track of who was who, ignored them, and tried to pretend she didn't care.

Aimoto took them up the back stairs, the ones that led directly to Tinati's main office. Trouble spotted at least two gun alcoves on the way up, and knew there was more security she couldn't see, hidden in the walls and ceiling and wired into the building's electrical system. At the top of the stair, Aimoto paused and said, apparently to thin air, "I've brought them, boss."

A voice answered almost instantly, "Come on in."

Aimoto pushed open the heavy door, gesturing for them to enter. Trouble stepped past him, Cerise still at her side, and caught a quick glimpse of the armor sandwiched in the door itself as she came into the room. Aimoto followed them in, set his back against the door, and waited. Trouble did not look back, knew better than to look back, but the skin between her shoulder blades tingled painfully, and she knew from the deliberately bored expression on Cerise's face that the other woman was just as aware of the big man's presence between them and the only visible exit.

Tinati was sitting at a standard executive desk, beautifully polished red-toned wood supporting a black-glass display top. A few papers were scattered across the surface, but the viewspace and the work areas were conspicuously clear. Tinati was a slim man, not very tall, not quite dwarfed by his high-backed chair, and well dressed, looked like an Ivy League lawyer on the make.

"It's good to see you again, Tinati," Cerise said, breaking the silence.

Tinati looked at her without expression, steepling long and rather beautiful hands above the desk's viewspace. "And you, Cerise. Tell me, is this official, Multiplane's business, or is it personal?"

"A little of both," Cerise said again.

"I'd like to be a little clearer on that one," Tinati said.

Trouble said, "Why? It's not the clearest situation."

Tinati's eyes flickered toward her, but he looked back at Cerise. "Multiplane's involvement—complicates—my position."

Cerise took a deep breath. "Multiplane wants Trouble—there have been intrusions, as I'm sure you've heard. I want to make sure we get the right one."

"Ah." Tinati leaned back again, unfolding his hands. "Then I take it that resuming your old association is purely unofficial."

"So far," Cerise answered, with more certainty than she felt. Multiplane—or, more precisely, Coigne—would be extremely unhappy when they found out she'd been working with Trouble; only delivering the newTrouble's head on a virtual platter would have any chance of appeasing them.

"So I think I'm safe in saying this is the net's business," Tinati said. He looked at Trouble. "I don't mess with the net. It's not my bosses' policy, and it doesn't pay. I want that clearly understood. But if the net is cracking down on this new Trouble—well, I won't stand in your way. And I won't help, either. This is strictly the net's affair."

"What about your people?" Trouble asked. "I'm going to be asking questions. Your sanction, your forbearance, at the least, that would make a big difference." She was taking a chance, and she knew it, was not surprised when Tinati shook his head.

"What my people do is their business, up to the individual. I'm not for you, I'm not against you, I'm not involved. Don't make me get involved."

"As you say," Trouble answered, "it's the net's business."

"It's getting very close to real," Tinati said.

Cerise laughed, the sound loud in the quiet room. Even Tinati looked startled for an instant, and hid it quickly behind his lawyer's mask. "All we want is to resolve a problem, Tinati—one that's already a thorn in your side as well as ours."

"It's a straightforward deal," Trouble said. "We find him, I shop him to Treasury, and that's the end of it."

"I hope so," Tinati said. "I hope it's that simple, Trouble. I don't appreciate complications."

"If there are any complications," Trouble said, "they'll come from you."

Tinati studied her for a long moment, nodded at last. "As I said, this is the net's business. I don't interfere with the net."

"Until it interferes with you," Cerise said, and sounded almost happy.

"I'm glad we understand each other," Tinati said, and there was more than a hint of irony in his tone. "Kenny, will you show the ladies out?"

Aimoto led them back down the stairs and out into the bright sunlight of the Parcade. "Good to see you again, Ms. Cerise," he said, and disappeared back into the palace before the black-clad woman could answer.

"I bet," Trouble said, and started walking back down the Parcade. Cerise fell into step beside her.

"So now what?" she asked. "Bother some more dealers?"

Trouble considered the question, shook her head slowly. "No. No, I don't think it'd do much good. If anybody's going to tell us, it's going to be Mollie, and that's going to take time."

Cerise nodded. "I agree. So what, see what the nets are saying—see what's going on in the other Seahaven, maybe?"

Trouble smiled wryly, remembering her last visit to virtual Seahaven. "Maybe you better do that," she said. "I'm not exactly *persona grata* there just at the moment."

"Can't imagine why."

"Let me know what you find out," Trouble said, and saw Cerise's expression go suddenly wooden. There had been too much of an echo of the old days, too much a reminder of the old give-and-take and where it had led them both, and she added, much too late, "If you wouldn't mind. Please."

"I'll be in touch," Cerise said, still stiff-faced, and lengthened her step with sudden angry energy, striding off down the Parcade toward the main road that led back to Seahaven. Trouble watched her go, knowing better than to call her back, and could have kicked herself for her own clumsiness. She had always given the orders on jobs like this—she was good at the jobs where the real world intersected the virtual, better than Cerise, and better than Cerise, too, when it came to vengeance. Cerise enjoyed the chase, but lost interest once the catch was made. It had always been Trouble, in the end, who'd made the kills. It was old knowledge, not even regret anymore, and Trouble put it briskly aside, and with it the possibility that Cerise, too, might have changed. She started down the Parcade in Cerise's wake, not hurrying. She would let Cerise visit virtual Seahaven, all right, but she'd also run her own discreet checks, just in case. She could not forget, couldn't afford to forget, that they weren't a partnership anymore.

# SILK

# ∎ 9 ∎

CERISE FLOATS THROUGH the streets of Seahaven, frozen in a premature winter, the buildings white on black, heaped with snow. Even with a counterroutine in place, she feels the Mayor's cold, radiating up from the ice-rimed streets and the frozen canal that runs straight as a surveyor's line beside her. The same cold, damp and unpleasant, realer than IC(E), radiates from the building to her left, from the snow-heavy roof and the icicle-hung windows. She imagines her counterroutine as a cloak of fur, fur whiter than snow, greyer than ice, all soft warmth she's never really felt, and hugs it to her, cobbles a display and drapes her icon in barbaric luxury. She drifts on, wrapped in false fur, her feet not quite touching the slick-glazed surface, heading for the market plaza.

She slows as she gets closer, remembering the real Seahaven, remembering Trouble, Trouble giving her orders as though nothing had changed, as though she'd never walked out with all her worldly goods and left Cerise bewildered and angry, remembering, too, how good it had felt to be back together even just on the street, and wonders what she will do now. Find out what they are saying in the market about newTrouble, certainly; that she would do for herself, even if it weren't what Trouble wanted. But afterwards . . . She fingers a code in memory, the mailcode Silk had left her, wrapped in a glittering, Christmas-wrapped bomb. After that, perhaps, perhaps she will follow that code, and see what Silk has to say for herself.

The market plaza is busy, and she is glad of it, lets herself drift through the crowd, not hiding her presence, but not advertising it, either. She hears fragments of gossip, sees a silver sphere spring up briefly around a pair of icons—sees too the watchdog lunge for them—but hears nothing that she doesn't already know. Trouble—the original, her Trouble—is looking for the newTrouble, the one who usurped her name; the net is divided as to the rights of it, the snatches she hears uneasy, uncertain, but the lines are drawn. The only question left now is who will stand where. It is as she expected, *pretty much, and she turns along the message wall, readying a program she calls sticky fingers, lets it trawl past the gaudy surface. She feels it working, process translated as sensation, a vibration that becomes now and then a thump, as though she dragged a stick across an uneven surface. She is proud of this routine, of the quick-search, the codebreaker, that lets her scan the posted mail and steal quick-copies of those messages that match the search criteria. They will be imperfect, made on the fly, but she can reconstruct them later, and they will give her an idea of how the net is taking this.*

*She reaches the end of the wall, and feels the program shut itself down, slapping back into her hand, the stolen messages heavy in memory. She finds a departure node, lets herself out onto the net, hovers for an instant in the datastream, letting the bits pour past her like a river of gold. She should go home, or back to real-Sea-haven, where she can study the data that hangs in memory, but she reaches instead for the mailcode she has carried with her since she met Silk, and follows it instead, turning down the lines of light to-ward the unreal space where Silk has said she can be found.*

*Trouble walks the net like the ghost of herself, brainworm turned off, presenting a generic icon to the general view. The net lies flat before her, black lines and dots on silver, black-and-grey symbols scribed across her sight as the net relays its messages. It is slow, painfully so, like wading through mud; she is deaf and numb, swathed in the lack of sensation, and she feels her hands straining against the data gloves, muscles tightening as though, if she just works a little harder, she could feel again. She's been through this before and makes herself relax, but she can feel herself tense again as soon as her attention turns elsewhere. There is an ache behind her eyes, dull as black on silver, and she knows she will be sorry in the morning.*

*But she is effectively invisible in this guise, and most other net-walkers know nothing else; she can live with it for an hour or so, the time she needs to gather news. She turns toward the BBS—she slides along a thick black line, impervious to the data that she knows is flowing with her, past her, passes through a node like a great black gear, icons flickering above it to tell her who the parent users are, follows another, thicker line, and then a thinner, turning at* right angles, always, from grid to grid, and then she's on the floor of the BBS at last, a poor shadow of itself. Icons badge the air, offer other, smaller grids, or inner menu boards, and the view streams with brighter silver dots. She stops at one familiar display, where anyone can post a notice to the world. The board roils almost painfully in her sight, black print over silver-and-grey moire; a button hangs to her left, offering to clear the screen if she will log on, but she doesn't, prefers to keep her anonymity even as she squints at the distorted letters. The system is old, from the first days of the net; whoever is manager here still keeps the doors open to the world. She skims through three pages, then flips through a dozen more pretty much at random: her challenge has traveled even here, well into the bright lights, and it's made a lot of people nervous. Comment is divided, perhaps a third against and a third approving and a third deploring the situation altogether; perhaps half agree that new-Trouble had no right to take her name. Pretty much what she'd expected, she thinks, and she slips away again, riding the first major line out of the BBS. It's too crowded there, too painful to work without the brainworm to give depth and substance; she prefers the main net, the data highways, if she has to live without sensation.

She slides along a familiar gridline, watching for a starred intersection that will take her up another plane, deeper into the net. She reaches the intersection, makes the transfer, and codes flash before her eyes, icons and a stream of numbers warning her that another person, another icon, is overtaking her, signaling for her attention. She recognizes the main icon, and the contact code, sends codes of her own, and feels her secondary translator lock and mesh with the newcomer's.

*Hello, Trouble,* Arabesque's voice says, in her ear.

She frowns, wishing she had more to go on than just the sound— without the wire, all she has is the flat code that hangs in the air in front of her, black on silver. *Hello, Rachelle,* she answers, and knows she sounds less than enthusiastic.

*I thought you might like to know,* Arabesque says, and Trouble imagines she hears a hint of malice in her voice. *The Mayor's not best pleased with you.*

*The Mayor of Seahaven?* she asks, for want of a better question, wanting time to think, and Arabesque laughs.

*Is there another? He's saying—he floats it as a question, some- one else's name, but the word is he's behind it. He says you should be the one to be shopped, not newTrouble—you're not really one of us, he says, just another dyke on the wire, using it 'cause you're not good enough to run the net bare.* There is contempt in her voice, and anger: this touches her, too.

*What's the response?* Trouble asks, and is pleased to hear her- self dispassionate, as though she didn't really care.

*Not a lot of support,* Arabesque answers, and Trouble thinks she shrugged. *Maybe ten percent of what I saw, certainly no more than that.* There is a pause; Trouble waits, hating to be blind. *A lot of people were really shocked, Trouble, that's the good thing. They expected the Mayor to back you up, since he's always been so protective of his name.*

*What's he so pissed off about?* Trouble says.

*You've been making pretty free with his boards,* Arabesque says, *you and Cerise. And you've never been appropriately thank- ful.*

Trouble grimaces, feels her lips twist, knows the gesture is invisi- ble. *He's never done anything to be thanked for.*

*Whatever,* Arabesque says. *But I thought you ought to know what he was saying.*

*What's the name he's using? Can I prove it's him?*

*I doubt it. It's posted under Sasquatch—I couldn't prove it was the Mayor, but I'm morally certain it's him.*

Trouble considers this for a heartbeat, marshalling her options. *Thanks, Rachelle,* she says at last, regretting again her lack of available expression. *I'll keep on eye on this.*

*No problem,* Arabesque answers, and a codestring flashes as she breaks the connection. Trouble sees the code slide away, follow- ing a solid line, and turns away herself. There's not much more she needs to do; better, she thinks, to return home—take a circuitous route, lurk in any chat fora that are open, see what's being said— but still, return home, and wait for Blake to contact her.

Cerise finds the mailcode's reference point, pauses in the dataflow to scan the area: a flat and featureless plane, like an empty dance floor. It's not an ordinary node, that much is certain, and she steps out of the datastream expecting—something. As her foot touches the plane, color flares from that point of contact, shoots out across the virtual floor, turning it from a mere place-holder to squares of brick and stone and lush beds of flowers. They are blooming out of season, out of synch, chrysanthemums and crocuses sprouting together, beds of tulips set below roses in full riot, but that hardly seems to matter. The color, the image, spreads further, like dye in damp cloth, and a bench springs up, and then, beyond that, a fantastic steel and glass gazebo, bright as a birdcage against the illusory sky that wells up behind it. Cerise looks back over her shoulder, sees the air behind her shimmer like heat, reflecting the illusion like a trembling mirror: special-purpose IC(E), very sophisticated IC(E), triggered by the same routine that had set the image maker in motion. Was it my codes that triggered this, she thinks, or would anyone's touch have done it? It doesn't feel hostile—anyone who set a trap would hardly use this garden for a backdrop, she thinks, but she readies her defenses anyway, primary shield, dispersion routine copied from Trouble years before, the cutout that will drop her off the net if all else fails, and a voice sings from the gazebo.

*Hello, Cerise.*

It is the voice she knows as Silk's, and she starts slowly toward it, waiting for an icon to appear behind the glass and steel. She tastes the program around her, sampling the constructed images: no one she recognizes, not even fully Silk, though it holds a flavor of the work she'd sampled at their one meeting. And then she sees the icon clearly, the same girl-shape, all curves and black leather, standing hipshot in the doorway, one arm against the wall above her head.

*Hello, yourself,* Cerise answers, but her tone is warmer than the words, more appreciative than she'd meant. She keeps walking, past beds of tulips and something else she doesn't recognize, until she stands less than ten yards from the smiling icon.

*You like my place?* Silk asks, and Cerise hesitates, nods slowly at last.

*It's very nice,* she says, and judges her moment. *Technically.*

The icon twitches, but the expression stays the same for a long moment. Then, slowly, Silk lifts one eyebrow. *Only technically?*

*You're not a gardener,* Cerise answers, and allows herself a smile. There is a little pause, and then Silk returns the grin.

*You want to come in?*

*What did you have in mind?* Cerise asks, and keeps her distance. She lets the defensive programs fade from readiness, however, and Silk's grin changes, becomes sexy, open invitation.

*Come in and find out.*

Cerise hesitates, admitting the appeal but wary of it, of the stranger behind the icon, and Silk says, *Safe as houses.*

And safer than real sex, Cerise thinks, automatically, and adds, but not as safe as staying here. Trouble would have laughed, and walked away—or agreed, if the fancy took her. Cerise allows herself a smile. The old days are back again, she's stepping back into old habits as though there had never been a break—and that's a little too much, too fast, now, she needs a break from it, from Trouble. She takes a few steps forward, and Silk pulls herself gracefully upright, leaving just enough room for Cerise to step past her. She knows perfectly well what the mock-gazebo must contain, what she would consent to—the programs aren't difficult to find, are simplicity to write when both parties are on the wire, no need for complex suits and gloves, just the brainworm turning suggested fantasy to direct, directed input. She brushes past Silk, deliberately trailing a hand across the girl-shape's hip. She feel leather, cool and smooth as Silk's name against her palm, and Silk laughs and follows her in, offers her hand and in it a key.

Cerise hesitates only for an instant, less than a heartbeat, though Silk will see it, calls the routine from the depths of her toolkit, extends her own hand offering her own key. They touch, and Cerise feels the play of raw sensation like water shivering through her as the programs speak and calibrate one to the other. And then she feels Silk's hands on her breasts, delicate and possessive, reaches out to cup black leather hips and feels the shock of skin beneath her fingers. She closes her eyes—the programs have not matched, cannot match sight and touch—lets Silk's hand slip back along her shoulder blades, so that they are pulled body to body, breasts, bellies, and thighs touching, only Silk's hand against her breast dividing them. It's been a long time since she's played this game, a long time since there's been a presence on the net that excited her, and she is startled once again when she feels the distant ache between her legs, her body waking to stimulus, lagging behind the unreal sensations.

And then the brainworm has overridden that distraction, and she feels only the touch of Silk's hands, the whisper of Silk's skin under her own fingers. She pulls Silk closer still, feels the other woman lean back, straddling her, knees tight along her ribs, pubic hair and the wet warmth of her crotch just brushing Cerise's belly—there is no gravity, after all, no reference points, no reason to worry that she's gone somehow without noticing from standing to flat on her back—and Cerise smiles blind, runs both hands along Silk's thighs until her thumbs caress the inner join of thigh and groin, teasing along the edge of the tight-curled hair. And then Silk backs away, evading the touch, easing down along and then between Cerise's legs. Cerise tries to rise, to follow, but there is a hand on her breast and a hand on her belly, urging her down, and then a cheek against her own thigh and a tongue warm and eager between her legs. Cerise leans back, arching under hands and mouth, tangles her hands in Silk's hair, guiding her to the right spots.

*Greedy,* Silk says, sounds approving, and Cerise moans at the touch of breath and the moving lips. Then the tongue is back, busy and demanding, and Cerise arches harder against it, pressing herself against the other woman's mouth. She shudders, and then at last she's coming, riding the crest of her delight until the brainworm's trigger resets, and she shivers, unwillingly letting it end. She recovers slowly, body lagging behind her brain, and reaches for Silk, groping still with eyes closed, not wanting to end the illusion. There is nothing within her reach.

She opens her eyes, and gravity reasserts itself; she is standing again on the featureless plane, the IC(E) that walled it vanished, the illusion of a garden gone as well. She's been had, in more ways than one, and she sets a watchdog searching, just in case Silk has left a trail. The program returns a moment later, empty-jawed. She swears and recovers it, stands still for a long moment, staring at the grid of the net around her. Distantly, at a distance, she can feel her body trembling still, muscles relaxing only slowly in the aftermath of orgasm, but the brainworm has already recovered for her. Whatever it was about—and she can't be sure, it could be revenge on a syscop, revenge on a friend of Trouble's, or just some new game *invented by one more crazy—she will have to deal with consequences: there are never no consequences from something so meticulously prepared and executed. Stupid, she tells herself, it was stupid to agree—and then she strangles the thought stillborn. Stupid it may be, stupid it was, but it's done, and you'll have to deal with it. Trouble will be amused.*

*She turns away from the plane, launches herself to the nearest datastream and lets it carry her, at the same time letting her senses stretch until the din of the nets is almost painful. She will see/hear/feel Silk if she comes back, and recognize her; until then, she'll put out a few discreet inquiries. Once she knows what this was all about, why it happened, beyond her own foolhardy choice, then she'll know what has to be done about it. But the net is empty of significant data, and she lets the river of light carry her toward home.*

The hotel room was very quiet, and her legs had cramped. Cerise grimaced, knowing perfectly well why, and uncoiled herself cautiously from the chair. She was wet, as well as stiff, and remembered all too well why she'd never much liked virtual sex. She called up a text-analysis routine, and set it to work on the contents of the file she'd pulled from the message wall in virtual-Seahaven, and went into the bathroom to take a shower. She took her time about it, letting the hot water relax her tensed muscles, and emerged to wrap herself in a yukata just as the screen went blank, signaling that the program had completed its run. She frowned, and crossed to the media center, touched keys to open and read the re-created file. Most of it was old news, people passing messages, rumors, and gossip, about one or both Troubles, and she unwound the towel from around her still-wet hair, ran her fingers through the short strands to ease it into shape, not wanting to bother getting a comb, while the program displayed message after message. Then a strange name caught her eye, and the message attached to it seemed to leap out at her:

THE OLD TROUBLE IS THE ONE WHO IS CAUSING ALL THE PROBLEMS RIGHT NOW, AND I THINK SHE'S THE

ONE WHO SHOULD PAY FOR IT. SHE WAS OFF THE
NETS FOR YEARS; NOW SHE'S COME BACK AND
CLAIMS IT'S STILL HER RIGHT TO USE THE NAME?
COME ON! IF IT WEREN'T FOR HER, TREASURY
WOULDN'T BE SO INTERESTED IN THE NEW TROUBLE. I
SAY, IF ANYONE KNOWS WHERE SHE IS, REALWORLD,
THEY SHOULD TELL TREASURY AND GET IT OVER
WITH. THAT WAY WE CAN GET SOME PEACE AROUND
HERE AGAIN.

It was signed SASQUATCH and an icon she didn't recognize.

Cerise frowned, sat back down in front of the screen,
drawing the yukata closed around her, typed in a series of
commands that would retrieve all messages derived from
Sasquatch's. The sticky fingers routine had only picked up
some of them—not all of them, apparently, had contained
the trigger words she had selected—but she had gotten
enough to get a feel for what Seahaven's regulars were saying. Most, she was glad to see, disagreed, and she had gotten
most of one long posting that pointed out just what the new-
Trouble had done, but there was a small but vocal minority
who agreed with Sasquatch. And there was one final message from Sasquatch that made her frown even more deeply:

THE OLD TROUBLE IS STILL THE ONE CAUSING THE
PROBLEMS, AND SHE'S STILL NOT REALLY ALL THAT
GOOD, IF SHE HAS TO USE THE WIRE. SHE'S NOT ONE
OF US, SHE'S A POLITICAL. SO WHY ARE WE PROTECT-
ING HER?

*Political* was a familiar euphemism, one that had never
failed to draw at least a sour smile. Translated, Cerise
thought, Sasquatch is saying she's a dyke and on the wire,
and we don't have to take care of her. Wonderful. She flipped
quickly through the rest of the file—Sasquatch was not gathering much more support for his views, but at least one of
them was a name she recognized as local, metropolitan area
if not actually based in Seahaven. And that one was really all

Treasury would need to give them Trouble's approximate location. She shut down the program, saving the file in protected memory, and switched back into the communications net, tied herself in to Multiplane's files. Sasquatch was new to her, but one of her people might have encountered him before; she left the question in Baeyen's working volume, with a red flag attached to it marking it as urgent, and flipped out again into the main phone system. She should warn Trouble, too, though it was better not to contact her directly. She hesitated again, considering her options, then plugged herself back into the net, launched herself into the local system.

*She races through the spirals of light, finds the phone system and the hole that someone left in the stranded IC(E). This is a well-known trapdoor, at least in the shadows; she eases through it, still cautious, finds herself at last at the boards she wanted. She composes her message—SOMEONE NAMED SASQUATCH WANTS TO SELL YOU TO TREASURY; CONTACT ME ASAP—and lets a pocket routine translate it into voicemail. The next time Trouble picks up her phone, she will receive that message; Cerise smiles, a little wryly, thinking of Trouble's laughter when she hears about Silk, and turns again for home.*

Trouble walked back along the road that led to the Parcade, a twist of soft, greasy pretzel hot in her hand. She ate cautiously, trying not to spill either the butter or the mustard on herself, and watched the crowds out of the corner of her eye. It was getting dark, the sun just down behind the trees that edged the slough, the sky to the west flaming yellow and orange and red almost to the zenith. To the east, the stars were visible, and a sliver of moon, rising out of the ocean, cast a thin streak of light across the waves. The avenue was busy even on this side of the bridge, music spilling from the open doors of the two clubs—one playing intertech, the other playing speed, so that the bass lines met in a heavy, syncopated beat—and the food vendors were busy, their carts clustered around the public power points. She hadn't found much since she left the nets, hadn't had time to find much, but she was enjoying the return to Seahaven, to the crowds and the shops and the heavy salt air. And that, she told herself, was beside the point. She had bought her dinner—that had been her excuse for going out; it was time she went back to her room and waited for Blake, or any of the others, to call. She looked north anyway, toward the bridge at Harbormouth, wondering what Cerise was doing, if she were busy, if she wanted to come out on the town, but curbed that thought. It was too dangerous—and besides, she told herself, she was pissed at you when she left. Better let her calm down—better let us both calm down, let things cool down a little between us—before we try again. It was easy, too easy, to fall back into the old routines; the trouble is, she thought, I'm not sure I don't want to do just that.

" 'Cuse me?"

Trouble turned to face the speaker, automatically checking to make sure she hadn't somehow walked too close to the beach, and found herself facing a skinny black kid, hair carved into a tight cap. He was wearing a Net-God T-shirt, gold stylized chip design bright against black cotton, and the cuff of a VR glove protruded slightly from the pocket of his denim vest.

A cracker or a wannabe? she wondered, and said, "Yeah?" She kept her voice neutral, and was pleased when the kid didn't blink.

"You're Trouble?"

"That's right." There was no point hiding her name, she thought, not after she'd spent the morning making sure everyone knew she was back.

"I've got a message for you."

"Oh, yeah?" Trouble kept her voice and face expressionless, but inwardly felt herself snap to attention. "Who from?"

"Butch. Van Liesvelt."

Trouble nodded. "All right."

"Butch says Treasury's on to you. They know you're in Seahaven, so if you've put your name on anything, stay away from it." The kid took a deep breath, visibly recalling a memorized message. "He says he'll do what he can, but that isn't much. You're on your own."

"Shit." Trouble bit back the rest of the comment, thinking of the hardware left in her rooms—and it would have to be abandoned, she didn't dare go back—and managed a nod for the kid. "Thanks—tell Butch I appreciate the warning."

The kid grinned suddenly. "He also sent a call-card." He held out the silver rectangle, and Trouble took it, nodding slowly.

"Thanks," she said again, and meant it: the cards were as good as cash to gain access to the dataphone system; if she'd been given a card like that, at that age, she would have been sorely tempted to keep it. The kid's grin widened, as though he'd read the thought, and he slipped his hand out of the pocket of his jacket.

"I get a gold card as payment."

Trouble laughed. "Tell Butch thanks," she said again, and the kid nodded.

"I'll do that," he said, and turned away into the crowd.

Trouble watched him go, losing himself expertly among the strolling pedestrians and the knots of shoppers that eddied in front of the tiny storefronts, tried to think what she should do next. Try to retrieve her hardware, if she could: that was the obvious first step, probably too obvious. But she couldn't afford to lose the equipment without a struggle. She jammed her hands into the pockets of her jeans, started slowly back along the avenue toward the streets that led to the hostel. She stayed with the crowds most of the way, calling up old skills to hover always at the edge of a large group, so that at first glance she seemed to be part of it. A block from the hostel she turned down an alley that led between two fryshops, stepping carefully over the broken boxes and the rotted vegetables that slimed the pavement. It was a narrow space, narrowed further by the heaped trash, so that there was barely a clear path between the buildings. She walked carefully, letting her eyes adjust to the sudden darkness, and paused at the end of the alley to survey the street. The alley did not quite meet the end of Marcy Street, where the hostel stood, but came in at an angle to the cross street; the continuation of Marcy formed a dogleg in the opposite direction. From the mouth of the alley, she could just see the hostel's entrance and the runabout parked illegally across from it. She couldn't be sure, but she thought there were people sitting in the runabout, slumped low in their seats—even if there weren't, its very location betrayed it as a cop car. A good deal of the town's income came from parking fines; no local would be stupid enough to wait there, in a blatant no-stopping zone, without a guarantee of immunity.

She retraced her steps, wondering if she could get into the hostel through the back lots. It wasn't likely, but she had to try. She threaded her way along a residential street crowded with parked runabouts—all with bright-orange resident's stickers prominently displayed—and found a doorway at the end of the street, the alcove lamp not yet lit. She stepped into the shadows, pretending to examine the address board, and let her eyes travel beyond it to the street. From the alcove she could just see the wall that surrounded the hostel's small backyard—just sand, really, and brick paving—and, above the wall, the windows of the back rooms. Only a couple were occupied, the curtains drawn closed, light showing just at the edges of the rectangle, but she waited anyway, frowning into the dark. The stairway that ran from the yard to the main floor was dimly lit, as always, a single weak bulb burning behind amber glass, and she fixed her eyes on that, waiting. For a long time nothing moved, and then, quite suddenly, a head appeared, vanished again, as though someone had stepped up onto the bottom stair, and then stepped down again. Trouble swore under her breath, turned out of the alcove, and headed back down the narrow street, keeping close under the shadow of the houses. It could just be a resident of the hostel, out for a last smoke or a drink or waiting for a connection before the dealers stopped making deliveries, but this was not the time to take that chance. She would have to abandon the hardware, at least for now.

And that didn't leave her many options at all. She smoothed her frown with an effort, walked back down Ashworth toward the Parcade and the bank of phones that stood beside the palace, opposite the Ferris wheel. That was taking a risk, too, but Tinati didn't like the cops, used his influence to keep them off the Parcade as a matter of principle. She didn't think he would abandon that for her—she wasn't worth it, it wasn't worth it to him to meddle in what was, still, the net's affair. With the call-card and the telepad she carried in her pocket, she could contact Cerise, get her to help—unless it was Cerise who'd sold her.

She stumbled over a board that had worked itself loose from the walk, swore as much at the thought of betrayal as at the pain in her toe. But Cerise wouldn't do that, wouldn't shop her to Treasury; no matter how angry she was, no matter how long she'd worked for Multiplane, she was still loyal to the shadows, and this was shadow business. She would settle it on the net, and personally, not through the law. Trouble made herself keep walking, through the patches of light and shadow that swept across the sandy street in front of the palace, joined the crowd that hovered beside the bank of phones, forming a ragged queue. She took her place at the end, jammed her hands back into her pockets, running her fingers over the smooth case of the telepad. It was a busy night, maybe a dozen people waiting, another dozen hanging out, looking for work or just waiting for something to happen. She looked toward the palace, and saw Aimoto waiting in the shadow of the doorway: Tinati wasn't having any trouble tonight, that much was clear.

The line moved slowly, as it always did. A street vendor came by, selling cones of fried vegetables; she bought one and ate its contents piece by piece, feeling the greasy paper disintegrate under her fingers. Then at last she was at the head of the line and a phone came free, and she moved toward it without haste, crumpling the paper cone in one hand. She set the wadded paper on the ledge beneath the phone, tugged the cord to draw the baffles down into place, and reached for the telepad. She plugged it in, checking automatically for visible bugs, and touched a key to run a quick scan from the pad itself. It came up clean—she had expected nothing else; Tinati would make sure that the obvious bugs were dealt with, and anything else would be in the main system anyway—and she fed the call-card into the access slot. The miniscreen at the top of the phone lit, displaying a series of branching menus; at the same time, the image in the telepad's display shifted, showing a new series of codes and options. Trouble took a deep breath, and touched keys to route herself into the main phone system.

She found the subexchange she wanted quickly enough, for working blind, off the wire, and set her call chasing itself through the system, hoping to tangle any lurkers, before she typed in the codes that would give her access to The Willows and to Cerise's phone. Her screen flashed white instead of the expected green, and she felt a heartbeat's panic before she recognized what had happened. The white screen shifted, displayed voicemail codes, and she lifted the handset to hear the words.

"—named Sasquatch wants to sell you to Treasury, contact me ASAP."

The mechanical voice was unrecognizable, just a construct of the system, but the codes at the end of the message were perfectly familiar. Cerise, Trouble thought, and was surprised by the strength of her own relief. She had been almost certain that Cerise wouldn't sell her out, but it was good to know for sure. Then the other name hit her: if Arabesque was to be believed, "Sasquatch" was the Mayor, acting through another icon, another identity—and why the hell would he want to shop me? Trouble wondered. Not being respectful—that's not enough, not unless he's really crazy. I've got enough friends on the net who'll act for me, make his life miserable once they know it's him—and if Rachelle knows, the rest of the shadows will know soon enough.

The screen went green suddenly, her routine complete, contact made, no tracers sighted, and she lifted the handset again to hear the buzz of a hotel teleset.

Cerise answered on the fourth ring. "Yes?"

"Cerise," Trouble said, and didn't bother to hide the relief in her voice.

"Tr—" Cerise broke off before the word was even formed, said, smoothly, "There you are. I was hoping you'd call to-night."

"I got your message," Trouble said. "I'm afraid it came a little late."

"Did it, now?" Cerise was silent for a moment. "Do you need a ride, then?"

"And a place to stay," Trouble said.

"I figured."

There was another long pause, and Trouble looked un-easily at the telepad's screen. So far she didn't show any trac-ers, or any tap routines, but the telepad wasn't sophisticated enough to pick up anything more complicated than an active search. Passive monitors were slow, took a while to return the information they had gathered, but she would never know if one had been on her line.

"Right," Cerise said abruptly, and Trouble jerked herself back to attention. "I've got a couple of things to take care of first, but then I'll meet you—say by Joe's on the beachfront?"

Trouble frowned—Joe's was long gone, had been just a re-cent memory when she and Cerise had first come to Sea-haven—and hoped she was getting it right. "I'll be there. When?"

"Give me an hour," Cerise said, sounding grim, and cut the connection.

Trouble shut down her system, more slowly, trying to give herself time enough to think. She would go to the storefront where Joe's had been—it was as good a code as they could hope to come up with, on short notice—in an hour, and hope Cerise showed up. Or, more precisely, she thought, folding cables into a neat package, I'll hope I understood. Cerise will be there; that I can count on. All I have to do is stay out of sight for an hour.

She tucked the telepad and the call-card back into her pocket, and stepped out from under the baffles. The Parcade was still busy, would stay busy until well after midnight; she could lose herself in the crowds here. She walked slowly away from the bank of phones, turned into a video garden where the heavy music warred with the arrhythmic beep and jangle of game consoles. She found a table in the central space where she could watch the door, and settled herself to wait.

*Cerise runs the net like a bloodhound, head down on the scent of her own tracker. She sees it spark ahead of her, flickering red against the black-and-silver sky, follows its course along the datastreams. It was a good routine to begin with, and she has customized it, and knows her target intimately on top of that: it signals success within minutes, and she sweeps down to join it, sees Helling's icon on the horizon.*

*\*Max,\* she says, and the icon shifts, turns to face her. She throws a sphere around them, shutting out the net and his protests, over-riding him with casual force. There's no time to be subtle, or even polite, and she seals the sphere against his reflexive attempt to break it. \*I need Vess Mabry's realworld codes.\**

*\*What?\* Helling stops then, icebreaker half ready.*

*\*I need to talk to Mabry—I need his help, it's urgent.\**

*\*Trouble,\* Helling says, with absolute certainty, and dismisses the icebreaker.*

*\*How'd you guess?\* Cerise takes a breath. \*I need those codes, Max.\**

*\*I heard there was trouble from Seahaven, someone talking Treasury,\* Helling says.*

*\*Someone's shopped her,\* Cerise says, and bites her tongue to keep from saying more. Helling will help in his own good time, or not at all; she's already pushing him as far as she dares.*

*\*Do you really think Vess can help?\* Helling asks, and Cerise takes a breath, controls her response with an effort, clamping down on the brainworm's output.*

*\*I hope so. I want to make it Interpol's case, if I can—I've got some authority, through Multiplane.\* I hope, she adds silently, I hope it will be enough. But Mabry doesn't like Starling: she holds to that, and waits.*

*\*Shit,\* Helling says, half under his breath, and the icon gestures as though to dispel a lurking watchdog. \*Do you know who did it, shopped her, I mean?\**

*The codes, Max—* Cerise stops herself abruptly, answers, *Maybe. There was someone called Sasquatch who was advocating it. I imagine he or one of his friends went through with it.*

Helling shakes his head. *I don't know the name.*

*The codes.*

*All right.* Helling takes a deep breath, audible even over the net, reaches into memory to come out with a series of mail and phone codes displayed as a plain white square. Cerise accepts them, feels the numbers fizz against her fingers as she slides them into her own memory.

*There's business codes there,* Helling says, *and the home code. At this hour—* he glances sideways, conjuring an internal display*—try home first. Tell him I told you to.*

*Thanks,* Cerise says, and lifts her hand to dismiss the sphere.

*Hang on,* Helling says, and she stops, routine not yet invoked.

*If you want,* Helling goes on, *I can check out this Sasquatch. If he shopped her, I can put the word out.*

*Trouble is not universally loved,* Cerise says, and hears herself bitter: the same dislike is turned against her often enough. *Do you think it would help?*

*There's a lot of people who think she's right, this time,* Helling answers, and this time Cerise nods.

*Thanks, Max,* she says. *I appreciate it.* She lifts her hand again, dismisses the sphere, but to her surprise Helling does not immediately speed away.

*Just like the old days,* he says, and she can't tell, in the darkness of his thunderstorm, whether he is amused or angered by the thought. And then he's gone, icon snatched away on the datastream, and Cerise turns her attention to the codes he's given her.

The on-line address isn't far away, by common net reckoning. She sends a query, searching for him in the open pool, and is not surprised when the routine returns unanswered. Helling had said he would be at home, and he should know; better to try that address, off-line, and she turns up and into the nearest datastream, lets it carry her home.

The codes were waiting on her screen as she straightened in her chair and reached to detach the dollie-cord. She blinked at them, and switched out of the interface mode, running through files until she found the program she wanted. It was military in origin, grey-market in provenance, and very effective, would disguise the source of her call and give her a readout on anyone who tried to track her. She set it running, and found a cable to plug into the phoneset's i/o jack, then touched keys to route the call through the program. She pulled the yukata tighter around her, suddenly aware of the environmental system's chill, and ran one hand through her hair, vaguely startled to find that it had dried already. But there had been ample time for that; she had lost track of time on the net and worrying about Trouble. Numbers shifted on the screen—the program was having difficulty tying into the main trunk lines, was switching to a secondary system—and she wondered if she had time to dress.

A new icon appeared at that instant, and the handset beeped, signaling that her call had connected. She picked it up, feeling the sudden adrenaline surge tighten the muscles of her belly, and heard Mabry's voice saying, "Yes? Max, is that you?"

"It's Cerise," Cerise said. "Max gave me this number."

"Cerise." There was a little silence, and Cerise imagined the big man sitting up in bed, blinking and reaching for the light. Then Mabry laughed, not without humor, and said, "I don't suppose this has anything to do with a certain Treasury operation that's going down tonight."

Cerise revised her mental image, erased the bedroom, replaced it with office space, then killed that as well. "I don't suppose you're involved in that operation, Mr. Mabry?"

There was another, shorter pause, and Mabry said, "In point of fact, I'm not. My input was refused, with thanks."

Cerise drew a deep breath. If the Eurocops had been cut out of Treasury's plan, she might be able to use that old rivalry to her—and Trouble's—advantage. "Are you still interested in finding Trouble, then?"

"It depends on which one," Mabry said, dryly. "After all, you were pretty convincing that your Trouble wasn't the one causing the disturbances."

"Not—" Cerise bit off the rest of her comment—not my

Trouble, she would have said, and that was beginning not to be true anymore, if it ever had been—and said instead, "But my Trouble knows where your Trouble is."

"Does she." Mabry's voice was flat, not quite openly skeptical.

"Close enough," Cerise answered, and crossed her fingers against her thigh, grateful for the blind connection.

"What's the deal?"

Cerise took another deep breath. "Trouble—my Trouble— is willing to deal with you, give you what she knows, since she knows you'll find out it wasn't her causing all the trouble, and she can walk away clean."

"The statute of limitations hasn't run out on your earlier activities," Mabry said. "Didn't you know that was what this was about?"

"What?" Cerise made a face into the handset, annoyed that she'd betrayed her ignorance.

Mabry said, as though he'd expected her surprise, "Three years isn't long enough to reach limitations, Cerise, and Evans-Tindale didn't offer any amnesties. You—both of you—are still liable for—well, for quite a lot of things, if Treasury speaks true. Starling thinks he's got proof of a couple of them. Or someone gave him proof."

"What we did wasn't exactly illegal then," Cerise said. "The courts have ruled against retrofitting the laws."

She could hear Mabry shrug. "John Starling seems to think he can make it stick."

"Fuck him." Cerise made a face, regretting the betrayal, and Mabry laughed shortly.

"No, thank you. What do you want from me, Cerise?"

"I'm offering you a deal," Cerise said, as calmly as she could. "All you have to do is keep Trouble—my Trouble— out of Treasury's hands. You can have newTrouble. Even the Conventions give you plenty to charge him with."

"Can you deliver?" Mabry asked. "You said before, you and Trouble didn't part on the best of terms—not friendly, I think you said."

"Things change," Cerise said, with more confidence than

she felt. She could deliver Trouble. Trouble wasn't stupid; better to make a deal with Mabry than face Treasury. The question was, could they deliver newTrouble? She put the thought aside, said, "I can deliver, Mabry. Are you interested?"

"Maybe." There was a little pause, and then she heard Mabry sigh. "All right, yes, I'm interested. You say you can give me your Trouble, and newTrouble through her—precisely what does this entail?"

"You'll have to get Treasury off her—our—backs," Cerise answered, and did her best to keep the elation out of her voice. "How—that's your business, you'd know best. But do that and we'll give you everything we've got."

There was another, longer silence, and at last Mabry said, "All right, I can do that. You're in Seahaven, I presume?"

"Yes."

"It's going to take time to get there," Mabry said. "And to get some necessary paperwork taken care of. Can you keep Trouble out of Treasury's hands for another, say, twelve hours?"

"I can try," Cerise said.

"I can't get there any faster," Mabry said, and for the first time Cerise heard annoyance in his voice. "You'll have to do it."

"I'll try," Cerise said again. "That's the best I can promise, too."

"All right," Mabry said. "I will meet you in Seahaven—I will be at, what's it called, Eastman House? The hotel that isn't The Willows—"

"Eastman House," Cerise said.

"Eastman House," Mabry repeated. "I'll be there from ten A.M. on."

"We'll be there at ten," Cerise said.

"I'll expect you," Mabry said. "And, Cerise—thanks. I want this new Trouble very badly."

"So does John Starling," Cerise said, in spite of herself.

"But I really don't like to lose," Mabry answered. "I'll see you in Seahaven, Cerise." He broke the connection before she could think of a reply.

Cerise sat for a long moment, staring at the screen, while the program ran through its complicated disconnect routing. She would need the runabout, and all her hardware; Trouble was almost certainly without her equipment, or she would have made contact on the net. Money, too, and false ID, both of which she had, the money in a thin stack of bearer cards, the ID—several sets—tucked into protected memory. The machine beeped at her, signaling that the program had finished its run, and she bent over the keyboard to type the nonsense password that gave access to her most sensitive storage. The machine beeped again, flashed a warning, and she made a face and reached to disconnect it from the hotel systems. Not that I expect anyone to be watching, she thought, but it's better to be safe. She had set the program to force that choice—it was too easy to get careless otherwise—and a moment later, as the system acknowledged that it was isolated again, she typed the password a second time. This time, the space windowed, displaying a preliminary menu. She selected the IDs she wanted, and hit the series of commands that would dump the first to a standard datadisk. She waited until she was sure the transfer had begun, ID, work cards, health certificates, all the rest of the information that one accumulated over the years, and went into the bedroom to get dressed again.

The machine beeped at her before she had finished, and she went back out into the main room to give it another disk, buttoning her shirt as she went. It was a night for practical clothes, not display; she had chosen jeans and a plain shirt and a man-styled jacket, nothing to mark her either as a cracker or as law, just another of Seahaven's residents out for the evening. She inspected herself in the mirror, one eye still on the whirring transfer drive, and nodded to herself: she would pass.

The machine beeped again, and she fed it the final disk, then went back into the bedroom to collect her money. All things considered, it was likely to be an expensive evening—

Trouble always had been an expensive date. Cerise smiled to herself, remembering an evening that had begun with dinner and ended in the emergency room, with nearly five hundred citiscrip scattered to the winds in between. That had been the first time she'd fully appreciated that Trouble had earned her name off the nets as well as on. . . . The machine beeped a final time, and she returned to the media console, collected the last disk and began breaking the system down into components that she could carry in a single inconspicuous bag. She left some of the heavier pieces—the diskwriter and the printer/recorder, as well as the secondary memory box— slung the bag easily over her shoulder, and reached for the handset to call for her runabout to be brought up to the door.

Trouble leaned back in her chair, staring into the dregs of her drink, and wondered if she could avoid ordering another. It was a virgin drink, sweet and sickly, getting you high with sugar rather than alcohol, but she'd had more than enough of it. She glanced at the clock, displayed in a box that hung above the garden like a stadium scoreboard, slung from a network of poles and wires. Still twenty minutes before she could leave to meet Cerise. She looked away, avoiding the waiter's eye, and saw a movement in the doorway, a shift of the light as though someone very big had entered. She turned her head to see more clearly, and saw Aimoto threading his way between the tables, broad face drawn into a faint, fastidious frown. Maybe it's not for me, she thought, without hope, but was not surprised when Aimoto stopped beside her table, leaning down slightly to be sure he saw her face.

Trouble gestured politely to the empty chair, was equally unsurprised when he shook his head.

"Not a social call, I'm afraid," he said. "Mr. Tinati sent me."

"Of course," Trouble said.

"He's had word that Treasury will be taking a look-see down the Parcade real soon now," Aimoto went on, "and he would prefer that you not be found here."

"That's good of him," Trouble said, and allowed the irony

to color her voice. Tinati wouldn't care about her, whether or not Treasury found her; but any arrests here, on the Parcade, would polarize the net, and the last thing Tinati wanted was upheaval in the shadows that gave him most of his livelihood. The last time the shadows had been divided over an issue—and that had been years ago, back when the brainworm was first made reliable, and crackers on the wire had started to take jobs away from the old school—the fallout had brought down half a dozen crooked securities dealers and a Mob-run credit card ring, all shopped to the cops by crackers out to hurt on-line enemies.

"Mr. Tinati would appreciate your cooperation," Aimoto said, and lifted a hand to signal the waiter.

There wasn't much point in fighting, Trouble thought, at least not now. She said, "We're even, then. I appreciate the warning."

The waiter came bustling over, slip in hand, and Aimoto said, "She'll be leaving now."

The waiter's eyes went wide, but he controlled himself instantly, reached for the touchpad slung at his waist. "That's five even."

Trouble reached into her pocket, pulled out a folder of citiscrip, but Aimoto frowned and waved it away.

"Mr. Tinati insists," he said, and handed the waiter a royal blue foil. "That's all set."

"Thanks," the waiter said, eyes widening even further—the foil was worth more than twice the bill—and backed away.

Aimoto was still waiting with outward patience, and Trouble pushed herself slowly to her feet.

"I'll see you out," Aimoto said.

"That won't be necessary."

"I insist."

Which meant, Trouble thought, that Tinati insisted. "Suit yourself," she said, and started for the exit. Aimoto followed easily through the maze of tables.

"I have a last errand to run," she said, and Aimoto shook his head.

"I'm sorry," he said, and Trouble made a face.

"Fine."

She stepped out onto the sand-streaked pavement, Aimoto still at her elbow. The Ferris wheel sent neon shadows chasing along the length of the street, clashing with the bright lights in the shopfronts. She walked through the patches of light and shadow, Aimoto matching her step for step, and was aware of the faces watching discreetly from the doorways. It was a conspicuous expulsion, the sheriff walking the gunslinger right out of town, and she didn't quite know if she was amused or infuriated by it. In its own way it was a compliment, an acknowledgment of her importance; and besides, she was grateful for the warning.

She stopped at the head of the Parcade, where the seawall loomed ahead and the main street ran left back into Seahaven, and right toward the lesser towns and the dead beaches of the Plantation. Aimoto stopped half a pace behind her, hands in the pockets of his jacket, standing wide-legged in the exact center of the road. Trouble looked back at him, the night air cold on her face and bared forearms, said, "Tell Tinati I'll remember this." She kept her voice absolutely neutral, let the meaning lie ambiguous, and Aimoto inclined his head politely.

"I'll tell him."

Trouble nodded back, and turned left, walking down into the shadows that lay between the mouth of the Parcade and the bars and food shops still open along the avenue. Out of sight of the Parcade, she let herself shiver—the land breeze was still up, but the air was autumn cold—and rolled her sleeves down. It was still early to go to Joe's—or to the empty storefront that had been Joe's years before—but she started toward it anyway, keeping close under the shadow of the darkened stores.

The streets were nearly empty here, between the Parcade and the busy part of the avenue, no other pedestrians in sight and only a few parked cars. A black runabout swept past, lights blazing, and she had to make an effort to keep from looking after it, to see if it would turn down the Parcade. She hesitated as she approached the avenue, torn between risking the occasional mugger or druggie in the dark side streets and taking the chance of being recognized in the bright lights of the avenue. Treasury was more of a danger: better to chance the muggers, she decided, and turned down the first side street, working her way toward the beachfront stores. The streetlights were dimmed here, to save on the town's electricity, and she walked carefully, making sure she had room to run. Not that it would make much difference, not in Seahaven where guns were cheap and the natives made a game of evading the federal restrictions, but it made her feel better. Still, she was glad to reach the knot of stores and food shops that still survived on the beachfront.

The stores were closed by now, of course, heavy grilles drawn over the display screens and doorways, but the food shops were still fairly active. Most of the customers here were fishermen or midshift workers—cleaners and waiters, mostly, on their way home from The Willows or Eastman House—gathered in knots along white-topped counters. Trouble glanced casually at them as she passed, was aware of the hard stares that watched her. The vest—the jeans too, with the man-style shirt, but mostly the vest—marked her as a cracker, part of the crowd from the Parcade, and they were wary of her presence. Not hostile, not yet—it would take more than just walking past to make them willing to risk the net's anger, especially when most of them would be living on the edge, their credit too vulnerable already—but she kept her pace steady, did not even think of stopping.

She passed under the last of the brighter streetlights, moved out into the shadows where the lights were dimmed and the storefronts were covered with sheets of plywood instead of the grilles and barriers of a healthy business. Joe's—Cowboy Joe's, it had been, and then Geisha Jo's before it was just Joe's—had been five or six storefronts down, toward the barricaded pier that led out to the ruins of the Pavilion Bandstand. She slowed her steps, glancing cautiously into the dark doorways, saw only a single hunched shape, possibly male, drunk or drugged in the corner of the boarded-over door to a store that, she vaguely remembered, had once sold jewelry. Joe's had been two doors further down, and she looked over her shoulder, checking for surveillance or ordinary lurkers, before she stopped outside the graffiti-covered shell of the building.

The door itself had been removed, and the sheet of plywood that covered the entrance was reinforced by three heavier boards nailed haphazardly across the doorway. The entrance was slightly recessed, like most of the shopfronts along the beachfront, and she stepped back into its shadows, planting her back against the crumbling stone, one shoulder against the rough wood of the barricading boards. Sand from the beach grated underfoot, and she shifted her feet until she found safer footing on the worn concrete. In the distance she could hear the whine of a siren, moving toward the Parcade, and she wished again that she'd had a chance to talk to one of the dealers on the Parcade. Not that a gun would do her much good, not against Treasury; it was good only against the hopeless druggies, if then, and she shook the thought away. In the distance she heard a runabout's engine, faintly at first, and then more strongly, coming closer along the beachfront. She froze for an instant—too soon for it to be Cerise, and too high-powered; more likely to be a cop, either local or from the hotel—and then began frantically to strip out of the vest. She wadded it behind her, heedless of the expensive fabrics and Konstenten's complex work, let herself slide down the wall until she was huddled in the corner, knees up, head down on her folded arms. She slowed her breathing as the car came closer, heard the engine whine as the driver shifted into a lower gear, and then the distant crackle of a two-way radio turned low. Only the hopeless came here, and she could fake it, the sodden slump, mercifully oblivious; there were always a few homeless sleeping in doorways, even in Seahaven.

The runabout was coming closer now, engine loud and stressed, and the light of a searchlight played across the doorway, brilliant even to closed eyes. Trouble held her pose with an effort that made her shoulders tremble against the concrete, the light flaring red behind her eyelids, kept her forehead pressed against her knees and arms. The light played across her, across to the other corner of the doorway, then fixed again on her for a moment longer before it swept away. She made herself keep breathing, slow and snoring, and was not too surprised when the light suddenly flared again. She stayed still, and at last the light swung away. A moment later, the engine noise strengthened, and the runabout pulled away. She stayed as she was, counting slowly to a hundred, and then to a hundred again, before she dared lift her head.

The street was empty, only the sound of the waves beyond the seawall and the faint counterpoint of music drifting down from the few still-open shops to disturb the sudden quiet. Then, in the distance, she heard a runabout's engine, lighter-toned than the first, and coming from Seahaven proper. She cocked her head to one side, trying to judge the sound, but couldn't be sure. She stayed where she was, lowered her head to her arms, torn between fear and the irrational conviction that, this time, it had to be Cerise, and heard the runabout pull steadily closer, heard the chunk of gears as the driver slowed still further. She braced herself for the flare of a searchlight, heard the runabout slide to a stop opposite the doorway. Trouble lifted her head warily, to see a dark-blue runabout and a single figure at the controls, a vague shape behind the thick glass. Then the driver reached forward, touched controls, and a light came on over the driver's station, throwing a dim blue light across Cerise's face. Trouble drew a deep sigh of relief, and scrambled to her feet, dragging the vest from behind her back. She shrugged it on as she moved out of the alcove, and Cerise leaned across the seat to unlock the passenger door. Trouble ducked into the runabout, grateful for its warmth, and pulled the door closed behind her. Cerise flicked off the overhead light, and eased the runabout back into motion, saying, "You do know how to liven up an evening."

I TRY," TROUBLE ANSWERED, and let herself relax against the seat cushions.

Cerise slanted a glance in her direction, her face little more than a pale blur in the dark, but Trouble could hear the amusement in her voice, translated it to one of her quirky smiles. "You succeed, believe me."

"Thanks." Trouble slumped further down in her seat.

Cerise glanced over her shoulder, checking for other cars, and swung south onto Ashworth Avenue. Trouble sat up again, startled, and Cerise said, "Treasury's got a cop watching the bridge. I didn't want to chance it. I've made us a deal, Trouble, but we're going to have to stay out of the way until tomorrow morning."

"What sort of deal?" Trouble asked. "And what makes you think Treasury won't be watching on the way out of town?"

Cerise grinned again, the expression vivid in the flash of neon from one of the still-open bars. "They're relying on the checkpoint a little too heavily. Their man put a note on the transponder, saying there was only one person in the car. I jimmied it, so it says two people. Since they really don't expect you to get legitimate help—"

"Since when were you legitimate?"

"Since I quit you," Cerise answered. "But since Treasury doesn't expect you to get help, I doubt they'll be checking corporate cars too closely. They should be concentrating on the Parcade and the hostels."

"You hope," Trouble murmured, and saw the smaller woman shrug.

"It seemed a reasonable risk."

Trouble nodded, watching the neon circle of the Ferris wheel looming ahead. If Treasury was willing to risk trouble on the Parcade, risk the net rallying against them and behind her, then surely their security would be tighter, here at the edge of town—but Treasury had always been blind to the nuances of possibility on the nets, despite recruiting these days from among the netwalkers. And besides, she thought, with a fleeting, wry grin, there wasn't that much reason to think that the nets would rally to her. She was still a little outré, a little outside the rules; it was even odds what would happen in the fallout from a real raid. And if Treasury played it even halfway cool, there were a lot of people who would be glad of the excuse not to act.

The runabout slowed, and Trouble held herself motionless. Ahead, an orange-and-white barrier ran halfway across the avenue, its markings ambiguous, either police or road crew. A single figure stood in the funnel of light from a street lantern, the runabout's headlights reflecting from his orange-and-white vest, but, glancing sideways, Trouble could just see the nose of a police van waiting in the shadows of a side street.

"I see it," Cerise said, almost cheerfully, and slowed still further. Trouble held herself motionless as light flashed briefly across her window—more than just light, she knew, probably a quick-scan as well, checking for additional bodies. The transponder beeped softly, lights flickering briefly in the heads-up display, and Cerise gave a sigh of relief. The man standing by the barrier waved them forward, and Cerise opened the throttle slowly, easing the runabout past the end of the barrier. Trouble looked back, toward the Parcade, and caught a quick glimpse of blue-suited figures moving down the center of the street, while the Parcade's denizens scrambled to get out of the way, scurrying for cover.

Cerise swung the runabout back into its proper lane, and opened the throttle. The engine sounded briefly louder, but the baffling cut out the worst of the noise. Trouble let herself relax again, and said, "So where to?"

"Ah." Cerise kept her eyes on the road, watching for trouble on the badly lit side streets and potholes in the roadway. The people who lived in the Sands weren't precisely fond of the crackers and the suits who came to Seahaven, and didn't make much distinction between them. "That's a little bit of a problem. The deal I made, we can't meet Mabry until tomorrow morning, and I don't think it would be a good idea for you to show up at Eastman House before then. Or at any of the hostels. My thought was, we head out to the flyway, head north to the first truck stop, sleep over in a capsule there."

Trouble shook her head. "There's a new cop-shop right at the head of the access road, there at the rotary. I'd bet anything they'll have them watching for me, too. Maybe a roadblock."

Cerise hesitated, swerved without thinking to avoid a pothole, and reached for the miniature keypad that controlled the communications system. She tuned it to the police channels, let the voices mumble in the speaker and the code strings stream through the data display at the base of the windscreen, to the right of the main grid display. "You're probably right—I'm seeing talk from a roadblock, anyway, and it looks to be in the right place. That doesn't leave much of an option, though."

"The Plantation," Trouble agreed.

"The glass is bulletproof," Cerise said, thoughtfully. "If any of the drug gangs are crazy enough to risk the beaches. Users are mostly jackals; if we stay alert we shouldn't have any problems with them. And if we can follow some of the old paving, we should be all right as far as chem-sands go."

"Great," Trouble said. "If the has-beens don't get us, the ecology will."

"You got a better idea?"

Trouble shook her head. "Not offhand."

Cerise smiled. "The Plantation is it, then."

Trouble nodded, smiled reluctantly. It was an eerie place, dangerous, and she shivered, remembering a video she had seen. An old man had walked along a beach, suited to the waist against the reeking sands and the seaweeds that smoldered sullenly under the low sun. The beach was absolutely empty, which had not seemed strange—beaches were always empty, in her memory—until she listened to the species that the old man—he had been a marine biologist, she remembered—had remembered studying there, back before the Hundred-Year Winter. A few, he had said, a few were still around, it was still possible to find specimens, but every year, there were fewer and fewer. They were dying before his eyes, and there seemed to be nothing anyone could do. Since the beaches had become increasingly poisonous, the normal tourists had—with good reason—taken their business elsewhere; that left only the drug gangs, who sometimes risked landing a smaller cargo along the chemical-laced shores, and the people who had absolutely nowhere else to go. The beaches, and the Plantation in particular, were a favorite spot for double suicide. She scowled, turned her head to watch the houses sliding past outside the runabout's window. The streetlights gave only a thin illumination, the houses mostly dark now: it was getting late, and the people who still lived here worked long hours to try to get out. Beyond the houses, she could just see faint glow of fog over the marsh, fog lit by the phosphorescent algae that choked the channels.

"What is this deal?" she asked, and looked determinedly away from the scarred land.

"I'll tell you when we get to the Plantation," Cerise answered.

"That good."

Cerise grinned. "You'll like it. It's certainly better than the alternative."

"What alternative?" Trouble said, but smiled.

"Precisely."

Trouble let the silence fall between them, the old, companionable quiet, tilted her head again to see out through the runabout's windows. Ahead, the road was empty, unlit except for the sweep of the headlights; the seawall, a piled heap of rock and sand, loomed to the left of the road, and here and there the rocks were stained as though with oil or burning. The last town had ended some way back, and the only sign of human settlement was the road itself. To the right of the pavement, the land dropped steeply into the marsh. In the distance, just at the edge of the headlights' reach, she could see the first glimmer of the sign that marked the turnoff that led back to Southbrook. It loomed quickly, vivid green and white in the runabout's headlights, and Cerise slowed slightly, scanning her display for any signs of surveillance. Trouble saw the same codes, nodded her appreciation of Multiplane's equipment.

"Nice package."

"I installed it," Cerise answered. "It had better be."

Ahead, the road was sand-drifted, the tire tracks that swept off to the right, drawing a curved clear line through the grit, making the general traffic pattern obvious. Cerise slowed the runabout, switched her lights to their maximum beam, and reached across to trigger a security package under the dash.

"You want me to keep an eye on that?" Trouble asked.

"Yeah, thanks," Cerise said, and switched the display to the passenger's side of the windshield. "You've got IR, broadcast scanner, gross motion detectors—those won't be much good until we stop, though."

Trouble nodded, watching codes and symbols flicker across the screen, pale blue against the dark. Beyond the windscreen, the headlights swept across sand etched into low hills bound by clumps of straggling, sickly-looking grass. A broken barrel, the metal rotted into rusty lace where it had touched the sand, lay in the center of the drifted roadway, and Cerise swerved to avoid it. The beam swept across more grass and sand, and the foundation of a tourist pavilion, but nothing seemed to be moving in the shadows. "There's a turnoff ahead," Trouble said, more to break the silence than anything else. "Used to be one of the parking lots."

"I see it," Cerise answered, and a moment later swung the runabout off the main road.

The sand was deeper here, loud under the wheels, and Trouble said, "How're your tires rated?"

"They're supposed to stand chem-sand," Cerise answered. "I'm not getting out to sweep, though."

"Probably wise."

Cerise nodded, preoccupied, and swung the runabout

through a half-circle on the invisible paving, looking for a landmark. She found it almost at once, the remains of another shack that had once been a parking attendant's booth. There was more left here, or at least the collapse had left a stub of one wall standing. A sheet of metal that had been the roof rested against that wall. The metal was rotting from the ground up, like any metal left too long in contact with the sand, but the cracked asphalt of the parking lot had protected it from the worst of the damage.

"Getting anything?" Cerise asked, and Trouble shook her head, eyes fixed on the readouts at the base of the windscreen.

"Not as far as I can tell. Nothing on IR, anyway."

"Right," Cerise said, and eased the runabout forward again, swinging around the ruin to slide the vehicle neatly into its protective shadow. Trouble caught a quick glimpse of trash, food wrappers, and half a bright beer can before Cerise killed the lights.

"Popular spot," she said, and Cerise shrugged.

"Probably courting. Or else cops or Coast Guard."

"There's a happy thought."

Cerise shrugged again, shutting down the runabout's primary systems. "If they were here recently, they probably won't be back—or at least not this late in the evening." She left the motor running on standby—there was enough fuel in the cells to last, and she wanted the option of a quick getaway if they needed it—and leaned back in the driver's seat. She had left the security systems running as well, and letters and code symbols danced in staccato patterns along the base of the windscreen. She watched the familiar movements, feeling the tiredness set in, tugging at her back and shoulders—less exhaustion, maybe, than the sheer release of tension. Not that it was over yet, she reminded herself. They still had to get back to Seahaven in time to meet Mabry.

"So," Trouble said. "What's this deal you've made?"

Cerise smiled wryly, grateful for the darkness. "Ah. I figured the main thing was to get Treasury off your back, right?"

"Right," Trouble said, after a moment.

"So I went to Vess Mabry—the guy from Interpol. I told you about him." Cerise took a deep breath. "He's looking for newTrouble, too, and I said if he'd get Treasury off your back, we'd give him newTrouble."

There was a long silence then, and Cerise wondered if she'd gone too far. She looked sideways, away from the flickering codes of the heads-up display, but couldn't read the expression on the other woman's face. Trouble said, at last, "It's a nice thought, Cerise, but we don't have newTrouble."

Cerise let out an almost soundless sigh and said, "But we're more likely to get him than Treasury, so far. Or Interpol."

"True enough." Trouble did not move, staring through the ghostly displays that signaled monotonously. Her eyes were adjusting to the dark; she could make out the shadows of the distant trees, a horizon faintly darker than the sky, and a few low hillocks that must be the remains of beach buildings. Some of the brightest stars were visible through the thin clouds, but she did not bother to crane her neck to find the few constellations that she knew. She could give Interpol newTrouble, she was sure of that. The only question was, would she? She smiled faintly, very aware of Cerise's silent presence in the seat beside her. Cerise hadn't left her much choice—Cerise was always thorough—but in this case she was also right, however much it might annoy Trouble to admit it. Mabry was the only person who could get Treasury off their backs long enough to track down newTrouble. And it would be one in Treasury's eye.

"So what next?" she asked, and heard Cerise stir against the seat cushions, as though she had finally relaxed. The sound was obscurely comforting—it was nice not to be taken completely for granted—and Trouble shifted so that she was leaning half against the locked door. From that angle, she could see Cerise as well as the flickering band of security readings. The pale face was just a blur, the expression unreadable, but Trouble could hear a certain renewed ease in the other woman's voice.

"Next we meet Mabry," Cerise said.

"Which may be harder than it looks."

"Possibly," Cerise admitted. "He'll be at Eastman House by ten tomorrow morning."

"And what are we supposed to do with ourselves in the meantime?" The moment the words were spoken, Trouble wished she could recall them. In the old days, there would have been no question about Cerise's answer, no matter what they ended up doing—which probably wouldn't have been fucking; sex on the ruined beach, even in the car, was probably a stupid thing even to think about. Now, however, she felt an odd, unexpected constraint.

It was almost a minute before Cerise answered, and the same restraint was very audible in her voice as well. "Have you heard from Mollie yet?"

"Not yet," Trouble answered, grateful for the diversion. "I didn't expect to so soon. Did you find anything on the net?"

Cerise laughed, barely a breath of sound. "Not a lot. How about you?"

"The major news," Trouble said sourly, "seemed to be that a few people don't like me."

"Surprise, surprise," Cerise murmured, but with only a touch of her usual teasing note. "No sign of newTrouble?"

"No." Trouble looked more closely at her, hearing something not quite right in the other woman's voice, but unable, quite, to recognize it. It sounded almost as though she were amused, but not quite. The last time Cerise had sounded like that had been the time she'd tumbled into and out of an affair with a man. "He seems to have gone to ground."

"That shows more sense than I'd've expected," Cerise said. She took a deep breath, well aware of Trouble's reaction. "I've met someone who might be able to help us there."

"You didn't," Trouble said, and her own laughter was very close to the surface.

Cerise glared at her, didn't pretend not to understand. "Yes, I did, yes, I got hustled, and yes, she was very good. But she's of newTrouble's generation, and from something she said, I think she may know him."

"Who is she?"

"She calls herself Silk." In spite of herself, Cerise felt a flash of memory, pure sensation stabbing through her as though the name tripped something in the brainworm.

"I don't know her," Trouble said, shaking her head. "On the wire, I assume?"

"Do you think someone off the wire could hustle me?" There was arrogance in the answer, as well as a certain defensiveness.

Trouble shrugged. "You never know. Your tastes could've changed. A text-only interface is supposed to be fun—or so they tell me."

"Fuck you."

"Do you think this Silk would help you?" Trouble asked, ignoring the insult.

"That I don't know," Cerise answered. "She—was out to hustle me from the beginning, I'm sure of it, but I don't know if I was a trophy or just for fun."

"But you think it's worth a try," Trouble said, and suddenly wasn't sure if she wanted Cerise to approach Silk after all. Before it wouldn't have mattered, any more than the sex had mattered—and it doesn't matter now, she told herself firmly. Their affair was over, had been over for years. But it didn't feel as though it was over, felt more as though it had never ended, as though the time in between had been a suspension of reality, less than a dream. To be sitting here, in a car parked on the ruined paving of the old Plantation, discussing with Cerise how to sell another cracker to Treasury— to be in the shadows again, with Cerise. That was where she had always belonged, should always have been. Except that the shadows weren't what they had been, any more than either of them had remained entirely the same.

"It's always worth a try," Cerise said, and Trouble dragged her attention back to the present, annoyed that she'd let her own exhaustion distract her so far. "Besides, even if she doesn't help, she may lead us to newTrouble anyway."

"You said she was good?"

"We're better."

Trouble shifted again against the door, searching for a more comfortable angle, and failed to find one. She hunched her shoulders and let her head rest against the chill glass, said, "So, how do we get back into Seahaven tomorrow morning?"

"Ah."

"You haven't worked that out yet," Trouble said, with sudden certainty. She remembered that tone from the old days, the false confidence, and knew enough to dread it.

"I was more worried about keeping you away from Treasury tonight," Cerise said. She took a deep breath. "I thought we could probably slip in with the morning rush—there seem to be a lot of people who live in the other towns who come in to work. Besides, the last thing they'd expect is for you to come back after you've got away."

"True," Trouble said, mostly appeased. It would probably work—would have to work, she amended silently, and smiled.

"What are you grinning at?" Cerise asked.

"Nothing," Trouble said, and even in the darkness could see Cerise's quick frown. "I just don't believe we're doing this, that's all."

Cerise paused, still frowning, and then, slowly, her expression eased. "Me neither, sweetheart." She had spoken without thought, the casual endearment easy on her tongue, and for a heartbeat she didn't realize what she had done. Then Trouble stirred, shifting against the padding, and Cerise made a face, looked away as though she could find some apology in the dark outside the car. The security crawl stayed monotonously clear, offering no change of subject, and the silence stretched between them.

"Do you know, I've fucking missed you?" Trouble said, and sounded at once surprised and annoyed by the thought.

Cerise looked back at her, surprised into laughter and the truth. "Well, I've missed you, too. Even if you did walk out on me."

"I screwed up," Trouble said, quite seriously. "And I know I screwed up. I'm sorry."

And that, Cerise thought, was one thing you had to say for Trouble. She could make even the most inarticulate of apologies sound better than sincere. "It's OK," she said, vaguely, and thought almost that it might be.

"How is Multiplane to work for?" Trouble said, after a moment.

Cerise shrugged, even though the gesture would be all but invisible in the darkness. "The company's all right, they let me handle the net pretty much the way I want. My immediate boss is a bit of a bastard, though. He's got a real problem with this intrusion, and I don't know why. He really wants you, or newTrouble; he doesn't really care which."

Trouble frowned. "But since I didn't do it—"

"He doesn't seem to care," Cerise said. "And I still don't know why."

Trouble said, slowly, "I don't mean to be naive, not being corporate myself, but setting me up for this would seem to be counterproductive. Word's bound to get around that he got the wrong person, and that'll only make him look like a fool on the nets."

"Make me look like a neo, too," Cerise agreed. Could that be it? she wondered. To get rid of me? It didn't sound like Coigne—for one thing, she was still useful, and it wasn't like Coigne to waste any resources—but it was the best, the only, explanation she'd been able to come up with so far. Not that there was anyone currently in Multiplane's security division who could replace her. . . . Or was it Trouble he was really after, not so much as a cracker, but as the symbol she had been in the old days, the time before Evans-Tindale, of the worm and its carriers? Or, maybe even more, of the symbol she was becoming, of the net acting to police itself? No, she thought, that couldn't be right, Coigne had wanted Trouble caught before all this started.

"You think that's the point, getting rid of you?" Trouble asked, and Cerise shrugged again.

"It could be, I suppose. But, let's face it, I'd be hard to replace."

"God, you're arrogant."

"But truthful," Cerise answered, and saw Trouble grin, baring white teeth. "I suppose it could really be you he's after," she went on. "You're making quite a stir these days, got the nets cooperating again, almost."

"The timing's off," Trouble answered. "So, other than your boss maybe trying to get rid of you, you like working in the light?"

"Other than that, it's a great job," Cerise said, and stifled a sudden yawn. "How was life among the artists?"

"All right." Trouble felt her own face stiffen as she fought to suppress an answering yawn, and gave up, stretching awkwardly against the seat and the door of the car. "I spent a lot of time fiddling with printer drivers."

"So what did they do, these artists?" Cerise asked, after a moment's sleepy hesitation.

"Lot of different things," Trouble answered. "A lot of printmakers, graphic artists—one fractalist. Then there were a bunch of potters and a quiltmaker, a couple of writers, too."

"Must have been interesting."

Trouble shrugged, wondering if she would be able to explain. It had been, well, dull, but that wasn't quite the word, either. More that she'd missed whatever it was she'd had in the shadows, whatever it was she'd had with Cerise—and that, she realized suddenly, was the real problem. She had missed Cerise, not just the work, the netwalking, though they had been good at that, but also the time off-line, the sex and the shared living. There had been nothing, or more precisely, no one, not even Konstenten, who had been able to provide her with that necessary partnership. She realized abruptly that Cerise was watching her through the dark, her posture more alert, and said, "Interesting enough, some of the time. There was a lot of politics."

"There always is," Cerise said. "Still, I bet you found someone to keep you company." In spite of her attempt to sound cheerful and offhand, the words came out charged with a vague jealousy she hadn't known existed.

Trouble glanced warily at her, wondering if she'd heard correctly, said, "A few dates here and there, nothing serious. Nothing even close to serious." There was a bitterness in her own voice that startled her, even as she watched sidelong for Cerise's reaction. "How about you?"

Cerise felt her own half-admitted uncertainty fade slightly. "Corporate life doesn't exactly make it easy for queers."

Trouble made a skeptical noise, and Cerise said, hearing herself defensive, "You know what I mean. Marriage or nothing, that's what they want—somebody they can check out, make sure is reliable."

Trouble nodded. There didn't seem to be much else to say, and she glanced at the security display—still nothing moving, except the random flicker of wind in the straggling shrubs at the edge of the pavement—and then at the sky. It was still very dark, no sign of even false dawn, and she suppressed another yawn. "You should maybe try to get some sleep," she said.

Cerise looked at her, sounded surprised when she answered. "I suppose I ought."

"Even an hour or two might help," Trouble said, and could see the movement of Cerise's head that meant the other woman had made a face at her.

"I know you're right," Cerise said, after a moment. "And I'm just tired enough to be annoyed about it."

Trouble smiled in spite of herself, in spite of her own exhaustion and the still-present tension. Cerise had never been very good about rest, had always been unbearable without enough sleep. . . . She said, "Get some sleep," and heard rather than saw Cerise shift again, so that she hunched down further in the driver's seat. There was a brief silence, and then Cerise twisted sideways, struggling to reach the catch that controlled the seat. She found it at last, fingertips just able to hook around the slick metal of the lever, lowered the seat back until it stood at a near-forty-five degree angle. She hesitated then, wanting to lower it completely—the runabout, bought on a corporate account, had the expensive seats that could convert to an uncomfortable sleeping platform as needed—but decided that it would mean taking too much of a risk. If there was trouble, if anyone challenged them, here in the Plantation, she would need to be able to drive out instantly. She could drive with the seat at this angle, but not with it stretched out into a sort of bed. She settled herself more comfortably, turning herself half toward Trouble, and let her eyes close. She had been more tired than she had realized, could already feel herself drifting into sleep, and stirred half in protest.

"Easy," Trouble said, and reached across the gearbox to touch Cerise's outflung hand. "Don't worry, just get some sleep." She ran her hand lightly along the other woman's arm. Cerise smiled, not fully sure if she was dreaming, the gentle touch the product of her own imagination, but let herself be reassured. There would be time enough to worry later, to sort out her own feelings, if there was anything that needed to be sorted out; for now, she needed to sleep.

Trouble watched her burrow deeper into the unyielding padding, heard her breathing shift almost at once toward sleep. Cerise's skin was cool under her touch, the fingers almost cold, and she ran her hand back up toward the other woman's elbow. Cerise did not stir, not even when Trouble ran one finger lightly over the other's forearm, feeling for the lump where the bone had been broken and grown back thicker than before. The once-familiar bump was there, oddly reassuring, and Trouble ran her thumb along the other side of Cerise's arm, feeling for the other bone beneath the skin. She could barely feel the bone, couldn't find the second lump that she knew must be there—Cerise had broken both bones that night, when the runabout finally missed a turn—and Cerise shifted uneasily under her touch, mumbling an incoherent protest. Trouble released her, but did not take her hand away completely. The feeling of Cerise's skin beneath her fingers was too pleasant, too comforting, to be lightly given up. Cerise shifted again, this time with a noise that might almost have been pleasure, and stretched her arm out along the gearbox. Trouble ran her fingers lightly along the offered arm, wished with sudden intensity that she could do more. This was not the time for sex, she knew that perfectly well, wasn't even sure it was sex she wanted, more like some way just to hold her, lie with her, feel the whole length of their bodies wound together, like in the old days after a job had gone wrong, or well, or they hadn't had work at all. . . . And if they had been somewhere safe, Trouble admitted, they would have made love. She wanted it even now, distinctly, memory as well as the sensation of Cerise's skin beneath her fingers arousing her, wet warmth spreading between her legs. She closed her eyes for an instant, remembering the touch of Cerise's lips—the simple, deceptively chaste kiss, just the touch of lips against her own that never failed to send her, send both of them, wild. I want her back, she acknowledged silently, and shook her head at the inadequacy of those words. It's not just that I want her back, I want her to want me back, too. I want what we had, the old days, when we were perfectly matched and the world knew it. When no one could challenge us, and we'd never challenge each other.

She shook the thought away, annoyed that she was getting maudlin in her old age, made herself look back at the security readouts. Nothing had changed, nothing was moving outside the car, though the sky was growing faintly lighter, back toward the ocean, but she made herself watch three cycles through, concentrating on the readings. Then she looked deliberately away from Cerise, made herself concentrate on the deal with Mabry. It wasn't impossible, at least not on the face of it: she could probably give him newTrouble without too much hassle, especially if people like Helling and van Liesvelt and Arabesque, and even Fate and Nova, backed her up on the nets. Most of the net would simply be glad that someone had solved the problem, however it was done; the important people in the shadows would know that she was right, the newTrouble was the real danger—taking someone's name and programs, cracking for the sheer joy of it, without thought of profit or consequences, running viruses, too, if Mabry was right—and would let Fate and Butch convince them of it, no matter how much they might dislike her. And maybe, just maybe, she could use even that grudged agreement to make a new place for herself on the changed nets, in the bright lights.

The only question that remained, then, was whether she could do it. And that would be no problem, she admitted silently. Maybe once she would have had regrets, but not now. It wasn't just that it was him or her, not even a question of revenge, really, though she was angry enough still to look forward to seeing him fall. It wasn't even that she resented him dragging her back into the business, though God knew she ought to be; if anything, she was grateful, glad in spite of herself, in spite of everything, to be back in the shadows, back with Cerise for however long. It was more—it was simply that newTrouble was a danger, not just to her but to the shadows, and, in the end, to all the nets. There were still too many people who were afraid of a technology that eluded them, still more who would never have access and resented and feared it in equal measures. Mobilize those groups just once, find a demagogue who could lead them—and there were always demagogues—and the nets would find themselves destroyed. Given enough incentive, the nets could be regulated, access deliberately slowed and stifled, checkpoints at every intersection. The hardware existed; it would be expensive, monumentally expensive, but if enough people could be frightened badly enough, it would seem cheap in the end. If the net did not police itself, did not, in the end, declare that there were limits, things that were by definition unacceptable, the rest of the world would do it for them, and that would be the beginning of the end. Evans-Tindale had been a step toward outside control. It was time that the nets created a standard of their own—the Amsterdam Conventions had been of the nets, not just about them.

And listen to you, she chided, and managed a crooked smile. You've been out in the bright lights too long, sweetie, taken your syscop's license entirely too seriously. At the very least, you're more tired than you ever thought, to be thinking like that. But the quirked smile faded almost as quickly as it had appeared. You had to draw lines, and that choice was in itself dangerous; all boundaries had a double edge, were like swords that could always be turned against you in the end. But you still had to choose.

She made a face again, annoyed at her own pomposity, more angry at her fear. There were no other choices; Cerise and the Treasury between them had seen to that. More than that, newTrouble himself had guaranteed it. She looked again at the readouts crawling along the base of the windscreen, watched a full cycle without really seeing the flickering symbols, then looked back to the east where the first signs of dawn were beginning to appear. Whatever else happened, she'd made her choice.

What was left of the night passed without incident. Trouble fought to stay awake, and lost, caught herself more than once dropping toward full sleep, but managed to keep half alert, slipping only into an eyes-open drowse. As the eastern horizon grew lighter, waking grew easier, and she was aware, belatedly, that she was hungry. She turned stiffly in the seat to see if there was food in the back seats, but found nothing. Beside her, Cerise shifted slightly, settled again to sleep. There was no point in waking her yet; it would be hours before they could leave the Plantation—before there would be enough traffic on the roads to cover their departure—but Trouble suppressed the urge to reach for her hand again. Then Cerise opened her eyes, smiled sleepily, and reached out to take Trouble's hand in her own. Before Trouble could move toward her or away, she was asleep again. Obscurely comforted, and perversely more awake, Trouble settled back to her watch.

She woke Cerise when the runabout's chronometer read six o'clock, waited patiently while Cerise stretched and grumbled, rubbing at puffy eyes. Trouble let her complain for a few minutes, listening to the semicoherent muttering, said at last, "Yeah, well, I'm hungry, too, sweetheart, and I need to pee, which is something I really don't want to try here, given what happens when ammonia hits chem-sand. So, when do you think we can get moving?"

Cerise reached down to adjust the seat, brought it back to a normal driving position. "Switch on the radio, will you? Find something with traffic reports."

Trouble did as she was told, trying to ignore the pressure in her bladder, fiddled with the communications console until she found a local radio station. Traffic reports were already being broadcast—light traffic on the access roads, getting heavy on the flyways, no serious delays at the border tolls or the bridge tolls into the city—and Cerise nodded thoughtfully.

"I think we can chance it."

She touched the switch that brought the runabout's motor off standby, eased the machine into gear. The low sun glared through a thin haze of cloud, starting a headache behind her eyes; she made a face, and swung the runabout out from the shadow of the ruined building. She needed sleep, she knew, and a shower, wondered briefly if she could pass any remaining roadblocks in this state. She would simply have to, though: there weren't any other options. Hopefully, the traffic would be heavy enough to hide one more runabout—and it should be, she thought. The locals who worked in the city, people from the Sands and Southbrook and all the other little towns along the coast, not just Seahaven, would have to leave now if they were to make the usual eight-thirty starting time. There should be plenty of traffic to obscure their presence. You hope, she added silently, and carefully did not smile. Trouble would not, in her current mood, be much amused.

At the entrance to the Plantation, Cerise slowed the car, checking the line of traffic feeding toward her. As the radio had promised, it wasn't too heavy as yet; there were breaks in the line of runabouts and light trucks, and she slid her own runabout into a gap, matching the general speed with practiced ease.

"I wonder what they think we're doing?" Trouble muttered.

"More like what they think we've been doing," Cerise answered, her attention on the controls. "People do go to the Plantation, you know."

"Yeah, for sex, drugs, and suicide," Trouble answered.

"Well, we weren't killing ourselves," Cerise said, and to her surprise, Trouble grinned.

"And nobody much cares about the rest, yeah, I know. Except maybe the cops."

"They shouldn't be worrying about commuters," Cerise said, with more confidence than she felt. "After last night, they should be too short on manpower to worry about commuters."

"You hope," Trouble said, and shifted uncomfortably against the seat.

"Yeah," Cerise said, and opened the throttle as the line of runabouts picked up speed.

They crossed the causeway through the marsh in silence, only the inconsequential babble of the radio rising above the noise of the runabout's engine. As they approached the rotary, Trouble held her breath, but the fast-tank parked outside the cop-shop stayed motionless, only the revolving blue light at the top of its carapace to remind drivers that it was manned and ready. Cerise took the runabout through the rotary at an unexpectedly decorous pace, did not pick up speed again until they were on the main road that led back to the flyway. She stopped at the first truck plaza they came to, this one just outside Southbrook proper, where they paid for the use of shower and toilets. Clean again, Cerise refused to eat there, claiming that there was a better plaza further along the flyway, and Trouble was too tired to argue. To her surprise, however, Cerise was right: the Eight-Ball Café, built on a median set between the two lanes of the flyway, proved to be both clean and relatively friendly. The food was good, too, as was the coffee, and Trouble gorged in silence. It was trucker food, thick and greasy sausage and fried bread, fried eggs and potatoes, unhealthy and enormously satisfying; she looked up at last, dredging the last slice of toast through the runnels of egg yolk, to find Cerise grinning at her.

"Feel better?"

"Some," Trouble admitted, and added, with cheerful malice, "I didn't get any sleep last night, remember?"

"Someone had to keep watch," Cerise said, without apparent guilt.

"So now what?"

Cerise shrugged. "Kill some time, I suppose—you could always eat another breakfast—until we can head back to Seahaven."

Trouble refused the offer of food, and Cerise paid their bill without complaint. After that, they found themselves in the deserted game room, and spent ten in citiscrip learning the Super-Lyrior table. Once they'd figured out the rules—imperfectly explained on the casing display and in the single help screen—they spent another five in citiscrip before they'd mastered the system, and embarked on a series of free games that lasted until the manager, free of the breakfast rush, arrived to suggest they move on. It was past nine by then; Cerise accepted the order meekly enough, and Trouble followed her back out onto the paving. The lot was all but empty now, a couple of big rigs parked to one side, windows opaqued to let the drivers sleep; the sun, finally free of the early morning fog, was startlingly warm. In the distance, on the western horizon, the trees glowed red and orange against the sky. Trouble glanced back once, looking east, and saw the sea like a wide blue line beyond the housetops. From here it looked pristine, the pale rim of the beach bleached by distance, and she looked away again, made uncomfortable by the knowledge that it was all illusion.

It was not a difficult journey to Seahaven after all. Cerise got them back onto the flyway without incident—it was a left entrance and a long ramp that wasn't always long enough, from the look of the dark stains on the concrete barriers where the ramp ended—and then dawdled in the slow lane, driving on manual just a few kilometers above the local minimum, until they reached the Seahaven turnoff. She switched to grid control then—no use annoying the local authorities or drawing attention to themselves before they had to—and let the grid take them back down to Eastman House.

They arrived a little after ten, turned the runabout over to the man on duty at the door—Cerise hesitated, just a little, but knew better than to do anything out of the ordinary—and made their way into the lobby. Trouble caught her breath, recognizing the man slumped on one of the low couches under the disapproving eyes of the staff, glanced instinctively backwards to see Bennet Levy emerging from the bellman's cubicle beside the door.

"Cerise," she said, and Cerise said, loudly, "Hello, Mabry."

A big man, broad-shouldered and heavy-bodied, with a mass of greying, disreputable curls, turned away from the main desk and smiled, showing teeth. "Hello, Cerise. And this must be your—former partner."

"Christ," Levy said, not quite under his breath, and Starling, who had levered himself up off the low couch with unexpected grace, said gently, "I'm sorry, Vess, this is Treasury business."

"I'm afraid not," Mabry said. "I have authority in this country to make arrests, and I'm taking Ms.—Trouble—into custody as a material witness." He eyed the Treasury agent shrewdly, added, "I'm sorry, John, but you're chasing the wrong one."

"You've made a deal," Starling said, and Mabry nodded. Trouble, watching, couldn't quite read the Treasury agent's expression, thought for a moment she almost saw relief mingling with the chagrin.

"That's right. And you can take it up with your superiors if you have any questions," Mabry said. The words could have been hostile, but his relaxed tone and easy stance robbed them of much of the offense.

"You know we'll have to, Vess," Starling said.

"I know. But can we call a truce until you've settled it?"

"And you know I can't do that, either." Starling sighed, looked past Trouble to his partner. It was a speaking look, and Trouble barely restrained herself from turning to see

Levy's expression. "Give me your word you won't leave the hotel until I've got my bosses' reading, and I'll let you get breakfast."

"Done," Mabry said, and, as Starling stared at him expectantly, added, "You have my word."

It was all, in the end, unexpectedly civilized. Starling vanished into one of the shielded communications cubicles to call his superiors, while Levy, his face set into a stony mask of disapproval, followed them upstairs to Mabry's room. There, Mabry ordered breakfast for them all, over Cerise's polite and Trouble's more definite protests, and they sat in silence, eating and drinking the near-infinite pots of coffee until at last Starling reappeared.

"Is it all arranged?" Mabry asked, and Starling shrugged.

"My bosses would appreciate some help with the eventual prosecutions—you understand, they don't want to cause you trouble over jurisdictions, but this has been a stateside problem as well. . . ."

He let his voice trail off suggestively, and Mabry nodded in perfect understanding. "My bosses are well aware of the value of international cooperation, John. I'm positive there will be no objection to my sharing any data I receive with you. Just so long as we are able to prosecute as well. One of the—incidents—comes under Singapore's jurisdiction, you understand."

In spite of herself, Trouble had to bite back the urge to whistle, and knew her eyebrows rose. Singapore's cracker laws were some of the most stringent in the notoriously strict Asian Circle; trying a case there, with the kind of evidence Mabry already had—not to mention what she herself could supply—practically guaranteed not only a conviction but a definite prison term.

Levy made a noise that might have been approving, and Starling gave an appreciative nod. "We weren't aware that Singapore had jurisdiction in any of the cases."

Mabry smiled. "We only got the ruling thirty hours ago ourselves."

"Good enough," Starling said, suddenly brisk. "Then we'll leave you to it, Vess. Good hunting."

"Thank you," Mabry said, and shut the door firmly behind them.

"Singapore," Cerise said, after a moment. "Who's the complainant?"

Mabry smiled placidly at her, poured himself another cup of coffee. "KMS."

"That won't hold," Cerise said.

"Probably not," Mabry agreed. "But it would be nice if it did."

Trouble watched them warily, not sure she liked the cold-blooded discussion—it was a fellow cracker they were talking about, and, no matter how dangerous newTrouble had become, personally and generally across the nets, it was still unnerving to hear them plotting his effective demise.

"So you're Trouble," Mabry said, after a moment. "I'm Vesselin Mabry."

"So I gathered." Trouble kept her voice neutral, was remotely pleased with the effect.

Mabry smiled. "So. You've agreed to help me find new-Trouble. Can I ask why?"

"Does it matter?" Trouble answered, and managed a smile to take the sting from the words.

"Probably not," Mabry agreed, still placid. "As long as I get him."

Trouble frowned again, and Cerise said hastily, "I assume we're free to do as we please now, Vess?"

"Do you have the information I want?" Mabry asked.

Trouble did not bother to hide her sneer.

Cerise said, "Ah. You wouldn't be threatening me, would you, Vess?"

"No threat," Mabry said, and contrived to sound hurt by the accusation. "But I would like to know."

Trouble glanced at Cerise, saw the other woman's head tilt in an all-but-imperceptible nod. "We're waiting to get it."

"When?" Mabry asked.

"That I can't say," Trouble answered. "We have a bunch of inquiries out, and it just depends on who talks to us first."

"Treasury may have made some people a little wary," Mabry said, not without bitterness.

"Or pissed off enough to talk," Cerise said.

"One would hope so," Mabry said.

"The first thing that I want to do," Trouble said, "is get some clean clothes—I assume my belongings are still back at the hostel?"

Mabry shrugged.

"If not," Cerise said, with a sudden, malicious grin, "we can have some serious fun getting them back."

Trouble smiled in spite of herself. "Speak for yourself. But then I can check in with some people."

"And I can talk to the nets," Cerise agreed.

Trouble's grin widened. "Going to go looking for Silk?"

"Not for that," Cerise said, and sounded suddenly grim.

"Silk," Mabry said, and there was something in his voice that made both women look curiously at him. "What do you know about Silk?"

"Cerise knows a lot more than I do," Trouble said.

Cerise shrugged, frowning at the sudden intensity of Mabry's stare. "I—met Silk on the net a while back. She and I had an extremely brief fling. But I think she knows newTrouble, and I owe her a bad turn, so . . . I thought I'd make some hard inquiries into her connections."

" 'Her'?" Mabry said, and laughed suddenly, without humor. "The Silk I knew—know of—was a boy."

Cerise quirked a smile at him, trying to choose her words carefully beneath the careless tone. "So you got hustled, too."

"Not me," Mabry said, still with a tight, unfriendly smile. "Max did."

"So which is it, I wonder?" Cerise said. There was no use in being embarrassed; sex and gender confusion was one of the hazards of the nets, something a few people enjoyed exploiting while most of the net tried to minimize the inevitable mistakes. Even so, she felt a brief, unwanted flash of something between annoyance and shame: bad enough to be hustled, she thought, but by a boy?

Mabry shrugged. "I admit, I don't really know. Except that he—she?—is an accomplished bitch, any way you care to name. I should like to have words with him—her."

Trouble looked at Cerise, wondering just what Mabry meant, how much of a threat he intended. Cerise looked back, lifted one shoulder in a fractional shrug. Who knows? her expression said, and Trouble repressed a sigh. The last thing they needed was for some personal vendetta of Mabry's to screw up what already promised to be a very tricky deal.

Mabry said, "The trouble with Silk wasn't just that he likes being an obsession, or that Max was well and truly obsessed there for a week or so. But he talked Max into doing him a favor Max shouldn't even have listened to, and very nearly got Max involved in some very dirty security work. Which came close to costing Max his license—the license that I put my neck on the line to get for him."

"Ah," Cerise said, and looked at Trouble. "Max has gone into security work, consulting. I didn't know if you'd heard."

"I'd heard something," Trouble said. That explained a lot, right there: if Silk had hustled Helling, and then used him to get codes or other information—well, she thought, if it had been my lover, I'd want to see his ass kicked, all right. I can't blame Mabry. And if his reputation is on the line as well . . .

"So, Cerise," Mabry said, and forced a smile that looked more like a grimace, "if you can get Silk to give you anything, especially if you can make him—her, whatever—look like the bitch it is, I would personally enjoy seeing it. But I'd be very careful."

"I intend to be," Cerise said. "I certainly intend to be."

# ■ 11 ■

SOMEWHAT TO TROUBLE'S surprise, her room was still
available, and Valentine was not nearly as hostile as
Trouble herself would have been, faced with Treasury
on her doorstep. The room had been searched, of course—
there had been at least a hint of a warrant, Valentine said,
shrugging—but nothing seemed to be missing, for which
Trouble, at least, was grateful. She took a second shower and
found fresh clothes, then checked the machine setup. She ran
the programs she had left set mostly as a matter of habit,
checking for searches in her own working volumes. Nothing
showed, which meant only that Starling, at least, was good at
his job. The thought was depressing; she shoved it away, and
crossed to the window to stare out into the dusty street. Seahaven looked pretty much as usual, though she wondered
what the Parcade would be like, if Treasury had been its
usual self the night before. She stood for a moment, watching
a trio of older women making their way along the sidewalk,
jackets with The Willows' logo slung over their shoulders.
They looked tired, moved as though they had been working
all night, feet in low-heeled shoes scuffing against the paving.

Trouble sighed, went back into the bathroom for her medi-
cal kit. She carried stimulants—what cracker didn't, for the
long nights on the net, designer drugs that didn't interfere
with perception—and she found the tube after a few mo-
ments' search, swallowed two of the tiny pink pills, and
washed it down with the dregs of her coffee. Then she collected her keys and the important components of her machine—she wasn't leaving that behind, not again, no matter
how much protection Mabry had promised—and started
down the stairs, heading for the Parcade.

The Parcade was quieter even than she had anticipated,
half the storefronts still metal-shuttered even though open-

ing time had come and gone. There were fewer people than usual loitering in the arcade doorways or waiting under the shadow of the boardwalks' awnings, and most of them, Trouble guessed, would belong to Tinati's goon squad. One of them stared after her for a long moment, and she braced herself, waiting to be thrown out again, but the man said nothing, in the end. Trouble kept walking, feeling the stare between her shoulder blades, was glad when she reached the entrance to Blake's shop. It was open—it was hard to intimidate Mollie Blake—but the girl behind the counter had been reinforced by a tall, skinny black man. He didn't move as Trouble came into the showroom, but his attention sharpened visibly. Trouble nodded politely, careful to include both of them in the gesture, and said, "Is Mollie around?"

The girl said, in a colorless voice, "Just a minute." She reached under the counter, touched controls, and reached for the thin wire of the mike, bringing it in front of her mouth. "Boss? Trouble's here."

The response was inaudible, of course, but the girl grinned suddenly. She controlled herself in an instant, but there was still a certain amusement in her voice as she went on. "Boss says you should go straight up."

The guard moved silently to open the door, and Trouble saw the sudden bulge of muscles under his skin. Blake didn't skimp on her security, she decided, and was grateful that he hadn't been ordered to toss her out on her ear. She started up the stairs, heard the second door open above her, and looked up to see Nova silhouetted in the doorway.

"You sure live up to your name," she said, and moved back out of the way.

Trouble stepped past her, into the sudden pleasant light of Blake's loft. The worktable was lit this time, and there was a device eviscerated on the working platform, sectioned into neat, unrecognizable pieces. Blake looked up, stood, stretching.

"So," she said. "Was this your way of convincing me I ought to hurry?"

"Not likely," Trouble said, electing to take the question at face value. "Caused me more trouble than that's worth, and probably annoyed Tinati on top of it. I don't need that grief, too."

"Nobody needs that kind of grief," Nova said from the doorway. "We had to hire his security this morning, just to prove our goodwill."

Blake ignored her. "I'm surprised you're still walking around this morning."

Trouble took a deep breath. "I made a deal," she said flatly. "Not with Treasury."

"Oh?"

That was Nova again, and Blake said, "Shut up, will you? Or say something useful."

Trouble went on as though there had been no interruption. "This is a multinational problem, Mollie. Interpol has an interest, and their guy has a good name—Cerise knows him, for one, and Max Helling. And he deals with it under the Conventions, not Evans-Tinsdale."

Blake nodded. "What exactly is the deal?"

"I give him newTrouble, he gets Treasury off my back," Trouble said. "And before you say anything, Mollie, remember, I asked the nets. And off the nets, too. And I'm not going to go down for the sake of some punk kid who's a stranger to me and most of the net."

"I know you did," Blake said.

Nova said, "It's been a little weird on the nets. When were you last on?"

Trouble glanced at her, unable to read the odd smile on her broad face, and shrugged. "It's been, what, fifteen hours? Maybe twenty."

Nova's smile widened. "You've got friends coming out of the woodwork, sunshine, and not just the worms, either. A lot of people were real pissed that it was you got shopped, and not the kid. That Sasquatch, whoever he is, he's lying low, and there hasn't been a whiff of newTrouble."

"I'm flattered," Trouble said. "But I could've used that help a little earlier."

Nova shrugged, still grinning, and Blake said, "Be that as

it may—" She stopped abruptly, tried again. "I am not particularly pleased with the situation, either. It's—you might say it's very bad for business, in more ways than one, and the sooner the Mayor realizes that, the better for him. So: you were right, Trouble, I have done business with your pretender. Walk-in business—he lives around here somewhere. The word is, he lives in one of the secure complexes up north of the highway interchange, I don't know which one. But I'm sure you can find that out easily enough."

Trouble nodded, her thoughts already racing ahead. "The ones on the headland, you mean?"

"Those are the ones," Blake agreed.

"Fucking expensive place to live," Trouble said. The kind of security, electronic and real, that those slim buildings provided for their tenants didn't come cheaply; when you coupled that with luxury flats, full services, and proximity to The Willows and its direct air link to most of the coast, and then added in a very limited number of available spaces—rents would be in the thousands-per-month, and buy-in would be in the millions.

"I know," Blake said. "And no, I don't know where he gets the money."

Nova gave a nasty laugh, and Blake glared at her. Nova subsided, and Blake looked back at Trouble. "What my partner is trying to say is, he's a kid—newTrouble, I mean. Really a kid, maybe seventeen, eighteen, something like that. And he is very pretty, if you like them sweet-faced and skinny."

"Sounds like a chicken-hawk's dream," Trouble said.

"That could be it," Blake agreed, "someone paying to keep him, and him cracking on the side."

"No other way he could afford it," Nova muttered, and when Blake turned on her, she spread her hands. "Look, Moll, there's no way he could afford that, even cracking—even if he was selling what he steals. Just no way. Someone's got to be paying his bills."

Blake shook her head. "Your mind's in the gutter—"

"Except when it comes out to feed," Nova said.

Blake looked back at Trouble. "He doesn't feel like a hustler. He's a cocky punk, but not in that style. And no, before you ask, I don't know how else he could afford a Headlands apartment. But he doesn't act like a hustler."

"Thanks," Trouble said, turned her head to include Nova in the glance. "I appreciate your help."

"You and yours didn't leave us much choice," Blake said, but she was smiling. "Good luck."

"I hope you get the little bastard," Nova said, sweetly, and held open the door.

"So do I," Trouble said, and went back down the stairs to the shop, and out into the sunlight of the Parcade.

*Cerise strides the patterns of the Bazaar, knee-deep in a fog of images. She has always been noticeable, now more than ever, and she wades through a stream of messages, bioware selectively deaf, ignoring all but the very few names she has chosen to recognize. It does not impede her progress, this glittering chaff that ebbs and flows, her illusory movement cutting illusory eddies in its broken-mirror surface—she's too good for that—but it is a nuisance, makes it hard to spot the thing she knows is there. Person, she corrects herself, but it's hard still to see that spot of nothing, that negative icon, as the person she knows it to be. Mabry—as she supposes she should have, could have guessed, had she thought about it—is following her as discreetly as he's able. She considers the question as she winds through the alleys of the Bazaar, idly brushing away the occasional bit of advertising that flies too close. She could be rid of him, if she wanted; it wouldn't be easy, but she's good enough, and she very nearly takes the first step toward the funhouse hidden behind the deceptively plain Willander icon, before she thinks again. It might be better, in the long run, to let him follow, let him shadow her—let him find Silk and contrive his own revenge.*

*She changes her step, turns instead for a confection like a tent, low swooping walls and draped ceiling all of a light that shimmers like iridescent satin. She sees the walls sway toward her, feels the touch of an identity check like a warm hand at her pulse points, and the door rises for her: an expensive effect, but effective enough. She steps inside, wondering what Mabry will do, and feels her shadow hesitate and then retreat into the crowd of users, where even her best passive surveyors can't find him against the background noise. He will be waiting when she returns, however; that is more certain than taxes, and she hides a smile at the thought, moving into rose-scented shadow.*

Inside, the light has the same tint of roses, overlaid on the silver haze of a security sphere. She looks around once, noting the visible icons and the one that is invisible, blanked out, lurking behind a screen of light, and then nods to the shape that bows stiffly in her general direction.

*Cerise,* it says, a shape like a man made out of steel pipes, and Cerise answers, *Tin Man.* She is more interested in the invisible icon, but the amenities have to be observed.

*You have been a busy girl,* the Tin Man observes. *Tell me, does the course of true love still run smooth?*

*I've been busy,* Cerise agrees, *and the rest is none of your business.*

The Tin Man achieves something like a leer, an accomplishment for someone not on the wire. *Oh, come now, I've always been very fond of Trouble.*

*I doubt it's mutual.* There is no point in subtlety with him. Cerise looks at him without expression, allows the contempt to spill like acid into the air between them, then looks past him, fixing her eyes on the spot where the invisible icon is lurking. *It's not you I came to talk with.''*

*Sorry?* The Tin Man sounds genuinely surprised, and a part of her admires the act.

*I didn't come to talk to you,* Cerise said, with infinite patience. *Where's Dorothy?*

The Tin Man's icon doesn't change—he's not wired, any more than the invisible one is wired—but Cerise can hear the sudden anger in his voice. The Tin Man's proud of being straight, resents the insinuation, and Cerise hides a smile.

*Don't know any Dorothy,* he says, and Cerise allows the smile to show. *If it's herself you want to talk to, I'll see if she's willing.*

She'll be willing, Cerise thinks, but judges she's pushed hard enough already. The Tin Man's icon vanishes, though she can feel his presence, this faint tingle of electricity against her skin, and she looks around the rose-lit room again. The shimmering silver walls *have closed in, sealing her off from the rest of the nets: a necessary precaution, but one that always makes her uneasy, at least when she doesn't control the program. She controls herself instead—she can break this program if she has to, has ice-cutters in her toolkit that will destroy better security than this—and resigns herself to wait in patience.*

*At last the Tin Man reappears, bowing so that his silver-tubing fingers brush the rose-scented floor. \*This way,\* he says, and a blackness opens beside him, an oval doorway into nothing.*

*Cerise lifts an eyebrow—it was a cheap effect, and they both know it—and steps through into emptiness.*

*For a long moment the light doesn't appear, no light, no sound, no sense, and Cerise frowns, readying a program to strip the disguise from within the sphere of the security. She counts to ten, slowly, then reaches into the toolkit for the routine. As she had expected, light returns, dull, white light like the light in an office, and with it the rest of the illusion. She is standing in a featureless white sphere, and at the center of it hangs a plaintext symbol, blue reversed crescent and a blue disk like a planet trapped between its horns. The edges of the symbol flicker faintly, fizzing red. Cerise regards it without affection, picturing the woman behind the symbol: thin and bony, iron-grey hair cut close to the skull, face scraped clean of makeup while her body is constrained by the drab jeans-and-T-shirt of a mainline cracker. Ms. Cool has been around for years, from before the brainworm, and she's made a place for herself on the nets, but she's not fond of anyone, and especially not of women, at least not women on the wire.*

*\*Cerise,\* she says, in a voice electronically distorted to a timbre like scraping wire. \*What do you want?\**

*Cerise grits her teeth behind the mask of her cartoon-icon, hopes that the brainworm has not translated the fleeting emotion, dislike, and intimidation, or something very like it. \*Word is, you know everyone's location on the nets. I'm looking for Silk.\**

*\*Word is,\* Ms. Cool says, the electric voice nasty, \*you already have a mailcode.\**

*\*Had,\* Cerise corrects, and keeps her own voice level only with an effort. The space defined by Silk's code had been empty, as she'd expected, the trail long cold; she has wasted minutes searching, she*

and her watchdogs, before she'd admitted defeat and the necessity of bargaining with Ms. Cool.

The icon hanging opposite her does not change, not even a shift of color, but Cerise imagines that the other woman would have smiled had she been able. *If Silk's dumped you, it's not my business to put the two of you back together. Besides, what would Trouble say?*

*I manage my own sex life, thanks,* Cerise says. *This is business.* She hesitates, gauging the insult. *I didn't think Silk was one to pass up business—any more than you.*

Ms. Cool ignores her, doesn't answer for a long moment, just the icon hanging blind in the blank white space. Cerise keeps a grip on herself, masters her impatience, and waits unmoving. At last, without the flicker of anything to anticipate the response, Ms. Cool says, *I have a code. But there's a price.*

*There always is.* Cerise speaks without thinking, sees no reason to regret the words.

*Multiplane's security is good,* Ms. Cool says. *And I need information.*

Cerise laughs aloud. *My security's good, you mean. And it's no deal.*

*You might want to hear the full offer,* Ms. Cool says, and Cerise gestures for her to continue. *And don't think I can't break your IC(E), girl, but I have other fish to fry.*

That is almost certainly a lie and they both know it, but Cerise gives no sign, and Ms. Cool goes on without a breath.

*And I'm not after trade secrets, you'd be surprised how little market there is for them. What I want is personnel information, nothing more. Just a simple file, not even the classified version. On a man named Derrick Coigne.*

Coigne. Cerise barely stops herself from speaking the name aloud, feels the surprise congeal around her, the sensation doubly vivid in the blank room. That was different, Coigne was different, it might even help her to pass that information on to Ms. Cool—and this was probably just what Ms. Cool wanted her to think. Ms. Cool's favors are rarely simple, simply given or simply achieved; besides, even a general-access internal file contained information that outsiders were not supposed to see. Multiplane has more secrets than she knows, more enmities and rivalries and obscure alliances than even she can monitor, even watching the internal nets as she does—but there's no choice this time, she tells herself. She needs Silk's codes, some location, and she needs them now or she would never have come to Ms. Cool, because if she doesn't get them, if she and Trouble don't find newTrouble, and soon, the whole messy business with Treasury will begin all over again. And that she, they, cannot afford; she will not risk it, risk losing Trouble, not again.

She has made the decision almost before she's realized it, as though there was no decision to be made, no choice at all. The only question left is whether she will keep her bargain, get Ms. Cool the files she wants, or, more precisely, how she will go about keeping both the bargain and her job. And if she loses the job, she thinks, it will be worth it—and that is a thought she doesn't want and can't right now afford, and she puts it aside without even the acknowledgment of a frown. *Coigne,* she says, aloud this time, still playing for time. *Why would anyone want Coigne's files?*

*Don't be stupid, girl,* Ms. Cool says. *Anyway, the whys don't matter. It's a straight deal, my code for his file. Are you willing?*

*I'm interested,* Cerise corrects. *But I'm not—in the office right now. You'd have to take it on trust.*

*I don't do business that way.*

*In this case, you don't have a choice.* Cerise stops, takes a deep breath, makes her tone ever so faintly conciliatory—anything more would be suspicious. *Even I don't have access from outside.*

There is another silence, another of Ms. Cool's periods of inattention, and Cerise finds herself holding her breath. She hides a frown, and makes herself breathe, counting heartbeats; she reaches a hundred, an eternity, before Ms. Cool speaks. *All right. We'll do it your way. But if you cross me, Cerise . . .*

Cerise doesn't answer, because there's nothing she can say. They stand silent for another moment, and then Ms. Cool says again, *All right.* The icon flickers and a mailcode appears; Cerise plucks it out of the air, feeling the numbers tingle against her fingers. She tucks it into her toolkit, carefully compartmentalizing just in case, and looks back at the icon.

*You owe me,* Ms. Cool says, softly, and Cerise nods.

*I owe you,* she agrees, and closes her mind to the consequences.

*The blank sphere splits open around her, and the icon vanishes. Cerise steps backward, and is abruptly in the center of the rose-colored tent. The Tin Man sneers at her from a corner.*

*Get what you wanted?*

*Do you care?* Cerise asks, with a grin, and adds, *Ask your boss, if you really want to know.* She walks past him without another word, brushes through illusory curtains that hum for an instant under her touch as though they held a swarm of bees. She steps out into the gaudy light and noise of the Bazaar, follows the meandering path between the heaped icons and the crude-drawn storefronts that lie behind the piles of advertising, and is aware again of the negative icon following her. Mabry is still with her. She keeps walking, wondering if she should try to lose him, but perhaps, she thinks, a witness would be advisable. She finds a sheltered spot, checks the mailcode Ms. Cool has given her—an unfamiliar string, an unfamiliar part of the net—and calls a new routine, lets it absorb the mailcode, and follows it as it runs.

The tracer leads her back out into the main highways of the net, as she had expected. She lets herself absorb the new perspective, the rivers of neon fire, streams and falls of light, here and there a flurry of white and red, lights tossed like water over rapids, then strides out into the nearest node, lets the force of the traffic carry her away. She can see, and feel, the tracer ahead of her, sorting through the junctions for her, follows its path that glows green to the eye and warm to the touch, and at the fourth node calls a halt. The tracer whines in protest—it, they, are nearing the end of its programmed road, and it seems almost eager to finish its work—but Cerise waits anyway, listening, sniffing, for a hint of the negative icon. It is there, as she had known it would be: Mabry, still with her, following at a distance just discreet enough. She sighs then, and steps from mainstream to local net, follows the tracer down the last wide road of light, until they emerge together at the mailcode's volume. The tracer vanishes, and Cerise is left alone, except for the ghost of the invisible icon lurking in the distance.

There is IC(E), of course, both obvious spikes and coils of it, walling off all but a staging area, and subtler strands of it, hair-thin tripwires and delicate poison darts. She frowns for an instant, considering the problem, then evokes a routine from her toolkit. It *spreads, slow and thick, meaningless codes and numbers oozing like molasses, clogging the more delicate traps, overloading the fine triggers until one by one the traps fire or fizzle, releasing payloads that are lost at once in the sea of garbage. Cerise watches carefully, recording the pattern of the traps—there's always something to be learned from even amateur work, and this is good, better than a mere amateur—then steps across to the main barrier. She studies it for a moment—the same hand built it that forged the subtler traps—considering how to proceed. She has two choices, discreet and overt, and after only an instant's thought chooses the obvious approach. Silk needs to know she's pursued, that she has not acted, cannot act, with impunity—and besides, Cerise thinks, and smiles, she herself has watchdogs in her toolkit that can follow anyone. If Silk panics, and runs, the watchdog will follow, and with any luck Silk will run to newTrouble. She evokes the watchdog then, sets its chameleon routine and leaves it sleeping, less of a presence on the net than Mabry's invisible non-icon, and turns her attention to the IC(E).*

*Under other circumstances she would take her time, thread the glittering razors' maze of it, but she's already betrayed her presence by neutralizing the first array of traps. She selects the best icebreaker she owns. She didn't write the main structure, but she has modified it until it fits her hand, her style, like a velvet glove. She draws it on, feeling the power surge through it as the program wakes and tests the IC(E), then sweeps her hand across the first bright coil of program. The shock of it jolts her to her elbow, numb tingling as though she'd hit a nerve; she grimaces, calls more power. She touches it again, and this time the IC(E) cracks and shatters under her touch, falling away in chunks like broken glass. At the edges of the breach, the broken ends of the matrix flare, and then fade, like embers in the wind. She reaches out again, seizes another handful of the brittle glittering IC(E), enjoying the feeling as it cracks and falls like dust at her feet. Once more, and she is through, emerging into the echoing silence of an empty node.*

*She has expected that, predicted the emptiness when there was no counter to her first assault on the volume's defenses, but she checks anyway, letting her own countersecurity programs survey the area. There is nothing more than the routine maintenance programs, anonymous and mainstream, nothing to betray their owner's hand, and she steps out into the empty space. It is flat, featureless, grey floor, white dome/ceiling, all standard, not even a hot-spot to trigger a new environment or a private stash of files. Which is all pretty much as she has expected: she scans anyway, and this time finds the button, dulled almost to invisibility. She checks for links to IC(E), finds none, but readies a defensive program anyway before she triggers whatever lies behind the routine.*

*Grass sprouts underfoot, and a pavilion shimmers into place: the scene of her earlier seduction. She makes a face, but lets the program run, until the stage is complete, if empty, no sign of Silk behind the clever trappings. She scans again, ignoring the demanding memory—better to have Trouble, in spite of everything—finds a storage cache and a single file. She studies the guard program carefully, selects a tool, and freezes the lock into immobility. It can neither close nor destroy its contents; she pries it gently open, and scans the file. It is a working draft of a program, a model for iconage, and she seals a copy carefully into her working memory. It could be bait, a poison trap that carries some unpleasant virus, and she doesn't have the time to risk that now.*

*There is nothing else she needs, not here, and the mere fact that she's been here is message enough for Silk. She hesitates, contemplating a message, and at last tosses a copy of her icon out into the empty space. It hangs in the air, the cartoon shape glowing against the blank walls: if Silk knows what's good for her, she'll contact me, Cerise thinks, and turns away. And if she doesn't—there's always the watchdog. She walks out through the shattered IC(E), feels the ghostly touch of the watchdog, warm against her ankle, reassuring her of its presence. Mabry, too, is still with her, but she ignores him, and turns again for home.*

Trouble sat cross-legged on her chair, left hand still nursing the elbow that stung and tingled from the feedback of the IC(E) surrounding The Willows' databases. Voices spilled in through the open window, kids' shouts high and clear as they played basketball in the lot behind the Chinese restaurant, mixing with the periodic drone of runabouts' engines, but she ignored them all, staring at the numbers that filled her display screen. It was bad enough that she hadn't been able to break through the IC(E) on-line—not only did her elbow hurt, but the same pins-and-needles sensation trembled through her hands, slowing her fingers on the keyboard and controls. The numbers did not change, and she glared at them a moment longer before moving on to the next screen. The news was no better there: most of the Headlands apartments were controlled by The Willows, and the information on tenants' names and rents and who actually paid the bills was buried in The Willows' most secure databases. She had already proved that she couldn't break that IC(E)—almost unconsciously, she ran her hand over her sore elbow, imagining a bruise beneath the skin even though she knew perfectly well that the tingling was in her nerves, in the brainworm itself—which left her only the slow, unreliable road through the city records. And that wasn't even cracking, she thought, bitterly; it was more like panning for gold, sifting huge amounts of raw information through a datasieve in the hopes first that the information you wanted was actually there, and then that you'd built the sieve correctly to catch it. Most crackers didn't have the patience for the technique—hell, she wasn't sure she had the patience for it anymore—but she'd already exhausted all the other options.

She made a face at the screen, dumped the information back to the disk, then called up another file. This one contained the latest access codes for most of the East Coast city databases—it was one of those things the wannabes cracked out of the systems and posted, just to prove they could do it—and, as she had hoped, the Seahaven/Southbrook/Sands joint administrative district computer was on the list, less than twenty hours old. The codes indicated that it was an older machine, without the additional security packages that most of the larger cities had installed in the past year. She lifted an eyebrow at that—she would have expected The Willows either to provide the program or at least to insist that the town governments install it—but experience had taught her to be grateful for small mercies. She copied the code, and went looking for her datasieve. She found it at last, on a subsidiary disk, and brought it into working memory, opened it, then stared at the matrix, considering the parameters. This was something that Cerise was particularly good at, designing search routines, and she stood up abruptly, reached for the handset before she could change her mind. There was no point in not contacting Cerise, not now, but she still felt oddly embarrassed by the sudden strength of her need to work with the other woman. She punched in the numbers with more force than necessary, steeling herself for the buzzing of an empty line, and was startled when Cerise herself answered.

"Yes?"

"It's me."

"Figures," Cerise said.

Trouble could hear her relax, and imagined her sudden smile. "I need your help with something," she said, and Cerise laughed softly.

"Do you want to talk about it?"

"Not on the phone, no," Trouble answered.

"Ah. Well, I have some news for you, too," Cerise said. "Shall I come to you?"

Trouble looked around the little room, reminded again that Treasury had been there the night before. She had swept for bugs and taps again as soon as she returned, with no result, but Treasury was good. There was no reason to take unnecessary chances. "Probably not," she said, with some reluctance. "Why don't I meet you back at your place?"

"I'll be expecting you," Cerise answered, and the line went dead.

Trouble walked back across the bridge into Seahaven proper, her portable system and the disk-bound toolkit heavy on her shoulder, and threaded her way through the crowd of shoppers along Ashworth Avenue. They were mostly corporate, out on holiday, mixed with a few of the richer locals, and she was glad when she reached the entrance to Eastman House. Cerise had left word at the desk; the attendant, another young woman, sallow and thin, not flattered by the deep red uniform jacket, motioned for Trouble to take the elevator. Trouble nodded her thanks, and went through into the lobby. The elevator came quickly enough—Eastman House didn't seem to be particularly busy at the moment—and she found herself hurrying down the hallway toward Cerise's room. She made a face, but did not slow her step until she was right outside the door. She knocked, and was obscurely pleased when Cerise answered instantly.

"So what's up?" she asked, and stepped back out of the doorway.

Trouble followed her in, impressed again by the expensive furniture and the view of the slough and the trees through the enormous window. The sunlight spilled across the carpet, and the tide waters gleamed like steel in the channels of the marsh; the trees were red and gold and green against the sky. Cerise closed the door, and Trouble turned again to look at her, as slim and expensive as the furniture and the view, vivid against the decorous cream walls. She bit down the sudden flood of desire, said, "I've got a line on newTrouble."

"Have you now?" Cerise said, soft-voiced, and grinned suddenly. "I didn't find Silk. I left a watchdog, though, that may help."

"Mine's in the real world," Trouble said. "Mollie says he lives in one of the Headlands apartments."

"The fancy towers?" Cerise asked. "How the hell does he afford that?"

"That's what I've been wondering, and so have Mollie and Nova," Trouble answered. "Mollie says she doesn't think he's hustling."

"And he's not selling what he takes off the nets," Cerise said, her eyebrows drawing down into a faint, unconscious frown. "I'd trust Blake to know a hustler when she sees one."

"Exactly."

Cerise nodded, looked back at Trouble. "So what did you want, sweetheart?"

Trouble grinned. "I already tried The Willows' IC(E)— they own the Headlands, did you know that? I didn't."

"I might've guessed," Cerise muttered. "How's your head?"

"It's not my head that hurts, it's my elbow," Trouble said, with perfect truth. "I didn't get very far—I didn't think it would be smart to push it."

Cerise nodded again. "So how do you want to play it?"

Trouble felt a brief thrill of pleasure. It was flattering for Cerise to assume that if Trouble couldn't break that IC(E), neither could she; more than that, it was like the old days, the casual trust, making it easier to ask. "I think we're going to have to go through the city database, and that was always your specialty. You want to help me program the sieve?"

"God," Cerise said, "that takes me back. I don't think I own one anymore, certainly not in this memory." She gestured vaguely toward her system, snugged up against the main media console.

"Working in the light's got you spoiled," Trouble said. "As it happens . . ." She let her voice trail off, and slipped the heavy bag from her shoulder.

"Help yourself," Cerise said, and went to the console, typed in codes to open the system. After a moment's search, Trouble found the disk she wanted, and fed it into the drive Cerise indicated. A light flickered on, and Cerise typed the run codes before Trouble could recite them.

"Your memory's good," she said, startled, and Cerise looked up at her, eyes hooded.

"You better believe it, darling."

That sounded promising, looked promising. Trouble shivered in spite of herself, said quickly, "The code's already in there, I downloaded it an hour or so ago. It was eighteen hours old then, so it should still be all right."

Cerise nodded. "They usually change every twenty-four hours up here," she said absently, her fingers already busy on the keys, calling up the main program and the search routine. "So. What do we know about this newTrouble?"

"He's young," Trouble answered promptly.

"How young?"

Trouble shrugged one shoulder, thinking. "Under twenty-five, would be my guess, probably younger. Mollie said he looked sixteen, seventeen.''

"Can I bring it down to twenty, do you think?'' Cerise asked, her hands poised over the keyboard. Trouble came to stand behind her, staring at the search screen.

"Make it twenty-one,'' she said, after a moment. "I've just got a feeling he isn't legal yet.''

Cerise nodded, entered the number in the correct box. "I wonder if he lives alone?''

"Alone or with one other person,'' Trouble said.

"Yeah, that would be my thought, too,'' Cerise said. "Should I be looking for a keeper, maybe put an age restriction on the household?''

Trouble hesitated, tempted—despite what Blake had said, she had to think that someone was paying newTrouble's bills—but shook her head. "I have to trust Mollie,'' she said. "And she says he's not a hustler.''

"That doesn't mean he's not being kept,'' Cerise argued, but moved on to the next field. "Profession or professions?''

"God, I don't know.''

"Well, what would you tell the IRS?''

"As little as possible,'' Trouble said. "I don't know, consultant, maybe? Technical trades/miscellaneous?''

"You know, I'm inclined to leave it blank for now,'' Cerise said. "I'll use that to sort the results later.''

"You're the wizard at this,'' Trouble said, with perfect truth, and Cerise smiled up at her.

"I know.''

"And modest, too,'' Trouble said, not quite under her breath. Cerise laughed, and turned her attention back to the screen. She worked quickly now, pausing only to ask a quick question now and then. Trouble did her best to answer, but knew that her responses were less than adequate. When at last Cerise was finished, she leaned back in her chair, shaking her head.

"I'm going to get at least thirty names out of this, even restricting it by location, maybe as many as fifty. How're we going to sort it out?''

"I don't know," Trouble admitted. "I liked your idea of sorting by profession—"

"Assuming that newTrouble lists himself as something technie," Cerise said. "What do you call yourself, sweetie?"

"A syscop," Trouble answered.

"Before, I meant."

"I know." Trouble looked away from the screen. In the old days, she had described herself on the government forms as a clerk-typist, freelance; Cerise had called herself a grade-three secretary, Trouble remembered, and not for the first time wondered if the other woman had actually trained as office staff. She said, "There must be a way we could check it out— or we could just hand it over to Mabry as is, I suppose."

"You don't sound any more eager than I am," Cerise said.

"Well, I wouldn't feel like I was living up to my part of the bargain," Trouble said. "And I really don't want him to think that way."

"Yes," Cerise said. She frowned at the screen, touched more keys to dump her responses into the main search matrix. "Let me start this running, then we can talk."

Trouble nodded, stayed leaning over the other woman's shoulder to watch as Cerise keyed in the first series of access codes. The regional database prompts appeared after a moment, and she keyed in the next codes. Even working off the wire, completely outside the nets' virtual space, her work was precise and efficient, and Trouble caught herself watching again in fascination. Cerise found the main search program almost at once, and touched more keys to insinuate her own program, replacing the preset parameters with her own datasieve. There was a momentary hesitation, and then the system accepted her override. The screen went blank, the prompts replaced with a holding pattern. Trouble eyed it warily—she distrusted anything that tied up a machine long enough for the authorities to complete a trace, no matter how necessary she knew it to be—and Cerise pushed her chair away.

"This is going to take a while," she said. "You want a drink?"

"Yeah, thanks." Trouble watched her move to the low cabinet, touch her thumb to the cheap lock and open the main compartment. "Wine?"

Cerise turned back to her, already holding two half-sized bottles. "The glasses are in the bathroom."

"How elegant," Trouble said, but went to collect the tumblers. The sinkboard was cluttered with familiar items, brush, toothbrush, a dozen black-lacquer containers of makeup, all the same expensive brand Cerise had always used. Some things don't change, she thought, and brought the glasses back out into the main room. Cerise handed her one of the bottles, accepted a glass, and they poured the wine in companionable silence.

"Well," Cerise said, after a moment, and held up her glass in silent toast.

Trouble matched the gesture, old habit, tasted the wine cautiously. It was better than they had ever been able to afford—better than she had been able to afford on her syscop's salary—and she took a longer swallow, savoring it.

"Expense accounts are a wonderful thing," Cerise said, with a rather bitter smile.

"Useful, certainly," Trouble said. "Is Multiplane really going to pay for all this?"

"It's on their account," Cerise answered.

The silence returned, broken only by the occasional whirring of the machine's main drive as it accessed some other part of the program. Cerise turned to look at the screen, grateful for the interruption, saw that the holding screen had been replaced by something else, and went to see to it. Trouble trailed behind her, still holding her glass of wine, watched over the other's shoulder while she stored the file—a massive one, Trouble saw without surprise—and extricated herself from the system. Cerise didn't look up when she had finished, but recalled the main program and set up a second search routine.

"Sorting by profession?" Trouble asked after a moment, wanting to break the silence. Cerise nodded, preoccupied, fingers busy on the keys, and Trouble resigned herself to wait. To her surprise, however, Cerise touched a final sequence that dumped the new file into the sort queue, and pushed herself back from the machine.

"Yeah. I've set it up to break the list down by job listing, technie stuff at the top, and so on, but then we'll have to go over it by hand."

Trouble nodded. "Fun."

"Oh, yeah."

Trouble stared for a moment longer at the screen, its numbers now replaced by a mindless swirl of color. "How long, do you think?"

Cerise shrugged. "I don't know. Fifteen, twenty minutes?"

"That long."

"It's a complicated file, and a complicated search," Cerise said, annoyed.

"Sorry."

The silence was less amiable this time. Trouble turned away from the media center, frowning slightly, found Cerise scowling back at her from across the room. Trouble felt her own frown deepening, temper rising in response to Cerise's irritation, wondered suddenly what had happened to the ease they had felt—was it only that morning? I'm not letting this happen again, she thought, smoothed her expression with an effort. She took another swallow of the wine, said, "I did miss you."

Cerise's eyebrows flicked upward in surprise. It was on the tip of her tongue to remind Trouble that she had been the one who left—but she'd said that before, and Trouble had apologized, too. "Well," she said. "I missed you, too."

It was her turn to sound unreasonably annoyed, and Trouble laughed softly. Cerise stared at her for a moment, then, reluctantly, smiled back. "So now what?" she asked, and Trouble put her glass down, took a step toward her.

"What did you have in mind?"

"Ah," Cerise said, and put her own glass aside. "Well."

"Back rub?" Trouble asked, too brightly, and Cerise grinned.

"No. Come here."

Trouble held out her arms instead, and Cerise moved toward her as though hypnotized, caught Trouble in a firm embrace. Trouble returned the hug, awkwardly, hampered by the other woman's hold, and was very aware that Cerise was staring up at her, still grinning, daring her to pull away. They were close in height, but Trouble was the taller; she clung to that illusion of advantage as Cerise worked one arm free, reached up to tilt the other woman's face down to meet her own lips. Her kiss was momentarily chaste, lips closed and cool, deliberately so, and she smiled again as Trouble's eyes flickered closed.

Trouble caught her breath, pulled away for an instant, a familiar ache beginning between her legs, set one hand deliberately on Cerise's breast, feeling the nipple hard beneath her palm, distinct even through the fabric of her shirt and bra. The bra was a surprise—Cerise had never used to wear one before, but then, they had both filled out since the old days, gotten older, gotten better—but the rest was startlingly familiar. They made their way into the bedroom somehow, locked in a stumbling embrace, still competing to end up on top because that was what had always turned them on, fumbled with shirts and jeans until at last Cerise sprawled back against the pillows. She was naked to the waist, shirt discarded somewhere on the floor, bra tangled under her, jeans half unbuttoned already, and Trouble sat back on her heels, too caught by the swell of breast and belly for a moment to even think of shrugging out of her own clothes. She had forgotten, somehow—had always forgotten, had always relearned, each time she saw Cerise naked—just how fine her body was, the alabaster skin and the dark brown-pink aureoles, the sleek black hair now tousled around her face.

"Come here, then," Cerise said, and reached for the taller woman, drawing her down against her own embrace. Trouble came to her willingly, wrapping arms and legs around her, grunted in surprise as Cerise rolled deftly, so that she straddled Trouble's hips.

"My turn," Cerise said, and Trouble let herself be peeled out of the tangle of shirt and bra. Cerise slid her fingers under the waistband of Trouble's jeans, fingers cool against hot skin, then, suddenly impatient, tugged the zipper open, dragged jeans and underwear down around Trouble's hips. Trouble arched upward, ready to cooperate, but Cerise left the material where it was, tangled just below Trouble's crotch, and leaned forward, drawing her breasts down the other woman's body. Trouble whimpered softly—it had been a long time, too long—and she should know better, should stop now, but Cerise's touch dissolved all thoughts of safety. She pulled Cerise down hard against her. Cerise grinned—Trouble could feel the movement of her mouth against her breast—and slid her hand down between Trouble's legs. Trouble closed her eyes, giving herself up to the sensations, the too-slow touch, easing between her labia, thumb circling her clit while a finger pressed and entered her. Cerise mumbled something, sounded approving, tongue busy on Trouble's right nipple, and Trouble whimpered again, wriggling to try to get the busy fingers just where she needed them. For a moment, it seemed as though Cerise would ignore her, worse, had forgotten, but then her hand shifted, fingers settling to a familiar rhythm, and Trouble let herself be carried away, shuddering to her climax against Cerise's hand.

Trouble lay still for a long moment, savoring the slow relaxation, the warmth of Cerise's hand still cupped against her vulva, the weight of the other woman's body sprawled half across her, head tucked comfortably just above her breast. She ran her hand down Cerise's spine, felt the other woman shift slightly, as though she would have purred. And then the handset beside the bed beeped gently, echoed an instant later by a louder buzz from the media console.

"Fuck," Cerise said, her mouth still against Trouble's breast.

"We just did that," Trouble said, unable to resist.

"You may have done," Cerise said, and twisted free of Trouble's embrace, reaching for the handset.

"So don't answer," Trouble said.

Cerise glared at her, and lifted the handset. "Yes?"

Trouble rolled onto her side, automatically pulling up her jeans, and grimaced at the soggy fabric between her legs. She had been stupid, and the knowledge of it chilled her to the bone. She didn't believe in taking chances, not when she knew the odds, not even with Cerise. "Who is it?" she asked, and Cerise mouthed, *Mabry*. Trouble groaned softly, and reached for her shirt, began disentangling it from her vest. What they'd done was relatively safe, but gloves would've been safer, and she found herself staring at Cerise's delicate hands, looking for cuts. Three years was a long time, long enough for anything to happen.

Cerise said aloud, "Yes, we have some of the information you were looking for." She stopped, listening, and made a face. "Yeah, why don't you come on up?" She listened again, nodded, and said, "All right." Trouble rolled her eyes, and Cerise put the headset down with exquisite care.

"Hell, Cerise," Trouble said.

"You think you're disappointed?" Cerise said, and reached for her clothes. "You owe me, sweetheart."

"No problem," Trouble said, and meant it. "When's he coming?"

"He's on his way," Cerise said, and gave a rueful smile. "Timing is everything."

They managed to dress before Mabry knocked at the door, but only just. Trouble ran her fingers through her hair, well aware that it was even more disheveled than usual, and Cerise gave herself a disapproving look in the mirror as she went to answer the door.

"You said you had something for us?" she asked even before Mabry was fully into the room.

Mabry looked around once, eyebrows lifting in what might have been amusement. Trouble glared at him, daring him to say anything, and the big man looked away.

"You wanted to see more examples of newTrouble's work," he said. "I brought some. You said you had something for me?"

"It's just finishing," Trouble said, without looking at the screen.

"We have a rough address," Cerise said. "It's just a matter of narrowing it down."

"That's very good," Mabry said, in what seemed to be genuine surprise. "I'm impressed."

"It's nice to have friends," Trouble said.

"So," Cerise said. "What have we got?" She crossed to the media center and leaned over the screen, frowning slightly. Trouble moved to join her, saw the list of names now neatly sorted by probabilities, and looked back at Mabry.

"Can I see your disk?"

Mabry handed it to her silently, and she stooped to collect her own carryall, discarded on the floor by the media center. She seated herself on the couch, stretching to reach a power node, and hastily rigged a working system. She slipped the disk into a drive, flipped through the files. Most of them were Treasury or Eurocop dissections of viruses or intrusion techniques, but a couple were straight transcripts of intrusion and pursuit. Those she paged through more slowly, frowning more deeply now. She was only dimly aware of the click of keys as Cerise worked her way through the list, or of Mabry still standing by the main door, hands shoved deep into his pockets. There was something familiar about the hand in the files, something familiar about the way the programs were constructed and the way newTrouble approached a job—not just that he had stolen from her work, that she could see and discount, torn between annoyance and flattery. But there was something about the stranger, about one exchange between newTrouble and a pursuing syscop— the flare of an icon, an exchange of insults, and then the quick and contemptuous disappearance—that reminded her of something, someone, she could not quite place. She ran her fingers through her hair, flipped back to an earlier file, looking for a file that dissected one of newTrouble's icebreakers. The autopsy was well done, more sophisticated than the usual run of cops' work, and she went through it slowly, line by line. This was familiar, too, though not quite in the same way as the intrusion she had been tracing; this time, at least, she could put a name to the model.

"This is the Mayor's work," she said aloud, and was startled when Mabry answered.

"The Mayor? Of Seahaven?"

"It can't be the Mayor's," Cerise said, ignoring Mabry. "He'd never give anything of his to newTrouble."

"It's still the Mayor's work," Trouble said.

"Surely he—newTrouble—could have stolen it?" Mabry asked.

Trouble shook her head as Cerise came to join her, leaning down over her shoulder to study the little screen. "You don't steal from the Mayor," she said. "First, he'd never forgive you, would hunt you to the day you died—"

"Which wouldn't be very far off," Cerise said.

"—and, second, you'd have to break his IC(E) to do it." Trouble shook her head again. "The Mayor—virtual-Seahaven's his own private fortress. There are parts where he doesn't need IC(E), the programming is so idiosyncratic. Nobody's ever stolen anything from him. Not anything important."

"That is the Mayor's hand," Cerise said, leaned further forward so that her arm was resting on Trouble's shoulder. Trouble was briefly aware of the scent of her, sex and sweat and perfume.

"Take a look at this one," she said, and touched the controls to recall the first file. "It looks like the Mayor, too, a little, but there's something else. . . ."

"It reminds me of Silk," Cerise said.

"Silk?" That was Mabry again, moving in from the doorway.

Cerise brushed past him to retrieve a disk from the media center. "Take a look at this," she said, and handed it to Trouble.

Trouble took it, fed it into the secondary drive, and waited while the machine absorbed the contents. There was a lock on the main file, and Cerise leaned past her, breast nudging against her shoulder, to touch the codes that released it. Trouble nodded her thanks, and opened the file. It was a work-in-progress, blocks of as-yet-unwritten code replaced

with cryptically labeled placeholders, but the basic intent
was clear enough. It was a display program, mostly iconage,
but married to the bones of a decent-looking icepick: a showoff program, Trouble thought, the sort of thing kids wrote, to
prove what they could do. It would work its way through
someone's IC(E)—probably without alerting security; even
in the skeletal state, she could see that it was a pick, not a
hammer—and then, in the heart of a supposedly secure system, unfurl its iconage. And probably something else, too,
she realized suddenly, looking at the missing pieces of code.
There was certainly a place for a viral payload.

"It's a clever piece of work," she said aloud. "And it looks
like newTrouble, all right. What's good is brilliant, but
there's some sloppy work around the edges."

"He's added code he didn't write," Mabry said. "See,
there and there, those timers—and he hasn't bothered to inte-
grate it."

"I got this," Cerise said, deliberately, "out of Silk's space.
Silk's work."

"You think they're the same person?" Trouble asked.

Cerise closed her eyes, trying to recapture the feeling of the
first intrusion, her sense of that hand, compared it to the
sense she'd had of Silk, in their two meetings. Bearing in
mind that Silk had meant to hustle her, had overlaid her—
his?—program with deliberate seduction, while the intruder
had been after other game—yes, there had been a hint of
Trouble, her own Trouble and the imposter's version of that
hand, in Silk's approach. It was, she acknowledged, one reason she had fallen for it so easily. "Yeah," she said aloud.
"Yes, I think so."

"And there's a connection to the Mayor as well?" Mabry
asked. His voice was tight, controlled, and Cerise looked
warily at him.

Trouble said, still looking at the screen, "If he's using the
Mayor's routines, the Mayor sold or gave them to him. I'm
sure of that."

Cerise nodded, but her eyes were still on Mabry. Mabry
smiled, turned away from the couch, and leaned in over the

screen set up below the media center. "How is your list set up?" he asked.

Cerise followed him, frowning now. "By profession, technie stuff first, then by age and number in household within each category."

"Run me a search, will you?" Mabry asked. "By co-lessor or primary leaseholder, probably the leaseholder. The name is Eytan Novross."

Cerise lifted an eyebrow, but did as he asked, saying, "Who's Novross?"

Mabry smiled, not pleasantly. "Eytan Novross is the Mayor of Seahaven."

Trouble set her machine aside and came to join them, resting one hand on the back of Cerise's chair. "I thought nobody knew who the Mayor was, realworld."

"We've known for years," Mabry said. "We just couldn't—can't—prove anything against him. The space that Novross runs is perfectly clean, or has been every time we've gained access. But it is Seahaven, and he's the Mayor, there's no question about it."

"Do you think he'd be stupid enough to have an obvious connection with newTrouble?" Trouble asked.

"It's worth a try, at any rate," Mabry said, and there was something in his voice that made Trouble look sharply at him. He knew something, all right, something that he wasn't telling—

"Got it, by God," Cerise said. "Look there."

The record filled the screen, drawn perhaps from census, perhaps from the tax forms, the record of owner and inhabitants of one of the Headlands apartments. Not the most expensive of the buildings, Trouble saw without surprise, but not the cheapest, either. And even the cheapest of those flats were worth more than she could afford. Eytan Novross was listed as the owner, a further screen indicating that he paid taxes and mortgage promptly and without complaint; the occupant, however, was listed as James Tilsen, student. "He's seventeen," she said aloud, and Mabry shrugged.

"We figured he was young."

Not that young, I didn't, Trouble thought, not really, and bit back the words because they weren't—quite—true. She had been seventeen when she first made a name for herself in the shadows. It was more that she had forgotten, as she herself had gotten older, just how young the competition would always be. It was hard not to feel a little guilty when you slapped down a rival, if you thought too much about their age. . . .

"You really think this is newTrouble?" Cerise asked.

Mabry nodded again. "Yes. I'm sure of it."

It was there again, in his voice, the certainty. "You knew this," Trouble said aloud. "You knew there was a connection."

Mabry looked at her, heavy face empty of emotion, and Cerise said, "Ah. I think you're right, Trouble." Her voice hardened. "Give, Mabry."

Mabry hesitated a moment longer, grimaced. "We knew that Novross—the Mayor—was paying to house and feed this kid, a kid, anyway. We looked into it pretty thoroughly, of course—the boy was well underage—but everything was scrupulously aboveboard. Novross lives elsewhere—he's on the move a lot, but he rents in Harborside or by the Parcade, anyplace he can get power for the hardware—and does not, absolutely does not, sleep with the kid."

Cerise lifted an eyebrow at that, and Mabry scowled, looked fleetingly ashamed. "Do you think that wasn't the first thing Treasury—and us, too—checked out? They thought—it would have been a good arrest. Tilsen was fifteen when he moved in."

Trouble looked away, torn. Fifteen was too damn young, most of the time, ninety percent of the time, but she resented the certainty that it would have been the queer relationship that made a conviction certain. If newTrouble had been a girl—if it had been me, she thought, with a sudden chill—it would have been a different matter.

"You mean he's just being paternal?" Cerise asked, and the disbelief was plain in her voice. "The Mayor?"

Mabry shrugged, looked even more uncomfortable. "There

was a sting set up, too, nice young-looking guy. He said Novross nearly panicked when he said he'd sleep with him, told him no in no uncertain terms. Said he was above all that, above sex, but our man thought he was too scared to do it. So, paternal or not, I don't think he's sleeping with the kid."

Trouble looked at him without affection. This was the part of a syscop's work that she disliked—but that, she told herself, was pure sentiment. NewTrouble, whatever his age, whatever his relationship with the Mayor, had done his best to destroy her and steal her name and reputation. That, in the end, was all that mattered. Still, at the moment, her victory felt a little hollow.

"What happens now?" she asked, and Mabry shrugged again.

"I get a warrant, and go see Tilsen," he said. "With any luck, he brings down the Mayor as well."

That wasn't in the bargain, Trouble thought, but Cerise's eyes were on her, and she said nothing.

"Do you think that's likely?" Cerise asked, and heard the ambivalence in her own voice.

"Look," Mabry said, "the Mayor is the source of half of what's illegal in this sector of the nets—on the nets in general. Seahaven, his Seahaven, is worse than the City of London for data laundering. Do you have a problem with shutting him down?"

The two women looked at each other, each one knowing better than to speak for the other, and then Cerise gestured impatiently. Trouble said, "I suppose not. But it'll be a weird world without Seahaven."

Cerise nodded.

"Maybe," Mabry said. He turned away from the media center, stopped again with his hand on the door controls. "One thing, though. If you screw up this arrest, the deal is off."

"You don't need to threaten me," Cerise said.

"It wasn't you I was talking to," Mabry answered, and was gone.

When the door had closed behind him, Cerise looked back

at Trouble, one eyebrow rising in question. "You weren't thinking of warning him, were you? NewTrouble, I mean."

"No, not really," Trouble said. She sighed, and walked back to the couch, began shutting down the system there. "It's just—it makes a difference, knowing his name."

Cerise nodded. "I know."

"And I never wanted to close down Seahaven," Trouble said.

"Christ, no." Cerise took a deep breath. "Except I never liked the Mayor. . . ."

Trouble smiled. "No more do I. But—" She broke off, shaking her head, coiled an errant cable around her fingers. "Damn it, I don't like the way the net's changing. I don't trust these guys who come in out of the bright lights and plan to fix everything, clean up the mess—who knows what they're going to shut down next, the arts links?"

"You're overreacting," Cerise said, and made herself sound certain because she wasn't sure at all that Trouble wasn't right.

"You don't think so."

"No," Cerise admitted, after a moment. "But it's already changed. It changed when the law did, back when you said, when you had the sense to leave. This is just mopping up."

Trouble nodded, slowly, looked down at the components strewn beside her on the couch to hide the old, still-fierce pain. Cerise was right, of course: that had been why she herself had left the nets, left Cerise, because the virtual frontier had closed, its shadows bounded and mapped by the new web of laws that allowed the realworld to exert its authority. Once, there had been a chance that the nets, the virtual world, might expand to contain and control the real, but that had ended. All that was left for them was to try to preserve the good things of the nets within the confines of the realworld. "So what do we do now?" she asked, meaning afterwards, and Cerise smiled, deliberately misunderstanding.

"What about a last walk on the wild side?" she asked, and Trouble smiled back, grateful to have her question deflected. "Care for a trip to Seahaven?"

# SHOWDOWN

# · 12 ·

*T*HEY WALK THE nets like the echoes of a dream, icons oddly twinned, disparate but somehow matched. The roads of light glow before them, around them, the datastreams coursing across the black and midnight sweep that is the net itself. The patterns are somewhat different this night, as every night, different in the details, the intersections and nodes where the information is traded, created, recreated, but the greater shape remains much the same. The high-speed lines swirl past, rigid geometry walled in strands of IC(E); corporate preserves loom out of nothing, their public spaces open, deliberately inviting, while discreet IC(E) walls them round, keeping secrets in. It's a strange feeling, to be together again with no job in hand, just the desire to be out on the nets, and Trouble lets Cerise take the lead for now, walking them down the fields of light. They pass familiar walls, junction nodes they know, that every netwalker knows, from the shadows or the light, and Trouble half turns, expecting them to head down a primary lead, down toward the BBS and the doors that lead to Seahaven.

Instead, Cerise turns a different way, toward a node shrouded in IC(E), and Trouble has to scramble to keep up with her. Cerise pauses, waits, and passes them both through together. There is something familiar about the IC(E), Trouble thinks, but Cerise is already flickering ahead of her, and she has to hurry again to catch up. Cerise's hand? she wonders. Cerise's work? But Cerise is in no mood to talk, not now, and Trouble follows, close behind. The IC(E) is tight here, sharp geometry edged with sparks of light, clear and dangerous, and it's only Cerise's company that takes them through unscathed. Not that I couldn't break it, Trouble thinks, even so deep in it, I could break free—but it wouldn't be easy, and it wouldn't be elegant. And, most of all, it would be more than obvious.

They are inside a preliminary wall, she realizes, at the edge of a major system. This is the space that you could reach most easily from the outside world, where the daily exchange of business takes place; no one cares much about that, and she catches herself looking ahead, toward the central core, a tall cylinder walled in with IC(E) so tight it looks like seamless glass. Light refracts from it, the core of the codewall invisible within the dazzle, only a thin line of purple, close to the base, to indicate that there is access at all. It is even more familiar, there is something about it, about the look of it, the taste of steel in the wind, even the brightness that flares back from it, that catches in her memory. It feels a bit like Cerise's work, she thinks, but then there's something more.

*This is Multiplane,* she says aloud, and sees icon-Cerise nod its cartoon head.

*I need to pick up something,* she says, and turns away. Trouble feels her invoke a mail routine, sees the packet flash from her hand and vanish against the cylinder, absorbed through its gleaming skin. She feels the IC(E) respond, too, and this time she knows what it is. It's been remade, more than once, but this is the wall, the design that first caught Cerise's eye. She hadn't bothered to find out, then, whose IC(E) it was that Cerise wanted to crack; it hadn't mattered, not after Evans-Tindale passed. But this was it, or its grand-daughter program: Multiplane's IC(E), Multiplane's security, and that explained, more clearly than any words, how Cerise had come to work for Multiplane, and why.

She opens her mouth to say something, anything, she's not sure what, just something to say, I know, I'm sorry—to say once again, I let you down. I screwed it up—but the IC(E) flickers again, and there is something in icon-Cerise's hand, briefly visible before she stows it again in her toolkit. And the time for words is past, at least for now. Trouble sighs, and follows Cerise, close enough that their icons make a single shadow, back out of the IC(E) to the main roads of the net.

Outside Multiplane's enclave—dim to the eye, here on the out-side, unexpectedly discreet, now that she knows what, who, lies within—Cerise hesitates for the first time, turns to face her, the car-toon-woman shading to pink against the neon-streaked sky.

*Where away?*

Trouble shrugs, sees and feels the mock-uncertainty appear on the net, carried by the brainworm. *The BBS? Or shall we try Sea-haven?*

*The cartoon-woman grins, pale shadow of Cerise's smile. \*Sea-haven sounds like fun,\* she says, and her voice is sharp and feral.*

*She has always liked a challenge, Trouble thinks, maybe even more than me. But the Mayor's mine. She doesn't say it—doesn't need to say it, she thinks, but knows it's more that she doesn't dare, for fear Cerise will claim him too. She swings away without speaking, finds a line of light and lets herself fall into the datastream, carried away in its embrace. Cerise moves with her, less than a heartbeat behind, and they are carried together down toward the BBS.*

*As the streams slow, joining together, the competing flow and press of data filling every available channel, Trouble lets herself slide free, dropping down into the main plane of the Bazaar. She feels the virtual floor beneath her feet, and in the same instant the filters cut in and she is standing among the icon-shops, a swirl of adverteasing winding around her body. Cerise is there in the same moment, batting idly at a too-importunate image. It bursts in a shower of chaff, black and white confetti-shapes spelling out a man-ufacturer's name, and Cerise brushes them away as well.*

*\*Where was it last?\* Trouble asks, delighting in the old ease, that she doesn't have to be specific, and Cerise slants a smile to her, the icon-face sweeter than the tone of her voice.*

*\*I went through Maggie-May's. But I doubt he'll let us in.\**

*\*We could be subtle,\* Trouble says, and lets her tone carry her preference. \*Try to fake him out. Or we could force it.\**

*\*Subtlety's wasted on the Mayor,\* Cerise answers. \*Besides, you've never been subtle in your life.\**

*\*So let's go and see if he'll let us in,\* Trouble says.*

*They move along the corridors of the Bazaar, past glowing tents and boards where messages, images and text and sound, each over-laid with an icon or a name-sign, bloom like flowers against light-less walls. Trouble feels her muscles tense, relaxes with an effort, working her shoulders against the constraints of a chair she cannot truly feel. She sees Cerise's image flicker, and guesses she is doing the same. The Mayor's IC(E) is always good, some of the best; as she told Mabry, there are places where the interface alone, the structure of his dictated reality, is enough protection. To think of cracking it is maybe crazy, but it's every cracker's dream.*

*And then again, she thinks, it may not be necessary. The Mayor
may still let them in, at least to the main volume; the point, she
supposes, is to prove that she, that they, she and Cerise together, are
still the best, are back better than before.* They reach Maggie-May's
together, to find the space dark and empty, a hole in the illusion
where the shop icon had been. There is no notice, just the haze of
black-and-silver static, but Cerise turns, circling, calls to an icon
Trouble doesn't recognize. She directs her message, shutting out
other ears, and Trouble bridles, but then the stranger answers, uneasy, flicks away as soon as icon-Cerise nods.

*She had some trouble with Treasury,* Cerise says, and Trouble
imagines the twist of her smile.

*So any word on a doorway?*

*The usual suspects,* Cerise begins, and then the air opens in
front of them, through the hole where Maggie-May's had been.
Through the oval, bright as a window, they can see the streets of
Seahaven—a dry place today, bathed in a hot, hard light.

*A dare?* Cerise murmurs, and the icon cannot match the hunting note in her voice.

*Certainly that,* Trouble says, and steps through before she can
change her mind.

The hole seals itself instantly behind her, a soundless thump and
concussion of hot air that emphasizes the finality of the closing.
Trouble wastes a single second on a curse, anger at her own stupidity, the sheer arrogance that tempted her to take this chance, then
swings in a quick circle, surveying this Seahaven. It is remade
today in stark simplicity, dirt road and sunlight and flat-fronted
wooden buildings, a double line of them along the single road, the
only road today, that leads straight to the Mayor's Aztec temple. If
there are other netwalkers, she doesn't see them, though she thinks
she feels a passive presence, watchers lurking beneath the shell of
the images. But if they are that far buried, they can neither hurt nor
hinder; she dismisses them from conscious thought, lifts her head to
survey the temple. The Mayor will be waiting there—And then she
has the image, belatedly, the grade-B western's final scene, and she
grins in spite of herself, wishing her icon remade as she could re-
make it, given time, and starts walking, slow and easy, hands at her
side, up the dusty road toward the Mayor's citadel.

* * *

Cerise swears as the door slams shut against her, reaches out to catch the codewall, and swears again as IC(E) sparks against her fingers, driving into the receptive nerves. She pulls back instantly, stands for a moment with numbed hands, wincing at the sensation of blood rushing back into damaged tissue. And there may be real damage this time, not just the illusion of it, detached pain flowing along the wires from the brainworm: it was serious IC(E), the kind she knows enough to fear. She works her fingers cautiously, feeling pain beneath the tingling, then reaches for a program. Her hand fumbles for an instant with the toolkit, briefly clumsy, and then the brainworm's override cuts in and she feels clear sensation return. She chooses an icepick, and then a couple of lesser routines, frowns and peels the illusion away so that she is looking at the code symbols that make up the wall of IC(E) itself. It is complex, definitely the Mayor's work, his best work, maybe, and despair touches her, cold beneath the adrenaline high. But she's good herself, and knows it, has become something of an expert on IC(E) in the years with Multiplane, and she knows where to begin unraveling. She touches probe to code, and watches the patterns dance, marshaling forces to repel her pretend-invasion. She touches it again, differently, and sees a different pattern respond, a new defense writhing across the symbols. She touches it a third time, betting with herself that she knows what will happen, and the IC(E) answers as she predicted, a flash of light that would have shocked an unwary netwalker off the nets, overloading the cutout circuits. She knows the system now, knows its important parameters, and that means she can break it. All she needs, she thinks, and it becomes a kind of mantra, all she needs is time. There may not be time, Trouble may not have the time to spare, but she puts the fear aside, concentrating entirely on the codes in front of her. All she needs is time.

Trouble walks, and readies her programs, her best defense and the needle-sharp icepick that doubles as a disrupter, her best tool to unravel other people's work. She calls them to hand, but leaves them uninvoked. She can feel the tingle of IC(E) to either side, hidden behind the false-front buildings, smells the cold, damp-metal tang of it, incongruous beneath the dry heat that bathes her. She ignores it, however—disdains it, really, wouldn't deign to escape, to walk away from this challenge—and keeps going, and at last the Mayor comes out to meet her, a thin black-clad shape of a man, a shadow against the bright stone of his stair-stepped temple. He stands on the first platform like a priest, high enough to dominate, not so high that he cannot reach her, and Trouble curls her lip at him, lets the worm carry her contempt, strong enough that even he must feel it.

She sees she's struck home as the worm carries his response, a deepening heat, and then the flattening of the light, as though he's exerting himself to keep control.

*Hello, Trouble,* he says, and despite the apparent distance his voice is close and conversational.

*Hello, Mayor,* she answers, and keeps her voice equally calm. She stops where she is, perhaps forty virtual meters from the base of the pyramid. The first platform, where he stands, is four meters above her head, and if she goes much closer, she will have to crane her neck to see him properly. *Quite a greeting.*

*You've earned it,* the Mayor says grimly, and Trouble manages a grin she doesn't feel.

*Nobody messes with me,* she says, and, remembering the lurkers, *not even you—Sasquatch.*

It is a shot at random, following Arabesque's word, and she is remotely pleased when the Mayor waves his working hand, waving away the charge without denying it.

*You've done quite enough, Trouble,* he says. *This has to stop. This time I'm giving you fair warning, and if you don't listen, I will bring you down.*

*That's been tried,* Trouble said, the anger swelling in her. *You tried to shop me, and you blew it. And the worst of it is, I'm the one who's been wronged here. It was my name your little friend stole, my programs he tried to use, me he tried to blame. The only thing I've done is to defend myself.* She shook her head. *I didn't start this, Mayor, and you know it. But I will finish it.*

She hears her own absolute certainty reflected across the net, feels the distant stirring, like indrawn breath, as that same certainty reaches the lurkers. The Mayor's icon cannot frown, but she senses the change of expression in the air around her.

*I'm making this my business,* he says at last. *NewTrouble is *my business, and I will deal with it. But in my own way, not yours. Leave it to me.*

Trouble shakes her head, too angry to think of conciliation. *No. You had your chance, Mayor, you don't get another one.*

*And who do you think you are?* the Mayor demands, stung at last into real response. *You're nobody, just another half-competent bitch queer who thinks she's good because she has a brainworm. You haven't earned what you have, you haven't worked for it the way the rest of us have, the real crackers, you just had it handed to you direct-to-brain. You don't have any right to dictate to me.*

*Fuck you,* Trouble says, and then regrets it, the easy, unthinking answer, shoves the mistake away as unimportant and irretrievable. She takes a breath, mastering her own anger, looking for the words that will reach beyond him, that will touch the lurkers. *You know damn well that's not how the wire works, and if you weren't afraid of it, you'd have one yourself. It's just the same as the implants, just like the dollie-slots, but it gives me an edge, yeah, because I'm not afraid of it, of what I can do with it. Or of you.* She stops then, breathing hard, pins him with her best glare because she's told a lie. She is afraid—she'd be a fool not to be, he's maintained Seahaven in the face of the law and the bright lights for ten years, and she's never been entirely a fool. *NewTrouble's a menace,* she says again, one last attempt at rational argument even though she knows it's useless, at least if Mabry's right. If newTrouble is this boy the Mayor's been keeping—and he must be, there's no other reason for him to behave this way, no matter how much he hates, fears, the wire—then he'll do whatever he can to protect him, no matter what. *The Eurocops know who he is, you know, they'll have him—*

*You sold him,* the Mayor says.

*You sold me.* Trouble blinks up at him, staring into false sunlight burning down out of a dust-white sky. The Mayor's icon loses all resolution against that sky and the white stone of the pyramid; even the lions and eagles that crown the corners of each step have lost their distinct outlines. She risks a backward glance, sees the storefronts fading, faintly translucent, a hint of the white light shining through. She hesitates, weighing her words, and strikes. *If you can't hack the rules . . .*

There is no warning, not even a drawn breath, and the Mayor strikes. She is half expecting it, had known it would be now if ever, but even so the blow—icepick? clawhammer?—hits hard, sending electric shivers through her defenses. She winces, feels the effect like pins-and-needles all along her limbs, dispatches her own icepick more or less at random, buying time. It slides harmlessly off the Mayor's IC(E), kicking back painfully into her palm. She feels the jolt of it to her elbow, but readies it, and another, a different program, heart jolting against her ribs. She can taste adrenaline, and fear, knows and doesn't care that the lurkers will feel it, too. There's no time to worry about it: the Mayor's clawhammer probes again, and she calls a secondary codewall into existence, reinforcing her defense. It takes excruciating time, like a gunfight in slow motion, too much time, either to attack or defend. The trick, she knows, is to stay with her decision, never succumb to the temptation to second-guess, choose another program—that and knowing when to cut and run.

Cerise worries at the Mayor's IC(E), working alternately with her best icepick—a custom job, her own creation—and the lighter probes, assessing her progress. She's getting there, the watchdogs muzzled or damped off, the alarms garotted, the traps spiked or circumvented, but there's still a lot to do—meters of it, in the brainworm's projection, and she hesitates for a moment, tempted to try an all-out assault. But common sense prevails—she's good, but so is the Mayor; in an even match, the one who rushes first will, inevitably, lose—and she reaches for the icepick again, applies it to a stubborn knot of code. It resists, the feedback singing in her sore fingers, but then she's found the inevitable weakness, and pries the program open. Its mechanism is clear, and she applies a routine from her toolkit, freezing it, and the section of the IC(E) that it controls, into immobility. That clears another meter or so of the IC(E), and she takes a cautious step forward, into the hollow she has cleared in the wall of code.

And then, behind her, she hears/feels a shift of air, a change in the net, and swings around faster than thought, sees a familiar shape hovering, on the verge of flight.

*Silk,* she says, and knows in that instant she is wrong, that this

is newTrouble, the boy James Tilsen, as much as it is Silk. He, the
icon, flinches, turns to run, and she reacts without thought, without hesitation, throws her sphere around them both, sealing them
inside. She sees/feels him collide with the IC(E), rebound, his pain
skittering briefly in echo across the net, and he turns to face her,
eyes wide. She tastes his fear, the faint echo of it tainting the net,
and then it's gone, he has himself under control, and there's only
the icon facing her across the silver sphere. It's an ordinary icon,
generic man-shape roughly clad in leather, and there's no reflection
at all of Silk, except perhaps the hint of sensuality, the scent of
burnt-sugar sex bittersweet to the tongue. He waits, braced in case
she lets the sphere drop even for an instant, and she smiles at him,
covering her own anxiety. The icepick is working still, slower because she isn't there to direct it, but it will work on until the wall is
breached. Her concern now must be with him.

*Silk,* she says again, because it frightened him, and sees him
flinch again. *Going to see the Mayor?* She gets no answer—as
indeed she expected none, goes on anyway, needing to force the
issue. *You can take me with you.*

*No way,* the icon answers, sounds almost indignant, and flings
himself sideways, at the same moment loosing a disrupter against
her.

She parries, awkward but effective, and her guardian watchdog
pounces on the stunned fragments, neutralizing them as it begins
to consume the code. Her sphere holds, too, and Silk shakes himself,
turns at bay.

*Well,* Cerise says, and smiles, not nicely. Silk waits, says nothing. *Take me with you.*

There is another pause, and then Silk looks away, voice gone sul-
len. *All right. Loose the sphere.*

*Not yet,* Cerise says, grim, and pulls a long-unused tool from
her kit. She flicks it into existence, tunes it to Silk's icon, and feels
the leash slap home. Silk winces, but she ignores it, makes sure the
tie is fast, testing methodically before she releases the sphere. The
sphere vanishes, and she sees the codewall exposed, her icepick still
burrowing slow and stubborn into the knotted code.

*Well,* she says again, and looks at Silk. He looks back at her, the
icon showing the hip-shot stance, the defiant stare that she remem-

bers, and she thinks again of the touch of her—his—hands. He's playing a dangerous game, reminding her of that, and a part of her admires his arrogance before she slaps the thought away. *Open the door.*

There is a last, minuscule pause, and then he steps forward. She calls back the icepick, in the same moment shortening the leash that holds him to her, and sees him reach deep into the violated code. Something sparks, and then the system recognizes him, his icon. The codewall vanishes, all but a few patches, segments of the wall already so eroded by her work that they can no longer respond even to legitimate stimulus. Seahaven opens before them, a dusty street lined with the tall false fronts of the frontier town, and they pass through together into the sudden heat. Silk tugs once at the leash, little more than an experiment, and she controls it instantly.

*Walk,* she says, and they start together up the long street.

The clawhammer slides away with a noise like a needle scoring plastic, and Trouble feels the sickening scrape of it against the code-wall, bringing a skidding pain like the deliberate scratch of a pin. That means the wall is damaged, though only slightly. She feels the self-seal routine kick in, knows already that it won't be finished in time, that she will rely on the inner wall. Her icepick returns to the attack, slower now, probing the convoluted codes. The Mayor brushes at it, but it finds a weak point and fastens on, burrowing, fretting loose the imperfect fragments, digging into the wall. The Mayor dispatches a watchdog—not one of his specials, with all its fancy iconage; this one's a killer, plain sphere covering code that will shred almost any other program. The icepick keeps burrowing, blindly, oblivious to the watchdog chewing at its heels, and for a moment Trouble thinks it might succeed. And then the watchdog reaches vital code: the icepicks slows and fades, dissolves into direction-less fragments.

Trouble swears, and feels a new touch, a cold mouth like a leech's full of glassy teeth, against her skin. She swears again, under her breath, knowing what's happened—she was concentrating on her own attack, forgot to keep an eye out for sleepers, and now she has one on her, already burrowed through the first codewall and onto her main defense. She stays calm with an effort, hating the touch of it, cold with the pain of a dozen razors' cuts, calls the watchdog she bought from Jesse. For a long moment she waits, the cold pain gnawing at her, and then the watchdog catches hold, and the sleeper vanishes. The Mayor's watchdog lurches forward, and her own program turns to meet it. She winces, unable to tell which one will win, but makes herself look away, reaches into her toolkit for another attack. This one's a hammer, slow and crude, but she sets it bashing, hoping to distract the Mayor. She parries his icepick, looses a copy of the disrupter on it, and feels a lucky blow: the icepick shatters, scattering fragments. She ducks, but feels a few of them slap against her skin, distinct points of pain like bee stings.

She brushes them away, reaches for another program, triggers its response, another kind of icepick, to join the hammer already at work. The Mayor swats at the hammer, but it's sturdy, resilient, bounces back each time he slaps it away. Trouble allows herself a quick smile, seeing that, looses a second copy of her icepick, hoping to overwhelm his defenses, then turns her attention to her own systems and the icepick worrying at her shields. Her watchdog is still tangled in fight, and she calls another copy, sets it to work.

*Trouble!*

Cerise's voice, she thinks, but does not dare glance back toward it, just in case it's some trick of the Mayor's and then a second voice echoes, a voice she's never heard, clear and young.

*Eytan!*

For an instant she can't think who it means, and then remembers—the Mayor's name is Eytan—but the Mayor's already turning, leaping down like a superhero from the first level of his temple. He carries the cloud of his attackers with him for an instant, but then gestures stiffly, and the space of Seahaven itself twists and swirls around him like a twist of wind, and Trouble's programs are gone. She freezes for half a heartbeat, appalled at the casual power, the sheer scale of the Mayor's creations, and then her mind is working again, and she sees, knows, what he's betrayed. Seahaven is fluid space—that much they'd all always known, that it was entirely the Mayor's whim and so controllable from somewhere, but this, this sweeping destruction, proves that the control points are everywhere, and everywhere potent, potentially universal. And, therefore, potentially accessible to any cracker.

*Jamie—* the Mayor begins, and Cerise's voice rides over his words, sharp as the crack of a whip.

*Be careful, sunshine, I've got a leash on him. Trouble, are you all right?*

*Fine,* Trouble answers, shortly, not surprised even now by the rescue—figuring the odds are still even, with Cerise here, since she's brought newTrouble with her.

The Mayor says again, *Jamie,* and fear and anger both are sharp in his voice, crackle on the net like the scent of lightning.

Silk/newTrouble says, *I'm sorry—* and the Mayor's voice cuts into whatever else he might have said.

*You're wired,* he says, and Trouble risks a look backward, over her shoulder to where Cerise's familiar icon stands beside a generic man-shape rough-clad in black, not quite matching the Mayor's severity.

*You little bastard,* the Mayor says, voice flat again, the anger damped to a hint of sulphur. *When— How—?* And he stops, with what would have been the shake of a head if he'd himself been on the wire.

*I'm sorry,* Silk/newTrouble says again, and sounds terribly young.

*You cunt,* the Mayor says, and the icon's working hand convulses. *Go home.* The fabric of Seahaven warps again, twists and distorts and in an eyeblink wraps itself around Silk/newTrouble's icon. Cerise swears, incoherent, lifts a hand to jerk short the leash, and the program kicks back, broken at the source. The section of image knots tighter, space stretching around it, painful to the eye, and then relaxes, smoothing out to restore the stark frontier town as though it had never changed. Silk/newTrouble is gone.

Cerise curses again, shakes a stinging hand, and Trouble swings back to face the Mayor. The ground roils under her feet, tipping her sideways, the air goes gluey, multileaved and flaking yellow-tinged as isinglass; she struggles for breath and balance, goes to her knees in the dust that rises to engulf her. Cerise calls something, but her voice is muffled, and Trouble closes her mind to it, concentrating on the space that has enfolded her. She closes her eyes as well, cutting off the visuals that threaten to override her system, feels the pressure on her lungs ease because she lacks the visual cue of dust to reinforce thick air. She could hit the panic button, drop off the net completely, she'd be safe then, but that would mean losing, admitting herself beaten. She reaches blindly into the spaces around her, groping spread-fingered for the hot spots, the control points that will allow her to break free of this program. She trips an emergency control, dangerous but necessary, kicks the brainworm to full power, full receptivity, and feels the heat and the thick air clog her lungs, illusion but dangerous, warning her of slower dangers. She ignores that, reaches out again, fingers trailing across illusory lumps and tingling wires, every touch magnified, and finally touches a hot spot, palms its burning circle in her left hand. She finds a second even as she analyzes the first, and cups them both, working through the system. The feeling is familiar beneath the generic heat, a system like systems she has used before. She shifts her left hand slightly, then her right, and feels the system controls wrap themselves around her fingers. She gestures—the old-style code, the old netwalker symbols—and feels some of the pressure ease from around her. She gestures again, with more confidence this time, and the wall of images unravels around her.

Cerise says, *Christ, you gave me a scare.* She lets her hands fall, lets another icepick flick back into obscurity.

Trouble takes a deep breath, ignoring the heat that lingers along with the fear, looks up at the Mayor's palace. It turns a blank face to the rest of Seahaven, the usual windows and doors sealed with stone, even the battling statues vanished from the corners of the platforms. *NewTrouble?* she asks, and Cerise shrugs.

*Bounced him out of Seahaven—right off the nets, I think. Are you all right?*

*Fine,* Trouble says, sourly, not thinking, then looks at Cerise in apology. *I'm all right. But we have to do something about the Mayor.*

*Yeah, but what?* Cerise scowls, scanning the illusory space, empty now except for the icons. They have waited a long time, by the reckoning of the nets; the walls will be sealed tight, all the IC(E) in place and fully armed.

*Go after him,* Trouble says.

Cerise hesitates, her hands still stinging from the first wall of IC(E), knowing it would be smarter to take the draw and run, leave the Mayor to Mabry, to Treasury and the Eurocops. But that's not either of their styles—and there is Silk to think about. He's on the wire, one of them, doubly family, maybe, and she feels responsible. She nods slowly, works her hands again. The fingers that held the leash feel thick and clumsy, and worry stabs through her.

*Are you OK?* Trouble asks, her tone sharpening, and Cerise nods again.

*Caught some IC(E) getting in here,* she says, careful to keep her voice casual. Trouble looks at her, uncertain, searching, and she forces a smile. *Stung my fingers a little, nothing more.*

*All right,* Trouble says, and her tone is doubtful, but she starts toward the temple.

*Wait,* Cerise says, and reaches into her toolkit, triggers the iconage editor she had carried since she first went into the business. Trouble cocks her head to one side, but asks no questions; Cerise grins, and triggers a sequence, spinning an image into the air around them. Her touch is clumsy, but the shape that forms is recognizable enough: a gunfighter's silhouette, battered ten-gallon hat and loose cap-shouldered duster, dark against the Mayor's walls.

Trouble laughs softly. *Shouldn't the hat be white?* she says, and makes the change. *What brought this on?*

*Blame the Mayor,* Cerise says, and gestures at the fading frontier town around him. *I thought I'd beat him at his own game.*

After a moment Trouble nods, and reaches for the icon, drawing it over herself like a suit of clothes. Cerise spins a second copy for herself—she keeps the black hat, but her kerchief is her own hot fuchsia, a single point of vivid contrast—and dons it, too.

*He picked the game,* Cerise says, and looks at Trouble remade, at an icon that seems suddenly more herself than the dancing harlequin had ever been. Trouble looks back at her as though she'd read the thought, and the icon's wry mouth twists into a sudden smile.

*When were we ever the good guys?* she asks, and reaches for her toolkit.

Cerise doesn't answer, moves to join her, to examine the featureless surface. Weren't we always? she thinks, and runs one hand across the temple face, feeling sun-warmed stone beneath her palm. She finds a protruding bit of code, a defect, where the image has been corrupted—perhaps by collateral damage from the fight, per-

*haps just by wear and tear, by constant usage; whatever the cause, she catches hold of it, levers away the skin of the image. It comes away with a ripping sound, just a small patch of the illusion, perhaps as big as a man's outspread hand. In that one spot, the code-wall lies exposed, and she frowns, studying its pattern. Trouble moves up beside her, but she's barely aware of the other's presence, concentrating on the codes. It was made by the same hand that made the outer wall; there are similarities of style and shape, but otherwise it's not much like that first barrier, a tighter, leaner code concealing a colder IC(E). She hesitates for an instant, thinking of the first wall, of her sore hands, then shakes herself, makes herself contemplate the exposed patterns.*

Trouble reaches past the other icon's shoulder, carrying the icon of a sleeper. She releases it beside the open patch of code, bends close to watch it apply itself to the codewall. For a moment it seems to make headway, and then the IC(E) reasserts itself. The sleeper slows, frozen, drops away to shatter against the illusory dirt.

*It shouldn't've done that,* Trouble says, irrelevantly—she hates illusions that don't quite work—and Cerise leans closer to the opening.

*Try this,* she says, and touches a probe to a single strand of code. She is still clumsy, a little less accurate than she needs to be, but the codewall sings under her touch, a deep bass note that reverberates through their bones. She's found a hot spot within the wall of IC(E), a space that give access to a deeper layer of control, a structure more fundamental than the IC(E).

*Careless,* Trouble says, meaning the Mayor, and reaches for the same point, delicately brushes the same bit of code. The music answers again, true and deep as some great bell. She takes a breath, bracing herself for the necessary attack, the necessary risk, and Cerise touches her arm.

*Let me,* Cerise says.

Trouble hesitates, recognizing the logic—Cerise's hands are already burned; she herself is unhurt, and should remain so, to deal with the Mayor—and in that instant Cerise reaches past her, deep into the maze of coded IC(E). Light flares, momentarily blinding, and Cerise winces at the numbing chill that wraps around her. The cold dims her tactile sense, masking those receptors, but she gropes *anyway* toward the faint heat of the control points. And then she has it, and the light fades, dims, and then vanishes completely, revealing a new world within the temple walls.

\*Nice,\* Trouble says, and Cerise smiles, rubbing her hands to warm them. For a moment she thinks it's nothing more than cold, nothing more than an illusion of the brainworm, but then she feels something beneath the cool, a faint, distant ache, all the more worrisome because she's sure it's real.

\*Let's get on with it,\* she says, and Trouble looks more closely at her.

\*You all right?\*

\*Yeah,\* Cerise answers, and, when Trouble says nothing, just keeps looking. \*I'm OK. Let's go.\*

\*OK,\* Trouble agrees, not entirely certain, but closes off her concern, and steps through the opening.

She catches her breath as the new illusion takes hold of her, spins her perspective, and then she has compensated, steadies herself against the brainworm's insistence that she is upside down and sideways. She closes her eyes, lets herself go limp, and the brainworm and the temple-space together turn her right, so that when she opens her eyes she is standing perpendicular to the opening Cerise made, looking out at a world that hangs at a bizarre angle. Cerise's icon performs the same maneuver, spinning against the bright opening until it's oriented with the strict and sober geometry, drab black and a grey that isn't even close to silver, that makes up the Mayor's private space. Satisfied that Cerise is with her, Trouble turns, scanning the net around her for traps and watchdogs. She sees nothing, the brainworm finds nothing it can translate to sound or smell or taste, not even the wet-steel tang of IC(E).

\*Weird,\* Cerise says, and Trouble nods, knowing exactly what is meant.

A pattern, a line like a road, brighter grey than the planes that wall in this entrance space, stretches away from them, edged with thinner lines of black. It zigzags through the irregular slabs that rise like trees, like the stones of Stonehenge, disappears into an illusory far distance: the temple, like most virtual spaces, is bigger on the inside than the outside, and even with the brainworm's assistance, sight fails before the road ends. A shiver of light, like a dusting of stars, runs beneath the bright surface, shooting away into the interior, flickering in and out of sight between the irregularly spaced planes. Trouble catches her breath, looking instantly for watchdogs, for attacking programs, but there's still nothing, just the pure still sense of the code itself in the air around her.

*I suppose that's an invitation,* Cerise says.

Trouble nods again, still searching for IC(E), grateful that her brainworm is still tuned high. *I feel like Dorothy,* she says, and steps out onto the path. Another flicker of light runs away beneath her feet, like ripples on the surface of a pool; to either side of the grey band, the illusory floor drops away—not a surprise, but she walks carefully nonetheless.

*That wasn't Kansas back there,* Cerise mutters, and follows. The same scattering of light ripples away from her, and Trouble feels the faint warmth of it rush fugitive under her own feet.

*Might've been,* Trouble says, as much to chase away her fears as because she thinks so, and takes another few cautious steps. *Old Kansas, in the old days. Where the hell is the IC(E)?*

Cerise shakes her head, the brainworm carrying the gesture like a scent of oil, a taste of peppermint. *Worry about that when we find it—or when it finds us.*

Her voice is grimmer than her words, but Trouble laughs anyway, and keeps walking, lines of silver rippling away from her along the grey slab that is the path. There's still no sign of IC(E), though the plane that was the floor drops further away below them until it vanishes in a haze like black fog—she would say that the path is rising, but the brainworm denies that, tells her she is walking straight and level. Slabs of featureless grey, some narrow as sheets of steel, others thick as stone, rise on either side, set at angles to the walkway; ahead, the path jogs sharply left, around a stone pillar that looks almost blue, the blue of a shadow, among the shaded greys. And still there's nothing else, no watchdogs—she glances back in spite of herself, the fuchsia spark of Cerise's neckerchief the only color in the bleak grey-and-black, almost painful to the eye, sees only Cerise, the icon's face set in a faint, unhappy frown. And no IC(E) either, not even the hint of it drifting up from the black fog virtual meters below the walkway. The lights beneath her feet, the silver ripples like moonlight on water, aren't IC(E) either, aren't anything that she recognizes; she is getting used to them, though, and has to make an effort now to feel their fugitive warmth as they flicker away from her along the narrow path.

The blue-grey monolith looms ahead, its edges smoothed, rounded not by weather, nature, but as though ground by some massive machine. Trouble eyes it warily, suspecting a trap, dispatches a copy of a watchdog toward it. The program—stripped down to carry more features, its icon little more than a red disk—floats cautiously toward it, circles it, and returns again.

*Passive system?* Cerise says from behind her, and Trouble shrugs.

*This program's supposed to catch those as well,* she answers, but they both know that it's hard to simulate the output of a brainworm, the usual trigger for passive IC(E). A watchdog, even a complex one, is still only a limited program, and therefore, inevitably, imperfect.

Cerise makes a noise that is almost a laugh, short and angry, but says nothing. Trouble starts walking again, her best defensive routines invoked ready, trembling in her hands. She feels a tremor beneath her feet, a shudder different from the passage of the wavelets of light, and fixes her eyes on the hulking stone. It stays precisely as it is, releases nothing, no program or IC(E), just the blue-grey bulk of it beside the brighter grey of the path. Trouble hesitates, still watching, then starts to step past it, along the path that turns sharply left around it.

Her foot reaches out, but in the wrong direction, sliding somehow off the edge of the path. She staggers, trying to correct, but, though she can see the path plainly, can feel it still solid under one foot, she still reaches in the wrong direction, throwing herself even more off-balance. She can feel herself falling, flails backward, back toward the security of the walkway, and then she feels Cerise's hands tight on her shoulders, dragging her back and down, so that they both stumble heavily, Cerise collapsing backward into a sitting position, Trouble in her lap. Cerise grabs for the edge of the path—it's wide here, but nothing's wide enough, not at that moment—and swears again as she cuts her fingers, grabbing a raw program edge.

*Jesus Christ,* Trouble says, splays her own hands firmly on the path, grateful for the solidity beneath her touch. *What the hell was that?* So this is what the other crackers had tried to describe, the ones who'd tried to crack Seahaven, what they meant when they said the architecture of the Mayor's space defended itself, without IC(E)—without anything except a cracker's overconfidence and fear to help it along.

Cerise untangles herself from the other woman's icon, shaking her right hand—it feels bruised only, this time, but the accumulated aches are beginning to amount to a constant pain, warning her to be more careful. *What happened?*

*I—don't know,* Trouble answers, and sounds almost surprised. She studies the path, still turning sharply to the left, and levers herself up onto hands and knees. For a moment she feels distinctly silly—crackers, real crackers, do not crawl through the architecture they are exploring—but dismisses the thought, focusing on the walkway in front of her. She reaches out again, feels Cerise's hands close with reassuring strength on her ankles, and reaches again to the left. Her hand goes right, against her will, against all common sense; she frowns, concentrating, tries to bring her hand to the walk, and finds her hand jigging back and forth, unable to obey.

*IC(E)?* Cerise asks, but her tone says she already knows it isn't.

Trouble answers anyway, *Not like any I've ever seen.* She reaches out again, and again she misses, but this time she's closer. She grits her teeth, lays her hand flat against the surface of the walk, and slides it forward, following the path. Silver ripples fan out ahead of her, teasing, showing her the way she should go, but her hand obstinately refuses to obey, slips from side to side, advancing in fits and starts that bring her closer and closer to the right-hand edge of the walk. She is almost at the end of her reach, braces herself on that hand and shuffles forward, Cerise still clinging to her ankles, then reaches out again. There is something familiar about this, the halting progress, the way her eyes and her senses do not match—

*It's a mirror,* Cerise says. *God damn.*

*That's it,* Trouble says, and the illusive memory appears: a child's toy, a puzzle, a box with a hidden mirror and a series of figures to trace. You reached in from the side, and looked through *the plate in the top, not realizing that you were looking not at your hand but at its mirror image. She had fought with the thing for hours, her finger jittering from side to side as she tried to figure out how to do what she could so plainly see, her shoulders tightening with sheer frustration, until at last she'd mastered it. The problem was, she couldn't quite remember how she'd done it. She inches forward another few dozen centimeters, her hand still flat on the walkway's surface, reaches out again and slides suddenly off the edge of the plane. She falls forward, catches herself clumsily, and hears Cerise swearing again behind her.*

\*I'm OK,\* she says, and tries to pull her hand back. For a moment she can't do it; the movement that should work just leaves her flailing in nothingness, and then, quite suddenly, she has it, and slides forward another meter, two meters, crawling, scrambling on hands and knees to get as far as she can before she loses the knack of it. Cerise follows, clumsily, a reassuring weight on her legs and ankles. Then at last they've turned the corner and the intangible pressure vanishes, as though the mirror is behind them and they are once again looking at the walkway itself.

\*Through the looking glass,\* Cerise says, and releases her hold on Trouble's ankles.

\*Yeah,\* Trouble says, and pushes herself cautiously to her feet. \*But what happens when we hit IC(E)?\*

Cerise looks at her and doesn't answer, stands up more slowly, scanning the volume around them. There is still no hint of IC(E), none of the metallic taste to the wind. \*You don't suppose there isn't any.\*

\*No,\* Trouble says, and Cerise smiles.

\*Neither do I. But we'll have to deal with it when we find it, won't we?\*

Trouble grins back, acknowledging the too-obvious logic of the other's answer. It hides real concern, and real danger, and they both know it—but, as Cerise said, there's no point in trying to anticipate it. Ahead, the walkway stretches empty, the silver ripples running ahead of their footsteps, travels perhaps fifteen, twenty virtual meters before it zigs again to skirt an encroaching plane. Trouble eyes that distant monolith warily, but starts walking toward it, feeling the walkway steady again underfoot.

*She slows as she comes up on the turn, takes the time to check for IC(E)—there's no sense in taking any risks, not here, not now—and, as she'd expected, finds nothing. She slides a foot forward, testing the path, takes five cautious, shuffling steps before she finds the point where the image reverses. She makes a sound, a sharp intake of breath, and Cerise's hands close reassuringly tight around her waist.*

*How do you want to work it?* Cerise asks.

*Trouble doesn't answer, but eases her foot forward, manages to take a step without going too far wrong, drifting too far to the left and the path's edge. She takes a second step, Cerise braced behind her, ready to save them both, and then a third, and a fourth. It's easier this time, something about the reflection is simpler, so that she passes through the backward space still standing, and draws Cerise after her onto the new straightaway.*

*Nice,* Cerise says. *She works her shoulders, loosening tight muscles, looks ahead toward the next pillar, and the monolith beyond that, where the path begins to zig back and forth at irregular and ever-decreasing intervals.* *That, however—*

*Yeah,* Trouble answers. *I see it.* *And she can smell something, too, they both can, the first faint whiff of IC(E) in the wind. For an instant she wonders if it's worth it, if there's anything real to be gained in this pursuit—after all, even if she, they, win, defeat the Mayor, the nets will turn a blind eye, say it's because she was on the wire, or because there were two of them, anything to pretend it wasn't a defeat, not of their hero—but she's come too far to turn back now. She wants to win, to prove to herself if to no one else that she is better than the Mayor, and there's newTrouble to consider as well. He is on the wire, family in that sense if not the other, and she owes him, as she would owe van Liesvelt or Arabesque, or, better example, Fate. For me, then, she thinks, and maybe for the kid, too.*

*It's still a long way off,* Cerise says. *She stands in the center of the walkway, eyes fixed on the middle distance, on nothing in particular, tasting the wind. This is something she's good at, better than Trouble, better than anyone they know, and she takes her time, teasing all the information she can out of the hint of a flavor.* *Stationary, too, but powerful. I don't recognize the style from here, but that may change as we get closer.*

*Trouble nods, grateful for the insight—she can taste only the presence of the distant IC(E), not the subtle shifts and delicate differences—makes herself say, \*You don't have to come.\**

*Cerise looks at her blankly for an instant. \*Don't be stupid.\**

*Trouble hasn't expected any other answer, but she's momentarily startled by the intensity of her relief, grins because she can't find the words. Cerise smiles back, touches her shoulder once, gently, the gesture carried through the brainworm, then looks ahead.*

*\*Let's go.\**

*They make their way along the elevated pathway, slowing each time they come to a mirror reflection of a turn. Trouble is getting the knack of them now, as she learned to read the distorted reflection in the childhood toy, and she moves with more confidence, making her way around the corners now with only the occasional misstep. To either side, the black fog rises higher, though it's impossible to tell if that's because the floor, whatever, wherever, that may be, is rising too. It isn't IC(E), however, and Trouble ignores it, concentrating on the maze ahead of them as the turns come closer together, offering less and less chance to recover from the effort of the previous corner. At least once, she thinks, they must have crossed their own path, but the mirror-display, the mirrored perception, makes it impossible for her to be certain. Cerise follows grimly, holding tight to Trouble's icon, fighting an unexpected nausea. The abrupt shifts in perception, the effort of changing her point of view almost as soon as she's settled on one, is overloading her system; her inner ear can't quite keep up with the brainworm's transmissions, and the pain in her hands is a nagging distraction.*

*\*Hang on,\* she says at last, and Trouble stops, looking back over her shoulder, eyebrows rising in question. Cerise ignores it, concentrates on her own system, and resets the brainworm, lowering the intensity of its display.*

*\*You all right?\* Trouble asks, and Cerise nods, impatient with herself.*

*\*I needed to reset,\* she says. \*I'm OK now.\**

*Trouble hesitates, remembering—almost too late, she thinks—that Cerise has had troubles before with rapidly shifting perceptual fields, something like vertigo when her brainworm is set at its higher levels, but knows, too, that she has to trust Cerise. She nods*

*back, starts again toward the next obstacle, three turns in quick
succession that seem almost to loop the path back on itself, and feels
the touch of a vagrant breeze on her face, cool against her skin. With
that warning breeze, like the first soft breeze that comes before a
storm, comes the smell of IC(E), damp metal, the tang of copper like
the taste of fear.*

*Shit,* she says, half to herself.

Cerise says, *The center, there, at that loop.* She sounds a little
better, freed from the full intensity of the brainworm's input; her
tone is detached, analytical, too calm to be afraid.

Trouble considers the apparently empty space, the source of the
vagrant wind, of the scent of IC(E), and the loop of walkway that
seems to circle around it. She can only see so far, trace a portion of
the line, before she loses her place, as though it is some kind of
Möbius strip, or, worse yet, derived from one of the etchings be-
loved of crackers, where perspective twists and impossibly separate
things are in fact intimately connected—where the waterfall is its
own source and figures climb both sides of a stairway. It's no wonder no one's ever beaten the Mayor, she thinks, on the wire or not,
then puts the fear aside. This has to be the Mayor's inner sanctum,
and she refuses to allow that it might not be—even the Mayor has
technical limits, storage limits, she thinks, no matter how much
time and space he's liberated from other sources, and this has to be
it. And if it isn't, she thinks, well, I'll keep going.

*Any sense of what it is?* To her, the IC(E) is just inchoate
IC(E), the indistinguishable unspecific taste that means poison,
danger.

Cerise tilts her head to one side, considers. *The Mayor's work,*
she says, and Trouble snorts.

*Tell me something I don't know.*

*The Mayor's work,* Cerise goes on, placidly, as though the
other hasn't spoken, *very like the outer walls, only woven
tighter—reminds me a bit of my own work at Multiplane, too, but I
can't quite tell you how.*

*You should be flattered,* Trouble says.

*If it's mine,* Cerise answers. *It could be an illusion, trying to
sucker us in.*

*That's a nasty thought,* Trouble says, and Cerise shrugs.

\*I've some mirrors of my own—to make you think my IC(E) is set like yours, not the kind we've been playing with—in our inner walls. It tends to confuse people.\*

That would be an understatement, Trouble thinks, trying to imagine reaching for what should be a familiar program and feeling the jolt of hard IC(E). She says, \*I'll watch it, then,\* and she keeps walking, on toward the place where the fabric of the Mayor's world shimmers and turns back on itself. Underfoot, the silver ripples are brighter, and she catches an occasional glimpse of their light toward the end of the walkway, as though all the wavelets that they have set dancing have collected there beneath the surface of the walk.

As she slides a cautious foot into the first turn, she finds herself reaching once again in the wrong direction, tries to pull back as she has done before, and finds herself suddenly trapped, her out-stretched leg jogging back and forth without making any progress. Cerise reaches to steady her, a comfortable weight, hands rock solid on her shoulder and waist, and Trouble struggles to bring herself into alignment with the walkway. Her foot obstinately refuses to move the way she wants it; instead, she slides closer in spite of herself to the edge of the walk.

\*Easy,\* Cerise says, her own voice strained, and Trouble feels the hand on her shoulder move to her waist, Cerise's weight thrown backward to anchor them both.

Trouble doesn't answer, tries again, and again stands frustrated, muscles knotting as she tries to bring her foot back to the left. It's worse than any force field, because she knows there's nothing there, nothing really blocking her way—but then, none of it's real. She takes a deep breath, closes her eyes, and edges her foot forward a dozen centimeters, opens her eyes again to see that she has gone in the right direction, has actually taken a step the way she wants to go. And that gives her the answer.

\*We'll have to crawl,\* she says, and Cerise releases her.

\*You're going to have to guide me,\* she says, and Trouble nods.

\*I can do it.\* She drops to her knees without waiting for an an-swer, and Cerise copies her, wraps a hand tightly in the skirt of the icon's long coat. Trouble nods, grateful for the protection—one good thing about iconage, you don't have to worry about your clothes being ripped away when they should protect you; they're an *integral part of any image—then reaches forward, eyes open, and sees her hand stray to the edge of the walk. She flattens her hand against it, careful not to put her weight on it, to avoid the jagged edge of the unfinished program, then closes her eyes and runs her hand forward, keeping the edge centered in her palm. She brings her hand in again, until she can just feel the edge of the walk against the edge of her hand, and draws her body up to meet it, Cerise's weight heavy on her legs and hips. She opens her eyes again, half afraid to look, half afraid that in spite of the evidence of her senses she will be off the path and falling, careening down into the black fog, and finds herself perhaps half a meter further along the walk, not quite past the turn. She closes her eyes again, reaches out, the program edge scratching along her palm, draws her body after, and checks her position. Still safe, still making progress, though without dignity or grace, and she manages a breathless laugh before she starts again. She reaches out again, repeats the process, and this time she's through the perceptual mirror, Cerise still clinging to her coat. Trouble turns back, grabs the hand that is clinging to the icon-coat, and pulls her through. Cerise, eyes closed tight, accepts the help, comes scrambling through, silver light radiating from her.*

*What the hell were you laughing about?* she demands, scowling, pushes herself up onto one knee.

*Us,* Trouble says, *how we must look.*

Cerise gives her a sour look. *Yeah, I bet the Mayor thinks it's funny, too.*

That stings, and Trouble has a sudden vision of how they must look from outside, two cowboy-hatted icons crawling, more clumsy than children, on a grey-and-silver bridge through a black-and-grey geometric universe. It is silly, and she hates looking foolish—and then she laughs again, acknowledging the absurdity. It may look stupid, they may look like clowns, unskilled mimes trying to act out some strange disaster, but they've come further into the Mayor's world than anyone else has, than anyone she's ever known or heard about in all the years she's been on the net. *I don't think he's laughing,* she says, and knows absolutely that it's true.

Cerise looks sour for a heartbeat longer, then, slowly, returns the smile. She pushes herself upright, holds out her hand to help Trouble to her feet. *He better not be,* she says, and looks left, off the *edge of the walkway. The smell of IC(E) is stronger now, and she can feel its dank weight, but no corresponding icon stands visible. She considers probing it, trying to force some image to emerge, but decides against it. There are still two more turns to the walk, and logically it will eventually lead to the wall of IC(E), and whatever it is the IC(E) protects: she'll wait until then to try her probes.*

*The next turn is much the same, the distortion perhaps a little more complex, and Trouble feels her way along the walk with her hand. Cerise follows, eyes closed tight, letting the other woman pull her along through the mismatch of vision and sense that leaves her seasick, and then, as she crawls, dragged at Trouble's heels, she catches a first faint sound, the rustle and stir of watchdogs, search-and-destroy programs moving somewhere in the distance.*

*\*Trouble,\* she says, and Trouble says, \*I hear.\**

*She pulls herself to her feet, turns to pull Cerise up as well, and the first of the programs pops into sight. Cerise studies it, goes intent and still, analyzing the taste of it. She reaches into her toolkit, selects a counterroutine and sets it loose, releases a second and a third copy as well to patrol the space between them. The first copy churns toward the watchdog, meets and tangles it; the programs fall, turning slowly end over end, but she doesn't bother to watch the end. She reaches into her toolkit again, evokes another version, and then her own icepick, queues them ready for use. She has movable IC(E) as well, a variation of the privacy sphere, and far more effective, but she holds it ready, not yet deploying it.*

*\*How many?\* Trouble asks, and Cerise shrugs.*

*\*Five that I can be sure of, maybe more. Now what?\**

*Trouble takes a deep breath, looks over her shoulder at the final corner, where the walkway seems to turn back on itself and the smell, the cold of IC(E) is strongest, then looks back at Cerise and the watchdogs, arrowing down on them. \*Why the hell did he wait until now?\* she says, and is briefly angry at the irrelevance. To her surprise, Cerise grins.*

*\*I think we've got him worried,\* she says. \*Those aren't part of the main program.\**

*\*That's something,\* Trouble says, looks back at the final corner, deceptively ordinary. She knows what will happen if she tries to step through it, to walk the path as it stands, she's tried it before,*

*practiced it all along the length of this walkway, and that means, she thinks, that this one will be different, somehow. The Mayor would have to be a fool to use the same method, the same kind of program, here where it matters most, and the Mayor has never been a fool. And there was the IC(E) to deal with, as well. \*Can you watch my back?\* she says, and Cerise glances at her.*

\*How do you mean?\*

\*Keep those off my back until I can figure out how to turn the corner, get to the IC(E) so I can break it.\*

Cerise nods. \*I can do that.\*

\*Thanks,\* Trouble says. \*Stay close.\*

She moves cautiously toward the last corner, testing each step, ready to throw herself backward as soon as she finds the point where the mirror's reflection begins. Cerise follows, walking backward so that she can keep an eye on her own counterroutines and on the approaching watchdogs. They are swarming in from every direction now, more and more of them visible in the distance—the Mayor has evoked multiple copies, more copies than she's ever seen before in any one volume of the net, and she spins a few more copies of her counterroutine into the air around her. The second watchdog engages a counterroutine, and then the third; the programs are well matched, the counterroutine damaging the watchdog beyond function even as it itself is destroyed. She looses another copy, and another, eyeing the oncoming wave of watchdogs: the icons, simple half-spheres, coded red and yellow for warning, brighten the dark volume.

Trouble reaches out again, and, finally, feels her hand slide in the wrong direction, out away from the walkway. \*Found it,\* she says, and hears Cerise sigh in relief.

\*I'm rigging our own codewall,\* she says, \*my own IC(E).\* As she speaks, she sets the program running, sees the first clear-glass spokes of the lattice spin themselves out of thin air, and stoops to guide the forming wall. Her counterroutines fan out from it to face the watchdogs, backed by the secondary counters and then by a brace of icepicks. She will be able to release some of her programs through the IC(E)—it's programmed to let them through—but that opening is a weakness that the Mayor may be able to exploit, if he can analyze the wall's construction in time. She closes her mind to *that thought, and concentrates on the wall itself. The spikes of IC(E) are stronger now, thicker, building on each other like crystals growing out of a solution, and she guides the pattern, walling herself and Trouble inside a glittering dome.*

*Trouble looks back over her shoulder, sees them encased in shards of bright glass—tinged here and there with purple, with fuchsia, a reinforcement lattice within the main system. She can leave the defense to Cerise—she has no choice, and anyway Cerise is the better at running IC(E); it's always been her specialty and she's had the time at Multiplane to hone her skills. Her own job is to concentrate on the Mayor, to root him out of the heart of his system, so that all of this, all the effort and anger, won't have been in vain. She reaches out again, feels her hand stop as though she's hit a barrier, knows it's only the mismatch of sight and reality. She takes a deep breath, concentrates, and eases forward into chaos.*

# • 13 •

THIS TIME THE *disorientation is worse, so that she can barely move at all, muscles throbbing with useless effort. Then, as she starts to pull back, to try again, her hand moves by chance as she wants it to go, straight ahead along the path traced by the walkway. She freezes in sudden understanding, her hand still outstretched toward the invisible IC(E). The silver ripples are puddled under her feet, solid silver that shimmers like cloth in a breeze. This time the mirror has inverted her perception as well as reversed it, or at least partly so; she must reach down to move ahead, as well as right to go left. But knowing isn't the same as doing: she tries to take a step, and nearly falls, saves herself only by a graceless twist. There's only one thing she can do, what she's been doing all along, and she drops again to her knees, eyes closed, and gropes forward, running her hand across the surface of the walkway. It seems to rise slightly under her fingers, and she slides cautiously forward, not daring to open her eyes. She finds first one edge, and then the other, sweeping her hand back and forth like a blind woman's cane, slides forward again on her knees. She reaches out, and her fingers shock painfully against hard IC(E), the pain of it driving up into her shoulder and down into her ribs.*

She cries out, eyes flying open, and sees the world flung sideways around her, the walkway twisted like a Möbius strip, so that Cerise and the wall of their IC(E) hangs at an impossible angle. In the same instant an illusion of gravity tugs at her, so that she can feel herself on the verge of falling, a heartbeat, a second, a fraction of a second away from losing her grip on the walkway and spilling out into empty space. She squeezes her eyes shut, and the worst of the sensations vanishes. The pain in her arm returns, but the pins-and-needles feeling is already fading: just a warning, really, this time, just to let her know this IC(E) is diamond-hard.

She clings there, the red-black darkness behind her eyelids a perverse comfort, bracing herself to try again. She needs to see the Mayor's IC(E) to breach it, needs to find a control point and destroy the illusion of invisibility, but to do that, she has to open her eyes. *Tune the worm lower?* she thinks, and discards the thought as quickly as it forms. She needs the full input, the full intensity and range of sensation, if she's to beat the Mayor. She opens her eyes, swallowing nausea, makes herself ignore the tugging gravity, her palms flat on the walkway's cool surface. She can still feel herself starting to fall, resists the temptation to go with that illusion, and flattens her whole body against the path, pressing herself, hips and thighs and breasts and shoulders, into the silver surface as though she would embrace it. She lays her cheek against the rippling light, imagines she feels the faint ebb and flow of it against her skin. The falling sensation recedes a little, and she shifts her head to study the invisible IC(E) and the illusion that protects it.

The shield is very well made, a seamless, recursive image, the walkway twisting back on itself; its surface stretches without flaw, without a glitch in the code to give her a handle. And even if she found one, she thinks, she couldn't reach it, not lying flat like this, trapped by the illusion that surrounds her. . . . She suppresses the thought, shifts her head again. Gravity clutches harder with each fractional movement, threatening to pry her from her place. She tells herself it is unreal, an image, a sensation, transmitted by the brainworm; tells herself then that she is coated in glue, that she will stick to the walkway, that she cannot fall. Slowly, she reaches out

*again, sliding her hand along the cool and silver-rippling surface,
gropes for the control points she has found before. She finds nothing, just the inchoate, general presence—not even warmth, just the
tremor of movement—of the silver ripples that have gathered there
under her body. She starts to reach for the IC(E), to try a blind assault, but stops herself, makes herself pause again and think. There
is something about the way the light moves beneath her body, something familiar in the faint sensation. . . .*

And then she has it, the source of the memory and of the answer
all in one: the light is an echo, incomplete and nearly insubstantial,
of the bright control points she has seen outside the pyramid. Either
it hides the control points in its diffuse light or it is in itself a control mechanism, fragile and ephemeral, hard to manipulate but as
effective as any more permanent node. She lies very still, letting the
sensations seep through her, the gentle pulse gather against her
skin. No control points are hidden in the seashell flicker; the light
itself, the cool delicate ripples of it, is the mechanism. She presses
her hand flat, as though she would force it through the rigid surface,
spreads her fingers and watches the ripples spread and then return,
rebounding from the edge of the invisible IC(E). She shifts her hand
again, wriggling her fingers, feels the ripples build, bouncing back
from the IC(E), from the walkway's edge, from the surface of her
body. The feedback swells, a flush of heat now present in the walk
beneath her hand, where the program has to manifest in order to
maintain control of the illusion. She waits, letting the substance
build, and feels an override cut in, emerging to banish the program
before it can be manipulated. She closes her hand, feeling the pulse
of the override strum through her body, and her fingers sink deep
into the solid warmth of a temporary control point. She twists her
hand, shuts off the override, and the program vanishes, leaving her
abruptly chilled. But the control point stays warm in the palm of
her hand, as though she holds a handful of embers.

And that's all she needs. The Mayor set his reality to respond to
these controls; she adjusts it, carefully, feels gravity vanish and
then return, oriented now so that she can stand straight against it,
feel its pull through the soles of her feet. She strips away the illusion
covering the IC(E), and a wall like a tangle of thornbrush spun
from glass blinks into existence in front of her. The light that

streams from it is all but blinding, hiding detail. She blinks, eyes watering, looks away, and in that instant the control point evaporates in her hand. She braces herself for the return of the illusions she has banished, but the walkway stays beneath her, and the wall of IC(E) remains. She studies it, head cocked to one side, does her best to ignore time passing, the knowledge that there's only Cerise watching her back, keeping back the active defenses. The pattern of the thorn wall shifts and shimmers, writhing as though alive, as though with heat, and then, quite suddenly, she sees it, sees the key. It is like Cerise's work, just as Cerise said, the complexity of the system elaborated and reelaborated from a matrix Trouble remembers all too well. She smiles, tasting triumph, reaches into the glittering hedge; the spines stab her hand, and then skid painfully along her arm as she reaches deep into the tangled code, leaving dark trails like blood against her skin. She ignores them, ignores the pain shivering through her, finds the single branch that is the key to the pattern. She takes it in two fingers, delicately, presses down and away. The glass resists, impossibly, bends and stretches, and then, suddenly overloaded, snaps like a brittle twig. The wall of IC(E) vanishes as though it had never been.

She stands at the edge of a space so mundane that it must mirror reality, a room crowded with hardware, a room with a desk and a lamp and a single window that shows rooftops and the arc of the Parcade Ferris wheel. The Mayor stands in the center of that space, frozen in the heart of his machines, at one with his machines, clothed in sheets of chips and wrapped with flickers of wire, each hand splayed wide across control mechanisms impossibly magnified, so that with the flick of a finger he shifts electrons, changes, recreates his world. They stand facing each other for an instant, perhaps six heartbeats, Trouble smiling, knowing now she has him, the Mayor's face unchanging, still the blank icon, but she can feel the same knowledge chilling him. And then he closes his hands, the magnified controls shattering, spinning away, and the illusion winks out, disappears, and the Mayor with it, dropping away from the net leaving nothingness behind, an empty hole, so that Trouble has to fight to stay where she was, not fall off the nets after him.

*You bastard,* she shouts after him, knowing it's useless, *you cowardly son of a bitch—*

*And she stops as abruptly as she's begun, standing on the edge of nothing, an absence of virtuality, because he's beaten her after all. By running like this he's denied her her only chance to prove herself, because the Mayor's friends will always say—the net itself may always say—that she never faced him directly, and that if she had, she would have lost. It won't matter that he ran, that he was the one who chose not to meet her; it will always be her failure— and maybe it is my fault, she thinks, I should've known, should've stopped him—*

*She shoves that thought aside, furious with herself for allowing it—it is not her fault, not her choice or her cowardice, but the Mayor's, and there will be plenty of people who'll see it—and turns back, toward the space where Cerise still stands behind her guardian IC(E), the icon braced, stance utterly intent, absorbed in the delicate and deadly ballet of battling programs that Trouble can only just make out, distorted, through the glasslike wall.*

*Cerise turns her head, the icon's head, as though she senses some change in the air behind her. \*Trouble—?\**

*\*He's run out on me,\* Trouble says, furious, and Cerise looks back at the programs struggling on the other side, struggling against, her wall of IC(E). The icebreakers are moving more slowly now, by rote programming rather than the Mayor's hand; the watchdogs, too, are suddenly clumsy, awkward against the counterroutines' attacks.*

*\*Any data?\* she asks, and Trouble shakes her head, staring into the hole. When the Mayor dropped off-line, he took his immediate volume with him; with it, she thinks, she is certain, went all the vital data. The air is empty, tasteless, around her.*

*\*No,\* she says, voice flat. \*There's no point in staying. Let's go.\**

*Cerise grins and nods, closes her fists tight over the emergency control. Trouble copies her, and the world, the Mayor's world, blinks out around them.*

Trouble sat up abruptly, wincing from a stiff shoulder, reached angrily for the datacord and jerked it out of her dollie-slot. Cerise copied her, more slowly, her fingers clumsy and stiff. She freed herself from the machine, and then laid her hands flat against the edge of the table, studying them warily. As she had feared, the knuckles were swollen, the fingers puffy as though with heat. She grimaced, recognizing a familiar injury, and Trouble reached across to touch her shoulder.

"You OK?"

"Froze my fingers a little," Cerise said, and Trouble winced again, this time in sympathy.

"You should see a doctor—"

"In this town?" Cerise managed a laugh. "I might as well post a sign on the net that I've been cracking." She bent her fingers cautiously, made a face at the jarring pain. "Maybe Mabry can recommend someone."

"We should find him," Trouble said, grimly. "He must've missed newTrouble at the flat—"

The door slammed open as though the locks had never been set, bounced against the far wall. Mabry caught it one-handed, flung it closed again behind him, practically in the face of the frightened desk clerk. Trouble caught a brief glimpse of her pale, red-lipped face and the master key hanging in a nerveless hand before the door had shut, and Mabry was in the room.

"You've blown it," he said. "I warned you, and the deal's off. Cerise, I expected better of you—"

"Hold it," Trouble began, her own temper rising, and Cerise said, "Wait a minute, Mabry. We didn't warn the kid."

"Then how the hell did you know he was warned?" Mabry glared at them impartially, one hand still knotted in a fist at his side.

"Because we ended up chasing him on the nets," Cerise said, impatiently. "What happened?"

Mabry stared at her for a moment, then took a deep breath, visibly controlling his temper. "We lost the kid—he was coming up to the flat, and something spooked him. He got off the elevator a couple floors early, and then we think he went back down the fire stairs while we were still figuring out what happened. He must've jimmied the alarms. And if either of you had anything to do with it—"

"We didn't," Cerise said. "My word, Vess."

Mabry was silent for another long moment, then, slowly, nodded. "For now."

"We went to Seahaven," Trouble said, and hoped he wouldn't ask why. "The Mayor challenged me, and then the kid showed up—"

"He was running from you, Vess," Cerise interjected. "I don't know where he was, realworld, but it was after he'd got away from you."

Mabry nodded again, as though that explained something. "Go on."

"The Mayor bounced him right off the net," Trouble said. "And then he jumped me. We went after the Mayor."

"Why the hell didn't you go for the kid?" Mabry muttered.

"I told you," Trouble said, "the Mayor dumped him off-line. Like he'd tripped the emergency cutout. We couldn't follow him."

"And we've lost Novross." Mabry's other hand tightened briefly to a fist, and then, with an effort, he made himself relax. "All right. I want everything you can tell me about the Mayor, about the boy, about this encounter." He gave a singularly mirthless grin. "After all, you still haven't given me newTrouble."

"Don't threaten me," Trouble began, bit off anything else she would have said.

Cerise said, softly, "We kept our part of the bargain, Vess. You wouldn't want to break yours."

Mabry made a face, waved the words away. "All right, yes, sorry. But this is important. If we lose the Mayor now, if he gets a chance to run, start over somewhere else—"

"All right," Trouble said. "All right." She closed her eyes, calling up the memory of the Mayor's virtuality, spaces within spaces, the western town and the Aztec temple that contained the walkway and its mirrors, that in turn contained the last small space, the volume that had vanished with the Mayor. She could almost see it now, the machines and the Mayor merged, and the dull room that contained them, table and lamp and the window that overlooked the Parcade—

"I can find him," she said aloud, and felt a surge of glee. He hadn't beaten her after all; he had betrayed himself instead, and she could prove it. Both Mabry and Cerise were looking at her, Mabry frankly skeptical, Cerise wary, and she grinned at both of them. "The last volume, the one at the very end of the path, Cerise—it was based on his realworld location, I'm sure of it. You wouldn't construct something like that unless you were copying something real, it was too plain, too mundane for it not to be real." She broke off, took a deep breath, controlling her excitement. "The point is, there was a window, with a view of the Parcade. If we can find the view, I can find the Mayor."

There was another silence, and then Cerise moved, swinging back to the media center, swollen fingers clumsy on the controls. "There's a tourist mock-up of the town, supposed to let you see what your rooms will be like, what the views will be, that sort of thing." Her hand slipped, jarring her fingers, and she swore under her breath, scowling at the screen.

"Let me," Mabry said, and Cerise stepped reluctantly aside. Mabry finished entering the codes, triggered a three-dimensional model of the town.

"What did you see?" Cerise asked, and gestured for Mabry to call up the inquiry screen.

"He was overlooking the Parcade," Trouble said. "The western end, with the Ferris wheel. There were houses in the way, so you couldn't see the street itself, just the Ferris wheel."

"How many streets?" Cerise asked. Mabry seated himself at the controls, heavy face intent on the screen and the menu of questions.

Trouble frowned, trying to remember. "Three, maybe? I think there were three rows of roofs, anyway."

"How high up were you?" Cerise asked.

"High," Trouble answered. "At least two stories, maybe three or four—the nearest building was a little away, you'd be looking down on it."

Cerise nodded, looked at Mabry. "Run it, see what it comes up with."

Mabry did as he was told. The model vanished, to be replaced by a swirling paisley pattern.

"Come on," Cerise murmured, staring at the screen. "Come on."

Trouble leaned over Mabry's other shoulder and willed the holding pattern to clear. After what seemed an interminable time, the paisley swirls vanished, and a message appeared: NO EXACT MATCH AVAILABLE. "Oh, shit," Trouble said, and turned away.

"See if there's a possible location," Cerise said calmly to Mabry, and the big man touched keys, frowning slightly. The holding pattern reappeared, but only for a moment, then was replaced by a section of the city model—four, maybe five blocks of nondescript houses, on the far side of the Harbormouth bridge, where the solid land fell away into the Slough. A message appeared with it: SIMILAR VIEWS EXIST IN THIS APPROXIMATE AREA.

"Now, that's more like it," Cerise said, and Trouble turned back to the screen.

"That's where I'd expect to find him," she agreed.

Cerise nodded, studying the image. "A view of the Ferris wheel, you said, and a bunch of housetops."

"Yeah."

"What about there?" Mabry asked, and slid the cursor across the screen to circle a tall rectangle colored the pale green of a rooming house.

"Why not?" Cerise said.

Mabry touched keys, and images flickered across the screen as he moved the cursor from floor to floor of the rooming house. All were views from the windows that faced the Parcade; all showed housetops and the Ferris wheel above them in the distance. "Well?"

Trouble shook her head. "Definitely not there." She studied the screen, trying to imagine what it would take to transform the images she had just seen to the one she remembered. "What about that one?"

Mabry touched keys again, calling up the views attached to the house she had selected. Trouble watched them through, but shook her head again. "It's close, though. Try next door."

Mabry worked his way down the street, selecting two more houses, shook his head as the images from the third popped onto the screen. "This of course assumes that he'll stay put long enough for us to catch him. Even if we find the place, he'll be long gone."

Cerise looked at Trouble, who said nothing, her eyes fixed on the screen. Cerise said, carefully, "I'm not so sure about that, Mabry. There's no real reason for him to run—he doesn't know what, if anything, Trouble saw, and he doesn't know we know Seahaven. He's been invisible for a long time, and he's got hardware there—it must be substantial, to run Seahaven. I think he'll stay."

"It would be stupid," Mabry said, but he sounded slightly more optimistic than he had. "Where next?"

Trouble pointed, touching a house across the street from the one they had viewed before. "That one."

Mabry selected it, ran the images, moving up from the ground floor. Trouble held her breath as the pointer reached the top two floors, relaxed with a sigh.

"That's it."

"You're sure?" Mabry asked, but he was already calling up the address.

"Of course I'm sure," Trouble answered. "That's the view I saw, anyway."

"That's near where Blake used to live," Cerise said, and shook the thought away as irrelevant.

Mabry shoved himself away from the media center, not bothering to shut down the program. "Your phone? I need to call—"

"We're coming with you," Trouble said, and pointed to the handset resting on the coffee table.

Mabry picked it up, began punching numbers. "Do you think that's wise? I thought you had a reputation to uphold."

Cerise grinned at that, reached across the keyboard to close down the system. "Oh, we have reputations, all right—"

"—and I fully intend to keep mine," Trouble finished. "Nobody crosses me, Mabry. Nobody."

"Suit yourself," Mabry answered, and turned away to speak softly into the handset.

Cerise looked at Trouble, lowered her voice cautiously. "You sure you're sure?"

Trouble nodded again, knowing the question she was being asked. After all this, Cerise was saying, after being dragged back into the shadows and finding out again that she had a taste for it, did she really want to throw herself irrevocably into the bright lights, turn herself into nothing more than a syscop? "I'm sure," she said, and Mabry tossed the handset onto the couch.

"Let's go," he said, and swept out of the room without looking back.

Trouble followed, said over her shoulder, so softly Cerise wasn't for a second sure she had heard correctly, "I want to be in at the kill. If I've gone over to the enemy, I want to do it right."

Cerise hesitated, shook her head, uncertain of her feelings, or at best sure only of one thing, that she would see this through to the end. She followed both of them down the emergency stairs and out into the lobby.

Mabry had commandeered a car from the local cops, unmarked but with police equipment, sophisticated net monitors and local tie-ins, prominent on its control boards. There was a driver as well, a skinny, nondescript young man with pale brown hair and a recruit's flashes below The Willows' insignia on his shoulder. He looked momentarily as though he might protest, seeing the two women, but Mabry said, "You have the address?"

The young man swallowed whatever he had been going to say. "Yes, sir."

"Then let's go." Mabry climbed into the front seat beside the driver, and Trouble and Cerise scrambled into the narrow passenger compartment. "You notified Treasury as well?"

The driver put the car into gear, edged forward out of the

driveway in front of Eastman House. "Yes, sir. They're on their way."

"Good," Mabry said, and leaned back against his seat. Trouble looked at Cerise, saw the other woman's pale face intent on the road. Then Cerise looked at her, dark eyes wary, and they both heard the sound of sirens, distant now, but coming quickly closer.

"What the hell?" Trouble said, softly, and Mabry leaned forward to query one of the systems plugged into the main board.

"—hostage situation—" The voice blared from a speaker, and Mabry reached hastily for a datacord and plugged it in, cutting off the voice.

"Who the hell can he be holding hostage?" Cerise asked. "Not Silk, surely."

"Who'd care?" Trouble agreed, her eyes on Mabry.

The big man glanced back at her, his expression unreadable. "He's tied into the city computers. Threatens to erase system software if he's attacked. Can he do it?"

Trouble nodded slowly, remembering the sheer scale of virtual Seahaven, of the power, hardware and software, that the Mayor needed to maintain the illusion. Turn that power on a city system, and no IC(E) would be sufficient; at that scale, brute force alone would be enough to shatter the city's coding, leave all the files, all the city systems, open and vulnerable.

"Does The Willows care?" Cerise asked, with a smile that did not touch her eyes.

Mabry's eyes flicked toward her, and then away again. "The Willows is tied in to city services—drainage, the pump system, sewers, traffic control, all that. If Novross crashes those, The Willows doesn't have sufficient backup power to keep things running." He turned back to the control board, running one hand along a sensor strip. "Besides, the city systems contain the tax records."

"Ah." Cerise's smile widened into open contempt.

The sirens were louder now as they crossed the Harbormouth bridge, and the local cops had set up a hasty roadblock halfway down Ashworth Avenue. Other cops were fanning out from the roadblock, moving along the storefronts to shut down the businesses and force the citizens indoors. Out of harm's way, or, more likely, just out of their way, Cerise thought. Mabry extended his credentials to the waiting cop, a man in full armor under his coveralls, with a stunstick at his belt and a pellet gun slung across his shoulder.

"Where's Starling?"

The cop didn't answer at once, but studied the folder with its double ID carefully, checking both identification and warrant before he returned it to its owner. "Down by the house," he said. "He's directing the operation."

"Wonderful," Trouble muttered.

Mabry said nothing, gestured to the driver. The young man pulled the car sharply around the end of the barricade, and started down the narrow street.

The cops had removed some of the parked cars from this end of the road, though they'd left others in place as makeshift barricades. Two fast-tanks were pulled into place across the street, one with its rear treads resting precariously on the soft ground that edged the Slough, the other blocking the roadway entirely. A trio of armored cops—wearing state badges rather than The Willows' insignia—crouched in its shelter; a fourth man, equally armored, stepped out of its shadow and waved the car to the side of the road. The driver slowed obediently, and Mabry lowered his window to confer with the approaching officer.

Cerise laughed sharply. "You'd think the man was a fucking terrorist. Look at all this."

Mabry glanced back at her, then turned to hand his credentials to the armored man. "Where's Starling?"

"Mr. Mabry," the cop acknowledged, straightened slightly as though he would have saluted. "Mr. Starling wants to see you right away. Down there, sir." He pointed toward a third, smaller car, recognizable as police only by the way it was parked, slewed deliberately across the road to provide protection behind its bulk.

"I want to see Mr. Starling," Mabry said, and levered himself out of the car. "You two, wait here."

"Fine," Trouble said to his back. She watched him make his way down the street, broad-shouldered in his battered jacket, conspicuously casual among the armored and uniformed police huddling behind the cars.

"What the fuck do they think they're doing?" Cerise demanded. "He's a cracker, not a gunrunner."

Trouble saw the driver's shoulders twitch, and a detached part of her admired the man's self-control. "Yeah," she said, deliberately provocative, "crackers don't generally go around shooting cops."

Cerise shook her head, still furious. "They got to be crazy, reacting like this." But that was Evans-Tindale for you: the laws had been written by people who feared the nets, and it was that same fear that made things escalate, spiraling out of control.

Another siren sounded, a deeper note this time, and Trouble twisted in her seat to stare back the way they'd come. A fire engine, one of the heavy tower trucks with a lift basket on the front and a massive ladder-and-hose station at the back, was making its way ponderously down the street. One of the armored cops shouted and waved, and the driver edged their car in closer to the curb to let the fire engine pass. There were more armored men clinging to its sides.

"All this for software?" Trouble said. "They've got to have backups."

The driver turned in his place, pale face very serious. "We can't let him get away with the threat—we don't dare let him crash the city systems."

"This isn't going to stop him," Cerise said. She shook her head again. "This is not how you deal with the net."

"They must have somebody trying to stop him on-line," Trouble said, but her tone was less confident than her words. All this hardware could only be an admission of failure, a desperate attempt to stop something that couldn't be dealt with in virtuality—and this would have to fail, too, she thought. If the Mayor really did hold Seahaven's systems hostage, really had gained control of them through the net, then the fastest, most surgically efficient realworld attack would be seconds, minutes too slow. Starling, at least, would know it; she wondered bleakly if any of the others realized just how ineffective they really were.

"Trouble!" That was Mabry, striding back toward the car, his jacket flying open around him. "Cerise!" He lifted a hand, beckoning, and the driver popped the rear doors.

"Bet you he wants us to go cracking for him," Cerise said, and swung herself neatly out of the compartment.

Trouble followed more slowly. "I don't make bets on a sure thing."

"We have a problem," Mabry said.

"No shit," Cerise murmured.

Mabry pretended he hadn't heard. "Novross does seem to have control of the city systems. Starling and his lot have been trying to dig him out for the past half hour."

He tilted his head toward a black van that sat behind the line of cars. A cable snaked from a shielded port and disappeared into the door of the nearest building: Treasury's special netwalkers, Trouble realized.

"They haven't made much progress, but they're still working on it," Mabry said. "But the main thing is, Novross wants to talk to you."

He was looking directly at Trouble, but even so she frowned in confusion. "To me?"

"To you," Mabry agreed.

Trouble looked at Cerise, who shrugged, looked back at Mabry. "Why?"

"I don't know," Mabry answered. "He's not precisely forthcoming on the matter. But he wants to talk to you—he says he'll negotiate with you. And only you."

"I doubt that," Cerise said.

"She's right," Trouble said, and dredged a smile from somewhere. "We're not exactly on friendly terms. But I can crack his IC(E)—let me in that van, and I'll get him off the nets." It wouldn't be that easy, she knew, would take time and effort and probably more tools than she had with her, though Treasury might have some of what she would need—

Mabry shook his head. "It's not on, Trouble. I'm sorry. Starling thinks his men can handle it, but he needs time. They need time. And Novross wants to talk to you."

"He could kill her," Cerise said sharply. "Did you think of that? Or is that what Starling has in mind?"

"He's promised full cover," Mabry said. Behind him, machinery whined, and the fire engine's bucket rose jerkily into the air, swinging slightly from side to side. An armored figure was just visible over the edge of the bucket, gauntleted hand cupped to a headset in his helmet. The bucket rose higher, swung slightly sideways, so that the men in the bucket—there were two of them, Trouble realized—had the Mayor's windows in their field of fire. "And I intend to hold him to it."

"Not good enough," Cerise said.

"What exactly am I supposed to do?" Trouble asked.

"Keep him talking," Mabry answered. "Buy us time."

"How?"

"He said he wants to negotiate," Mabry said, "so negotiate. Offer him—whatever it is he wants, I suppose. No, offer passage out of the country, then we can haggle over how and where. Try to keep his mind off the nets. He'll probably have demands of his own, anyway, so see what they are and we'll go from there."

"Great," Trouble said. "I'm not a fucking negotiator, I don't know what I'm doing—" And I don't want to get myself killed, not by the Mayor, not after I've won—not for The Willows, anyway.

"He says," Mabry said, "and I emphasize I don't know if it's true, but he says he has a line to the local nuke. He says he can override local controls, cause a catastrophic failure."

"You don't think he does," Trouble said.

"No." Mabry's face twisted in a grimace half of frustration, half of rage. "And I don't think Starling does, either. But it's fucking useful for him, gives him access to all of this." He gestured broadly, the sweep of his hand including the tanks and the fire engine and the huddling cops. In the distance,

Trouble could hear the beat of a military helicopter, sweeping down from the base to the north. "And I—we can't afford to take that chance."

He was right about that, Trouble thought reluctantly. She tilted her head, looked up at the Mayor's building: just another cheap Seahaven rooming house, paint peeling on the sides where it was less likely to be seen. The Mayor's windows, uncurtained, unshaded, unlike all the others in the building, turned blank glass to the street. I should say no, she thought. Starling's just trying to use me, use this threat to get me to do what he wants, maybe even get me killed, just like he's used it to call out all this, local cops and state and God knows what all else. It was all but impossible to get into a nuke's internal systems, even for the Mayor—they were built to stand up against all intrusion attempts, there were cutouts and realtime requirements, and the crucial systems were supposed to be completely disconnected from the nets. But if they weren't, if the Mayor had gained access . . . He was just crazy enough, just desperate enough, to try something, and no one could stand by and let that happen. She shied away from the image that presented itself, out of ancient video, smoke billowing from a broken dome, radiation fires smothered in concrete; that wouldn't be what happened, not quite, but the area would be poisoned worse than it already was. And no one had ever honestly calculated the probable deaths. She looked back over her shoulder at Starling, still standing in the lee of the unmarked police car, conferring with Levy and a man in armor, not knowing whom she resented more, the Mayor or Starling himself.

"You'd still be better off with me running the nets," she said.

"I don't doubt it," Mabry snapped. "But that's not the deal."

Trouble took a deep breath. "I want complete immunity, all charges past and present dropped."

"Done." Mabry nodded, with decision. "I will see to it personally."

"And for Cerise as well."

"Agreed."

"He'll fucking kill you," Cerise said. "Trouble, don't do it."

Trouble looked at her, swallowing her own cold fear. "Look. He's one of us, a cracker, a netwalker. Since when did we start carrying guns?"

"I did."

"You weren't exactly representative."

"Neither's he."

"That was a long time ago, and in the city. And it's not the same. It's not the Mayor's style." Trouble took another long breath, tasting salt and the ubiquitous oil. The air was thickening, fog swirling in from the sea: not a good time for that, she thought, and automatically squinted upward, looking for the helicopter. It was still there, a dark shape against the white sky, but when she looked east, the outlines of the beachfront buildings were already blurred. "He doesn't gain anything by killing me—"

"Except personal satisfaction," Cerise snapped.

"Yeah." Trouble shivered, told herself it was only the first wisps of fog. "But he loses his chance to walk out of here."

"Do you really think Starling would let him walk?" Cerise asked. "Do you really think he thinks Starling will let him walk? Trouble—" She broke off abruptly, the rest of the sentence unspoken. I'm not losing you now, she would have said, not again, and this was not the time for declarations.

"But if he really can get into the nuke?" Trouble said.

"There's no way he can," Cerise said. "No fucking way."

Trouble looked at her, and Cerise made a face, answered her own question. "Except he's the Mayor, and if anyone can, it's him, and we can't take that risk anyway. Not on this coastline." She sighed. "All right, do it. But I'm coming with you."

"He said alone," Mabry interjected. It was no more than a token protest, but Cerise turned on him anyway.

"So get me in there without him knowing it, sunshine. I thought you people were supposed to be good. And I want a gun."

"All right," Mabry said. "Let's go."

They followed him down the narrow street, Mabry careful to keep the line of parked cars and runabouts between them and the rooming house. The cops, local and state, clustered in twos and threes behind the inadequate barricades, looked up as they passed, but their expressions were invisible behind the dark-tinted faceplates. Starling came to meet them, Levy and the armored stranger—probably some kind of senior police officer, Trouble thought, just from the amount of braid and badges, but she recognized only The Willows' insignia among the clutter—following a few steps behind.

"Well?" Starling asked, and Mabry nodded.

Trouble said, "I understand he wants to talk to me. Is that right?" In spite of her efforts at control, her voice came out too loud, uncertain.

Starling said, "That's right. I gather you've agreed."

"I want all charges past and present dropped," Trouble said, "for both me and Cerise."

"That can be arranged," Starling said.

"I've agreed to it," Mabry said, mildly, and Starling's lips tightened momentarily.

"All right."

"Now," Trouble said. "Just what is it you want me to do?"

"I just want you to keep him talking," Starling said. "Distract him while we isolate him on the net, so that the rest of our people can move in." He nodded to the fire engine. "We've got a sniper team there. They can take him out as soon as we're sure the nets are safe."

"That wasn't in the plan, John," Mabry said.

"You'd be better off letting us run the nets," Trouble said, without much hope. "We've beaten him before."

"No, thanks," Levy said.

Starling said, "It's you he wants to talk to. There's nothing I can do about that."

"But there are some things you can do about protection," Trouble said.

Starling waved his hand again, a broader gesture taking in

not only the snipers but the men crouching behind the lines of cars. "You'll have backup."

Except when I'm inside, Trouble thought. But the men in the fire engine's bucket would provide some cover, as much as she could reasonably expect.

Cerise said, "Yes. Well. I'm going with her."

Starling frowned, and Trouble said, "It's not negotiable."

"He said alone," Starling began, and Mabry shook his head.

"It can be done, John. It's better this way."

"And I want a gun," Cerise said.

Starling sighed, looked at Levy. "Ben?"

Levy reached into his jacket, freed his pistol from the shoulder holster, and reluctantly held it out butt first. "Do you know how to use this?"

Cerise took it, automatically checking the magazine— full—then cocked it, putting the safety on. "Oh, yes."

"Then let's get on with it," Starling said. "Mabry, you take Ms.—Cerise—around to the front door. Keep behind the cars, he can't see down into the street too well." Mabry nodded, motioned for Cerise to follow him. "Ms. Carless—Trouble. We'll wait here."

Trouble nodded, not daring to speak for fear her voice would break, watched as Mabry and Cerise made their way cautiously across the street and disappeared finally behind the line of parked cars. At last there was a flicker of movement beside the doorway, and Levy sighed.

"They're in position."

"Right," Starling said, and reached for a handset. "Novross."

There was a long silence, not even the crackle of static, and Trouble wondered for an instant if she was off the hook at last. Then the machine clicked, and the Mayor's voice came clearly through the tiny speaker.

"I'm here."

"We've done as you asked," Starling said. "Trouble's here, and she's prepared to act as our representative."

There was another silence, shorter this time, and then the Mayor said, "About time. Send her up."

"She's on her way," Starling said, and looked at Trouble. "You're on."

"Thanks," Trouble said. She took a deep breath, and stepped out from behind the car. She did not believe, in spite of everything Cerise had said, that the Mayor had a gun; it wasn't his style, was unlike anything else he'd ever done, but even so, she felt an odd, tingling sensation on her forehead, and then between her breasts. It felt very real, so real that she looked down at herself, half expecting to see the bright dot of a targeting laser, but there was nothing there. She shivered again, convulsively, and wished she thought anyone would believe it was from the fog.

Cerise was waiting in the doorway, pressed against the wall under the shelter of the arch, out of the line of vision of the single securicam. It looked broken, blinded by too many nights in the salt air, but there was no point in taking chances. Trouble looked up at it, wondering if the lens were really as scratched as it appeared, looked back down at the locks and the intercom board with its list of names. Before she could decide if she should press the bell, the one marked "Novross" in a neat, orderly hand, the buzzer sounded, and she reached out almost automatically to push the door open. It gave under her hand, and Cerise slipped ahead of her into the darkened hallway. Trouble followed, letting the door close behind her.

The lights were out in the hallway, the only brightness filtering down through a distant skylight over the stairway. Cerise said, her voice little above a whisper, "They must've cut the power to the building."

"Which should've cut the net link," Trouble murmured.

Cerise nodded, managed a grim smile. "Except that he had a hidden line. Just like we had."

"Just like everyone," Trouble said, and started up the stairs. Cerise followed, silently, copying the other woman's movements, staying half a flight behind. She had the pistol out and ready, safety off, just in case; it was heavier than the one she had used, a heavier caliber, the weight awkward in her hands.

Trouble paused at the first landing, listening, but heard nothing, not even the usual noises of a building's miscellaneous machinery. She looked back, saw Cerise braced against the wall of the stair below, pistol held in both hands, the barrel tilted toward the ceiling. The sight was somewhat reassuring; Trouble forced a smile, and climbed the rest of the way to the third floor. There was only one door off the landing, and it was closed, but light showed through at the edges of the frame. So this is it, Trouble thought, but didn't move closer at once, looked around instead for cameras. She didn't see any, even in the shadows where the walls joined the high ceilings, but she was careful not to look back as she stepped up onto the landing. Cerise was behind her, there on the last landing; she could see what was happening well enough.

Trouble took a deep breath, and knocked on the white-painted door. For a crazy moment she thought she was going to giggle—it was too incongruous an image, her tapping on the metal door as though she were any visitor, this a normal visit—and she bit her lip hard, knowing that if she started laughing now it would be impossible to stop. The Mayor wouldn't understand, she thought, wouldn't be amused, and that realization was almost enough to send her over the edge.

"It's open," the Mayor's voice said from inside, and the desire to laugh vanished as quickly as it had appeared. This time, Trouble did look back, to see Cerise hurrying silently up the stairs, to flatten herself against the wall, just out of the line of sight from the doorway.

"I'm coming in," Trouble said, and heard herself shrill and nervous. She pressed lightly against the door, wary of booby traps, stories of bombs and electrical charges coming back to her from the old days, the Mayor's days, when crackers had fought their battles off the nets as well as on, but nothing happened. She turned the knob, wincing in advance of an explosion, and the door swung open with the gentle groan of imperfectly oiled hinges.

The Mayor was standing exactly as she'd seen him last, frozen in the heart of his machines, hands splayed wide over the control surfaces, wires and chip boards wreathing him. And then she saw the differences as well, recognized that there was only one wire, the long cable of a datacord running down from a socket at the back of his skull, saw too that the chip boards were portable flatscreens, propped awkwardly across the main machines. Whatever else he'd planned, this was a jury-rigged defense, Trouble realized. And a defense of his home, in some strange way: there was a table with a microwave on it in one corner, and a futon on the floor beneath the windows. A slight figure lay curled on that, asleep or unconscious, face turned toward the wall: newTrouble, she thought, Tilsen. So he was here all along.

"Trouble," the Mayor said, and she answered, "Mayor."

The lights were working here, a single, badly shaded bulb dangling over the central work space, throwing the Mayor's face into grotesque shadow. He was a thin man, cadaverously thin and pale, a shadow of light stubble further hollowing his cheeks, but his hands on the controls were sure and competent, his whole stance that of an El Greco prelate. Trouble stared at him, surprised at how much like his icon he was, and knew that he was staring just as curiously back at her.

"I suppose I shouldn't be that surprised." The Mayor's voice was slow, too, and faintly slurred, and Trouble realized that he was still at least half on-line, some part of his brain holding off Starling's men from the city systems. "You never really were one of us."

So that's the tack you're going to take, Trouble thought, and dredged a laugh from somewhere. "No," she said, "I'm not, and never was one of your kind. I'm better."

The Mayor frowned, magisterial, would, she thought, have shaken a finger at her had he been able to free himself from his boards. "Very cocky. How unwise. Where's your girlfriend?"

"Here," Cerise said, from the doorway. Trouble didn't dare look back, but saw the Mayor's frown deepen.

"I would advise against using that," he said, and one hand shifted on the board. A beam of ruby light shot from the ceiling, struck the worn floor just at Trouble's feet, blinked out as quickly as it had appeared. Smoke curled from the cheap tiles, and it was all Trouble could do not to take a step backward.

"You'll still be dead," Cerise said.

"And so will your friend," the Mayor answered. He fixed his eyes on Trouble, dismissing Cerise from his calculations. "I really didn't think you'd throw in with them. Not in the end."

"You didn't leave me any alternatives," Trouble said, stung more by the disappointment in his tone than by his words. "Christ, do you think I'm going to stand by and let you play silly buggers with the local nuke?"

"You believed that?" The Mayor gave a snort of contempt. "I thought you were at least technically literate. You should know it's not possible. They—" He jerked his head toward the window. "I'd expect them to fall for it, but not you. Not even you should be that ignorant."

Trouble felt herself flush, said, "Not so ignorant I couldn't break your IC(E), Mayor."

"That was the worm, not you," the Mayor answered. "But real technical knowledge? I should have known better than to expect it."

"Starling said you wanted to talk to me," Trouble said, through clenched teeth. "So what do you want?"

"I had thought," the Mayor began, and broke off, hands moving busily across the control surfaces. "But it doesn't matter. What I want now is to be rid of you. You're a disgrace to the nets, and the least I can do, the last thing I can do, is clean up the mess I inadvertently caused."

His eyes slid sideways, toward the boy on the bed, and in that instant Trouble flung herself backward. The laser spat fire, the beam striking the tiles where she had stood. Cerise fired in the same instant, the noise enormous in the high-ceilinged room, kept firing, and with her second shot the snipers fired, too, shattering the windows. Trouble flung herself down, hands instinctively covering her head against the rain of glass, saw the Mayor's body falling, torn, jerking with the impact of the bullets. Cerise screamed something, crouching against the wall by the door, a shriek that resolved itself at last into words.

"Stop it, you stupid bastards, stop firing! He's dead!"

Whether they heard her or not, the shooting stopped as abruptly as it had begun. Trouble lifted her head cautiously, saw the floor paved with glass like broken ice, and the Mayor's body sprawled bonelessly across his machines. A coil of smoke was rising from one of the consoles, and she crawled forward hastily, trying not to look at the body, groped for the kill switch and cut the power. The Mayor's hand hung down, almost close enough to touch; there was no blood on the thin fingers, but she could smell it, acrid and unmistakable, and kept her eyes down, not wanting to see the ruin of his body.

"Silk?" Cerise said, and Trouble looked at the slight figure on the futon. The glass has fallen all around him, shards glittering on his body, and she winced and moved toward him, sweeping the bits of glass awkwardly out of her way. She could hear footsteps on the stairs now, the heavy tread of running men, but she ignored them, began picking the slivers of glass carefully away from the mattress and the boy's clothes. Cerise came to join her, dropping the automatic on the floor beside her, picked flinchingly at the larger pieces.

"He doesn't seem to have been cut," Trouble said, doubtfully, grimaced as a sharp edge sliced her finger. She sucked at the cut, and Cerise brushed the last obvious pieces away from the mattress.

"Turn him over," she said, and her voice was sharp with fear.

There was something wrong with him, Trouble thought, as she helped Cerise ease the boneless weight onto its back, something very wrong about the way he moved, about the open, staring eyes. "I think he's dead," she said aloud, and groped for a pulse in the slim neck. He looked barely fifteen, not the seventeen Mabry had claimed for him, slim, sweet-faced, with huge brown eyes that stared sightlessly at the ceiling.

"Dead?" Cerise echoed.

"What happened?" Mabry said, and Trouble turned gratefully, to see armored cops crowding into the room behind Mabry and Starling.

"I don't know," she said. "The glass didn't cut him, not seriously—"

"Here," an armored man said, and held up an injector. Starling took it, inspected the label and the discolored tip, then made a face and handed it to Mabry.

"Gerumine," he said, and Mabry grunted.

"It's a euthanasiant," he said to Trouble. "I wonder if he took it himself, or if Novross gave it to him."

"You don't know that's what happened," Cerise protested automatically, pushed herself to her feet. Her hands were shaking, and she jammed them into her pockets.

"Well, he sure didn't take it," Starling answered, nodding to the Mayor. "And you two didn't, and the injector's been used. That doesn't leave many choices, does it?"

Trouble shivered again, stood slowly, glass crunching under her feet. "Jesus," she said, and then, "Why?"

"I don't know," Mabry said.

Cerise said, "He said he was cleaning up the mess, the mess he'd caused. I suppose Silk was part of it."

Like me, Trouble thought. It could've been me—fifteen years ago, it might have been me. The fog was thicker now, drifting in through the shattered windows, cold and wet on her skin.

Mabry touched her shoulder, turned her away from the two bodies, newTrouble's and the Mayor's, urged her toward the door. Trouble went unresisting, and Cerise followed more slowly, looking back toward the boy's body and the grey-jacketed medics kneeling beside it.

Mabry paused on the landing, touched Trouble's shoulder again. "This—incident—presents an opportunity for us, one that I don't want to see go to waste. It's important, Trouble, will you listen?"

Trouble made a noise that might have become laughter, bit her lip again to keep it from swelling to full hysterics. "I'm listening."

"Seahaven, virtual Seahaven, is without a Mayor now," Mabry said. "If we had somebody legal in charge, somebody we could trust—"

"Me?" Trouble said, and lifted a skeptical eyebrow.

"It would make sense," Mabry said. "You're an old-style netwalker, you've been a syscop, you beat the Mayor at his own game. The nets would have to respect your claim, and we'd be able to crack down on Seahaven."

Cerise grinned. "You shot the sheriff, Trouble, that means you get to be marshal."

"I'm still on the wire," Trouble said automatically. "People may not believe I beat him." But the idea was tempting: to have Seahaven for herself, to take over that space, that status, for her own . . . And there would be other opportunities too—maybe Mabry wouldn't approve, and Starling, Treasury, certainly wouldn't, but the possibilities cut both ways, not just not to return to the shadows, she'd come too far for that anyway, but to redefine the bright lights, begin again the action Evans-Tindale had cut short. From Seahaven, with Seahaven's sanctuary as a base and a passport, she could do anything.

Mabry said, "You could do it. Times are changing; the wire doesn't matter so much anymore—too many people have them now. And you've earned it. That's the thing nobody else can ever claim. You beat him."

Trouble nodded slowly. "It can't be this easy."

Mabry grinned, showing very white teeth. "Probably not," he admitted. "But in the long run, there isn't anybody else. And even Treasury isn't so stupid as to leave Seahaven untenanted, when they can have you in charge."

"All right," Trouble said, and nodded again. "All right, I'll do it. Conditionally."

"Of course," Mabry said.

Cerise turned away, left them talking, walked down the stairs as silently as she'd come. Her hands were aching now, worse than ever, from the recoil; she rested a hand on each shoulder to try to reduce the swelling, hugging herself against the cold and the irrational feeling of loss. Not that she'd lost anything, not necessarily, but Silk was dead, and the Mayor—though he was no loss—and Trouble would become Mayor in her turn—She bit off that thought, knowing she was being maudlin, hysterical, and not knowing how to stop. Should I go back to the hotel? she wondered, get my runabout and get out of here, or should I just start walking, keep walking until I feel safe again? The street was still full of cops, a knot of them standing beside the fire engine, its bucket once again fully retracted, armored men clustering around the two snipers in congratulation; there were more cops at each end of the street, their mottled grey uniforms blurred even further by the thickening fog. She should probably thank the snipers, too, Cerise knew; they had saved her life. But she couldn't quite bring herself to do it, couldn't quite get past the cold that filled her, and stood with her hands on her shoulders in the fog, wondering what to do.

"Cerise?" Trouble said from behind her. "Ah, your hands."

"Yours aren't in great shape, either," Cerise said, and Trouble looked down as though surprised to see the thin cuts that crisscrossed her palms and ran up the sides of her hands.

"It's the glass," she began, and Cerise said, "I was there, I know."

"I know." Trouble looked past her, toward the end of the street where the fog was thickest. "I wanted—I need to talk to you. Before I agree to this, there are some things I need to settle."

"Such as?" In spite of herself, Cerise heard the old bitterness, the old anger, in her voice, and Trouble grimaced.

"Look, how many times do I have to say I fucked up? I don't want to do it again, Cerise, I don't want to leave, or for you to leave me, OK? If I take Seahaven, will you run it with me?

"And if I won't?"

Trouble spread her hands. "Then—whatever. Is Multi-plane hiring?"

Cerise stared at her for a long moment, not sure she had heard correctly, then, slowly, she began to laugh. "I don't believe you said that."

"What's so goddamn funny?" Trouble glared at her, and Cerise got herself under control with an effort.

"I'm sorry. It's just—you giving up Seahaven? To work for Multiplane? You've got to be kidding."

"Will you run it with me?" Trouble asked.

Cerise nodded, slowly. "It's kind of a dumb question, sweetheart. Is there anybody who doesn't want Seahaven?"

Trouble nodded back, reached out, careful of Cerise's hands, touched first her shoulder and then her cheek. "It's not going to be the same."

"It never is," Cerise answered. She forced a smile, and a lighter tone, knowing perfectly well what Trouble meant: the old days were long gone, and there was no going back, no matter what the regrets. "You'll just have to bring the law in, Marshal, that's all."

"Thanks," Trouble said, sour-voiced, but she was smiling. They stood close together against the chilling fog, the sky grey as glass above them, waiting for Mabry to return.

# • 14 •

TROUBLE STANDS IN *the heart of Seahaven, her Seahaven now, on the patch of nothing, black and slick as glass, where the Mayor's palace once stood. She has kept the rest of the space the way he had it that last day, the dusty street and the false-fronted buildings, the heat and the sun and the dust, and she's kept the icon Cerise made for them, the dark gunfighter's shadow against the virtual sun. The control points, the space itself, eddy around her body like the kiss of the wind: a new sensation, still, the full power of the interface filtered through the brainworm, as though she has no skin, as though she walks naked through the sys-*

tem. It is a strange feeling, vulnerable and powerful all at once: she is getting used to it, and without it Seahaven would be less than it was. And that she cannot, will not, allow: she's come too far, risked too much, to let this space be anything but more than it was under the Mayor's rule.

Ahead of her, the street is busy, icons clustering by the wall, wood now, not stone, where the artists work and messages are posted, others clustering by the door to the saloon where the real business is done. She built that herself, borrowing from the memory of Miss Kitty's years before, and is pleased. Cerise is in there now— she can feel Cerise's presence even through the swirl of signals, the constant rumble along her nerves. There are plenty of others, too, and she stops, mostly because she can, the novelty not yet worn off, lets the brainworm and the fabric of Seahaven itself tell her who is talking there. Dargon is there; triumph enough in itself, that he'll still come to Seahaven even though he doesn't think, isn't sure, she's earned the right to it. Arabesque, too, like a taste of salt, and Helling, and a dozen others she sees as flickers of an icon, an eye-blink image in her mind. The shadows still come to Seahaven, and she doesn't, won't stop them, but she welcomes the bright lights as well.

That in itself has been enough to drive off some of the shadows, the ones who are deep enough in the shadows that they have their own outside system, their own network of protectors and enemies in the realworld. Of all of them, only Fate has ventured into Seahaven more than twice, and he hasn't brought his business with him. That brings a flicker of regret, but she quells that sternly. She can't afford it—more than that, she isn't the Mayor, this isn't his Seahaven anymore, and she will live by the rules she's made, not by his.

She sees the sky thin on the fringes of the townscape, where she sketched the echo of desert to blend into the artificial distance, feels in the same moment the slap of a door opening, like the sting of sand against her skin. She doesn't move, looks up instead, not recognizing the hand behind the flurry of code, and sees a shape like the silver sketch of a bird, brighter even than the heat of the sky. She has been more than half expecting him, but she waits, lets the icon fall to her own plane, before she moves to meet him. Her shadow goes *before her, falling across him like a chill wind, and she feels him turn, feels the dispersal routine ready in his hand.*

*Hello, Starling,* she says, and for the first time she thinks he might be afraid.

*Trouble.* Starling's voice is as it always was, the same easy tone, but Trouble feels the tension surrounding him, the tension of readied programs, carried on the live air of her Seahaven, and she has to hide her own elation.

*Welcome to Seahaven,* she says, and lets her shadow fade a little.

*We need to talk,* Starling says. *My bosses aren't exactly pleased with what you're doing.*

*Really?* Trouble doesn't bother to sound convincing. She feels a flicker in the air, doesn't have to look back to know that Cerise has come to the doorway of the saloon, stands looking out into the dusty street. *I don't know why not, they got what they wanted. Seahaven's not a refuge space anymore.*

*They expected a bit more cooperation,* Starling says. *Under the circumstances.*

Trouble shrugs, enjoying the easy play of her icon. *I've done what I can, under law. But I have a direct-drop open node on the Euronets that puts this space under the Conventions, not Evans-Tindale. I have to abide by those rules.*

And, she doesn't say, doesn't have to say, the Conventions protect the nets as much as they protect the realworld. It's not the clearest situation, and she knows it—there have been rulings for and against her open-node argument—but Starling knows it, too, and knows that the nets will be solidly behind her. Trouble can feel the quiver in the air that means that icons are gathering, the other netwalkers coming out to see what's going on, what Starling wants. She doesn't look back, but she can tell they fill the false windows of the saloon and gather on the boardwalks to either side of the street.

Starling says, *That argument's been overruled before. It won't hold up in court.*

*Maybe not,* Trouble says, *but maybe it will. Charge me and we'll see what the judges say.*

There is a little pause, and she feels Starling withdraw a little, *preparing his retreat.* *Give me half a chance. We'll be watching, believe me. Every transaction, every payday, every single packet of data that comes out of here—oh, yeah, we'll be watching.*

*Go ahead,* Trouble says. *I've nothing to hide. But I hope you plan to get warrants for all that.*

*Oh, yeah,* Starling says, grim-voiced. *I play by the rules, Trouble, remember that.*

*I don't forget,* Trouble says, but already he's moving away, turned his back to her, the blank side of the icon, heading for the nearest node. She lets him go, and the lurkers move warily away, giving him a wide berth. She feels the node open, and the icon flicks away. She sighs, acknowledging at least his competence—he will play by his rules, she'll give him that, and he'll do it well—and turns away.

Cerise says, *He wasn't pleased.*

*No,* Trouble says, and turns to face her, seeing the icons that still wait in the windows and the boardwalk. She ignores them, their presence a weight in the air around her, says, *Still, somebody has to do it.*

*I hope Max is right about this one,* Cerise says—the open-node defense was Helling's idea—and Trouble grins, lets the brainworm carry her pleasure onto the net.

*The law's ambiguous, statute law and common law both. Besides, the main thing is still to get the Conventions established—to get people to push for it again.*

Cerise shrugs—she's less certain of it than Trouble, of the ability of the net to cooperate and of the realworld to pass the laws they all need—but she's said that all before, says only, *Well, if anyone can do it, you can.*

*Someone has to,* Trouble says. She looks around at the space that is Seahaven, the careful details of the street and the buildings and the vivid artwork flattened slightly in the harsh light, tastes the dust and heat. It was bought with a death—whatever she thought of the Mayor, he's dead, and if it wasn't at her hands directly, it was close enough, and she wouldn't have the hardware or the software or the authority if he weren't dead—and she can feel that burden sometimes like a wall pressing in over the dome of the false sky that bounds the city. *Someone has to,* she says again, as if his ghost is

*somewhere in the machines that create this Seahaven, as if he might
have cared, and turns away, walks back down the vivid street, the
dust soft and almost real against her feet.*

The sun was sinking toward the horizon beyond the long
window, its pale disk almost obscured by the dull clouds.
Trouble watched it idly, saw the lower limb drop below the
last layer of cloud, and looked away, blinking, as the fen ran
suddenly with watery light and shadow.

"Impressive, isn't it?" The voice was sharply accented, not
of the educated class, and Trouble blinked again, trying to
drive away the green reflections that floated in her eyes. She
recognized the man; Mabry had pointed him out as one of
the conference's local sponsors, a senior Eurocop who was
smart enough to realize how useful the nets could be, but she
couldn't remember his name. The man—he wasn't very tall,
about her own height, with wavy hair that had gone grey at
the temples and eyebrows that arced like a bird's wing—
smiled as though he recognized her dilemma and held out
his hand. "Jack Callier. Regional chief constable."

"Mr. Callier." Trouble took his hand, warily, trying to remember what else Mabry had said about him. When she had
agreed to speak at the annual European Conference on Computers and the Law, she hadn't realized that cops' politics
were as complicated as the nets', and she still wasn't sure
enough of all the factions.

"I enjoyed your talk," Callier went on.

"Thanks," Trouble said, and waited. It wasn't that the
Eurocops had been hostile, exactly, but they didn't know her,
and the ones who did know her reputation knew her as a
cracker better than as the new marshal of Seahaven.

"I don't mind telling you it'd make my job easier, if your
lot signed the Conventions," Callier went on, with an easy
grin that invited confidences. "What do you think the
chances are of getting it past your legislature?"

Trouble shrugged, on familiar ground here, and felt herself relaxing in spite of herself. "Not this session, I'm afraid.
We haven't got the support right now, and no one wants to

risk a vote yet. As more and more of Congress is dollied-up, have the implants, I mean, we get more and more backers, but until enough of them have actually dealt with the nets, it's hard to explain why we need the Conventions when we've already got Evans-Tindale."

"I heard your people elected someone—a senator, was it?—who was on the wire." That was one of the few women there, a rawboned accentless woman called Dumesnil, who was a senior agent in Europol's computer intelligence division. "Hello, Jack."

Callier nodded. "I don't know if you know Anne Dumesnil, Ms. Carless?"

"Trouble. Please."

"And I'm Stingray," Dumesnil said. "Jack's not on the wire—or on anything, for that matter."

Trouble nodded, impressed—Stingray had made a name for herself on the Euronets, was accounted a force in tracking the software black markets, someone even the shadows spoke of with grudging respect. She looked across the room, looking for the other faces that had come out of the shadows: Cerise and Max Helling, standing by the buffet table, the pair of net cops that everyone called the Terrible Twins, a black woman whose hair was braided with functional-looking beads and wires, a man in a deliberately conservative suit and a mane of untidy dark hair. There still weren't enough of them to make policy, but at least they were there at all.

"I started out a street cop," Callier said. It had the sound of a set speech, something he'd practiced, and Trouble dragged her attention back to the conversation. "And a street cop I'll always be. At least at heart."

"Not in that suit," Dumesnil said, and Callier laughed. "So what about this congressman? Is it true?"

"Yes, but," Trouble said, "he's only a member of the House of Representatives, he was elected from a district that's not only historically liberal but also technophilic, and he got his worm when he was a subsidy student for a European corporation, and then only because he couldn't do his research without it. All very legal and aboveboard."

"Surely it's a start," Dumesnil said.

"I hope so," Trouble said.

"This must be quite a change for you," Callier said, and there was something in his voice that made Trouble look sharply at him. "Working the bright lights after all those years in the shadows. How do your old mates feel about it?"

Trouble looked at him for a moment longer, trying to assess what she was hearing in his voice. Challenge? she thought. Mockery? Something of both, but not quite either one. "Does it matter?"

"It might," Callier said.

Dumesnil stirred uneasily, but then said nothing.

Callier said, "I don't know about on the nets, but on the streets, turning cop's going over to the enemy."

"I suppose it's not that different," Trouble said. It took an effort to keep her tone level, detached, and she wished with sudden passion that Cerise were with her. Or maybe not: Cerise would take Callier apart, or try to, and that, she thought, was not the answer now.

"So how do you feel about it?" Callier asked. "Which one bothers you more, being legal or that you were in the shadows?"

"Jack," Dumesnil said, a warning in her tone.

"No, it's important," Callier said. He smiled suddenly, the unexpected gesture taking some of the sting out of his words. "It is important."

Trouble said, slowly, compelled in spite of herself by the change of pace and tone, "Yeah, it's a problem, my coming out of the shadows. It couldn't not be a problem. The way I figure it is, I was a kid when I started—I didn't have a lot of other choices, for reasons that are none of your business— and in a way I'm grateful to Evans-Tindale because that gave me the chance to get out. But I don't regret it, not exactly— I've done the best I can. I'm still trying, still trying to do what's right." She stopped abruptly, embarrassed by her own passion and her own lack of certainty, and saw Callier relax.

"I know what you mean," he said. "I was a right tearaway

when I was a kid, caused all kinds of trouble myself—nearly killed another kid once, just lucky I didn't." He saw Dumesnil looking at him, and grinned again, the expression wry, "Yeah, I didn't think you knew that, Annie."

"It doesn't fit you," Dumesnil said, expressionless.

"It's true. He pulled a knife on me, I hit him with a piece of pipe, broke his shoulder. I was aiming for his head." He looked back at Trouble. "But you got to grow up sometime."

Trouble nodded. She saw movement out of the corner of her eye, a shadow crossing against the cool greys and browns of the window, and turned to see Mabry making his way toward them, bulky against the dying light. She lifted a hand in greeting, but turned back to Callier. "Sooner or later," she said, and Callier nodded back. Mabry beckoned, and she excused herself, moved to join him, into the cool light of evening.

# SF & FANTASY FROM
# L.E. MODESITT, JR.

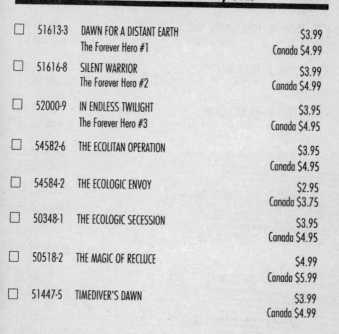

| ☐ | 51613-3 | DAWN FOR A DISTANT EARTH<br>The Forever Hero #1 | $3.99<br>Canada $4.99 |
| ☐ | 51616-8 | SILENT WARRIOR<br>The Forever Hero #2 | $3.99<br>Canada $4.99 |
| ☐ | 52000-9 | IN ENDLESS TWILIGHT<br>The Forever Hero #3 | $3.95<br>Canada $4.95 |
| ☐ | 54582-6 | THE ECOLITAN OPERATION | $3.95<br>Canada $4.95 |
| ☐ | 54584-2 | THE ECOLOGIC ENVOY | $2.95<br>Canada $3.75 |
| ☐ | 50348-1 | THE ECOLOGIC SECESSION | $3.95<br>Canada $4.95 |
| ☐ | 50518-2 | THE MAGIC OF RECLUCE | $4.99<br>Canada $5.99 |
| ☐ | 51447-5 | TIMEDIVER'S DAWN | $3.99<br>Canada $4.99 |

Buy them at your local bookstore or use this handy coupon:
Clip and mail this page with your order.

Publishers Book and Audio Mailing Service
P.O. Box 120159, Staten Island, NY 10312-0004

Please send me the book(s) I have checked above. I am enclosing $ _____
(Please add $1.50 for the first book, and $.50 for each additional book to cover postage and
handling. Send check or money order only — no CODs.)

Name _____

Address _____

City _____ State / Zip _____

Please allow six weeks for delivery. Prices subject to change without notice.

# SF AND FANTASY FROM ORSON SCOTT CARD

☐ 53365-8 THE CHANGED MAN $4.99
Canada $5.99

☐ 52304-0 CRUEL MIRACLES $4.99
Canada $5.99

☐ 51911-6 ENDER'S GAME $4.99
Canada $5.99

☐ 51685-0 FLUX $4.99
Canada $5.99

☐ 50086-5 THE FOLK OF THE FRINGE $4.95
Canada $5.95

☐ 51183-2 FUTURE ON FIRE $4.95
Canada $5.95

☐ 53351-8 HART'S HOPE $3.95
Canada $4.95

☐ 53259-7 THE MEMORY OF EARTH $5.99
Canada $6.99

Buy them at your local bookstore or use this handy coupon:
Clip and mail this page with your order.

Publishers Book and Audio Mailing Service
P.O. Box 120159, Staten Island, NY 10312-0004

Please send me the book(s) I have checked above. I am enclosing $ _____
(Please add $1.50 for the first book, and $.50 for each additional book to cover postage and handling. Send check or money order only—no CODs.)

Name _____

Address _____

City _____ State / Zip _____

Please allow six weeks for delivery. Prices subject to change without notice.

# THE BEST OF
# POUL ANDERSON

| | | | |
|---|---|---|---|
| ☐ | 51919-1 | ARMIES OF ELFLAND | $3.99 Canada $4.99 |
| ☐ | 50270-1 | BOAT OF A MILLION YEARS | $4.95 Canada $5.95 |
| ☐ | 53088-8 | CONFLICT | $2.95 Canada $3.50 |
| ☐ | 51536-6 | EXPLORATIONS | $3.99 Canada $4.99 |
| ☐ | 53050-0 | THE GODS LAUGHED | $2.95 Canada $3.50 |
| ☐ | 53091-8 | GUARDIANS OF TIME | $3.50 Canada $4.50 |
| ☐ | 53068-3 | HOKA! with Gordon Dickson | $2.95 Canada $3.50 |
| ☐ | 51814-4 | KINSHIP WITH THE STARS | $3.99 Canada $4.99 |
| ☐ | 52225-7 | A KNIGHT OF GHOSTS AND SHADOWS | $4.99 Canada $5.99 |

---

Buy them at your local bookstore or use this handy coupon:
Clip and mail this page with your order.

---

Publishers Book and Audio Mailing Service
P.O. Box 120159, Staten Island, NY 10312-0004

Please send me the book(s) I have checked above. I am enclosing $ _____
(Please add $1.50 for the first book, and $.50 for each additional book to cover postage and
handling. Send check or money order only — no CODs.)

Name _____
Address _____
City _____ State / Zip _____
Please allow six weeks for delivery. Prices subject to change without notice.

®

**Tor Books presents**

# COUNT GEIGER'S BLUES

by **Michael Bishop**

$12.95          89008-7

$17.95 Canada

"Michael Bishop('s). . . best book yet."

—*Locus*